Joseph Dawson

Peter Mackenzie

His Life and Labours

Joseph Dawson

Peter Mackenzie
His Life and Labours

ISBN/EAN: 9783337306748

Printed in Europe, USA, Canada, Australia, Japan

Cover: Foto ©Raphael Reischuk / pixelio.de

More available books at **www.hansebooks.com**

BY THE

Rev. JOSEPH DAWSON

AUTHOR OF

"THE FACE OF A SOUL" AND "THE SOUL OF THE SERMON" ETC.

FOURTH EDITION

London:

CHARLES H. KELLY

2, CASTLE ST., CITY RD.; AND 66, PATERNOSTER ROW, E.C.

1896

PREFACE

THIS biography was begun on December 16, 1895,
and completed on March 21, 1896,—a period
of three months and five days. Ordinarily such haste is
greatly to be deprecated, but in this case urgency of circumstance rendered it unavoidable. To have delayed
the publication of the book until the autumn would
have seriously jeopardised its success. The forced speed
at which it has been written will perhaps be accepted
in explanation, if not excuse, of such defects as may be
discernible in its style and contents. Every endeavour
has been made to ensure accuracy and fulness of detail,
and to furnish a satisfactory presentation of Mr.
Mackenzie's personality and work.

Grateful acknowledgments are hereby tendered to
the many friends who have kindly supplied information,
granted the use of letters, or in any way assisted in the
preparation of the work. The names of such have, as
far as practicable, been noted in connection with their
several contributions. Two persons, not so named,—
Mr. R. J. Phalp of Haswell, and Bailie Doig of
Dundee,—demand special thanks for valuable infor-

mation relating to Mr. Mackenzie's earlier life and surroundings.

It only remains to be added, that the aim of the writer has been to portray the hero of these pages in that larger outline clear to those who knew him best; and his gratification will be abundant if what has been to him a labour of love should succeed in securing for Mr. Mackenzie ampler appreciation as a man of genius, a friend of the people, and a servant of Jesus Christ.

BRADFORD, *March* 23, 1896.

CONTENTS

CHAPTER I
BIRTHPLACE AND CHILDHOOD—1824–1836 . . 1

CHAPTER II
WAXING INTO MANHOOD—1836–1844 12

CHAPTER III
FROM THE FARM TO THE MINE—1844–1845 . . . 22

CHAPTER IV
ENTRANCE ON MARRIED LIFE—1845–1847 . 32

CHAPTER V
DECISION FOR CHRIST—1847–1849 41

CHAPTER VI
GETTING UNDER WAY—1849–1850 . . 51

CHAPTER VII
FIRST ATTEMPTS AT PREACHING—1850–1852 . . . 59

CHAPTER VIII
EXPERIENCES AS A LOCAL PREACHER—1850–1852 . . 69

CHAPTER IX

PAGE

GROWING POPULARITY — EMIGRATION THWARTED — 1850-1854 79

CHAPTER X

BISHOP AUCKLAND AND REGIONS BEYOND—1854-1858 . 87

CHAPTER XI

PROPOSED FOR THE MINISTRY—1858 . 100

CHAPTER XII

THE YEAR AT DIDSBURY—1858-1859. . . 111

CHAPTER XIII

HIS FIRST CIRCUIT—BURNLEY—1859-1860 . . . 123

CHAPTER XIV

MONMOUTH, ROSS, AND FOREST OF DEAN—1860-1862 135

CHAPTER XV

AMONG THE WILTSHIRE VILLAGES—1862-1865 . 147

CHAPTER XVI

BACK TO THE NORTH—GATESHEAD—1865-1868 . 157

CHAPTER XVII

SUNDERLAND—SANS STREET—1868-1871 . . . 167

CHAPTER XVIII

NEWCASTLE-ON-TYNE—BLENHEIM STREET—1871-1874 . 173

CHAPTER XIX

LEEDS—ST. PETER'S—1874-1877 180

CHAPTER XX

LEEDS—WESLEY CIRCUIT—1877-1880. . 194

CHAPTER XXI

BRADFORD—SHIPLEY CIRCUIT—1880-1883   .   203

CHAPTER XXII

DEWSBURY CIRCUIT—1883-1886   .   .   214

CHAPTER XXIII

RETIREMENT FROM CIRCUIT WORK—1886-1895   222

CHAPTER XXIV

THE LAST DAYS   .   .   240

CHAPTER XXV

REST AT LAST   248

CHAPTER XXVI

THE MAN—HIS COURTESY   .   .   .   256

CHAPTER XXVII

THE MAN—HIS JOYOUSNESS   .   .   269

CHAPTER XXVIII

THE MAN—HIS GENEROSITY .   277

CHAPTER XXIX

THE MAN—DIVERS TRAITS AND INCIDENTS .   .   285

CHAPTER XXX

THE PREACHER—HIS MENTAL AND SPIRITUAL QUALITY   292

CHAPTER XXXI

THE PREACHER—ILLUSTRATION—HUMOUR—DELIVERY   .   298

CHAPTER XXXII

THE PREACHER—HIS PRAYERS   .   .   .   307

CONTENTS

CHAPTER XXXIII

THE LECTURER—TOIL AND TRAVEL .　.　.　312

CHAPTER XXXIV

THE LECTURER—DRAMATIC REALISATION　319

CHAPTER XXXV

THE LECTURER—HIS HUMOUR　326

APPENDIX

THE MAN AND HIS WORK　.　.　333

LIST OF ILLUSTRATIONS

	PAGE
SPITTAL, GLEN SHEE	3
TAY FERRY STEAMER	7
NEWPORT FROM THE WEST	17
MINER AT WORK	24
MINER AT REST	26
"HAND-PUTTER"	28
WHERE THE WIFE-BEATER WAS CHASTISED	33
MACKENZIE'S HOUSE WHEN FIRST MARRIED	37
PONY AND TUB	42
HASWELL COLLIERY	45
HASWELL CHAPEL	48
WHERE MACKENZIE LIVED WHEN CONVERTED—HOUSE ON RIGHT WITH CLOSED DOOR	52
CHAPEL LANE, HASWELL	63
MAIN STREET, HASWELL	71
MACKENZIE AT THIRTY	95
LITTLE DEAN HILL CHAPEL	136
WESLEY CHAPEL, CINDERFORD	138
MR. MACKENZIE'S DRAWING-ROOM	225
MR. MACKENZIE'S STUDY	233
REV. PETER MACKENZIE	257

LIFE OF PETER MACKENZIE

CHAPTER I

BIRTHPLACE AND CHILDHOOD—1824-1836

Autobiographical Scraps—Birthplace—Scenery of Glen Shee—
Early Influences—Journey to Dundee—Little Peter Lost—
Links of Comerton—Leuchars and Logie—Meagre Schooling
—Lesson of the Cock-crowing.

UNLIKE Rembrandt and other masters, among all
the canvases he painted, Peter Mackenzie included no portrait of himself. Ceaseless activities
crowded out of his life all possibility of autobiography.
What a story he might have written had leisure been
allowed to nurse him in her lap awhile before death
struck the pen for ever from his fingers !

He made a beginning, but it was a mere scrap ;
covering only five pages of note-paper, hurried in style,
and meagre in statement. Swiftly, indeed, must he
hurry on, when in so brief a chronicle he travels from
Glen Shee, in the north of Scotland, to Didsbury, on
the skirts of Manchester, and covers a period of over
thirty years. Yet, hurried and bare as the history is,
like a half-clad beggar in too much haste to gather

alms, what interest it awakens, and how valuable, in
the absence of other witnesses, are the few ragged,
disjointed details it lets fall for us as it scurries
onward !

I was born in Glen Shee, North Highlands of Scotland
on the 11th of November 1824.

Glen Shee is a romantic valley, flanked on the east
by Mount Blair, and on the west by Lamh Dearg,
through which the road from Blairgowrie climbs
patiently up towards Braemar, a distance of thirty-
five miles. The road is designated the Royal Route,
owing to its having been chosen by the Queen and
Prince Albert as the way to Balmoral before the
Deeside Railway was constructed. The surrounding
mountains rise to a height of from three to four
thousand feet, and listen with haughty brows to the
brawling of the river Shee in the valley below.
Before the road enters the glen, it clambers up a steep
hill, and beyond it hugs the shoulder of Cairnwall,
until, having threaded a sharp zigzag, called the Devil's
Elbow, and climbed to an elevation of two thousand
feet, it reaches the summit of the pass, near where
the small loch of Brotrachan sleeps quietly on the left.
This is the watershed, from which the road rapidly
descends, by Glenclunie, to Braemar.

The inn at the head of the glen is known as *The
Spittal*, a corruption of the word hospital, the name
having its origin in the fact that a hospice of the
monks or Hospitallers of St. John once stood here, and
served as a refuge for travellers.

Here, among these rugged mountains, the strength
and largeness of which seem to have passed into him,

SPITTAL, GLEN SHEE.

freshened by the free air, browned by the unhindered
sun, hardened by the wholesome fare common to the
household of the Scottish peasant, the man whose
course we have to follow through these pages spent
the first three years of his life, reminding us involun-
tarily of that other child, of whom Wordsworth
sang—

> Three years she grew in sun and shower.

And the poetry that lay at the heart of all his
thought and speech in after years would almost lead
one to picture him saying of himself, in the words of
the same writer—

> Not in vain,
> By day or star-light, thus from my first dawn
> Of childhood didst thou intertwine for me
> The passions that build up our human soul:
> Not with the mean and vulgar works of Man;
> But with high objects, with enduring things,
> With life and nature.

We catch the tone of our surroundings in childhood
as readily as the lake at midnight takes the imprint
of the stars, and it is hardly a freak of fancy to scent
in the strong bright speech of Peter Mackenzie some
of the breeziness and rugged vigour of his early
environment.

Left the Highlands for the Lowlands in the county of Fife
when three and a half years old.

Hurried little sojourner! How soon he was jostled
out of the nest of that quiet little valley! How early
those wanderings began that were to extend so
far and continue so long! "The child is father to

the man," and in that red-cheeked, barelegged
little mannikin, trudging by his father's side, or
borne, when tired, on the father's shoulder, or maybe
seated proudly on the cart that carries to a new
home the plain belongings of the Highland cotter,
see we not the rudiments of the after Peter—
man of many journeys — beginning to foreshadow
themselves ?

The route would be the same as that followed to-day;
for the road, having been constructed by General Wade,
dates further back than this journey of seventy years
ago.   It follows the right bank of the Shee to where that
stream joins the Ardle, to be known henceforth in its
fuller flow as the Ericht.   The scenery is grand and
picturesque, the Bridge of Calley, where the Ardle, as
if delighted at its approaching union with the Shee,
dances joyously over a rocky bed, being truly a
romantic spot.   Then is passed the mansion of Craig-
hall, said to be the Tullyveolan of *Waverley*, towering
from the edge of a precipice at a height of two
hundred and fifty feet above the river, and surrounded
by woods and rocks and fields that make a pleasing
combination of the sylvan and the rugged.   Thence
the road presses onward through Rattray and
Blairgowrie, and forward by Coupar-Angus, and a pass
in the Sidlaws, to Dundee.   All along the way, from
the wild Highland glen, downward through the rich,
peaceful valley, well watered by the Ericht and the
Isla, parents and child would travel in the company
of pleasant landscapes, and, let us hope, equally
pleasant thoughts.

How pathos is spattered with humour in our next
quotation !   How the older Peter — writing more

TAY FERRY STEAMER.

than sixty years afterwards—seems to chuckle at
the younger through its odd capitals !

In coming to Dundee, remember being lost in the town when
waiting for the boat. One of the Bobbies, the Gentlemen in
Blue, took care of me. All my sorrowing friends found me by
the assistance of the Bellman.

Fate evidently does not intend this child to be
ordinary : she rings the people up to look *for* him,
even as in later years she rang them up to look *at*
him. Other bairns keep the path, and pass on un-
noted ; this one loses his way, and all the town is
stirred. How came he to be lost ? The history does
not say ; but not unlikely the quick, prankish spirit
of after days was stirring in him then, making it
difficult for the parental eye to keep him within
range.

The boat for which they waited was the ferry that
crosses the river Tay to Newport in Fife, a distance
of nearly two miles. Steamers had been plying on
the ferry for six years prior to this date. Poor
strayed Peterkin ! Was he unconcerned, or did his
little heart heave and thump as he watched the wide
river and the distant hills, and the passing folk, and
saw none in whom his tearful eyes could spell the
name of friend ? The bellman of Dundee, too, at
this period, was a character and a wit, as bellmen
often are, and one cannot but query whether, through
any twinge of affinity, he had inkling, not of the
humour of the situation, but of the humorist in
embryo who was playing so prominent a part
in it.

Across the river our little hero was carried safely,

and some miles beyond, for his scanty history proceeds-—

Remember living on the Links of Comerton, by the sea. The storms, the wrecks, the dead men, and the big trees. The rabbits and the traps, the whins and sand.

Comerton Links are in the neighbourhood of Leuchars. They form a section of a vast plain, Tents Muir, extending from Tayport, on the south shore of the Firth of Tay, to the Firth of the Eden, and continued south of the Eden to the far-famed golf links of St. Andrews.

What a Victor Hugo-like grouping of the ghosts of memory looms upon us from the above extract, and how suggestive the order in which their shadows are made to pass before us! First, the large, dark, dreamy things that touch the poet in the man—the storms, the wrecks, the dead men, and the big trees; then, the common interests of the country child—rabbits, traps, furze bushes, and sand. Such a passage suggests at once Taine's characterisation of the style of the Saxon poet: " In his impassioned mind events are not bald, with the dry profundity of an exact description ; each fits in with its pomp of sound, shape, colouring. He emits the word that comes first to his lips without hesitation ; he leaps over wide intervals from idea to idea."

Again we read—

Lived at Leuchars and Logie, near Cupar-Fife. Went to school, remember the tasks that I could —— [The word is illegible. It looks like *supplant*. Probably he means the tasks he could evade], and the old dominie or schoolmaster.

Leuchars is a village on the road between Dundee and St. Andrews, and about seven miles distant from

the latter place. It has a primitive aspect, with
houses one storey high, covered with red tiles. The
parish church is remarkable as a fine specimen of
Norman architecture. A notable Scottish ecclesiastic,
the Rev. Alexander Henderson, who drafted the
famous Solemn League and Covenant, and was one of
the Scottish Commissioners that sat in the Assembly
of Divines at Westminster, was minister at Leuchars
before he removed to Edinburgh. Logie, the other
place named by Mackenzie, is also a rural Fife village
of no pretensions, unless it be that about a mile and
a half to the north of it, on the banks of the Moutrey,
stands the parish church of Kilmany, where Dr.
Chalmers first began his labours.

In these humble villages, "far from the madding
crowd," was laid the groundwork of Mackenzie's
education ; an education that was probably carried on
with far more zest in mature life than amid the mischievous distractions of boyhood. Measured by his
subsequent attainments, it cannot have been of a very
elaborate character. Probably it included no more
than the mere rudiments, reading, writing, and arithmetic, and the wonder will always remain how such
results as his life achieved could be produced with so
slender an equipment. It can only be understood as
we keep in mind that there is a higher teaching than
any school can supply, an education at the hands of
life itself, of which Mackenzie himself gives us a
suggestive hint in the quaint remark on another
Peter in one of his lectures : " Peter learned more from
the cock-crow in three minutes, than a classical tutor
could have taught him in a fortnight."

CHAPTER II

WAXING INTO MANHOOD—1836–1844

Ripening into Youth—Herd Laddie—First Good Impressions—
"Cotter's Saturday Night"—Revisits Old Scenes—Laird of
Logie—Hard Experiences—"More Jog than Trot"—Three
Times in Peril—Cupar Hirings—Saving and Giving—
Return to Dundee—Manhood.

WE have followed Mackenzie along the simple
paths of childhood by the welcome aid of his
milestone sort of notes. We have seen him open his
eyes on life, and look around him under the broad sky
and among the big mountains of his native glen; we
have heard him tell how the storm-maddened sea,
flinging its 'wrecks and dead upon the shore, the large
trees, spreading their arms across the road, or perchance stretched like stricken giants on the ground,
the timid rabbits peeping from under the gorse, or
scuttering among the sandhills, or caught in the fatal
trap, all left their varied impress on his mind. We
have gone with him to where

> In his noisy mansion skilled to rule,
> The village master taught his little school.

And now, as the pathway urges under more serious
skies, we have still to be guided by the meagre blurts

which his rapid pen flings upon the road. The child
has now disappeared in the youth, and in the next
extract we behold the lusty stripling, proud, doubtless, that he can do work and receive wages of his own.

Lived at Mildean about two years. During that time went
to service for ten shillings with Janet Fife, married to David
Lonley. Good man ; family prayer. Made my first good
impressions.

Mildean was probably a farm somewhere between
Cupar and Logie, where he acted in the capacity of
herd laddie, and the ten shillings would be his wages
for twelve months, with board and lodging in addition.
This was about the standard of remuneration for such
service at the time.

The reference to his "first good impressions" is
interesting and significant. We are prone to err in
our endeavours to trace the awakening of the life of
God in the human soul. We generally pin such
awakening down to a fixed point and a specified
agency, whereas it is usually a gradual process, the
outcome of many diversified impressions. This hard-
working David Lonley and his wife pursue the even
tenor of their way, and dream not that the unobtrusive piety of their home is silently moulding the
soul of their youthful helper. The mention of their
"family prayers" sets before us at once the scene so
vividly sketched by Burns in his "Cotter's Saturday
Night."

The cheerfu' supper done, wi' serious face,
  They round the ingle form a circle wide ;
The sire turns o'er, wi' patriarchal grace,
  The big ha' Bible, ance his father's pride :

> His bonnet rev'rently is laid aside,
>> His lyart haffets wearing thin and bare ;
> Those strains that once did sweet in Zion glide,
>> He wales a portion with judicious care,
> And "Let us worship God !" he says, with solemn air.

In the year 1868, Mackenzie revisited these scenes of his boyhood in company with Mr. Henry Reed, whom he always acknowledged as the means, under God, of bringing him to Christian decision. Recalling this visit, he writes in his autobiographical chronicle—

Went to see the old spot about '68. The time that I was first there would be about the year '36. [That is when he was about twelve years of age.] The old people remembered me and my boyish pranks and peculiar sayings. We had a good time, temporally and spiritually. They gave us curds and cream ; and prayer and thanks and backsheesh made it all right on both sides.

The distribution of what he humorously terms " backsheesh " was to Mackenzie, as is well known, what the dropping of showers is to the clouds, a natural and inevitable exercise. He began the practice early, and it grew upon him to the end. It would be easy to summon a cloud of witnesses from the cabmen, the railway porters, the engine-drivers, the servant-maids, and many others, upon whom his gratuities rained, not only in unusual profusion, but with an accompaniment of happy word or genial wish or appropriate prayer that won for them a doubly grateful acceptance.

Once more he carries us forward—

From Mildean to Logie. Lived there two years. The Laird of Logie said—that boy would be either a good man or a great scoundrel. The Laird was glad to see me after thirty years' absence, and delighted to hear that I was a minister.

The remembrance of his "boyish pranks and peculiar sayings," after so long a lapse of time as thirty years, and this prophecy of the laird, serve to show what, without such evidence, it would be natural to infer, that a character so accentuated in its singularity afterwards would begin early to manifest an angular formation. Peter the boy on the farm would no doubt be a true miniature representation of the points that, standing out more strikingly, won attention and popularity for Peter the preacher.

Again he gives us brief enlightenment—

During my stay at Logie the house took fire.—Great fear among the folk. In '37 went to place with Mr. Peter Barringalla. Got on pretty well. Plenty of hard work.

Though he "got on pretty well," his condition cannot have been greatly overcharged with comfort, for on the heels of this grateful exclamation comes the confession that the hen-roost was either within or so contiguous to the room in which he slept that, for reasons best left in a decent haze of reticence, he was often compelled to leave his bed and sit out the night by the kitchen fire. Poor lad! the hands that fortune held out to him were certainly not over-burdened with enjoyment. He had known little of the sweetness of home. As far as can be ascertained, his mother died when he was very young, and those hours in which he drowsed over the kitchen fire, with his much-needed rest so untowardly broken in upon, must sometimes have passed very dolefully. Fortunately, he was healthy and had a good appetite, which the nature of his employment tended to make even better, as is humorously illustrated in the following reminiscence, given by one who heard him relate it :—

"When I was a lad, I lived in farm service, and we had to get up very early to go to market. I had to get the conveyance ready, and put in two bundles of straw for the old man and the old woman to sit on. I was the driver, but the cart had no springs, and off we went jog-trot over a good many miles of rough road. I remember how the old woman gave the old man and me a sermon and lecture all in one. I can assure you we were all ready for a second breakfast when we got to our journey's end, for we had more jog than trot."

To return once more to the written record, we find—

I was very fond of the horses, and three times was placed in imminent peril. The cart backing against the wall ; the two carts that met, and I was between them ; the horse that struck out, hit me in the mouth, cut my lip, but did not disfigure me. I was too near him, etc. etc.

Laconic descriptions these of what at the time must have been exciting incidents. Would that time had been more liberal with him, and allowed him to enlarge on them in his own graphic manner! What a vivid description he would have given us of the burning house and the frightened folk of which he speaks! How we should have held our breath, as he made us see the youth against the wall and the cart going back upon him, or smitten in the face by the heels of the horse, or wedged without apparent hope of escape between the two carts that are closing on him like a vice. Too provoking, Peter, to fling these bald, exciting sentences at our heads, and leave us standing in

unsated curiosity! We might have been informed in what manner the miracles of deliverance were wrought; or is it better, after all, that each should work out his own conception of how, in the providence of God, this venturesome laddie was spared for greater things?

Once more the story proceeds—

Went home for a few months. Then hired myself at St. James's Market, Cupar of Fife, to David Arnot, Wester Colsel, near Auchtermuchty. Stayed three years as boy and man. Saved five pounds out of the thirteen that I had for three years' hard work.

Cupar is the county town of Fife, situated on the banks of the river Eden, thirteen miles south of Dundee. It is a clean, pleasant little place, with a population of about five thousand. St. James's Market is held in Cupar, about the month of August, for the hiring of servants and other business, and still commands a large gathering of people. Thirteen pounds for three years' service strikes us as a small sum; but from four to five pounds a year was the regular wage. The social condition of Scottish agricultural labourers sixty or seventy years ago was low. Ploughmen were hired by the year or half-year, the highest remuneration not exceeding eight or nine pounds per annum. For labourers in quarries, and other kinds of out-door workers, the wages ranged from eight to nine shillings a week. Houses were small and poor, food plain; peasemeal, oatmeal and potatoes forming the staple diet.

It speaks volumes for the careful habits of this youth of sixteen or seventeen, that out of so scanty a pittance for three years of hard work he should be able to save five pounds. The proverbial Scottish thrift was evidently not lacking here. And how may it be accounted for that Peter Mackenzie, Scottish by birth, and with the national proclivity for saving, strengthened in him by the hard, penurious experiences of his youth, should develop into one of the freest of givers ? Explain it as we may, the fact should always stand to his credit, that his was a generosity that triumphed not only over the natural selfishness of the human heart, but over a national tendency that early experience might have been expected to harden into habit.

After having expended so little over him in the shape of wages, and received so much from him in that of hard work, it is not surprising that he should be able to write of his employers—

They were pleased to see me when I went back after some thirty years' absence. Henry Reed, Esq., and his good wife were with us. We prayed, and parted for ever as regards this world.

He means that he and his company parted for ever from his old employers and acquaintances. His next removal was to bring him into contact with town life, and to judge from his own words, and from other evidence, the new experience was not altogether beneficial. Continuing his chronicle, he writes—

Went to Dundee. Lived two years. Neither did nor got much good, but saw a good deal of town life. We had a dairy and a coal yard, and cart on the quay-side. Left there in '44 for Oxclose, in the county of Durham.

There is indubitable evidence that he lived in Dundee from May 1842 until July 1844, for there are records of his having had to answer before the authorities for furious riding, and also for striking with his whip a fellow-carter's horse, and starting it off in a dangerous scamper. Such escapades reveal to us not a vicious disposition, but a nature fraught with a mischievous energy it was difficult to hold in check.

Born, as we have seen, in 1824, he departs from Dundee for the North of England in 1844; that is as a young man of twenty. These fragmentary auto-biographical notes, of which nearly the whole has now been quoted, set before us, then, with sundry intermissions, the leading events of the first twenty years of his life. What emerges for us, as the record closes, is a brawny young fellow, with muscles hardened by manual labour; with keen dark eyes that look out upon us unabashed from an open, pleasant face, and that dance with the play of a rollicking humour. We see, too, a heart in which the seed of the kingdom of God has been sown through the influence of at least one godly Scottish home, and where, though retarded by less pure and kindly ministries, it will continue to grow, and, in due season, bring forth fruit.

CHAPTER III

FROM THE FARM TO THE MINE—1844–1845

The Book of Job on Mining—Into the Pit—Darkness and Silence
—Miner at Work—" Hand-Putters "—Training of Mackenzie
—Influence of Environment—Son of Soil and Rock—
Methodism, Mining, and Agriculture—Colliery Phraseology
—" Men like Pigs "—Year at Oxclose—Good-heartedness—
Incident of the Harvest Field.

IN the twenty-eighth chapter of the Book of Job
there is a magnificent description of the toils and
discoveries of the ancient miner, as he digs into the
heart of the earth in search of the precious metals.
" In a few deft strokes," says the Rev. Samuel Cox,
" the writer brings out the pathos of the miner's life
and occupation—its peril, its loneliness, its remoteness
even from those who stand nearest to it."

He maketh an end of darkness,
And searcheth through all its limits
For the stones of darkness and the blackness of death ;
He sinketh a shaft far from the habitations of men,
He is forgotten by those who walk above,
He swingeth suspended afar from men :

He putteth forth his hand against the quartz,
He turneth up the mountains from their base ;
He cutteth out canals among the rocks ;

And his eye detecteth every precious thing;
He bindeth up the waters so that they weep not,
And bringeth that which is hidden to light.

That is the poetry of mining; the prose is steeped in a yet deeper pathos. If the hardship of the miner's life of old, searching for gold, or silver, or copper in some lonely region like the wilds of Sinai, was great, that of the modern miner, digging for coal, discloses even a sterner condition; and forty years ago it held in its black heart a still vaster armoury of perils and privations.

Let us picture its details. Borne by the cage that glides with the stealthiness of a snake down into the cavernous jaws of earth, the miner threads his way in the glimmer of a frightened candle, or the duller gleam of a carefully-guarded lamp, often with his body bent and crouched into the semblance of some misshapen creature, along rugged, interminable galleries hewn out of the solid rock by the toil and sweat of past generations. Around him presses a padding of thickest gloom, and within the gloom a voiceless quiet, eager, whenever the cranch of his footstep on the roadway ceases, to fold him in its ghostly arms. What a silence, dumb as the lips of death, a huge encircling thing, with hollow, tongueless heart, out of which issue no sounds, save such as make the stillness more sepulchral—the creaking of strained timber, or the dripping of water, or the moan of liberated gas!

Farther and yet farther into this weird, sunless depth does he make his way, cramped and perspiring, hugging his heavy tools, until he arrives at what is termed " the face " of the coal, where all farther advance is barred. The face is the limit to which the gallery in which he finds himself has been carried. Here his mate, or " marrow," toiled yesterday.   In the rock are traces of his pick, and on the floor of the passage lie still perchance some of the fruits of his excavations in the form of a heap of loose coals.

Here the man we have followed drops his tools, wipes the sweat from his brow, swallows a hasty sip from his tin of cold tea or coffee, and then, one by one, lays aside his rough flannel garments, until nought

MINER AT WORK.

remains save his heavy shoes, his coarse stockings, his short breeches, and a thin armless shirt that covers loosely his chest and shoulders.   In the dim glimmer of the candle we can descry how labour has knotted the muscles into firmness and might, and how unfriendly blows and bruises, followed by the tattooing of the black dust, have wrought uncomely scrawls upon his skin.

And now the toil of the day begins. Into that hard, rocky face he must dig his laborious way. Striding half double, or squatted on a rough wooden " cracket," or seat, which raises him a few inches from the floor, or crouching almost flat upon the ground, he plies his various picks, slowly carving a deep gash at the bottom and another at the side of the seam, until a huge segment of the coal is on two sides severed from its surrounding, and ready through the push of some explosive to be dislodged.

Now a hole is drilled at the unhewn corner, a charge of gunpowder inserted, a match applied, and so lighted as to leave a moment for the workman to find shelter from the explosion, and then, if " the shot " proves effective, he returns through the blinding, suffocating smoke, to find the floor of the gallery covered with a huge heap of shattered spoils. This loose, broken coal he at once shovels into the " tubs " or small waggons that convey it along dark, rumbling ways to the mouth of the shaft, and thence to the good daylight above.

In the collieries of the North of England forty years ago, the youth who brought these tubs or waggons to the hewer and took them away when filled was called a " hand-putter." His work was to push the heavy vehicles with hands and head along the low, dreary passages that led to where the hewers were engaged, and back again to the " flat " or station, whence they were dragged by horses or ponies along the more lofty galleries to the mouth of the mine.

Here, then, tugging and toiling amid these hard conditions, surrounded by men and youths of rough ways and ofttimes uncomely speech, we find our

Scottish laddie in the year 1844, and we cannot but pause to reflect on the wonderful training through which Providence is ordering that he shall pass.

For nearly twenty years he has drunk the sweetness and the glory of the fresh air and the bountiful sun, in regions where the black fingers of modern industry have not fouled either. He has seen the dew on the grass, and heard the lark in the sky, and

MINER AT REST.

caught the young look on the face of the sun at early dawn. The smell of the fresh earth, that most primitive of odours, pungent, invigorating, the wholesome heritage of the tiller of the ground, has been his. And now he is made to enter into the fellowship of silence and gloom, broken in upon by ugly toil and unshapely noise. He has scanned the face of the earth as only the patient farmer knows how, and now, as far as man is so permitted, he plunges into her bosom and listens to the beating of her mighty heart.

Training of no trivial order must there have been in all this. An old dweller in a wild Yorkshire valley, when asked why the people were so stolid, answered, "You see they have been bred and born among these rocks and scrogs, and they have gone into them." Things pass into us whether we will or no, especially the things among which we move in the opening days of life, and our nature receives more fully than we dream of the imprint of the outward. Peter Mackenzie was, in his early years, first a son of the soil, and then a son of the rock, and it is not simply a poetical vagary that discerns in him afterwards the wholesome freshness of the one and the enduring hardness of the other.

Such training not only moulded the man, but stretched serviceable links of fellowship between himself and others. To agriculture and mining belong two of the most numerous classes of British workpeople, and in the work of fashioning these to spiritual issues, the Methodist Church has borne no inglorious part. The warmth with which it has expounded, and the sociable forms in which it has given expression to Christian doctrine and experience, have enabled it to capture them by thousands, and among the ministers to whom these classes have turned with appreciation and affection, few, if any, have occupied a higher place than Peter Mackenzie. Born and fashioned among these children of the people, never ashamed of acknowledging his connection with them, impregnated with their spirit, conversant with their ways, not free even from their faults, he was enabled

to make them feel, in fuller measure concerning him
than they felt concerning most, that he was one of
themselves. The colliery vernacular probably never
had such an innings as it obtained in his sermons
and lectures, and the aptitude with which he manipu-
lated its stock expressions when addressing an audience
of pitmen, lent wonderful vividness to his diction.
How expressive to remark, when puzzled by a theo-

"HAND-PUTTER."

logical question, that he could not get his pick round
it! On one occasion he was relating how he had
taken part in the opening services of a new chapel,
his being the sixth service of the series. The five
ministers who had preceded him were the best men
that could be secured. He likened them to hewers
who had worked so well, and filled their tubs so full,
that when these tubs had to pass under the low

planks supporting the roof, much of the coal was raked off, and all he could do in coming after them was to gather up their leavings. In this way, however, he succeeded in scraping together no less a sum than £87, which he considered a good day's work for an old miner. On his last visit to Haswell, in returning thanks to the chairman, who was also the colliery manager, and who had not by a lengthened introduction robbed him of any part of his lecture, he said : " The chairman has behaved in a most gentlemanly manner. He did not take away my steel pick, nor rob me of my shovel, and he left me a ' led tub ' for a start." A " led " or leading tub is an empty tub left for the hewer by his mate from the day before, and is in several ways a great convenience. Both master and men understood Peter's terminology, and enjoyed it immensely. How the knowledge he had gained on the farm could also be happily utilised is well illustrated by the remark made when addressing an audience in which sons of the soil were numerous : " Some men are like pigs : they never look up till they are laid on their backs." At a harvest thanksgiving, too, on a week-day afternoon in October 1895, how effectively he provoked gladness and gratitude among the countrymen in his congregation during prayer, when he exclaimed : " Thou hast blest Thy servants in the fields. They sowed a handful, and they have reaped an armful ! They stuck in half a potato, and they dug up a boiling."

It was at Oxclose, near Washington, in the county of Durham, that, as a " hand-putter," Mackenzie, with three other young men who had accompanied him from Scotland, was introduced to the work of the mine.

He remained there a year, and then removed to Haswell, a colliery village in the same county, consisting at that time mainly of one long street of miners' cottages and small shops, with a few smaller streets or rows abutting from it on either hand. In one of these, called Chapel Lane, Peter played many good-natured pranks in those lively, but never wicked, earlier years. He soon became at Haswell what he had also been at Oxclose, a great favourite with his fellow-workmen, one of whom says: "He was always a canny sort of chap: the most he liked was fiddling and dancing." The word "canny" in the vocabulary of the North of England has not exactly the same significance as in Scotch, but leans more to kindliness, geniality, and general good-nature.

Miners in those days had their location in the pit settled each quarter by the drawing of lots. These lots, or "cavils," would vary greatly in quality, some being unremunerative and disagreeable, while others were of a more favourable nature. Two men generally worked a "cavil" together as mates, taking successive spells or "shifts," which in former days lasted from eight to nine hours, but are now considerably abridged. It seldom happened that these work-mates would be peers in strength and dexterity, yet it was customary for what they earned to be regarded as common to both, to be shared equally when the pay-day came round. In a matter of this sort, how generous-hearted a man Mackenzie was, even in those unregenerate days, was strikingly evident. Of powerful build and agile movement, he was able to accomplish more than an ordinary workman, but he was never known to begrudge extra labour, nor to hesitate for a moment to divide his earnings equally with his mate, even when that mate chanced to be an old and very much feebler man. In a similarly disinterested spirit, it was a common thing for him to share his " bait," or provision of food and drink, with any fellow-worker who seemed not to have enough. No wonder his mates admired him, for there was never a spell of hard work to be undertaken, or a deed of kindness to be done, but he was always ready.

The disastrous strike among the miners in 1844, shortly before Mackenzie came to England, had sadly disorganised industry and trade throughout the counties of Durham and Northumberland, and brought impoverishment and privation to many families. In these circumstances, wives and mothers often sought to supplement the scanty earnings of husband and father by employment in the harvest-field, shearing the corn with a sickle, and binding it into sheaves. One fine day, young Mackenzie was leaning over a fence, watching the harvesters at their work. His quick eye caught sight of a poor delicate woman, struggling vainly to keep pace with her stronger-armed companions. His tender heart was touched at once. The fence was cleared at a bound, and, stepping up to the astonished woman, he said, " Let me have your sickle, hinny, and I'll gie ye a hand while ye straighten your back a bit." One who witnessed the incident said that the willing heart and practised arm of the young miner soon completed the woman's task, and enabled her to take a welcome and greatly needed rest.

CHAPTER IV

Punishing a Wife-Beater—Dancing Parties—The Public-House
Then and Now—Mackenzie's Father—His Marriage—Books
and Bowling—A Quoit Match—Sacrifices of his Family.

THE kindly spirit that prompted his deed of helpfulness in the harvest-field led Mackenzie about this time to enter on a somewhat more difficult adventure. There lived in the village a man of violent, overbearing disposition, whose hapless wife suffered much from his brutal behaviour. One day, as he was using the woman in a shameful manner, outside his house, Mackenzie happened to pass. The young Scotsman was not yet a Christian, but he had a noble soul, a soul that hated tyranny, so he paused to remonstrate. The infuriated brute not only declined to abate his cruelty to the woman, but threatened also to punish her defender. The latter was no pugilist, but he took the cowardly boaster in hand at once, and conferred upon him a very much needed thrashing. He has been spoken of as addicted to fighting before his conversion, but it was not so. This was really the first and last encounter of the sort he ever had. "Didn't I dust the coward's jacket for him?" he exclaimed years afterwards, to a friend who had witnessed the incident, and to whom he was recounting it. The man whom he thus chastised was not prosperously circumstanced in after years, and it was entirely like Mackenzie that, whenever he went to Haswell to preach and lecture, he invariably sought the poor fellow out, treated him to the public tea, and rendered him other assistance to an extent only known between themselves.

WHERE THE WIFE BEATER WAS CHASTISED.

Since his settlement in England, that is, for a period of about a year and a half, Mackenzie had lived as a single man in lodgings, but he now began to take steps towards obtaining a home of his own. Not far from where he lodged dwelt John Thompson and his wife, a respectable, industrious couple, employed in agriculture, and it was upon one of their daughters that the choice of the young miner fell.

Dancing parties were common at the public-houses
in the district. They were frequently held in
connection with what was called a " Wife's Feast ";
that is, a tea given by some married woman to a
number of friends of both sexes. After tea, dancing
would begin to the inspiring strains of some local
fiddler—one famous scraper of the catgut being a
man named Tom Lamb, who rode on a donkey from
one of these gatherings to another. The fiddler's fee
up to a certain hour was paid by the publican. If
the party waxed merry, and more dancing was
demanded than had been agreed upon, then the door
of the room was locked, and a hat passed round for
contributions, and so long as the pocket of the
fiddler was thus replenished, so long were his strains
lengthened out. Harvest festivals were also favourite
occasions for the indulgence of this form of amusement, of which Mackenzie and his sweetheart were
both passionately fond. It was at one of these
dancing parties that they first became acquainted.

It may not be amiss to remind the reader that in
those days public-houses were often the only place
where refreshments could be obtained and social
gatherings held. The café and coffee-tavern were as
yet unborn. The moral influence of the public-house
then is not to be measured by what it is to-day,
especially in large towns, nor was the feeling in
regard to it the same. I remember, when a boy,
going frequently with my father and mother to
Durham market, and when the business was finished,
retiring with them, as a matter of course, to a small
inn, where they partook of refreshments, in the form
of bread and cheese and ale ; nor, good people as

they were, was such a practice regarded as at all unbecoming.

The temperance movement has created a different sentiment. It has placed the public-house to some extent under a ban, while sundry changes in our social habits and conditions have also tended to render its character less reputable, and its employment in social functions less desirable. It may be worth consideration, however, whether in severing completely one section of the people from the public-house, and leaving another section to be its patrons, we have not on the one hand stiffened unduly the sense of virtue, and on the other over-emphasised the appearance of laxity. It might not be unprofitable to ask whether a wise and loving adoption of the Master's policy in relation to those whom we regard as morally deficient, would not be mutually beneficial. Be this as it may, it must be borne in mind that attendance at such festive gatherings as we have described did not then wear the same moral or even social complexion as would be indicated by it now.

About this time the father of Peter Mackenzie travelled from Dundee to Haswell, in the hope of inducing his son to return to Scotland. Mackenzie, however, preferred to remain in his present employment. The remuneration was probably larger than he could hope to win in agricultural labour, and, moreover, his affections were partly engaged, and as a consequence, the colliery village had grown more attractive. His mother having died when he was quite a child, his father had married a second time, and it would seem that the family relations were hardly of such a nature as to tempt him back. But, though the father was disappointed, and had to return to Dundee without him, friendly intercourse was not broken. In after years, when the son was a popular minister in the Gateshead circuit, the old man came and sojourned with him for a few weeks, and perhaps on other occasions. Under date November 10, 1869, I find the following brief record in his own hand concerning an appointment at Ryhope Colliery in the Sunderland circuit:— "Missionary Meeting. Not there—Scotland—father's funeral"; from which it would appear that the father died at this time, and that the son went to Dundee to render due respect to his memory.

"Eh, but ye're a braw lassie!" were the characteristic words with which the young miner saluted his sweetheart the first time he addressed her. Then followed a visit to the mother, and a conversation with her concerning her daughter, succeeded by a long first walk, round by Old Hetton, Houghton-le-Spring, and West Rainton, a distance of many miles, on a lovely Sabbath afternoon, terminating only when the evening shadows had flung their sombre mantles over field and wood.

After a courtship of a year and a half, and a never-forgotten visit to Durham city to purchase the ring, Mary Thompson and Peter Mackenzie were quietly married in Shadforth Church, on Sunday, April 25, 1847, the bride aged twenty and the bridegroom twenty-two. They set up housekeeping in a cottage of two rooms, an "upstairs and down," beginning thus a married life which, had it lasted seventeen months longer, was to have been honoured by the celebration of a golden wedding.

Mackenzie was at this time a very happy-go-lucky fellow, dancing, fiddling, and reading being his favourite pastimes. He never attained great proficiency on the violin, his most lively strains being, as one of his old companions puts it, "like pulling the cat's tail," still it was a great delight to him to let the merriment with which he was brimming over find vent through the squeaking strings and the accompanying clatter

MACKENZIE'S HOUSE WHEN FIRST MARRIED.

of heel and toe upon the floor. Some of the books from which he is remembered as reaping much enjoyment were the *Tales of the Borders* and *St. Clair of the Isles*. These and other volumes he secured the loan of from a friendly publican, and read aloud to a comrade during his illness in so lively a manner that he is spoken of as having acted as well as read the books.

In the out-door sports of the miners, especially the bowling practised in the lanes and on the commons, it was impossible that a man of his active and vivacious temperament should not be interested. The bowls consisted of whinstones dressed down into smooth round pellets of a specified weight, and as the winner in the game was the one who could throw the bowl the farthest distance, an exercise of arm demanding both strength and skill, picked men were often matched to contend against each other. In this sport Mackenzie, who was an adept at " handling the whin," would frequently be entered as a competitor against some fellow-workman for a few shillings, but he never indulged in big matches as a professional gambler.

Quoits was another favourite game among the colliers, and an incident is recorded in connection therewith that illustrates Mackenzie's determination to succeed in whatever he undertook. A great quoit match had recently been played between Tom Charlton, a miner, and Tom Brown, a Tyne keelman, at which Mackenzie was present. A few evenings afterwards, in a public-house which he frequented, the conversation turned on quoits, and in reply to some remarks of a miner, named William Rawlings, Mackenzie asserted that he could play quoits quite as well as he, Rawlings, could. Rawlings, who was considered a good player, retorted that he could easily become the champion if there were no better competitors than Mackenzie. The outcome of the contention was that he was matched to play Rawlings for £2 a side, the match to take place a month after the final deposit. He had shown no special skill in the game up to this time, but during the period intervening, he practised so incessantly that when the appointed day arrived victory was easy.

Amid all this apparent indifference to a higher life, better thoughts were working in his mind. For months before his conversion, partly, no doubt, as the result of his Scottish training and impressions, he was in the habit of reading the Bible aloud on Sunday evenings, and would not infrequently remark to his wife, that while this might be good as far as it went, still, he thought, they ought to attend a place of worship.

On his last visit to Haswell, he went once more to see the cottage in which his married life began. After surveying it for a moment, he laughed and said, " Look at it !   There it is—and *that's* the place to which the popular lecturer brought his bride ! "   And then he passed on, murmuring something about not despising the day of small things.

Mrs. Mackenzie is a woman of kind heart and good sense.   Her educational opportunities, like those of her husband, were exceedingly limited, and after days did not provide her with such prompting and facilities for self-improvement as they brought to him.   It is possible that at the beginning of his ministerial career she found it difficult at all times to adapt herself adequately to the new condition of things. The change was tremendous.   To be lifted all at once from the life and associations of a mining village to a position that involved entrance upon a wholly novel range of manners and ideas, was no ordinary trial of mind and character, and the wonder is, not that there might be hesitancy at first in sustaining the new demands, but that they met with so fair, and, on the whole, satisfying a response.   Her unobtrusive ministries as wife and mother, during the many years her husband left her to travel to and fro throughout the land, deserve more generous recognition than they have sometimes received. While he was footing it bravely on the boards, stimulated, as all men in such a position are, by the blaze and shouts of popularity, she was working quietly in the dim light behind the scenes, little known, and but faintly appreciated by the public for whom her husband was using up his strength.

In estimating the service rendered by Peter Mackenzie to the Wesleyan Methodist Church, there must not only be a column in which we place the number of his converts, and a second in which we write down his financial achievements, but a third in which we shall vainly endeavour to register the losses laid upon his family by his almost uninterrupted absence from home, and their consequent deprivation of fatherly influence and example. A solemn responsibility is undertaken by the religious public when for forty years it lays appropriating hands on nearly the whole of a man's time, and leaves him only snatched moments in which to fulfil his duties as husband and father. It may be questioned, indeed, whether any man acts wisely in acceding so fully to such demands; whether, without inflicting injury on himself and others, he can sacrifice the claims of home to those of pulpit and platform. Whatever view is taken of the matter, it must never be overlooked that the wife and children of Peter Mackenzie relinquished no small part of the true wealth of life when they gave up so ungrudgingly, and for so long a period, the brightness and charm of a presence that carried warmth and sparkle everywhere.

CHAPTER V

DECISION FOR CHRIST—1847–1849

Never a Vicious Character—His Donkey—"Houghton Feast"—
Good Company—A Curious Wager—His Integrity—Mining
Reminiscences —Squire Reed—His Conversion—An Exciting
Scene—A Shout from the Gallery.

"MY husband, in his younger days," says Mrs.
Mackenzie, "was full of life and kindliness,
but I never knew him to be a swearer, or a drinker,
or a fighter." "Before his conversion," writes one
who knew him well, "he was known to all around as
a hearty, good-tempered, jolly young fellow, physically
strong, with a good constitution and a cheerful disposition. His ready wit and genial humour made
him a striking personality among his mates in the pit,
and the soul of merriment in their amusements and
social gatherings." His love for dancing has already
been referred to. He was what his oldest friends
describe as "a clinking dancer,"—nimble in action
and graceful in movement.

In addition to the sports already named, donkey-
racing was a prevailing form of amusement among
the colliers. Shetland ponies had been recently
introduced into the pit, and the donkeys which they
superseded were sold at a nominal cost to the work-

men. Mackenzie owned one for some time, and as might be expected, was not content to have a commonplace, ordinarily - behaved animal, but must needs keep one of an untamed nature and restive habits. It was while adding one more to the already long list of wicked tricks which this creature had been taught in the mine, that he gained, through a bite, the crooked finger which he carried to his grave.

PONY AND TUB.

I remember him relating to me how he went once to Houghton-le-Spring, to enjoy what was called "The Feast," a species of rustic fair and merrymaking held annually. He sported for the occasion a pair of white pantaloons, and what was his chagrin, on returning from the fair to the inn where he had stabled his donkey, to find saddle and bridle gone, and as if that were not enough provocation, the perverse animal had rolled itself vigorously in the mire of the inn yard, and was not fit to lay a hand upon. White trousers and a mud - plastered donkey formed an incongruous combination, and the disgusted sportsman returned home with the conviction that the way of transgressors can not only be hard, but at times disagreeably soft. It was probably to this incident he alluded on his last visit to Haswell, when, in reply to one who was urging him to come to Houghton-le-Spring for a day, he answered playfully, "Nay, no more Houghtons for me! You behaved badly the last time I was at Houghton Feast. Somebody stole both my pad and bridle."

The ludicrous side of things, the humour that contrives to thrust the bright edge of its smile through all the tragedy of existence, had unceasing charm for him. A wealth of amusing anecdotes, enriched and garnished by his graphic recital of them, made him a constant fountain of entertainment to his companions. At the street-corner or round the alehouse table he would be the centre of a circle whose hilarity swelled into boisterous overflow beneath the charm of his witty sallies, his comical gestures, his laughable stories. It has often struck me that, in the wonderful vivacity of his nature, and the piquancy and charm of his conversation, there would be in those days a somewhat striking resemblance between him and his famous countryman—Burns.

One evening, when he and a number more were enjoying a merry time at the Grey Horse, one of the public-houses of the village, a wager was laid that Mackenzie would drink a pint of ale with a tablespoon in shorter time than one of his companions

could eat a penny roll of bread. They sat opposite
each other, and no sooner did the other man commence
operations, intending to abbreviate his task by bulky
bites, than Mackenzie also took up the game; but,
with every spoonful of ale, he made such comical
grimaces, that his opponent could neither masticate
nor swallow, and had no choice but to join his companions in shouts of uproarious laughter. Meanwhile
the Scotsman, who handled his spoon like one to
whom early familiarity with porridge had lent
dexterity, proceeded imperturbably with his task, and
won his wager in triumph.

Not only was he characterised at this time by a
constant flow of humour, but by an unbending
integrity. Whatever spiritual religion might have to
do for him afterwards, the task of converting him
into an honest man would not be laid upon its
shoulders. He hated all deceit and shams, and
admiring commendations of his inflexible uprightness
mingle with the gossip of the village still, even after
forty years of absence.

At that time, the identification of each miner's tub
by means of a "token" fastened inside was not in
vogue, but each as it came out from the hewer was
noted by a boy in a wooden book. Nor was it uncommon for unscrupulous men to insist on having
more tubs chalked to their credit than properly
belonged to them; a species of fraud not always avoided
by those from whom better things might have been
expected. The memory of an old miner who worked
near him dwells still, with a pride that has in it an
unconscious homage, on the fact that such methods of
adding a shilling or two to his wages were always

HASWELL COLLIERY.

scorned by Peter Mackenzie, even in his unconverted days.

On one occasion, when visiting the North, he was asked to call on a man with whom he had formerly worked in the pit, and who was now noted for religious fervour. To the surprise of those who made the request, Mackenzie declined. The reason he gave afterwards was this. Mackenzie was detained one night, when a hewer, to work near the shaft, while his mate went forward to their usual place of toil. During the shift an accident occurred which compelled those farthest in to suspend operations and return to their homes, but did not interfere with Mackenzie's toil. The natural thing, of course, would have been for his mate, when interrupted elsewhere, to join and assist him; indeed, he could not reach the shaft without passing close to the spot. What he did was to pass stealthily by, without a word of greeting or inquiry. No wonder that Mackenzie had scant respect for the man afterwards, in spite of his per-fervid ejaculations, saying, " I thought it rather mean ; for I made six shillings that night, of which he got three, and he made one and sixpence, of which I got ninepence."

In the year 1849, Mr. Henry Reed of Harrogate, commonly designated Squire Reed, a well-known and successful evangelist of a past generation, went to Haswell Colliery to conduct a series of special religious services. Mr. Reed, who had spent several years in Australia, was a man of considerable gifts, and a powerful preacher. The first Sunday morning service was thinly attended, but strenuous efforts were made during the afternoon to induce the villagers to attend, and in the evening things assumed a much more promising appearance, and quite a flutter of excitement passed through the congregation when one of the least likely men in the village was seen to enter and take a seat near the door. It was Peter Mackenzie, who, during his residence at the colliery, had not been known to attend any place of worship. His presence now was due to the earnest

HASWELL CHAPEL.

invitation of two simple-hearted men,—James Lumley and H. Elsbury,—who had called at his house and urged him to come to hear the mission preacher. He had given them a kindly welcome, and a promise of his presence at the evening service.

The sermon was cogent in its appeals, and of all the listeners, no one gave it greater heed than Peter Mackenzie. The truth went home to heart and conscience, and under the warm rain of its influence and the powerful stirring of the Divine Spirit, the good sowing of past days in the farmer's kitchen at Mildean, and of the Bible readings at his own fireside, began to germinate.

At the conclusion of the ordinary service, anxious glances were directed towards the stranger, to see whether there was likelihood of his remaining to the prayer - meeting, and when it was found that he waited, the feeling among those present rose to exultation. One of the friends, Mr. Matthew Young, spoke encouragingly to him, and then, while the hymn beginning,

> "Rock of Ages, cleft for me,"

was being sung, he went forward, knelt at the "penitent form," sought in earnest supplication the forgiveness of his sins, and consecrated himself to Jesus Christ, the Saviour of the world. One of his remembered petitions at that moment has in it an earnest and prophecy of the devotedness of his after days—"Lord, what wilt Thou have *me* to do?"

The scene has lived in the memory of all who witnessed it. The excitement was profound. Men little accustomed to ebullitions of emotion made the chapel echo with their prayers and exclamations. Mr. George Minto, a quiet, sedate man, lost all control of himself, and shouted a thanksgiving at the top of his voice; while Mr. Hunter, cashier of the colliery, one of the chief supporters of the church at the time, and also one of the grave, steady-going sort, stood over the penitent and wept like a child. It seemed, indeed, as if the conviction was driven home upon every mind that night, that a great trophy was being won for the Lord Jesus Christ, that a flame was being kindled in the village sanctuary, the gleam of which would blaze afar.

An incident characteristic of the fervour of Mackenzie's nature, and of the lasting impression made upon his mind by the experiences of that evening, has been communicated by Mr. George Parkinson of Sherburn. About twelve months after the events just related, Squire Reed was announced to preach in the Wesleyan chapel in the city of Durham, and Mackenzie, with others, walked from Haswell to hear him. During the service, Mr. Reed referred to the revival at Haswell, and spoke of a good Scottish brother who had been brought to Christ —a very promising case of conversion. " I wonder where he is now, whether he has held on his way," said the preacher; and in a loud voice from the gallery came Mackenzie's answer, " I am here, Mr. Reed. Praise the Lord, I am here ! "

CHAPTER VI

GETTING UNDER WAY—1849–1850

Hindrances—Sceptical Literature—A Persevering Class-Leader—
A Narrow Escape—The Monkey and Cromwell—His Reading—A Miner's Library—A Spiritual Impetus—His Exuberant Happiness—The Reform Agitation—Missionary
Meeting Incident—Introduced to Punshon—Happy Interruptions.

THE conversion of a man so well known, and whose
personality had made so deep a mark on the life
of the village, could not but create a sensation. That
the jovial miner should become a Methodist seemed
incredible, and many were inclined to regard it as
only another of the practical jokes of which he was
known to be especially fond. Time demonstrated the
reality of the change, however. It was evident that
he had become a new man in Christ Jesus. Without
leaving on him a shade of gloom, the frivolity passed
out of his life, and religious earnestness took its place.
The moor, with its bowls and betting, the street-corner,
the public-house, were all avoided; the thoughtless
desecration of the Sabbath became a thing of the past,
and amid new associations there was commenced a
new life.

It was not with unhindered steps, however, that he

walked at first.   A neighbour, who ought to have
known better, made strong efforts to undermine his
new-found faith in Christ.   This man, it seems, was
in the habit of distributing sceptical literature, and
pressed its acceptance upon the new convert with
such persistency that for some two or three months

WHERE MACKENZIE LIVED WHEN CONVERTED—HOUSE ON RIGHT
WITH CLOSED DOOR.

his mind was considerably perturbed and his ardour
abated.   The strong accent of disapproval with which
Mackenzie always referred to this man afterwards
would seem to indicate that he was not one of that
nobler class of unbelievers, who are simply anxious
that the disciple should be able to give a reason for
the hope that is in him; but one of the baser sort,
who feel an unworthy delight in the mischievous
endeavour to unsettle the minds of others.

The leader in whose class Mackenzie began to meet was greatly concerned about him, and spared no pains to rescue him from this and other unfavourable influences, and to retain him in connection with the church. In this commendable endeavour he was seconded by Mrs. Mackenzie. She was shrewd enough to see how important it was that her husband should continue in the course he had entered upon, hence she furthered as far as in her lay, and to an extent that probably Mackenzie himself never knew, the effort that his class-leader made to preserve him from turning aside. Speaking of these endeavours and of the man who made them, Mackenzie said afterwards: " I tried hard to get rid of him, but it was impossible. If I missed my class-meeting, he would be at my house the following day, at a time most inconvenient to me, but a time that he considered to be the only chance of catching me. If likely to meet him in the street, I would either seek shelter in a friend's house, when one chanced to be near, or slip through an open-ing, and try to evade him by changing my route ; but I seemed to meet him at every turn."

An incident that occurred about this time, in con-nection with his daily occupation, seems to have made a deep impression upon his mind, and to have seconded very effectively the efforts of his ubiquitous leader. He had just finished the toil of the day, and was putting on his garments a few yards from the face of the coal, when a huge stone fell from the roof on the very spot where a few moments before he had been seated at work. What a wonderful deliver-ance ! How narrowly he had escaped the instant and cruel death which overtakes so many like workers, who, amid unsuspected perils, toil for their daily bread.

This deliverance reminds one not unnaturally of another with which Mackenzie used to illustrate one of his lectures, and which has been communicated by the Rev. Thomas H. Hill of Stirling. Mr. Hill says: "I remember, many years ago, hearing one of Peter's first lectures, at Melsonby, in the Darlington circuit. The lecture was on Providence, and in it he related a most remarkable incident in the life of Oliver Cromwell. Richard Cromwell, the father of Oliver, kept a monkey, who made himself very much at home in his master's house, and became head nurse to Oliver when an infant. One fine summer day, when the windows of the house were open, and Oliver sleeping peacefully in his cradle, in came the monkey through one of the windows, and, taking up the infant, climbed to the housetop, and there sat hugging and tossing up the baby with the kindness and care of a practised nurse 'Look at this picture!' cried Peter, with his wonderfully expressive face, and throwing up both hands and arms as if he held an infant there. 'Look at this picture! *The English Commonwealth in the arms of a monkey! The English Commonwealth in the arms of a monkey!*' The household of Cromwell were greatly alarmed, and how to recover the child could not tell. If they fired at the monkey, they might shoot the child; if they chased him, he might throw the child down. It was resolved at length to leave him alone, and, going out of sight, they waited to see what would be the result. After a good spell of nursing, down came the monkey with all possible care, and, passing again through the open window with the young Oliver in his arms, laid the little one in his cradle once more, without a broken bone in his body or even a scratch on his face."

It was natural that Mackenzie should be greatly moved by his own narrow escape from death, by what seemed to him almost a miraculous intervention of Divine Providence on his behalf. His heart went out towards God in a great swing of gratitude and fresh resolution. On reaching home, he found his pertinacious class-leader waiting with a special invitation; but coaxing and persuasion were no longer required. Filled with the recollection of his marvellous preservation, he went gladly to the meeting that evening; and resolved henceforth to give himself unbrokenly to the service of Jesus Christ.

He now sought with greater eagerness the fellowship of books, with an earnest desire for self-improvement, and probably with an unspoken wish to fit himself for future usefulness. The Bible and the Wesleyan hymn - book were then and ever afterwards great favourites, and it was impossible to hear him preach in after-life without recognising how deeply he had imbibed the spirit and letter of both. As a supplement to these, the local preachers, among whom he now formed companionships, were ever ready to place at his disposal whatever they possessed in the form of literary or theological treasures.

Their resources in this respect were not so scanty as a stranger to North of England colliery life would suppose. In many of those humble, unpretentious homes would be found, and, what is better, would be read and studied, selections of the best in English literature. I knew a miner of that day, and he was an example of many others, in whose library I could lay hands on Chambers's *Encyclopædia of English Literature*, Orr's *Circle of the Sciences*, editions of the best poets, treatises on philosophy and religion, besides yearly volumes of what were then some of the better and more popular magazines. Nor can I forget that the only man I have known who could claim to have gone five times through Milton's *Paradise Lost* was a collier from the county of Durham. The pastures on which Mackenzie would browse might be limited in extent, but it does not follow that the grass would be poor in quality. It was his custom to keep a box of books under the bed, and when sleep had repaired the energy wasted in the pit, he would, without rising, draw forth his treasures, and read for hours where he lay.

While this quiet intellectual cultivation was proceeding month by month, he received also a spiritual fillip in a revival of religion, the outcome of Sunday school sermons preached at Haswell by Mr. Thomas Elliott of Swalwell, a man widely known throughout all that district for the vigour and fervour of his pulpit ministrations. In this revival Mackenzie took a ready share as a worker, and, as an old acquaintance of his expresses it, the fire within him was fanned into a flame that never afterwards died out.

What we behold in him after this is an ardent, demonstrative disciple of Christ, filled with godly zeal and overflowing love, and especially remarkable for a joyous exultation of spirit, that found outlet in those explosive shouts of "Glory! Hallelujah! Praise the Lord!" and the like, which his lips never afterwards lost the knack of producing, and

which often broke alarmingly on people not accustomed
to such emphatic methods of expressing religious
emotion. As an illustration of this exuberance of
soul, it is related of him that he was one day sent
by the man in charge to assist a fellow-workman in
carrying from one part of the mine to another a
long heavy baulk of timber, such as is commonly
employed in supporting the roof. As the two crawled
along, almost crushed beneath their burden, they were
met by an old Methodist, who cried, " Hulloa, Peter,
how's tha gettin' on, lad ? " " Praise the Lord ! "
shouted Peter in reply. " Ay, but thou would praise
Him better with the baulk off thi back," rejoined his
friend. This was doubtless true enough, but all the
answer that could be evoked from the happy toiler
was, " Hallelujah ! Praise the Lord ! "

It was during these early years of Mackenzie's
religious life that the Methodist Church passed
through the strain of what is known as the Reform
Agitation. Two parties had come into existence,
with opposing views of ecclesiastical policy and pro-
cedure, and, as is common in such cases, personal
prejudices and antipathies were allowed to sharpen
the edge of public controversy. Strong feeling prevailed on both sides, and found vent at times in
bitter remarks. Fortunately for the growth of the
young convert, Haswell was but little disturbed; a
strong spiritual life dominating the little church,
and its work being more than usually prosperous.
When the annual missionary meeting came round,
the chapel was filled to overflowing, the deputation
for that year, 1850, being the Reverend William
Morley Punshon, then in the dawning flush of his

popularity in the Brunswick circuit, Newcastle-on-Tyne. The Rev. John Wilson, superintendent of the Durham circuit at the time, referred in his address to how that very day in the city one of the opposed party had pointed a finger at him and cried, "There goes an enemy of God!" Mr. Wilson went on to remark that he was not aware of being an enemy to anyone, unless it was the prince of darkness. Mackenzie, who was seated near the platform, called out immediately, "Ay, hinny, ye *are* an enemy, and lang may ye live to be an enemy to the prince of the power of the air!" His cry rang through the chapel, the audience cheered enthusiastically, and Punshon, joining heartily in the laughter and applause, made vigorous use of the incident in the eloquent and well-timed speech with which he followed that of the superintendent. At the close he shook hands with the impetuous miner, little dreaming that in a few years this unlettered and somewhat boisterous working man would, as lecturer and preacher, win a fame as wide as his own.

This faculty for happy interruption was one that Mackenzie never forfeited. I remember, years afterwards, when a serious discussion was proceeding in the District Synod anent a solitary station, the occupant of which was a brother unduly stout, he threw the meeting into roars of laughter by rising and saying with mock gravity, and in tones that gave unutterable raciness to the words, "I move, Mr. Chairman, that the ministerial staff be *reduced.*"

CHAPTER VII

FIRST ATTEMPTS AT PREACHING—1850–1852

Christian Development — Sunday School Work — Walk to
Sherburn Hill — His First Sermon — Interview with a
Hearer—Misgivings and Questionings—Wise Counsel—
How to get Warmed—His Dress and Appearance—"A
Bad Time"—Winning a Suit of Clothes—A Memorable
Watch-night.

IN every normal development of the religious life,
the convert passes by natural, almost insensible
steps into the worker; and, where there are suitable
gifts, the disciple develops into the apostle—the man
sent to others to tell of what has come to him. The
rock of the smitten heart cannot but send forth
streams of gratitude and helpful love. What form
the new-born activity shall take is usually decided
by the verdict of circumstance and ability. In a
large number of cases it is the Sunday school that
absorbs the early zeal and devotion, probably because
that form of endeavour is most easily accessible, and
is generally, though erroneously, supposed to require
but the minimum of qualification. This was the
service on which the converted miner at Haswell
tried his apprentice hand. "Worked in church and
school about one year," he says, in his autobiographical

notes. He also frequently accompanied the local preachers to their appointments, gleaning from them such instruction as was attainable on the way, and, doubtless, secretly anticipating and preparing for the time when he should himself be similarly employed.

That time came, perhaps somewhat unexpectedly, one Sunday afternoon in the year 1850. He had been requested by Mr. William Phalp, an intimate friend, to accompany him to the village of Sherburn Hill, at which place the latter was appointed to preach that day, afternoon and evening. Mr. Phalp has been for many years resident in Australia, but has confirmed the accuracy of this narrative in recent letters.

The two friends chatted together on the way, and Mr. Phalp, who was not feeling very well, asked Mackenzie, half in jest and half in earnest, whether he would take the service that afternoon. "Yes," answered his companion, "I will try. I have been asking the Lord about it, and I believe it is all right. I have an impression that I ought to preach." Mr. Phalp was hardly prepared for so ready an assent, and as he was himself but a probationer on the circuit plan, felt slightly uncertain about the course to which he was being committed. Having gone so far, however, it was difficult to retreat, and Mackenzie was allowed to take the pulpit. His appearance and dress were altogether unusual, while his abrupt, unconventional manner at once aroused attention, and possibly in some excited ridicule. But the stream of enthusiastic eloquence which he poured forth on the story of blind Bartimæus, moving the people to laughter and tears at will, held his audience spellbound, and from that hour he was marked out as one to whom the crowd would be glad to listen.

This account of Mr. Phalp's is substantiated by the relation of an interview between Mr. Cuthbert, then a resident at Sherburn Hill, and Mr. R. Garnett of Coxhoe, which the latter communicated recently to the *Northern Weekly Gazette*.

"I think, Mr. Cuthbert," remarked Mr. Garnett, "it was at Sherburn Hill, in the county of Durham, that Mr. Mackenzie made his first attempt at preaching?"

"Yes; I distinctly remember the time. It was in a building that was used both as schoolroom and chapel."

"Can you give any valid proof that the time you refer to was Mr. Mackenzie's first effort in the pulpit?"

"From his own statement at the time I am satisfied of this. In his apology at the beginning of his discourse, he reminded his hearers that they were not to expect much from him, as he had never been in a pulpit before, not even to snuff the candles. It may be necessary to explain that 'moulds' or 'dips,' forty or fifty years ago, were an indispensable requisite in village chapels during the long nights, and the snuffing very often had to be done in the pulpit by the preacher himself. If the manipulation was not very expertly performed, and any mishap took place, a general titter would pass through the congregation at the preacher's expense."

"Was there anything in the preacher or in his discourse that impressed you as being out of the ordinary?"

"I remember his intense earnestness, humour, and witty remarks made an impression on my mind which I have never forgotten."

"Do you remember if this, his first effort in the pulpit, was regarded by the congregation who heard him as a success, or was it considered a failure?"

"It was certainly regarded as a success, and much appreciated and talked about for a long time afterwards."

"Do you remember the subject of his discourse?"

"The subject, I think, was blind Bartimæus, but I cannot say positively."

"Do you remember anything as to his personal appearance."

"Yes, I remember distinctly. His appearance was that of a working man. He had on a short jacket, and looked somewhat odd and unclerical."

It is interesting to note that Mackenzie's first sermon was on a Bible, character, and those who watched his after career cannot but have observed that it was to this class of subject that his peculiar genius lent itself with most freedom and power; that, in both sermons and lectures, he was most effective when biographical and descriptive rather than when doctrinal or argumentative.

On the way home that night the two young men were not without disturbing thoughts. Mackenzie had begun well, and produced an exceedingly favourable impression, but had rule and usage been observed? He had occupied the pulpit almost by accident. Neither superintendent minister nor Local Preachers' Meeting had been conferred with. Would not trouble and difficulty arise?

CHAPEL LANE, HASWELL.

When Haswell was reached, they observed that the chapel was still lighted, and, proceeding thither, they encountered several of the leading brethren at the door, just leaving after a protracted prayer-meeting. A few were called aside for consultation, and after the young men had related the experiences of the day, Mr. George Wardle, a local preacher and one of the more sage and elderly, was appealed to. "Give yourself no concern, brother Phalp," he remarked very wisely. "The Local Preachers' Meeting may do as it pleases; this is a divine call. Brother Mackenzie is called to preach the gospel, and the local preachers will do their duty when the proper time comes." Sensible words, and fully supported by subsequent events. Before the Local Preachers' Meeting came round, Mackenzie's popularity was established, and his acceptance placed beyond dispute.

After this brief colloquy at the chapel door, one of the friends grasped Mackenzie by the hand, and congratulated him on having got into harness. In his reply, he related in a graphic manner the following incident, evidently gathered from his reading, and showing how the prompting to use what gifts he had was strong within him. In Northern Russia, two travellers driving a sleigh came upon a man who had fallen exhausted, and was lying helpless in the snow. The horses were stopped, and one of the travellers was eager to render assistance. The other declined. His more benevolent companion descended from the sleigh, and ceased not to tug and lift until he had placed the perishing one in it. The other, meanwhile, sat shivering in his furs, grumbling at the detention. "You ought to have helped," rejoined his friend, "and then you would have been as warm as I am."

"You see," observed the newly-fledged preacher, applying the incident, "when one does nothing, one grows cold. When you sit still in the gospel chariot, you get frozen up. If you want to be warm yourself, you must warm others." A teaching of which the whole of his subsequent career was a striking illustration.

The attire and general appearance of Mackenzie, during the days of his first pulpit efforts, can hardly be described as glaringly clerical. A fastidious taste would probably have shuddered when he stood up for the first time to address an audience at Haswell. The service was held in a cottage on a week-evening. Having done so well at Sherburn Hill, there was naturally a strong desire abroad to hear him. His appearance was certainly striking; in any but Peter it would have been accounted grotesque. Imagine a black coarse velvet coat, such as is now worn by sportsmen and gamekeepers; a blue vest, with two rows of buttons; broad - ribbed corduroy trousers, ripped from the bottom to the knee, and secured tight to the leg with fancy buttons, after the manner of gaiters; strong heavy boots; a coloured neckerchief, fastened in a gigantic bow; hair brushed into glossy obedience; and white handkerchief, well sprinkled with scent, crushed between the strong fingers or held fluttering aloft. To what singular uses, from the slaying of giants and Philistines to the persona-tion of babies, were the successors of that white handkerchief destined to lend themselves, and how the liking for perfume followed him to the end of his days!

When referring to this effort, years afterwards, he said, "There were too many locals there that night. I had a bad time." Such was not the impression of his hearers. They felt the service to be one of no ordinary power and success. The preacher's attire was not to them of great moment, convinced, as they were, that underneath the queer, staring garb there beat the heart of a true man and a genuine Christian, and that the uncouthness held in its crooked branches the promise of a notable aftergrowth.

As was customary, the house of one of the friends was resorted to after the service for social chat, and the company, being in a playful mood, chaffed Mackenzie about his unclerical appearance. "Ah," said he, "you would never guess how this suit came into my possession, but I will tell you." Then he related how certain sports were held near where he had lived in Scotland. One of these was a donkey race, the conditions of which were that not the first, but the last to arrive at the goal should be accounted winner. His rival and he exchanged animals at the start, and Mackenzie's interest was to urge his opponent's ass to go quicker than his own, a task in which he succeeded perfectly, his own donkey bringing up the rear, and winning for him the variegated suit as a prize.

The Watch-night Service of that year, at Haswell, was rendered memorable by sermons from the two young men, Mackenzie and Phalp. The chapel was filled. Both men, though direct opposites, were vigorous preachers, and each had made special preparation. Phalp preached on the parable of the barren fig tree, and Mackenzie on that of the man who had not on a wedding garment; and the older inhabitants speak of the service still, as one unparalleled in all their experience for its wealth of spiritual influence.

CHAPTER VIII

Worker in the Church—A Popular Probationer—His Preaching—
How he got a Commentary—Sociable Habits—Learning a
Tune—A Late Night and Early Morning—The Outwitted
Donkey—The Donkey Cart—A Suggested Frontispiece.

IN the autobiographical fragment already quoted
from, after recording his removal from Dundee
to Oxclose in 1844, Mackenzie continues :—

" Lived there nearly a year, then went to Haswell. Lived about
four years without Christ. Got converted in 1849, under Mr.
Reed. Worked in church and school about one year. Then
became a local preacher, was favourably received, saw good done,
and rejoiced exceedingly."

The exact date at which he became a local preacher
I have not been able to determine. It was probably
towards the end of 1850. A circuit plan, preserved
by himself, and where his name stands among those
on trial, is for the quarter beginning February 22,
and ending May 16, 1852. Impressive evidence
of his already abounding popularity, as well as of
his readiness in preparing sermons, is afforded by
the fact that on this plan, though still on trial, he

has no less than thirteen double appointments, with one afternoon in addition; in other words, he is not allowed one free Sunday during the whole of the quarter.

Mr. George Parkinson says of him at this time:—

" His early efforts as a local preacher were marked by striking originality of thought, apt illustration, and intense earnestness. His natural cheerfulness, wit, and humour were as irrepressible in the new life as they had been in the old, and as gifts of the Master, they went into the Master's service, to which he had given himself, with all that he was, and all that he might become. I was occasionally with him in conducting Sunday services, and have a vivid recollection of some of the sermons he then preached, and which I have the impression were never excelled in after years. One sermon on the final judgment especially impressed me, and another on John iii. 16, in which his own experience and appreciation of the love of God were strongly marked, and the pathos and tenderness of his own nature strikingly illustrated."

The books that aided him in those earlier years, among which are named Dwight's *Theology* and Whitfield's *Sermons*, were mostly borrowed from willing friends. Such biblical and homiletical apparatus as he could call his own was as yet limited to scanty proportions; but one aid that proved of great service came into his possession unexpectedly, and in rather an amusing manner.

A branch of the British and Foreign Bible Society was formed at Haswell, and, to give more efficiency to its operations, the village was divided into districts for regular visitation. The district appointed to Mackenzie and another young man, George Phalp, brother to William Phalp, was one that abounded with public-houses. The two young men went round systematically with sample Bibles, taking each house in turn, and Mackenzie's humour and geniality were valuable aids in securing orders. On entering the Oddfellows' Arms. the landlord, a professed infidel,

MAIN STREET, HASWELL.

opened on Mackenzie a teasing fire of chaff about his changed life, but found the object of his badinage quite a match for him in good-humoured and pointed repartee. When their samples were exhibited, the landlord said, " I have a better Bible in the house than any of these." Mackenzie asked to see it, and the book was produced. Observing how enviously he turned over the leaves and conned the pages, the landlord remarked good-naturedly, " Now, mate, have ye any swaps ? " That is, " Are you willing to exchange ? "   Mackenzie answered eagerly in the affirmative, a bargain was struck, and, handing the landlord one of the best of his samples, he departed with the newly-acquired treasure under his arm. When they got outside, he poked his companion in the ribs, and exclaimed laughingly, "The devil has outwitted himself again.   He has influenced that man to give me a Commentary." The book thus obtained proved to be a well-bound copy of Burkitt's *Notes on the New Testament*, and as the young local preacher possessed no such work of his own, but until now had always been indebted to the generosity of others, it will be understood with what joy he carried home a volume likely to prove so serviceable.   Better exegetical works could be found, at a subsequent period, in his library of nearly three thousand volumes, but the commentary so quaintly acquired was never disposed of, and stands on his shelves to-day.

The practice of consecrating all things to God in prayer, so notable in his ministerial career, was often exemplified in those early years.   His friend William Phalp, having recently married, set up house not far from Mackenzie.   As was customary among the villagers, the neighbours called to offer their congratulations to the young couple in their new home. Among the rest came Mackenzie ; and after surveying with pleasure the bright new furniture and attractive appearance of the house, he exclaimed, " Eh, but she's grand !   Has she been consecrated yet ? "   " She " is the term a miner naturally employs to describe the house in which he lives, the coal he hews, the colliery at which he works, and a multitude of other objects. In reply to his query, someone answered, "Not yet, Peter." "Then let us have her consecrated, friends," was the immediate rejoinder, and in a moment he was on his knees, pouring out an earnest and appropriate supplication for a blessing on the newly-married couple and all their belongings.

Mackenzie's contemporaries among the local preachers speak of him as having a propensity to remain to a late hour when out on the Sabbath fulfilling an appointment. He was exceedingly sociable, and the friends who entertained him delighted in his bright and genial society, and were eager to prolong his visits. On one occasion, when appointed to Coxhoe, eight miles distant, he agreed to meet the two brothers Phalp, who were, one at Kelloe and the other at Quarrington Hill, places from six to seven and a half miles away from Haswell in the same direction. The arrangement was that Peter was to proceed to Kelloe to supper, after which he and William would move on to Quarrington Hill for George, who was much younger, and just beginning to preach. Losing all sense of time in a prayer-meeting that seemed to have no end, and that was succeeded by singing and talk and cheery hospitality in the house of one of the Coxhoe friends, Mackenzie did not reach Kelloe, where his companion had waited two hours, until about ten o'clock. Turning their faces homeward, they called at Quarrington Hill, and satisfied the younger brother that he was not left behind. All three then proceeded to Thornley, where it suddenly occurred to Mackenzie that someone at Kelloe had spoken of a new prayer-meeting tune, which Michael Watson rejoiced in the knowledge of. Michael Watson was another friend, musical in his tastes, who resided at Thornley, and, despite all protest, Mackenzie insisted on proceeding to his house. It was eleven o'clock when the trio arrived at the door, and all was closed for the night. In response to a thrice-repeated knock, the inquiry came, "Who is there?" "Glory! hallelujah!" shouted the disturber. "Get up, lass!" cried Watson, in great glee, to his wife. "There's Peter at the door." The door was speedily opened, coffee prepared, and the interview prolonged until the new revival tune was mastered.

Thornley was not left behind until midnight, and when they arrived at Haswell, the caller (a man employed to waken the boys and men in the early morning) had already entered on his rounds, and was breaking the stillness with his unwelcome clatter and pitiless cry of "Get up, lad! call the lads up!" It was Mackenzie's turn to begin labour at this hour, so, without a moment's rest, after preaching probably three times, and walking sixteen miles, he had to lay aside his Sunday dress, clothe himself in working garb, and proceed literally from the pulpit to the mine. The same unpalatable portion awaited his companions.

About the middle of the shift, that is, about four in the morning, the two brothers had to pass the spot where Mackenzie was employed. He was hard at work, swinging his pick with a vigour that seemed to have in it no trace of the toil of the previous day. They stood for a few moments in quiet admiration, then one of them called, "How do you feel now,

Peter?" He threw down his pick, and, coming towards them, said, "Ah, lads, this won't do. We must get home sooner. She's hard. I have hardly strength to knock her down."

Such an experience was probably repeated at frequent intervals. It could hardly be avoided, in a circuit so wide that some of the appointments were as far as fifteen miles distant, with hardly any other alternative than trudging on foot. There were times when he was able to indulge in the luxury of a ride or a drive, but neither was of such an order as to excite greatly the envy of pedestrians, as the following incidents, supplied from several trustworthy sources, will show.

Having an appointment at Pelton Fell one Sunday, a distance of twelve miles, he borrowed a donkey of one of his friends, his own having by that time been disposed of. In returning, a brook had to be forded, and its usually narrow dimensions had been swollen by rain. The moon was at the full, and when the donkey reached the edge, its own reflection peered so uncannily up out of the water that it came to a sudden stop. "Whether he saw the Man-in-the-Moon," said Mackenzie, "or only his own shadow, I never could tell; but I coaxed him, clapped him, pressed him hard, said nice words to him, even put my shoulder against him and pushed like a ' putter down the dip,' all in vain. He would not stir. Then, thinking a little craft might be useful, I led him back a bit, put my coat off and wrapped it round his head and face, and after turning him round several times, so that he could not for the life of him tell the direction of the North Pole, I gradually brought him on to the path, and led him across the foot-bridge that crossed the stream, landing him safely on the other side before he knew where he was. I took off the blinkers, put on my coat, and, pricking up his ears, he trotted briskly on to Haswell, where we arrived in time for a short sleep, and then off to the pit."

On another occasion he started early on the donkey for Chester-le-Street, a somewhat similar journey Not far from the village, a man, whose very unpretentious residence he had to pass on the way, made a generous offer of his donkey-cart as an easier method of travel for so long a journey.

"But have ye any harness for the animal?" asked Peter.

"I've plenty of 'towts,'" answered the man, "and we can soon tie him in."

"Get him yoked, then!" said Peter.

"Towts" is a provincialism for rough hempen cords, by the help of which the donkey was duly fixed into some shattered old harness, and the preacher started once more on his way.

On reaching Chester-le-Street he drove up to the inn, called for the ostler, and gave the quadruped into his charge, requesting that he should be well fed. The man, examining the animal on both sides, stood amazed, and asked—

"How am I to get him out?"

"If you cannot loose him," said Peter, "cut him out, and deal gently with the brute, and we can tie him in again to-night."

One of the leaders, a saddler by trade, and who had considerable regard for the proprieties, happened to pass while this colloquy was proceeding, and was greatly impressed by the spectacle. He had heard of Peter Mackenzie, the man appointed that day, as an eccentric individual, and could not help murmuring to himself, "I hope this is not he." At the close of the morning service, however, his misgivings had begun to vanish, and in the evening, after very successful services, crowned with the salvation of souls, he was eager, with several others, to accompany the preacher to the inn, and see him safely started on his homeward journey. This was just what the preacher himself, remembering the shabbiness of his turnout, was most anxious to avoid. He thanked them heartily, protested there was no need for such kindness, and so on, but in vain. They were not to be shaken off, so, putting a good face on the matter, he led the way to the Lambton Arms. When the donkey had been strapped into his motley harness, and the eccentric preacher seated upon the cart, he cried, "Now, friends, just one verse before we start—

> When he first the work begun,
> Small and feeble was his day."

When relating the incident years afterwards, he suggested merrily that if ever his biography were written, there should be placed as a frontispiece a picture of himself in that donkey-cart, and underneath the words—

> When he first the work begun,
> Small and feeble was his day ;
> Now the word doth swiftly run,
> Now it wins its widening way.

Which merry suggestion shows at least one thing—

that while there may be men who climb high, and then blush to admit that they were ever low, Peter Mackenzie was free from the ignoble pride that is ashamed of the rock from which it was hewn, the pit from which it was digged.

CHAPTER IX

Demands on his Services—Rev. Joseph Hall's Recollection—"No
Houses to let in Heaven"—"A Locomotive Devil"—Heavy
Collection—Mr. George Parkinson's Testimony—Depressed
Condition of Industry—Carlyle's England—The Gold Fever—
Desire to Emigrate—Visit to the Rector—Frustrated again—
A Run for Life—Visit to Escomb—Reminiscences of Rev. E.
Dodd—Characteristics of his Preaching.

IT was impossible for a man so richly gifted as
Peter Mackenzie to remain shut up in a corner.
The Durham circuit, extensive as were its boundaries,
was not wide enough to hold him. His fame spread
abroad, and a demand for his services set in from all
the district round. School and chapel anniversaries
soon began to make heavy calls upon him. It has
not been without interest to me to discover that an
uncle of my own, Mr. William Burdess of Grange, in
the Durham circuit, a staunch old Methodist in his
day, was the first to seek Mackenzie to preach at an
anniversary. When reminded of this, only a year ago,
by Mr. John Burdess of Jarrow, he answered quickly,
and with as vivid a recollection of the occurrence as
if it had only transpired the day before, " Ay ; and a

wonderful figure I cut, with my velvet coat and red muffler, when I went into the pulpit."

As an evangelist his presence was even more eagerly sought for. He became a sort of religious stoker for the district, and wherever the fire of spiritual life and activity had burned low, his assistance was invoked to give it a new stir and fresh fuel. In this capacity he was often absent from home for weeks together, and extended his labours far beyond the immediate neighbourhood

The Rev. Joseph Hall writes :—

"I went to reside in Durham circuit in 1852, shortly after Mr. Mackenzie's name appeared on the plan, and found his services in great request on every hand. Myself and a few other young men walked several miles one Saturday evening to hear him at Coxhoe. The text was John iii. 14, 15 : ' And as Moses lifted up the serpent in the wilderness,' etc. It was a blessed time, and at the close of the service there was a rush—scores of penitents came forward in a few minutes.

"In those days I frequently heard Mackenzie preach, and there was always ' something to stick.' At Grange, near Durham, I heard him from John iii. 16. In speaking of the everlasting life, he said : ' Everything will last for ever in heaven, an everlast- ing throne, everlasting songs, everlasting palms, everlasting robes, everlasting habitations. You will never be turned out, and, bless you, you will never see it written up—*Houses to Let ;* for there shall be no more death, but everlasting life.'

" In preaching at Sherburn on the narrative of the Syro-Phœnician woman and her daughter, he said that when the girl had a worse fit than usual, certain present-day gentlemen would have said that it was because the moon was at the full, but not so—Satan was looking through her eyes and speaking through her lips ; in fact, she was a locomotive devil going about her mother's house.

"The people at Sherburn Hill had a great day one Sunday. Peter preached morning and afternoon in a marquee, and in the evening outside, as the crowd was so immense. The evening collection was so heavily weighted with copper that it required two men to carry the vessel in which it was removed."

These reminiscences of Mr. Hall throw an interesting light on the character of Mackenzie's preaching at that time, and enable us more intelligently to bring it into comparison with his style in later years. The following from Mr. George Parkinson also aids in the same direction :—

"The ready facilities offered by the Methodist Church for utilising the services and developing the talents of its members, afforded Peter Mackenzie the opportunity of active Christian usefulness among those of his own level of life, and at the beginning of his work as a local preacher he was the means of leading hundreds to God. Forty-five years have passed since he entered on his evangelistic labours in the colliery villages of Durham, but there are numbers yet to be met with who owe their conversion to his efforts, and many of them in their turn have led and are still leading others to Christ. I have known many men engaged in this work, but never a more single-minded soul - winner than Peter Mackenzie was in those days."

When the mind dwells on those years of glorious onslaught on the kingdom of evil, and on all that came in their train, it cannot but be grateful that a project formed by Mackenzie early in his Christian course was not carried out. Though not generally known, it is an undoubted and noteworthy fact, that his thoughts had been strongly drawn in the direction of emigration.

About the time of his beginning to preach, the condition of the industrial classes was extremely depressed. Among the miners, strong men were often not able to earn more than from eighteen to twenty shillings a week, while provisions were exceedingly dear—flour, for example, ranging from three shillings to three-and-sixpence a stone. Writing only a few years before, Thomas Carlyle, in his *Past and Present*, says: "The condition of England, on which many pamphlets are now in course of publication, and many thoughts unpublished are going on in every reflective head, is justly regarded as one of the most ominous, and withal one of the strangest, ever seen in this world. England is full of wealth, of multifarious produce, supply for human want in every kind; yet England is dying of inanition." Speaking of her fifteen million workers, he continues: "Some two millions, it is now counted, sit in workhouses, poor-law prisons; or have 'out-door relief' flung over the wall to them—the workhouse Bastille being filled to bursting, and the strong poor-law broken asunder by a stronger. They sit there, these many months now; their hope of deliverance as yet small."

The discovery of gold in Australia in 1851 caused

a sudden rush thitherward from nearly all parts of the Old World, but especially from Britain, and was not without its influence on the colliery villages of Durham and Northumberland, Indeed, it created in them a great excitement. The gold fever became an epidemic. Large numbers of miners emigrated, and several met with singular success. The reports sent home to Haswell by some of these men awakened in many minds a desire to share their good fortune ; and among those so influenced were Peter Mackenzie and his two friends, George and William Phalp.

Mackenzie was the only one of the three men who was married, though the other two were on the verge of being so. All three had fully decided to leave the country, and try their fortune in the colony of Victoria. They proposed to go as Government-assisted emigrants. The necessary papers had been obtained, and properly completed, with the exception of the rector's signature, whose place it was to testify to the respectability of their character. To obtain this signature, the three friends wended their way to the rectory at Easington, a distance of about two miles. On examining the papers, the clergyman discovered that they were all made out for married men. In reply to his inquiries, the two bachelor brothers stated that they were on the eve of marriage, that, indeed, their names had already been entered at the registrar's office. The rector waxed very indignant. What ! they were about to be married away from the church, and yet they had the effrontery to come to ask him to certify to their good conduct ! It was monstrous ! In vain did Mackenzie plead for his friends, urging that all the young folk desired and had intended was to be married quietly, and that, but for the greater publicity of it, they would be quite content to have the ceremony performed at the old church. His words were as rain upon rock. Ecclesiastical dignity was affronted. They had declared themselves to be Dissenters, and whatever was said after that only added to their offence. Mackenzie waxed eloquent, but the angry rector snatched up their papers, flung them indignantly back to them, flatly refused to append his name, and ordered them to leave the house.

This unlooked-for rejection ended for the present their emigration projects. Without the consciousness of what was involved in his action, the offended clergyman had rendered Methodism a signal service. Instead of helping him to become a digger of gold abroad, he had unwittingly aided in keeping Peter Mackenzie to dig in richer mines for nobler treasure at home.

About two years afterwards, a second endeavour on the part of the three friends to go out, this time at their own cost, was thwarted by the illness of one of them. William Phalp eventually sailed for Australia, where he did well, and still remains. His friend Mackenzie was exceedingly anxious to accompany him, but was prevented through lack of means.

Frustrated in his attempts to go abroad, he continued to labour with intense earnestness, and, as we have seen, with most gratifying success, at home. His library increased, his knowledge widened, his thinking attained greater order and strength, and every week made it growingly evident that preaching, not mining, the winning of souls from evil, rather than the winning of coal from the ground, was to be his vocation.

Meanwhile, though his spiritual life was so vigorous, and his efforts to save and strengthen others so successful, he was still made to feel at times that he had not yet passed beyond the possibility of returning to the old ways. More than once did he relate in the love-feast an exposure to spiritual peril about this period that almost wrecked him. He had been speaking at a meeting somewhere beyond Durham, and was on his way home. It had been hiring day, there were numbers of farm lads and lasses in the city, and at one public-house which he had to pass, a dance was in full swing. The fiddlers were waking merry strains, and the shouts and laughter of the revellers could be plainly heard. For a few moments Mackenzie stood and listened. As he did so, there swept through his veins a passionate longing for a draught of the old delights. The rhythm of dance and music seized his limbs, and he all but rushed inside to join the rollicking throng. The struggle was of brief duration, but his whole future seemed at that moment to tremble in the balance. Suddenly the sight of Bunyan's pilgrim fleeing from the City of Destruction flashed through his mind, and, thrusting his fingers into his ears, he ran from the place, crying, " Life ! life ! eternal life ! "

So was he preserved by the grace of God from having such writing placed against his name as is recorded of another: " Demas hath forsaken me, having loved this present evil world."

The next chapter describes Mackenzie's removal to the Bishop Auckland circuit, but the following testimony from the Rev. E. Dodds shows us that he was already no stranger there, and also furnishes interesting glimpses of his pulpit style :—

The little village of Escomb had the honour of introducing Mr. Mackenzie to the Bishop Auckland circuit. His fame as a popular preacher, who filled the chapels wherever appointed in the Durham circuit, reached there through a friend, a relative of my own, from Haswell, where Mr. Mackenzie then resided. This report issued in an invitation to preach anniversary sermons at Escomb. He arrived on the Saturday evening, and, according to announcement, preached that night. The text was Job xxxiii. 27-28 : "He looketh upon men, and if any say, I have sinned, and perverted that which was right, and it profited me not ; he will deliver his soul from going into the pit, and his life shall see the light." On the Sunday the little chapel was crowded with friends from far and near. The evening text was Prov. ix. 12 : "If thou be wise, thou shalt be wise for thyself : but if thou scornest, thou alone shalt bear it." These sermons, though by no means equal to many which followed, yet indicated very unmistakably the natural power which was soon to develop so gloriously and usefully in the pulpit.

He was blessed with a retentive memory, and a rare gift of imagination. His illustrations were graphic. Speaking of the impotence of all attacks against the truth of God, he said, " Ye might as well try to knock down Durham Cathedral with a pop-gun " ; and of the vision of God to those who pray—" The saint upon his knees can see farther than the tip-toed philosopher through Rosse's telescope." Again, of the might of angels—" One of them could take this globe of ours in the hollow of his hand, and skew it into the wilds of immensity, where neither man nor devil could ever find it any more." He had wit and pathos, and a natural eloquence which ministered very greatly to the effectiveness of his preaching. His choice of topics and texts was very varied, and sameness could never be laid to his charge. He was fond of Bunyan and some of the poets, and would sometimes quote Pollok by the page in the pulpit. Those who heard him in those days, can scarcely have forgotten his terrible sermon on Job xxxvi. 18 : "Because there is wrath, beware lest He take thee away with His stroke : then a great ransom cannot deliver thee."

His earnest reiteration of the word *Beware!* was very telling. It should be remembered that this was before the Revised Version had furnished a somewhat different reading of the passage. Despite eccentricities of manner and quaintness of utterance which did not suit all tastes, his preaching was exceedingly popular and useful.

CHAPTER X

Bishop Auckland—Removal from Haswell—Letters to Mr. P.
Cooper—Engagement as Circuit Missionary—Mr. Thomas
Greener's Recollections—Visit to London and Use made of
it—Variety in His Preaching—Testimony of Rev. Thomas
M'Cullagh—Plums for his Cake—Progress of Bishop Auckland Circuit—his Text-Book—Brief Extracts—Good Work
at Coundon and Crook—Visits to Ramshaw and Lanchester.

THE town of Bishop Auckland possesses "few if
any attractions," says a local Methodist historian,
"but its surroundings are acknowledged to be both
beautiful and picturesque. It is situated nearly in
the centre of the county of Durham, standing on an
elevation surrounded by other hills still higher: is
bounded on the north and west by the river Wear,
and on the south-east by the river Gaunless. In its
precincts is a very fine park, adjoining the main
entrance of which stands a venerable castle, for many
centuries the residence of the Bishops of Durham."

At the September Quarterly Meeting, 1854, of
this Bishop Auckland circuit, the following resolution
was adopted:—"That a committee be appointed to
arrange for the employment of Peter Mackenzie, as

follows: the two circuit ministers, the two circuit stewards, and a representative from every place in the circuit." Again, in March 1855, it was agreed— "That Peter Mackenzie be engaged as Circuit Missionary, on the same terms and under the same regulations as before." The circuit at the time when Peter Mackenzie made its acquaintance was large and laborious, comprising within its boundaries, besides Bishop Auckland itself, some twenty-one villages, chiefly occupied by colliers and ironworkers.

It was not as Circuit Missionary that Mackenzie went to Bishop Auckland in the first instance. While resident at Haswell, the continuous demands made upon him for evangelistic services made it very difficult for him to attend to his ordinary occupation. After a while, Mr. Philip Cooper, the under-manager at the colliery, kindly took him from the hard toil of hewing, and gave him employment not only lighter, but of such a nature as made it easier to arrange for his frequent absences. Other privileges, such as house and coals, were also allowed him, although his work in the pit grew increasingly irregular. In the year 1854, Mr. Cooper removed to the Black Boy Colliery, in the Bishop Auckland circuit, and, owing to his kindness and consideration, Mackenzie was induced to follow, and obtained employment under him at the same place. His own autobiographical record, after speaking of his becoming a local preacher at Haswell, is—

" Two or three years after went to the Bishop Auckland circuit. Preached and worked at the Black Boy for six months under P. Cooper. Was employed by the Auckland friends for some four years. Saw three or four hundred brought in."

Through Mr. R. P. Phalp, Mrs. Balderstone of Castle Eden has kindly favoured me with two letters written by Mackenzie to her father, Mr. P. Cooper, about this time. Mr. Cooper, himself a member of the Wesleyan Church, had evidently written Mackenzie about special services. The following is an extract from his reply :—

TO MR. P. COOPER.

HASWELL, *April* 18, 1854.

DEAR SIR,—Yours came to hand to-day, and I was glad to hear that all were well. Thank God for His goodness. We are doing nicely here too. . . . Matthew Child had his leg broken to-day ; he lives next door to me. Burne's son was killed on the waggon-way last Thursday, and my place came down to-day [the place in which he worked], but I got out. Dangers stand thick through all the ground to push us to the tomb. Lord, help us to number our days, and apply our hearts unto wisdom. God willing, I will be with you on Saturday, and I have no objection to preach Christ to the people. Such as I have I will give unto them, balm or brimstone, or both, if the Lord please. We had a good time at Pelton Fell on F. and S. Good companies, good influence, and souls saved. Hallelujah !

The next letter, in which he speaks of giving notice to leave his present employment, would seem to indicate that Mr. Cooper had engaged him for Black Boy Colliery during the visit referred to above, and that his removal was only a question of a few weeks.

TO MR. P. COOPER.

HASWELL, *April* 26, 1854.

DEAR SIR,—I got safe landed in Haswell again on Monday night, and found them all well, praise the Lord ! We had a very good day at Byer's Green [a village in the Bishop Auckland circuit]. Several were awakened. May the Sun of Righteousness ripen them for glory. A great many friends have been inquiring for you since I came back. Our pit has been off to-day. I preached in our chapel last night. Good company. I have not given in my notice yet. I should like to see the new plan. I hope that you are all well. May the blessing that maketh rich and addeth no sorrow, and the peace that passeth all understanding, and the presence of Him who dwelt in the bush be your portion for ever. Amen.

PETER MACKENZIE.

After living for about six months at Black Boy, Mackenzie removed to the large colliery village of Coundon, a few miles distant; where he lived when it was arranged that he should undertake the duties of Circuit Missionary. By this arrangement greater steadiness and concentration were imparted to his labours as an evangelist. Efforts that up to the present had been to a large extent desultory were brought within a more defined compass, focussed on a more limited area, with hope of more specific and abiding result. He became an auxiliary of the circuit staff, without the status and responsibility of a minister. But, though more regular in its character, his work was still mainly that of an evangelist: holding special services for a week or ten days at the various places in the circuit and also beyond its boundaries.

Mr. Thomas Greener of London, then resident in the circuit, has kindly furnished me with some interesting recollections of this period. He writes :—

Mr. Mackenzie's movements were at that time directed by a committee, of which I acted as secretary. Previous to this, his services were in great demand, applications reaching him from many quarters farther north, where he was well known. Always willing to oblige, he sometimes made arrangements that required almost superhuman efforts to carry them out. I remember, on one occasion he preached at Escomb on the Sunday morning at ten o'clock. After the service, he partook of some hasty refreshment, and, mounting a horse, which had been lent him for the occasion, he rode off at full speed for Chester-le-Street, in the Durham circuit, a distance of about twenty miles, where he was due to preach in the afternoon. From there he had to return for the evening service at Coundon, and was obliged to go to his work in the pit at a very early hour on the Monday morning.

It was under such circumstances that a committee was formed to free him from work in the mine, and to enable him to devote his whole time and strength to his evangelistic labours. The committee appointed a treasurer, to whom all moneys due from the places at which he laboured should be paid ; he, in return, having to defray the stipend and other expenses of the evangelist. As secretary I had to reply to all applications for his services, and soon found the duties to be very onerous, having often as many as twenty letters in a day, not only from places in our own circuit, but from other circuits far and near. These I had to tabulate in readiness for the committee, of which the superintendent minister was chairman. At the meeting Mr. Mackenzie's work was fixed for three months, and a list of the places handed to him, he always cheerfully carrying out the arrangements.

In July 1857, Mr. Mackenzie visited London, to carry on revival services in connection with Brixton Hill Chapel. This was in fulfilment of an application made by Mrs. Kirsop, then of London, who agreed to pay his expenses, not only for the time employed, but also for an extra week, that he might have the opportunity to see something of London.

An account of these services has been communicated by Mr. J. Reed of London, from which one gathers that they were of an exceedingly lively and effective character.

Mr. Greener continues :—

The visit was very successful so far as the evangelistic work was concerned, and the week's holiday was an immense treat. It was his first sight of London. He went about with eyes and ears open ; nothing seemed to escape him. How refreshing it was to hear him speak of that visit ! One use which he made of what he had seen, I shall never forget. On the first Sunday after his return, I went with him to a large village chapel, filled principally with pitmen and their wives and children. The packed and eager listeners were ready to welcome their old friend. He took for his text—" In My Father's house are many mansions." After a very lively introduction, he gave a description of the Crystal Palace, which, for clearness and fulness of detail, I have never heard surpassed ; making the Palace and the surrounding grounds live before the congregation. Then he went on to draw a vivid picture of Solomon's temple, which, if possible, riveted the attention of his audience even more intently. At this point he paused, and said, in a very solemn manner : " Those of us who are loving God with our whole heart, who are serving and honouring our Lord Jesus Christ, and are allowing ourselves to be filled with the Holy Ghost, may look forward with confidence to dwell in a mansion of God's own making, a house not built with hands, eternal in the heavens. Hallelujah ! Won't you keep on preparing to be worthy to live in such a mansion ? I have tried to show you a grand earthly man-built palace, also a temple of world-wide fame for its beauty. Look at them both again ! See them ! Grand as they are, compared with the mansion that Christ is preparing for us in the Father's House, they are just like *back pantries*.

You can imagine the effect on such an audience. Speaking for myself, I can never forget it. Only Mr. Mackenzie could have produced such an effect.

My acquaintance with Mr. Mackenzie began when he first came into the Bishop Auckland circuit. He was invited to hold three weeks' services at Toft Hill, now Etherley ; and stayed in my house during that time. He spent a certain portion of each day in visiting the families in the village, and preached every evening except Saturday. I attended all the services, and was very much struck with the variety of expression and phrase in those eighteen sermons. I did not detect any repetition. New thoughts and fresh illustrations were found in every discourse.

Many men, women, and children, during his four years' connection with the Bishop Auckland circuit, were brought into membership with the various societies. I know that the subsequent effect upon the character and action of large numbers was such as affords the best evidence for Christianity—that of turning men from darkness to light, from the power of Satan unto God. If Mr. Mackenzie had finished his course at the end of those four years, he would have lived to do a great work, and would have done it well.

To this testimony of Mr. Greener may be added very fittingly that of the Rev. Thomas M'Cullagh, second minister in the circuit when Mackenzie came into it, and who has written thus :—

He soon became remarkably popular, especially amongst the colliers and ironworkers about Bishop Auckland, with its episcopal castle and picturesque park. His labours were attended with great success. The plainness of his language, the adaptability of his illustrations to his collier congregations, the directness of his aim, and the unction of the Holy One brought home the word with power, and numerous conversions were the result. In prayer-meetings he agonised in oft-repeated prayers, body and soul. When with him on such occasions, I have seen vapour rising through his coat from the sweltering perspirations of the strong, well-knit frame beneath. I was so struck with his originality, wit, raciness, shrewdness, and withal simplicity and artlessness, that he soon won my admiration and affection. I found him athirst for knowledge, and teachable.

One day, in my study, he looked through a small volume of sermons by James Parsons of York, while I was writing a letter. Addressing me, he asked if I would lend him the book. I replied, "I will make you a present of it, if you will honestly confess for what purpose you want it."

"I want it," said he, "to get some plums for my cake."

There are few circuits in Methodism that have made such rapid strides, materially and spiritually, during the last forty years, as that of Bishop Auckland. Where, in Mackenzie's days, there was but one circuit, with only two ministers, there are now four—Crook, Spennymoor, and the Shildons having since then gained an independent existence; while the ministerial staff has increased from two to nine. How much of this gratifying progress is to be attributed to the spiritual impetus imparted by Mackenzie's labours it is impossible to say; but there can be no doubt that his enthusiastic fervour and

MACKENZIE AT THIRTY.

intense devotion gave to the work an onward push, of which it still reaps the benefit.

The committee under whose direction Mackenzie laboured did not, as we have seen, confine his labours within the boundaries of their own circuit. In response to numerous appeals, he was permitted to give at regular intervals a week or a fortnight to places at a distance. In this way the benefit of his services was extended to the Wolsingham, the Durham, the

Shotley Bridge, the Stokesley, the Barnard Castle, and other neighbouring circuits.

I have before me a manuscript volume, on the first page of which is inscribed, in Mackenzie's own hand-writing, the words—"Text Book. P. Mackenzie." Underneath this is written by his second daughter, who for years acted as his secretary, the words—"Dora Mackenzie. Given to me by father when he is done with it. May it be many a year yet!—1889."

How many hearts echo—alas, that it should be in vain!—that simple, tender-hearted, pathetic little wish!

The entries in this well-fingered little register, extending from 1856 to 1886, are of the briefest description; the records of a man too much engrossed in the action of life to stop to bestow upon it anything but the briefest comment and criticism. Brief as they are, however, comprising in most cases little more than the place, the date, the text, and about three words characterising the service, it is impossible to turn over the pages and scan the hasty jottings without feeling how deep and impassioned was the devotion of the man who made them, what longing for the salvation of men blazed quenchless in his soul. Here are a few of the comments on the work of those earlier years, taken almost at random.

> Very gracious move, thank God!
> Heavenly feeling.
> Glory to God! some seeking
> Many seeking.
> The Spirit's work.
> Souls saved.
> The Divine influence powerful.

> Lord save them !
> Good time. Glory !
> He will save souls.
> The Lord is working.
> A mighty coming.
> A glorious shower.
> Lord, save them by hundreds !

What copious and glowing pages these fervent ejaculations would enlarge into, could we place them in their full and proper setting of circumstances and emotion ; could we background them with the rich colouring of experience, and feeling, and incident, of which they are but the disjointed patches. Meagre scrawls and splashes as they are, imagination can spread them out and fill them in, can behold them grow into a space marked out for war, a field of battle crowded with contending hosts, waging deadly combat, and can see in the midst of the conflict a strong form moving to and fro, flaming with zeal for God and love for man ; now pleading for the intervention of Heaven, now smiting heavily the face of wrong, now cheering the faint-hearted, now kneeling tenderly by the wounded and comforting the mourner, now venting great shouts of triumph ; never tiring, never pausing, eager as a flame, impetuous as a cataract, resolute as fate, strong as one whose power is that of the Spirit of the living God.

At Coundon, where he resided, the Society greatly increased, and similarly pleasing effects were wrought in many others of the colliery villages. At Crook, now the head of a circuit, a very gracious work of God was developed and fostered ; many of the present office-bearers, including the circuit steward, being men who decided for Christ at that time. Mr. James

Elliott of Howdon-le-Wear informs me that it was the late Mr. John Kellett of Crook, brother to the Rev. Featherstone Kellett, who, impressed with Mackenzie's great fitness for such work, was one of those mainly instrumental in bringing about his employment as Circuit Missionary.

The Rev. William Lees, speaking of occasional services at this time in the Shotley Bridge circuit, describes Mackenzie's preaching as most impressive and original; and a writer in the *Methodist Recorder* says: "The respect in which he was held in the remotest villages was simply phenomenal, and anything that Peter—as he was familiarly called—either said or did was considered next to sacred. Whilst conducting a successful revival mission at the village of Ramshaw, at the western extremity of the present Shotley Bridge and Consett circuit, the ceiling of the chapel being low, he raised his fist too high, and left an indentation in the roof. Because Peter had made it, it had to remain as a memento of his visit and work there, and for more than thirty years, to the writer's knowledge, it was referred to with pride both by the preachers and people."

At Lanchester, in the same circuit, he held services for a week in 1857, and for a second week in the October of the same year. His own record of them is that there was a "mighty feeling," and that souls were saved, and this is amply borne out by the testimony of Mr. Robert Robinson, who describes them from personal recollection. There appears to have been great excitement, accompanied by physical manifestations, somewhat similar to those witnessed in Wesley's day. His preaching, as described by Mr.

Robinson, was of an awakening character, intensely earnest, and accompanied with great spiritual power; but in the prayer-meeting after the service, he never used pressure to bring people to decision, nor would he allow it to be used by others. Observing an over-zealous brother so engaged, he called out at the top of his voice, " Don't force them, Brother —— ! Don't force them ! "

About fifty conversions were the result of these services, and it is pleasing to have Mr. Robinson's testimony to the fact that, though nearly forty years have passed, yet, if we include those who during that time have died in the faith of Christ, about eighty per cent. of the awakened have maintained the spiritual life then kindled within them.

During the month of April 1857, and also part of May, Mackenzie appears to have taken his turn, Sunday and week-night, with the ministers at each of the places in the circuit; and on May 19th we have the following characteristic entry in his Text-Book :—

The commencement of my regular work again. Lord help me ! My soul shall live for Thee alone. O make me a man after Thine own heart ! Stand by me, and according to the ability that Thou hast given me, I will declare Thy will. I am Thine for ever ; I feel it. Glory be to Thee for ever and ever, world without end. Hallelujah to God and the Lamb !

So burned and was cherished in the quiet of his own chamber the fire that was carried forth and kindled to such high issues in others.

CHAPTER XI

Last Year in Bishop Auckland—Shall he enter the Ministry ?—
Fervour and Consecration—The District Synod—Recollec-
tions of the Rev. H. Mole—Scene at Family Prayer—Trial
Sermon—Call to Preach—Right Use of Scripture—Before
the July Committee—Rev. T. M'Cullagh's Story—His
Manuscript Sermon — Exuberant Thanks — Desire for a
Prayer-Meeting—Accepted by the Conference.

DURING the last of his four years' residence in the
Bishop Auckland circuit, Mackenzie was less
employed in special services, and filled what was
practically the position of third minister ; and at the
Quarterly Meeting in March 1858, he was " unani-
mously recommended to the Conference as a fit and
proper person to be received into the Wesleyan
ministry."

In the course of this semi-ministerial year, he had
occasionally to attend to the collection of moneys for
the superintendent, which to him was a new experience, and, speaking of the many things which
claimed the care and attention of the ministers in
addition to pulpit duties, he exclaimed, " I wonder
their sermons are not as dry as a stick."

In his *History of Methodism in the Bishop Auckland
Circuit*, Mr. Matthew Braithwaite observes :—

"Such was the demand for his labours, it soon became evident that his future life would have to be spent in the work of proclaiming the gospel, and whilst some thought he should go into the ministry, others were of opinion that he should continue as a lay evangelist. His being married increased the difficulty of his getting into the ministry, and the inquiry was made whether he could not be engaged by the Conference as a lay agent. This, however, could not be done, as there was no provision for such a class of workers in the Connexion at that time, and after much deliberation it was resolved that he should be recommended as a candidate for the ministry. The step was taken with some degree of hesitation, as it was contrary to the rules of Methodism to admit married men into the ranks of the ministry. No doubt his great usefulness in the position of a lay evangelist, and the urgency of those who believed the ministry was his right place, led the Conference to make special arrangements whereby he could be received, and it certainly has never had occasion to regret that Mr. Mackenzie was one of the several candidates the Bishop Auckland circuit recommended to its notice."

Among those " who believed that the ministry was his right place," the late Rev. Richard Brown, then superintendent of the circuit, was fortunately included. He was a scholarly man, logical and lawyer-like in the cast of his mind, not at all likely to be much in sympathy with the type of mental development represented by Mackenzie; yet he took up his case with great zeal, and argued and pushed it with great pertinacity and with ultimate success, and often expressed his deep conviction that he was rendering the Connexion good service by so doing.

The intense fervour of Mackenzie's own inner life at the time may be gathered from a record in his Text-Book :—

Coundon, March 22nd, 1858.—I received the seal of God's sanctifying power while reading Mrs. Palmer's *Faith and its Effects,* pages 111 and 112. Glory to God and the Lamb for ever !

> Thou from sin dost save me now,
> Thou wilt save me evermore.

I do believe, and I do possess the land of rest from inbred sin, the land of perfect holiness. Glory ! Glory ! Glory !

The May District Synod was held that year at Barnard Castle, and through the kindness of the Revs. W. Fern, R. H. Mole, and E. Dodds, all of whom were present, we are enabled to gather a fairly complete impression of the proceedings.

Mr. Mole writes :—

I am thinking of the past, of the memories that come with vividness and cheer ; my first District Meeting at Barnard Castle, in the year 1858 ; my home at Mr. John Steele's. There were three candidates for the ministry that year ; one of them, Peter Mackenzie, stayed with me. His remarkable and eccentric character was a continuous study for three days. I could not decide whether to admire or disapprove his sayings and doings. I felt tossed about, unable to understand this brother, so vivacious and energetic. One morning, at family prayers, when he was supplicating for a blessing on the District Meeting, the homes, and the church generally, such a manifestation of the Father's presence was given as thrilled our souls and bowed our spirits. There was weeping all around. Then, suddenly, thinking of Barnard Castle, he broke forth : "O Lord, Thou knowest the wants of this town. There are hundreds who never darken the door of the chapel, who are off to the bar-room, drinking and swearing and taking Thy name in vain. O hasten the time when they shall come to Thee ; when every publican's tap shall be stopped, when atheism shall have the ague, and infidelity turn blue."

Mr. Dodds, himself one of the candidates, says :—

On Wednesday, May 19, he preached his trial sermon, at five o'clock in the evening, in the schoolroom, when a large number of the ministers attended. The text was 2 Cor. viii. 9 : " For ye know the grace of our Lord Jesus Christ," etc. There was warmth and zeal and power in the service. The peculiarity of the hour and place of the service was doubtless owing to the fact that there were three candidates who had to deliver trial sermons. I had preached that morning at six o'clock, and the other brother had to preach the next morning at the same hour, while the Rev. Richard Brown occupied the pulpit in the chapel that evening.

Concerning the theological examination, Mr. Mole says :—

Then came the Thursday morning, when the candidates were to present themselves. Two came in quietly and decorously. Dear Peter, in his own inimitable way,—I can never forget it,— fell down on his knees, with uplifted hands, in silent prayer. Then he stood before us. There were old men there that day, men who had not shed a tear for many a year, stolid, thoughtful, and perhaps prejudiced ; cultured men were there, refined in taste and habit, the very acme of propriety ; young hearts were there, ready for the fray : but, concerning this man, filled with indescribable bewilderment. What would he prove to be ?

Two of the young men had spoken, and now Peter gave an account of his conversion. But the call to preach—what of that ? He told us that he could not believe it at first. He flew to prayer, and having, in a weak moment, promised some friends to go with them to a country appointment, he heard them asking for him below, while he was on his knees. Then, he said, he did what he would not recommend others to do—he opened his Bible, shut his eyes, placed his finger on a passage, pleading all the while for guidance, and then, opening his eyes, read : " While Peter thought on the vision, the Spirit said unto him, Behold, three men seek thee. Arise, therefore, and get thee down, and go with them, doubting nothing ; for I have sent them."

The unction and thrill of that moment can never be told. There was a silence electric in its power. I think, when it came to the vote, every hand was raised in his favour. None dared to say no.

Mr. Mackenzie preached again on the Friday evening from "This is a faithful saying, and worthy of all acceptation," etc. This was a different deliverance from the trial sermon, an evangelistic outburst, followed by a prayer-meeting, in which, now on the forms beseeching the people to come to Christ, and then on his knees praying, he sought with all earnestness to save some.

We had a walk to Rokeby, and having to shelter from the rain in a neighbouring house, Peter began to speak of Christ to the inmates, and then, outside, recited poetry "by the yard," and amongst other pieces, "Morn among the Mountains," in his dramatic, unequalled manner.

It will be observed that there is a slight discrepancy between the account of Mackenzie's first attempt to preach as related here, and that given on the authority of Mr. William Phalp in a previous chapter. This is hardly surprising after the lapse of so many years. The point has been thoroughly sifted, and Mr. Phalp's account may be taken as substantially accurate. It is possible that Mr. Phalp not only asked Mackenzie to preach when on the way to Sherburn Hill, but may have called at his house and said something to him on the subject before starting. Mr. R. J. Phalp, writing me on the point, says :—

"The two men Mr. Mackenzie refers to may have been Nathan Macree and my uncle, William Phalp. My father describes Macree as a simple-hearted man, an enthusiast in his way, and says that there is nothing more likely than that he may have asked Mr.

Mackenzie to preach unknown to my uncle, and that both may have afterwards called at Mr. Mackenzie's house. The three were inseparable companions. Macree died a few years ago, or might have cleared up the point."

There is another alternative available to those whose minds are yet unsatisfied. The service referred to by Mackenzie at the District Meeting, and subsequently at the Conference, may have been one of a later date. In spite of his successful attempt at Sherburn Hill, he still had serious misgivings, and considerable pressure had to be employed to ensure his continuance in the work; his fear being that he would not be able to sustain the demands it would make upon him. The existence of this timidity and reluctance at the commencement is confirmed by a letter from Mr. Thomas Elliott of Swalwell, who says:

"My first meeting with him was soon after he began to preach. I preached Sunday school sermons at Haswell, and it was decided to follow these up by special services, for which I remained. Mr. Mackenzie took one of the services during the week, his text being, 'Wilt thou be made whole?' At the end of his first division, he wished to close, but as I sat behind him in the pulpit, I held him between my knees, and compelled him to conclude a discourse which had a remarkable effect."

Let us hope that the guidance afforded to Mackenzie by the passage of Scripture on which his finger rested, marvellous as it was, will not encourage others to use their Bibles in a similar manner. Such a method of arriving at a decision seems to have struck even the raw young convert as somewhat dubious.

It was not the course he would have pursued in later life, and even at the District Meeting, he hesitated to recommend it to others. Enlightened views of what the Scriptures are, and of how their teaching is to be utilised, will lead us to drink in of their spirit rather than to lean upon the letter.

An incident, occurring in my own experience, has so appropriate a bearing on the point, that I may claim indulgence for recounting it here. I was meeting a class for the renewal of tickets one evening, and the subject conversed upon was the right use of Scripture. A young man, recently arrived in the town, said : " Before coming here, I lived in the south, and was uncertain whether I should remove. I prayed about it, and resolved to be guided by the words that met my eye on opening the Bible. The words were these—*To the north.* So I had no further doubt, but came at once." A good woman spoke next, and said : " Our young brother goes to his Bible for signs. I did so years ago, but was rebuked. I had received a great blessing, but could not accept it as a reality, so I prayed earnestly for assurance, and said in my prayer that I would take the first words my eye fell upon in the Bible as an answer. I did so, and the words were—' An evil and adulterous generation seeketh after a sign, and there shall be no sign given them.' I read the words, and have never gone to my Bible for a sign since."

Having been accepted by the District Synod, Mackenzie's next ordeal was an examination in London before the July Committee. The Rev. Thomas M'Cullagh gives interesting details of this portion of his career in an article in the *Church Record* :—

This examination in those days, 1858, lasted nearly a week. He sat first for his paper examination in Greek, Latin, French, English, mathematics, algebra, arithmetic, history, geography, etc. This was called the literary paper, after which came the theology paper. At the close he hastened to my house.

"Well, Peter," I asked, "how have you got on with your papers ?"

"Oh," he replied, "that literary paper! She was hard ! I couldn't get in my pick at all ; but when I got to the theology paper, I was able to hew a bit."

Knowing that some candidates found rejection a greater trial than they could well bear, I said to him—

"Now, Peter, you must not make too sure of passing ; your case is peculiar : you are thirty-four years of age, which is several years beyond the age at which candidates are received ; you have a wife and three children, and the Conference very seldom accepts a married candidate."

"I am not making sure, Mr. M'Cullagh."

"What will you do if you are rejected ?" I asked.

"I will go back to Bishop Auckland," he replied, "shouting Glory !"

I thought to myself, This man has in him the stuff of which saints and heroes are made. I went to the oral examination of the candidates, as a member of the committee, the only one of a large committee who knew Mr. Mackenzie personally. A small sub-committee reported, as usual, on the manuscript sermons of the candidates. The late John W. Greeves, when reporting Mr. Mackenzie's sermon, asked permission to read a few passages from the sermon itself. The paragraphs read excited much wonder and admiration by their simple and unborrowed beauty, and even sublimity. This is the only instance in which I have known this to have been done, although I have attended many of these examinations.

In reference to the manuscript sermon here spoken of by Mr. M'Cullagh, the following interesting particulars have been communicated by S. J. Inglis Smith, Apperley Bridge :—

My father, the late Robert Inglis, then at Spitalfields, was chairman of the Manuscript Committee for that year. Knowing something of the eccentricity of the candidate, already appreciated as a genius, the queer-looking document was passed. Evidently this was very gratifying to Mr. Mackenzie, for when he heard that he and his sermon had been accepted, he took a cab from Westminster Training College, where the candidates were billeted in those days, and drove to Spital Square. Unusual sounds were heard as a head was thrust out of the window of the cab— "Hallelujah ! here we are ! Stop, driver ! glory, glory !" Then, when he stepped out, there came another shout of "Glory ! Hallelujah ! Where is that blessed man of God ? I have come to thank him for passing my sermon." When my father appeared, the rough but jubilant and grateful Peter clasped him round, and almost danced for joy. When a little calmer, he was asked how he managed to write it all, not having been accustomed to use a pen. "Well," he answered, "glory to God ! I wrote a bit, and then I prayed a bit, then wrote more, but it was the hardest job I ever did in all my life." Then, with another loud shout of praise, he sprang into the cab, and the last we saw of him was his bright, happy face and waving arms, as he drove back to headquarters. This incident made an impression on all in the manse, and as it gives a glimpse of the goodness and gratitude of this noble man and true gentleman in heart, I am glad to put it on record for the first time.

Mr. John R. Langler says :—

At the July Examination of candidates for the ministry in 1858, Mr. Mackenzie, during an interval, was wandering about the Westminster Training College, in company with the late Rev. James Dixon, and found his way to the top of the octagonal turret which crowns the building. The sight of so many housetops, and the thought of the numbers of people who crowded the slums below, caused Mr. Mackenzie to seize his companion suddenly by the coat collar, and cry, "Down on your knees, brother Dixon !" while at the same moment he himself knelt on the leaden roof, and poured out his soul in loud and earnest prayer for the perishing multitudes. Mr. Dixon himself gave me this account of the first prayer-meeting held on the tower of Westminster College.

The Rev. E. Dodds, who sat with Mackenzie as a candidate at the July examination, says :—

An incident occurred which was for the moment amusing, but quite characteristic. He was not so much at ease in the treatment of the literary paper as with the theological, which remark would apply to others besides himself. The Rev. William Jackson, one of the secretaries of the Examining Committee, walked up the room, and perhaps detecting some perplexity in his appearance, said, "Well, Peter, how are you getting on?" To which Mackenzie promptly replied, "Oh, I should like to turn this into a prayer-meeting, sir." There was a titter through the room, but many, had they spoken their minds as frankly, would have responded Amen!

Looking down at his paper, Mr. Jackson said, "Why, Peter, you have not taken the easier questions." "No, sir," he answered; "I had to get into a softer seam." Mr. Jackson also states that in the committee the Rev. W. M. Bunting would have the manuscript sermon read, and when it was finished, he exclaimed, "Now, you *dare* not refuse that man."

The account given by Mr. M'Cullagh goes on to say :—

Mr. Mackenzie got the highest mark for his oral examination, for his theological paper, and for his manuscript sermon. I forget the exact marks he obtained for his District Meeting sermon and his July sermon; if not the highest, they were certainly high. For his literary paper he received a blank— nothing.

At the Conference of 1858 his case came up for settlement, and there was a considerable debate. I remember that Mr. Arthur pleaded eloquently that he should be accepted for the ministry, and asked what John Wesley would do in a case like this. Would he decline the services of such a man?

The Rev. Thomas Kent says :—

It was my privilege to attend the Conference of 1858, which was held in Hull, and of which the Rev. John Bowers was the President. The two things of which I have the most vivid recollection are, first, the remarkable sermon preached by the ex-President, the Rev. Francis A. West, in Waltham Street Chapel, from the words "Be ye filled with the Spirit"; and, second, the fact that in the list of candidates for the ministry, the name of Peter Mackenzie was included.

So deep and general was the interest which his case excited, that it occupied the attention of the Conference the greater part of a day. The Rev. William Arthur brought the discussion to a close by stating that he had heard Mr. Mackenzie preach, had also been in his company, and had opportunities of becoming acquainted with his spirit and character; and, said he, "It is my opinion that if you do not accept Mr. Mackenzie, you will commit a sin against God's providence." This utterance, coming from such a man as Mr. Arthur, at once settled the question, and Mr. Mackenzie was placed on the list of accepted candidates for that year.

He was to be sent to Didsbury College to be trained, and Mr. M'Cullagh relates that a friend of his met Mackenzie on his way thither, and asked him if his wife and children were to reside in the college with him.

"No," said he; "they have furnished a little cottage for me—all mahogany."

CHAPTER XII

THE YEAR AT DIDSBURY—1858–1859

No Technical Training — A-Might-Have-Been — Demand for
his Services—Unspoiled by Popularity—Appearance as a
Student—Asking the Doctor to Pray—Rev. A. Barber's
Description—A Night of Wrestling—Scenes at Grantham
—Reconsecration—Sunday Services—Attack on Public-
Houses—Brief Records—A Thousand Seeking.

ONE of the most remarkable features of Mackenzie's
life at college was the little time he spent there.
A house was taken for him and his family, but while
his residence was nominally at Didsbury, he practically
lived elsewhere.　In evangelistic work this was really
one of the busiest years of his life.

It soon became evident to the authorities that, for
a man at his age and with his temperament and
religious enthusiasm, hampered also by the disabilities
of the past, to settle down to hard grinding at the
elements of a literary and theological education, to
say nothing of classics, was scarcely to be expected;
hence they allowed him to give himself at once to the
work on which his mind and heart were so fully set.
Whether a special course of training might have been
devised for such a man, the aim of which would have

been to furnish him with hints and methods for after-study, rather than with the dry details of technical cultivation there and then, is a point on which we have hardly sufficient data to decide. It is difficult for training institutions, in their legitimate anxiety to overtake the wants of the many, to give special and individual attention to cases that manifest a departure from the ordinary type. Still, it is interesting to ponder for a moment what Mackenzie might have become, if it had been possible for that initial year, or a more extended period, to have given him some of those principles and methods in the acquisition and classification of knowledge of which every student knows the value. A Peter Mackenzie chipped and sand-papered into commonplace uniformity would have been a deplorable, if not an impossible spectacle; but a Peter Mackenzie guided by wise and sympathetic training into tracks along which his individuality might have marched with unfettered tread, and yet with even a grander sweep and surer step than that to which it did attain, would not have been an undesirable consummation.

A writer in the *Methodist Recorder* says : —

"It was soon seen, that it would be impossible to get Mr. Mackenzie to groove into college lines. Mr. Bowers, the President, was the very pink of pro-priety, a stickler for decorum, but, having a great admiration for honesty and earnestness, he wisely resolved to follow the indications of Providence. Applications for Mr. Mackenzie's services poured in, and the Governor-President, who was necessarily much away from Didsbury, gave his assistant, the Rev. Charles H. Kelly, full authority to enter into engagements for Mr. Mackenzie to preach through the year, irrespective of any college work. This, it is said, entailed on Mr. Kelly the task of answering nearly, if not more than a thousand letters. There were often letters in the teens and up to thirty in a day, asking for Mr. Mackenzie, or remonstrating that he could not be sent—he was not sent because a certain law in physics could not be set aside in his case, and one body could not be in two places in the same instant of time.

"But all this popularity did not spoil him. It did not make him talk of his piety. It did not make him boast; he never told people that he never preached without conversions, but people knew that he rarely, if ever, did. He retained his simple piety. He was constant in prayer. Wherever he went, he was the same humble, earnest Christian. During all this time he preached with great power. He had the magic witchery of genius. His sermons cost him more than people supposed. He read widely for them, thought much, and prepared carefully. He held congregations under a spell. Their interest was intense. There were times when men who had seen marvellous effects produced by oratory could have said that, whatever they had seen of public excitement was stone and ice to the burning interest that hung upon every word of this remarkable preacher. With the crowds his declamation, his entreaties, his eloquence, his happy hits had wonderful power; they listened, as to the words of life and death; they went to hear what they must do to escape the death that never dies, and how to flee from the inexorable wrath to come. They were eager to know what they must do to be saved; and they heard, for he told them in burning words, which they understood."

An interesting account is furnished by Mr. W. R. Burgess of Withington, of one of the first services conducted by Mackenzie as a student. Mr. Burgess describes it as his first service after going to Didsbury. This can hardly be correct, for, according to Mackenzie's own Text-Book, he was at Guisborough on the 5th of September 1858, at Barlow Moor on the 9th, at Accrington on the 12th, and did not go to Pendleton until the 19th. The date, however, is not a point of much importance. Mr. Burgess says :—

I have a very vivid recollection of it. It was at the Brunswick chapel, Pendleton, not the present elaborate structure, but the plain, unpretentious old building.

A student was appointed, and as he came the night before, his home was with an aunt of my wife. On the Sunday morning, waiting for my wife to accompany me to chapel, I stood looking through the window ; as I did so, I saw approaching the aunt referred to, accompanied by an extraordinary-looking personage. His dress and his deportment arrested attention. He had on a short black alpaca jacket, a soft black felt hat, a pair of short and shapeless trousers, and low shoes. His linen was clean but coarse, made, I think, of what formerly was called " Dowlas " linen. His burly form was in strong contrast with the somewhat diminutive lady by his side. I need not describe his features, which afterwards became so well known. There was the unconventional play of features, the same restless action of hands and fingers as they loosely hung by his side, which were characteristic. His appearance was so uncouth, so unparsonlike, so opposed to the trim and natty appearance usually associated with the name " Student," that I remember thinking, if not saying aloud, Bless me ! is that the student ? What will they send next ?

We went to chapel expecting anything but the food which was provided for us. His appearance in the pulpit excited attention, then surprise, some little amusement, wonder as to what was coming next. We were not accustomed to such vigorous and vivacious conduct. From head to foot he was all alive with a life so different from our own. The way he gave out the hymns made us prick up our ears and expect something out of the common. His reading of the lessons was accompanied by suggestive action. I may almost say he read with his hands as well as his tongue, as they were made to indicate almost as much as the tongue expressed. The second lesson was out of the First Epistle of St. John. His prayer was a revelation and a forecast of what was yet to come. We had a few men in those days who were not afraid or ashamed to respond when their hearts were touched, and many and deep were the responses that prayer called forth. His text was John iii. 16.

I must not attempt to describe the sermon. The subject was one in which he revelled. We were all fairly carried away with the stream of eloquence, of warning, and of appeal to which we had listened ; our mental attitude was revolutionised ; we had expected so little, we had received so much, and that of such excellent quality, that we marvelled, and felt constrained to ask, How knoweth this man these things ?

The effect of this service was electric. It was felt that a new power had come amongst us, and that we must utilise it promptly, and to the utmost. A series of special services was at once arranged for, to be conducted by Mr. Mackenzie. The power of the Holy Spirit was manifested, many were pricked to the heart, many were added to the Church.

The Rev. Alfred Barber, who was a student at the same time, says :—

"When Mr. Mackenzie had to take his turn in preaching before the Didsbury Institution authorities, as we were all accustomed to do, he chose for his text John iii. 16 : 'For God so loved the world,' etc. There was good and remarkable thought, beautiful language, and great unction. At the close, addressing himself to the theological tutor, the Rev. John Hannah, D.D., he stretched out his hands, quivering with emotion, and said, And now, the dear Doctor will give us his blessing.' Had any other student dared to make such a suggestion, he would have received a rebuke for his impertinence ; but such was the ardent and loving simplicity of good Peter Mackenzie, that the Doctor at once acceded."

It is impossible that there can have been any attempt at consecutive study during this year at Didsbury, for his Text-Book shows that, even in the September immediately following his admission to college, he was preaching, and in some cases holding special services at Guisborough, Accrington, Oswaldtwistle, Pendleton, and Blackburn. At Guisborough he records twelve as having been brought to decision, at Oswaldtwistle twelve, at Blackburn a number, while of Pendleton he writes, " I hope there will be a hundred at least that shall be found at the last to have got good at Pendleton." In the month of October he labours at Withington ; Regent Street and Irwell Street, Manchester ; Swinton ; Bishop Auckland ; Gravel Lane, Manchester ; and again at Pendleton. At all these places there is the usual record of success, with this note concerning Irwell Street: " A great many awakened. Glory to God and the Lamb! Surely there will be 50 forthcoming out of this week's labour. Lord, help them !" November and December find him at sundry places in the Wigan circuit, as also at Altringham, Bowdon, Sale, Chorley, Manchester, Grantham, Reeth, and Oakendale.

Speaking of this period, the Rev. Alfred Barber writes :—

From the first he was immensely popular. His preaching was very attractive. He drew to his ministry not merely the working and middle classes, but persons of position and wealth. Sir James Watt of Manchester, who entertained the Queen on her visit, was among his hearers, whilst ladies and gentlemen, with their man-servants and maid-servants, wept for their sins at the communion rail. Amongst the number might be seen a gentleman taking off his spectacles that the tears might flow more freely ; a delicate little Quakeress, daintily attired, seeking mercy from God ; Roman Catholics, carried away by the strange eloquence of the evangelist, confessing their sins ; and young ladies, who ordinarily would have scorned to mingle with the multitudes in such scenes of excitement, overwhelmed with distress of soul, penitently seeking the Saviour.

On one occasion, having no preaching appointment on the Sunday, I resolved to go to his assistance in Manchester, where he was conducting special services. The people never tired of his company, and it was difficult for him to be alone. A long and exhausting prayer-meeting followed the evening preaching, and the usual success in a number of souls seeking for salvation. Subsequently a great many friends sat down to supper in the house of our host. It was quite a social gathering. We were unable to retire to rest before two o'clock on the Monday morning. Mr. Mackenzie and I occupied the same room. Very quickly I fell asleep, but was soon to be roused. At the foot of the bed was Peter Mackenzie, praying as though his very life depended on the issue. It was a very cold night, freezing hard, yet, though thinly clad in his night apparel, the perspiration was streaming from his face. With all the energy of his nature he was wrestling with his Maker for the help he needed. I thought it better to leave him alone, and again fell asleep, only to be roused a second time, and to find my companion in the same position. "Peter," I exclaimed impulsively, "if you go on at this rate, you will kill yourself." He replied, meaning the people, "Well, if they will not leave me alone in the day, I must pray at night." The memory of that night of wrestling has followed me ever since.

In respect to Mackenzie's visit to Grantham in the December of that year, the Rev. George Barnley writes :—

During his first year of probation at Didsbury, Grantham asked for a fortnight's allotment of his services, and obtained it.

It fell to my lot to meet him at the station. Amongst the passengers no one appeared answering to my idea of the expected student. The nearest approach was a youngish, thick-set man, whose movements were quick and peculiar, and who swung himself round occasionally with a searching gaze, as if uncertain what course to take. Approaching him with an apology, and asking if his name was Mackenzie, his reply came—accompanied by a downward bend and a flinging upward of both hands above his head—"The same, sir," followed instantly by a "Hallelujah!" and "Glory!" such as startled the good people near, and fixed all eyes upon him. As we moved onward through a quiet street or two, these gestures and exclamations found frequent repetition. Arrived at the dwelling of his host, and entering by the shop, in which were many customers, his first proceeding was to make one of his downward bows, half-way to the ground, with arms upraised, and to cry, " Peace be to this house, and to everyone who dwells beneath its roof, as long as there is one brick left upon another ! " In the same breath, as he straightened himself and grasped the hand of his entertainer, came the ordinary salutation, but as Peter only could utter it, " How do you do, my dear sir ? "

Supper was ready, and we took our seats at the table, but the meal was unique, from its frequent interruptions, not only by short, sharp cries of " Hallelujah ! " and " Glory ! " and such remarks as " If we had been serving the devil, he would not have given us beef or mutton or any of the good things of this life," but by Peter dropping down from his seat and uttering a few impassioned words of prayer or praise, in which we all accompanied him as if it had been our regular habit. Before saying good-night, he insisted that two or three of the company should pray, and so contagious had the spirit of our visitor become, that responses waxed very loud. We learned afterwards that a policeman had paused under the window outside, wondering if some breach of the peace required his intervention.

Similarly exciting were the scenes night after night when the public services had closed. Mackenzie, having changed his clothes, was now ready for an hour or two of the most enthusiastic religious exercises I have ever known. The conversation was of the sprightliest, prayer the most fervent, and the singing such as carried the friends away heavenward, and during which

Peter's own face shone with wondrous radiance, while every nerve in his frame quivered, and to him a sudden translation to the better world would have been evidently the least possible change. Many conversions attended this fortnight of services; while the effect upon our people, especially those brought into closest companionship with the preacher, remained as a rich blessing for months and even years afterwards, and probably its traces have not even yet passed away.

The Rev. Thomas Kent speaks in a similar strain of services held at Bollington in the Macclesfield circuit, and describes Mackenzie's ministry as not only exceedingly popular, but wonderfully powerful and effective, especially among the young.

At the end of December 1858, Mackenzie inscribes the following record in his Text-Book :—

"Friday, the last night of 1858.—In looking back I see that goodness and mercy have followed me all the way. Glory, glory be to the Triune Deity for the blessings of the past year! The Lord has helped me through gloriously, thanks be to His Name! At the District Meeting He helped me, and at London He was with me, and here, in bringing me to Didsbury, I can see His divine love displayed. And, glory to His Name, He has awakened and converted sinners nearly every night that I have preached. To Thy Name be all the glory, O Lord! And now, O God the Father, Son, and Holy Ghost, here I give myself afresh to Thee, through the blood of the Everlasting Covenant. At the coming Conference, if I am spared, do what Thou wilt with me, only let Thy Name be glorified, either by using me or laying me aside. I am Thine for ever. My sins are forgiven through the blood of Christ, and Thou dost sanctify my soul from all iniquity, from all Thou dost my soul redeem.

In Jesus I believe, and shall believe myself to Him. Lord, fill me with Thy Spirit, and save souls by thousands for Jesus' sake.   Amen."

The year 1859 opens and continues with this evangelistic work at various places, some of them at a considerable distance from Didsbury, and of each one there is some brief, hopeful comment recorded.

Bolton.—This has been a wonderful week.   The Lord has been graciously pleased to answer the cry of His people, and souls have been saved by scores.   Glory to God and the Lamb for ever !   His kingdom is coming with mighty power.   Hallelujah ! hallelujah !

Runcorn.—Many coming to Jesus.   This has been a very happy week, and I have had divine help.   And my home has been a heaven upon earth, at Mr. T. Hazelhurst's.   May they be preserved as the apple of God's eye.   Amen.

Rawtenstall.—Mighty struggle, but God gave the victory.   I find that there is nothing like believing through the hardness, through the darkness ; the victory is certain to mighty faith.

Rawtenstall [*Later*].—Truly the Lord hath bared His arm in this circuit, the people have overcome through the blood of the Lamb.   About forty-one the last night.   Glory to God and the Lamb for ever !   Many very wonderful cases of conversion.   It will all be known at the last day, and God shall have all the glory through eternity.   He is worthy.   Honour for ever to His name.

Louth.—Salvation to our God and the Lamb for ever !   I believe that there has been everlasting good done here this week, fruit that shall be forthcoming in eternity.

Grimsby.—This has been a good week to many.   Some very glorious triumphs.   The power of God was manifested, and souls have been saved.   Hallelujah to Jesus !   He causeth us to glory in His salvation.

Speaking of a visit to Prescot, St. Helens circuit, during this busy year, the Rev. John I. Britten says :—

"One prominent feature of his work then was his attack upon the public-houses. He walked boldly into them, and I believe he visited almost every one in the place. If he saw a drunken man going in, he rushed up and tried to snatch him from the snare. If he saw one come out, he went in, and soundly, though kindly, rated the landlord. Then he would kneel down and plead, oh, so earnestly and tenderly, for the man. In some cases the landlord was wroth, and would turn him out, but he found it was only going 'from the frying-pan into the fire'; for Peter would fall on his knees on the road outside, and soon gather an astonished crowd as he made the street echo with his stentorian pleadings."

In the beginning of May he preached for a week respectively at Sunderland Street and Brunswick chapels, in the Macclesfield circuit, and the record is:—

Sunderland Street.—A good many in the net. I find them in a good way here. They pray short, and get hold on God, and there has been good done. To God be all the glory!

Brunswick.—Many in distress, and a few found peace. O that the Lord would lead them in safety, and land them in the world of light and joy, and the glory shall be His for ever.

That Mackenzie was occasionally at Didsbury during this year may be gathered from the following:—

Didsbury.—Spoke at the Missionary Meeting. Had a good time. Dr. Hannah spoke with great power, to the great benefit of all that heard him. Thanks be to God for such men.

Here are a few of the remaining records:—

Oldham.—Spoke at the Missionary Meeting. Kind-hearted ministers and warm-hearted members, thanks be to God.

Nantwich. May 7–12.—Souls saved. A large crowd of people, and many of them came from far.

George Street, Manchester, July 2.—Good time, and good was done, and £17 gathered for the chapel, thanks be to God.

Sherburn Hill, Durham, July 9.—A speech. A very great gathering. *July* 10.—A divine feeling all day, and good done, and I think they would realise £50, or rather better, for their chapel.

Lanchester, July 11.—Good times and good done. About £40 for the chapel. Lord, save !

Alnwick, July 12.—A very gracious feeling. Thanks be to God, He has a few names even in Sardis.

Hetton-le-Hole, July 17.—A great congregation. The chapel would not hold one-half of them, so we went into the field, and had the prayer-meeting in the chapel. About thirteen saved.

Ireland, Portadown, Aug. 24.—Gave an address out-of-doors, got a good congregation in ten minutes. Glory to God ! Preached in the chapel in the evening. Very bad singing. Felt some degree of liberty in preaching. Two or three striking cases.

Aug. 25. —Preached in the morning in the street ; gracious time. Went to Armagh. Felt well. Saw a good many striking cases. Preached from Acts ii. 38. Surely this is a work of God.

The story of this remarkable year cannot be better closed than with the final sentence of that brief autobiographical record, of which we gave the first in our opening chapter :—

Went from thence [Bishop Auckland] to Didsbury College. Saw about 1000 seeking mercy in the country during the year.

CHAPTER XIII

HIS FIRST CIRCUIT—BURNLEY—1859–1860

The Town and Neighbourhood of Burnley—Mackenzie not a
Stranger There—Letter to Mr. Braithwaite—Sermon at the
District Meeting—Fifteen Hundred People at 5 A.M.—
Mission Services at Padiham—"The Devil a Bankrupt"—
Revival Services at Barrowford—Chapel Speech at Nelson
—Work at Park Hill—Second Letter to Mr. Braithwaite—
The Penitent Thief—Bag and Baggage—Letters to Mrs.
Pincott—Missionary Speech : The Stream and Mr. Stagnant
—Success at Burnley—Regrettable Removal.

THE thriving town of Burnley, in Lancashire,
about thirty miles north of where he had
resided in 1858, with its cotton and worsted mills,
and sundry other industries, with numerous collieries
in its vicinity, and a population of impressionable,
good-hearted working people ready to be wrought
upon, was not an inappropriate place in which for
Mackenzie to curb the wanderings, though not the
spirit of the evangelist, and to enter on the steadier,
less exciting work of circuit life. He was well
received from the first; and speedily won as great
a popularity among the lively enthusiastic Lancashire
operatives as he had previously done among the
Durham miners. Homely, frank, warm-hearted, overflowing with good-nature, they took to him as the

coals take to a kindred flame, and soon blazed round him warmly and cheerfully.

He did not, in fact, go among them as an entire stranger. In the May of this same year, 1859, the District Synod had met at Burnley, and Mackenzie had preached to an immense congregation during its sittings. A letter written to an old Bishop Auckland friend gives us an interesting glimpse of that gathering, as well as of his own personality.

TO MR. MATTHEW BRAITHWAITE.

BOLLINGTON, MACCLESFIELD, *May* 23, 1859.

DEAR BROTHER IN JESUS,—I think that it is high time for me to write to you. I have thought of doing so again and again, yet it has always got put off. I hope that you will forgive me, nay, I am sure that you will. God bless you! Amen. We had a very good District Meeting at Burnley this last week. There are about 1200 increase, and about 1800 on trial. Thanks be to God for the times of refreshing that have come from His divine presence. I heard Luke Wiseman preach one night a most excellent sermon, great power attended the Word, the Holy Ghost filled the place. The Rev. P. Hardcastle held forth the next night. There was a great congregation, and it was a very good sermon. I preached in the morning at a quarter to five, to (it was supposed) 1500 people. I had a very good time, and there was a shout of a king in the camp. Hallelujah! Glory for ever! I have been a fortnight at Macclesfield, and souls have been saved every night. I came here on Saturday, and had a very good day on Sunday, a great many in distress, and about twenty professed liberty; to God be all the glory. We had a prayer-meeting last night, and there were about thirty in penitent grief, and some of them got made very happy, thanks be to God. Salvation is of the Lord. I was very much shocked to hear of the sudden removal of Mr. H——. O that it may stir us up to more diligence in divine things! Afflictions tell us that we are mortal, the death of others reminds us of our own, and loud speaks the silent grave. Everything in heaven and on earth and in hell unites to give emphasis to the language of inspiration—"Whatsoever thy hand findeth to do, do it with thy might." May the Lord help us, for Jesu's sake! Mrs. H—— and the dear family will need all the help they can get to enable them to bear this severe stroke. Let us remember them at the throne of grace, as none but God can fill up the gap that there has been made. May He dry their tears and comfort their hearts, and grant them His grace, that they may be enabled to acquiesce in the divine purpose, for it is among the all things that work together for good to them that love God. I shall be glad to hear from you. Drop me a line or two. Remember me to your dear family and the rest of the friends.—Yours, for ever,   P. MACKENZIE.

Not only had Mackenzie preached at Burnley during the District Synod; he had also held mission services at Padiham, then in the Burnley circuit, of which he writes: "Great congregations, glorious feeling, and souls saved. Glory to God and the Lamb!" The connection thus formed with Padiham was never afterwards broken; Mackenzie returning at frequent intervals to preach and lecture, and always to crowded audiences. Of one of these visits the Rev. William Allen (c) writes: "I heard him in the Padiham circuit. He described Satan tempting Christ with all the kingdoms of the world and the glory of them. 'Poor, bankrupt devil!' exclaimed Mr. Mackenzie; 'he wasn't worth a pig; he couldn't go into the swine until Christ gave him permission.' Speaking of the man healed in Decapolis requesting to follow Christ, 'Ah,' said Mr. Mackenzie, 'he wanted to be a travelling preacher, and the Lord appointed him to be a home missionary.'"

He had also in January of the same year conducted revival services at Barrowford, another place in the Burnley circuit. The record of these services is

most exultant. There were six sermons, and they
are characterised in order as follows :—" Good done—
Glory !—Hallelujah !—Praise the Lord !"—with a
concluding flourish of thanksgiving, applicable to the
whole—" Bless the Lord, O my soul, and all that is
within me shout His praise !"

A correspondent says there were several striking
conversions during these services, and, among the
rest, that of Mr. William Tunstill of Reedyford,
Nelson, now the senior lay treasurer of the Chapel
Committee. Mr. Tunstill has since remarked that
Mackenzie did more to develop Methodism in that
neighbourhood than any other individual.

After he had left the Burnley circuit, Mackenzie
was invited to attend a public meeting at Nelson to
advocate the desirability of a new Sunday school.
At that time the Sunday school was carried on in the
chapel, a building that would hold about four hundred.
Nelson was then a village of some two thousand
inhabitants, with no other Nonconformist place of
worship. The situation of the village made it capable
of immense development, being in close proximity to
the Lancashire and Yorkshire Railway, and the Leeds
and Liverpool Canal. Trade was then also fairly
good, and the people well employed. Mackenzie,
with the prescience of a prophet, grasped the
possibilities of the situation, and in the course of
his address said that they had asked him to speak
in behalf of a new school, but his vision took in a
much larger scheme. Why not go in for a new
chapel, and make the present chapel a school? The
suggestion was at once entertained, and the outcome
was the erection of the Carr Road Chapel; while

Nelson itself has expanded into a borough of twenty-seven thousand inhabitants.

Not only at Barrowford and Padiham had Mackenzie preached during his college year, but also at Park Hill in the same circuit. Of his first service there he writes : " A wonderful day : the chapel would not hold them. The collection amounted to £38, 5s. 8d., and, best of all, souls got brought to Jesus." After speaking in similarly glowing phraseology of two more services, he adds : " I have fallen in with great kindness here. May the Lord reward them ! Mr. Dugdale has given me a Bible, which I intend to use well by reading it regularly. May the precious Spirit grant me His gracious help, that I may learn the lessons of His grace. Amen."

To this kindness of Mr. Dugdale, and also to the services at Park Hill, reference is made in a second letter addressed to Mr. Braithwaite. The latter had evidently sought to impress him with the desirability of being less violently demonstrative in his pulpit action, and the letter shows how kindly he appreciated such counsel, however difficult it might be to adopt it.

TO MR. MATTHEW BRAITHWAITE.

STALEYBRIDGE, *June* 28, 1859.

HONOURED AND DEAR SIR,—I was so glad to hear from you. May heaven bless you for your many kindnesses, your fatherly care, and your godly counsel. I have many times endeavoured to act up to it, but alas, alas, how frail at best is living man, how puny all his purposes.

This being a fresh place, I went with the determination to act up to the old rule laid down by you, and, being doubly impressed with having read your letter, I thought that I should succeed, and so I did for some time, but towards the latter end, and in the application, I so far forgot myself that I literally broke the book-board. Down it went, with all its sacred contents, with a thundering crash upon the floor, shocking people's nerves, and producing a peculiar sensation amongst the congregation. I have resolved and re-resolved to do better, and I hope by divine help to succeed yet. There was a good feeling, and a few came forward in the prayer-meeting, and I think three got through. Glory to God and the Lamb! "There is joy in the presence of the angels of God over one sinner that repenteth." I had a good time at Padiham last Sunday. The chapel was full in the morning, a very gracious feeling in the evening. The people could not all get in, about 1600 would be in. It happened to be the day for the quarterly collection, so that they did very well. When they are all at work, generally they get about £4. This time, although they had been on strike for many weeks, they realised £14, and, best of all, about sixteen found liberty on the Monday night, and a good many more the other nights. I was at Park Hill the week before, and a good many found peace. Thomas Dugdale, Esq., gave me such a fine Bible, worth £1, 5s., and the friends gave me £3. I am sure I should be thankful, for the Lord's people are kind to me beyond all precedent. You were asking how many black coats were there that morning [referring to District Meeting service]. I cannot tell, but there was a great number. I gave them the thief. We bundled him up bag and baggage by the express, booking him right through; he never halted at Hell's junction, nor put on the brake at Purgatory, nor blew his whistle at Perdition, but went right to Paradise.

P. MACKENZIE.

There has been a discussion recently in one of the London dailies on Mr. Gladstone's use of the phrase " bag and baggage," and much learned breath has been expended in showing that he was not the first to employ the phrase. Few people, save pedants, ever imagined he was. It is quite pat here in Mackenzie's letter, and has, to my knowledge, been a common expression in the North of England for at least half a century.

From what has been said, it is fairly evident that Mackenzie did not enter the Burnley circuit a stranger. R. Harrison, Esq., J.P., Whalley, says :—

"His fame had gone before him, and such a scene as took place in the approaches to Wesley Chapel, an hour before the time of service, baffles all description. Although that noble edifice will contain 2000 persons, more than twice that number struggled to get in. After that day the trustees became greatly alarmed to find that this mass of persons rising at once to sing had caused the pillars supporting the gallery to give way. Experts were consulted, and before the famous preacher took the pulpit again, measures had been taken to secure its safety."

Miss Pincott of Scarborough has kindly forwarded letters, extracts from which afford partial glimpses of Mackenzie's life in Burnley. Of one, written before he went there, Miss Pincott says :—

"It was the means of my dear mother's conversion, who held on her way till God called her home, a little more than a year ago. I was converted under a powerful sermon he preached at Oldham Street Chapel, Manchester, on January 10, 1859. He has sometimes stayed all night at our house, and we have been awakened by his earnest, agonising prayers for the conversion of sinners."

In the letter to Mrs. Pincott, referred to above, Mackenzie says :—

While pleading your cause before the Lord, the promise was applied with power to my soul, as if the Lord had spoken it from heaven —"I have not appointed her to wrath, but to obtain salvation through Jesus Christ." The ear of faith could hear the beatings of the heart of Infinite Love, and Jesus said, in words sweeter than the music of heaven—"Blessed are they that mourn, for they shall be comforted." God is in deep earnest in asking you for your heart, and you must give it to Him as it is, and believe that God does take it, and praise Him for taking it. And while you believe, God seals it for His own, and unless you take it from Him again by doubting, He will keep it for ever.

TO MRS. PINCOTT.

BURNLEY, *Sept.* 17, 1859.

I should like to come and spend a day with you some time next week, but we are so throng giving the tickets that I cannot get away. But you are not forgotten at the throne of grace. O how sweet to feel the love of Jesus casting out all fear, filling the soul with unutterable delight, and giving strong foretastes of the happiness that we are to enjoy throughout eternity. . . The Town Missionary has just come in. I hear him downstairs, and shall have to go out to visit with him.

TO THE SAME.

BURNLEY, *Sept.* 30, 1859.

I am sorry that I have not been able to get to Manchester to see you before now, but the fact is that I have been shut up to this circuit, so that I could not get away. I am afraid I have worn your patience to a thread. May the Lord bless you! I hope you still feel the Saviour precious to you. He is always at hand, always looking, always listening, always disposed to help us, infinitely disposed, thanks to His name.

TO THE SAME.

BURNLEY, *Dec.* 29, 1859.

We had a very large gathering at the tea meeting; about a thousand people, and a very good meeting after. We have had our Quarter Day, and I am glad to inform you that we had an increase of between thirty and forty members, and about a hundred on trial. To God be all the glory. Amen and Amen. I have to preach at the Primitive Methodist Chapel this evening. I am praying that good may be done. My help is in the Lord.

That help I feel I need, and have faith to believe I shall have, so the devil may roar as loud as he likes.

TO THE SAME.

BURNLEY, *Jan.* 2, 1860.

I preached three times yesterday, and the Lord helped me. There were five penitents at night. Some of them wept aloud. The Lord saw and heard and answered, and good was done. Hallelujah! I am going to Padiham to preach this evening. May the Lord save sinners for Jesu's sake!

TO THE SAME.

BURNLEY, *Jan.* 4, 1860.

I have received both the books, for which I do desire to return my best thanks. . . I had a very good time at Padiham. We had some penitents, and last night at Park Hill one woman cried out for mercy, and a man got good, and there was a very glorious feeling. We have a bazaar here for the missions, it is open to-day and to-morrow. They realised £30 this morning. I hope that you are all happy, and that we shall have a glorious year of it.

TO THE SAME.

BURNLEY, *Jan.* 19, 1860.

We had a Town Missionary Meeting last night; it went off well, a very gracious feeling. On Sunday last I preached in the Burnley Chapel. There were a number of penitents, and a few of them found liberty through the blood of the Lamb. I am going to Wheatley Lane to-night, God willing, hoping to have a good time.

Mr. R. Harrison, writing of Mackenzie in Burnley, furnishes a reminiscence that illustrates well the delicate play of fancy that hardly ever failed to glint sunbeam-wise, even through the more sober phases of speech or sermon. The first platform speech he heard him deliver was in the Burnley Chapel, and in it he used the following illustration, though other memories have supplemented that of Mr. Harrison in the reproduction of it :—

THE STREAM AND MR. STAGNANT.

One morning a bright stream from the mountains passed a large sheet of water, which he would call Mr. Stagnant. 'Good-morning, my canny darling,' said Mr. Stagnant. 'Whither away in such haste?' 'Oh,' said the rill, 'I have a cupful of water, and I am going to the sea with it.' 'But,' said Mr. Stagnant, 'you had better be careful. We have had a very backward spring, and there is every prospect of a hot summer. I would therefore advise you to husband your resources.' 'If that is the case,' said the rill, 'there is all the more need for me to hasten on, and do good with the little I have; so good-morning, Mr. Stagnant.' The little rill ran on, blessing and being blest. It made such sweet music that other rills were attracted, and glad to join it. Trees gathered on its banks, and as though grateful for its moisture, spread their broad arms over it during the hot days of summer. The miller smiled on it, for it turned his wheel. The farmer was glad at its approach, for it made his pastures greener. The birds stooped and dipped their bills in it, and then soared higher and sang sweeter. And thus it ran on till it lost itself in the sea. But God drew up sufficient water from the sea, condensed it in the atmosphere, and, by means of His cloud-carriages, baptized ever and anon the mountain tops, so that the little rill never ran dry—January nor June, Christmas nor Midsummer. But what became of Mr. Stagnant? He had been quite right in his prophecy. There ensued an exceedingly hot summer; and he became foul and fetid and stench-full. Birds came within a dozen yards of him, and then wheeled round, sick and dizzy and faint. Many, as soon as they smelt his breath, turned aside, as though they had been plague-infected. Toads came and spat in his face. Hot cattle got three mouthfuls of him, and threw up their heels as though they had advanced thirty stages in the rinderpest. And Heaven, in mercy to man and beast, smote him with a hotter breath, and dried him clean up. 'There is that scattereth and yet increaseth; there is that withholdeth more than is meet, and it tendeth to poverty.'

Mackenzie's ministry in the Burnley circuit was remarkably successful. The congregations were immense, and the quarterly collections are said to have gone up two hundred per cent. On one occasion at Higham, he duplicated an experience of Wesley's at Haworth—the front window of the chapel was removed, so that he could address the crowd without, and yet be heard by the crowd within. A glance through his register of sermons and services shows that he hardly preached once during that year without having to record results in the form of visible decisions for Christ.

With all this success, it is difficult to understand why he should have been taken away at the end of the first year. That the extent to which people crowded to his services in town and country would deplete the ordinary congregations, and to some extent interfere with the regular work of the circuit, is quite conceivable, and that in this way there should have arisen rivalries and misunderstandings on the part of some is hardly matter for surprise ; but one cannot help regretting that some way of escaping the difficulty was not devised that would have created no sense of inequity in the mind of the worker, and not appeared to cast reflections on the work.

CHAPTER XIV

The Itinerancy a Creator of Contrasts—The Forest of Dean—
Its Natural Features—Methodism in Coleford—House and
Pay at Coleford—New Organ at Monmouth—An Alarmed
Hearer—"Cut it in Two, Brother"—Teaching the People to
Sing—A Blow in the Pulpit—Dark Walks Illuminated.

THERE is hardly a better creator of contrasts than
the Methodist itinerancy. At the beck of Conference a man is jerked from the soft breezes and
mellow landscapes of the Isle of Wight to the hard
hills of North Britain, or from the treeless wilds of
Shetland to the grateful umbrage of Warwickshire or
the wooded contours of Devon. Nor is the change
simply one of clime and country. The people vary as
greatly as the landscape, and the preacher finds himself as much in a new land of thought and habit and
usage, as of geographical site and conformation.

What a change for Mackenzie from the crowded
Lancashire town, with its smoky chimneys and
clattering mills, to the quiet folk, the sunny skies, the
rich, umbrageous hills and dales of Monmouthshire.
His new residence was at Coleford, in the Monmouth,
Ross, and Forest of Dean circuit, which then included
what are now the separate circuits of Ross and

Cinderford. "The Forest of Dean is the property of the Crown, and has been a royal domain as far back as the time of Edward the Confessor. It formerly covered all the triangular area between the Severn and the Wye, from Gloucester to Chepstow on the south-west, and from Gloucester along by the little river Leadon to Newent, and thence to Ross on the north-

LITTLE DEAN HILL CHAPEL.

west, which seem to be its natural, as in the days of Henry II. (A.D. 1200), they were its privileged . boundaries. The area of the Crown lands has diminished considerably in the last six hundred and fifty years, but the main features of the upland country between the rivers remain substantially the same." The scenery is charming, consisting of a succession of steep wooded hills and dells, with grand views of the Severn valley and the Cotswolds beyond, on the one hand, and on the other the beautiful cliffs and gorges of the Wye. This affluence of the picturesque is matched by an equal wealth of coal and iron below the surface, so that industries and natural beauty are brought into close relation, often to the detriment of the latter.

From an interesting article by the Rev. J. E. Harlow, in the last Winter Number of the *Methodist Recorder*, we learn that Coleford is in the heart of the Forest, and has three thousand inhabitants. It was visited by Wesley in 1756, and again in 1763. He rode from Chepstow to Coleford, and writes: "The wind being high, I consented to preach in their new room ; but, large as it was, it would not contain the people, who appeared to be not a little affected, of which they gave a sufficient proof, by filling the room at five in the morning."

"The next landmark of Methodism in Coleford," says Mr. Harlow, "may help to explain what had become of the Society visited by Mr. Wesley. In the year 1849, a Wesleyan chapel was opened by the Rev. Thomas Jackson and the Rev. Richard Roberts. That building superseded a Countess of Huntingdon church, which did not survive the disastrous events of that year."

In the house adjoining the chapel, Peter Mackenzie took up his abode at the Conference of 1860. "It was during the twilight of a day in the first week of September that Mr. Mackenzie, his wife and two daughters, and a lady friend, arrived at the quaint and quiet town of Coleford. A house had been hastily obtained and furnished, and into this the little party came. It was by no means a pretentious dwelling; this Peter seemed not to notice, but, true to his

WESLEY CHAPEL, CINDERFORD.

character, went straight upstairs with his family, and, kneeling down, dedicated his humble abode to God and the service of a Christian minister."

The change from Burnley must have been very great. There were long distances to be covered on roads lovely by day, but fearsome and uncanny by night, and the places to be ministered at were comparatively small and poor, and there were not the great masses of population to draw upon to which he had been accustomed. But there was no abatement of zeal, nor the faintest diminution of that cheery glow and whole-heartedness which he infused into all his labour. Mr. R. Harrison of Whalley, then of Burnley, remarks that Mackenzie wrote him soon after reaching his new appointment, and said, " I have walked fourteen miles. Two souls saved. Hallelujah ! I shall never have gout ! " If the secret of happiness consists in enjoying what we have, rather than in lamenting what we cannot get, then certainly Mackenzie had found it. Of him might be said, in the words of Goldsmith—

> Cheerful at morn he wakes from short repose,
> Breathes the keen air, and carols as he goes.

There is living still in Coleford a venerable local preacher, Mr. John Adams, who was born in 1809. This good brother paid a visit to London during the Conference of 1860, partly because of his interest in the circuit appointment. He had read the newspaper accounts of Mackenzie's admission into the ministry, and knew something of his work at Burnley, and, seeing his name down in the first draft of stations for the Monmouth circuit, felt anxious to secure him. As he loitered in the chapel yard, four ministers stood in a group: John Rattenbury, who had once been chairman of the district, Richard Roberts, who had opened the Coleford Chapel, Luke Wiseman, and the then superintendent of the Monmouth circuit. Mr. Adams approached them, and promised that, though no such provision existed then, it being a junior minister's appointment, yet, if Mr. Mackenzie were sent to reside at Coleford, a comfortable house should be found for him. Soon afterwards Mackenzie found himself the tenant of Mr. Adams in a furnished house, for which, however, he insisted on paying rent.

His residence at Coleford, and his work throughout the circuit, are gratefully and vividly remembered; the only regret being that the claims of outside places called him so frequently from home. Mrs. Mackenzie was the means of resuscitating the Sunday school at Coleford, which had been in a state of suspended animation for some years, and which has continued to flourish since. The appointment was such as afforded Mackenzie an opportunity of emulating Goldsmith's country parson, who was

> Passing rich on forty pounds a year.

The allowance was very small, only about fifty-six pounds per annum, but Mrs. Mackenzie bears most grateful testimony to the exceeding kindness of the people. Cream, eggs, potatoes, and all manner of eatables were poured upon them in abundance, so that they were enabled to say: "We have all, and abound, and are full, having received the things which were sent from you, an odour of a sweet smell, a sacrifice acceptable, well-pleasing to God."

I am indebted to Mr. Harlow for a rather interesting extract from the circuit steward's account-book, dated October 1, 1860. It is the first entry in connection with Mackenzie's name.

Rev. Peter Mackenzie	.	£2 10 0	{[Doubtless in respect of board.]
Quarterage	. . .	4 4 0	
Washing	. . .	1 11 6	
Books	. . . .	1 1 0	
Travelling expenses	.	0 15 0	
District „	. .	0 15 0	
Carriage of boxes	. .	2 0 0	
		£12 16 6	

The places in the circuit being so widely scattered, and the distances so great, some kind soul provided Mackenzie with a pony; and it is remembered that much amusement was created when, occasionally, he would ride along with his silk hat on his hand instead of on his head, so that the rattle thus made might urge the beast to a quicker pace.

His visits to Monmouth, the circuit town, were always occasions of interest and excitement. Not long previous to his arrival on the ground, an effort had been made to supersede the string band by a harmonium. A Mrs. Bullock, who lived at Hadnock farm, and a few others had even dared to dream of an organ. One Sunday Mrs. Bullock, in commenting on the attractiveness of the chapel, observed how pleasing it would be to see it crowded, and even went so far as to promise that when that not very likely contingency arose, she would be pleased to make a present of an organ. Soon afterwards the eccentric preacher arrived, and the chapel was crowded. Mrs. Bullock was at once reminded of her promise, and very generously fulfilled it.

Once Mackenzie preached at Monmouth to a packed congregation, on the Deluge. A retired army captain, a member of the Established Church, could only find a fragment of a seat at the end of a crowded pew. In illustrating the struggles of the people to escape the rising waters, some of the preacher's actions were so graphic and sensational, and in the rather high pulpit appeared so perilous, that the stranger, turning to the steward who had shown him in, whispered that he could not stand this. He was prevailed upon to remain, however, and afterwards never missed a service at which Mackenzie preached.

The prayer - meetings after service on Sunday evenings were remarkable. Numbers of strangers often remained in the galleries, and conversions were by no means infrequent. On one occasion a local preacher was too lengthy in his supplications. Mackenzie endured it for a while, and then cried out, " Cut it in two, brother, and begin again presently." Mr. John Histance, now in his eighty-first year, to whose good memory we are indebted for many of these reminiscences, says that he was greatly impressed in those days by the seriousness of Mackenzie's preaching. There was abundance of humour, but what always affected him and many others most, was the intense earnestness and pathos.

Mr. Isaiah Gadd of Wokingham also supplies recollections that throw a pleasant light on this period :—

" I well remember the coming of the Rev. Peter Mackenzie to the Monmouth circuit some thirty-five years ago. I was a lad in my teens, and my home was one of the beautiful villages near Monmouth.

This circuit of Methodism, as many a dear, good minister and local preacher has found, at the cost of shoe-leather and tired limbs, covered an immense area of country, running far towards the mountains of Wales on one side, and many miles right out to the villages of Herefordshire in a reverse direction. It spread up through the solemn woods and steep roads under the shadow of the great Buckstone Rock, and on into the Forest of Dean to Coleford, embracing nearly the whole of the Forest on to Lydney, with its switch-back roads, numerous quarries, disused pits and mines, many of them unkept and unprotected. This was the circuit to which Mr. Mackenzie came, and it was like the coming of a comet, and, as with John the Baptist, many people came out for to see, and we were soon conscious of a great stir on all sides.

"The first time I saw and heard Mr. Mackenzie was at our village chapel, five miles out from Monmouth, and about ten miles from Coleford. At the close of the morning service, coming down from the pulpit to the communion table, he urged the people that they should learn to sing well, so as to attract others to God's house. Taking out of his coat pocket a number of music leaflets, he said, ' Now this is a nice one,' and, suiting the action to the word, began to sing, ' I want to be an angel.' My elder brother, who had helped to lead the singing at the service with his concertina, and I, with my young, shrill voice, closed round the new minister, and while he poured forth a powerful lead, we each did our very best at that pretty, simple, and then new bit of music. By the time we had got through the verses the good people behind us were catching on, so that it ran 'like oil from vessel to vessel.' An unmistakable invitation to the afternoon service followed. Everybody was to tell somebody, and all were to bring their friends to help to make a good company. The short interval was soon over, and there was indeed a good company and a blessed service.

"When Mr. Mackenzie came out again to preach in the same little chapel, his fame had gone abroad, and the people crowded to the afternoon service so much that the building was packed from end to end. My father, in his desire to make room for others, had vacated his seat time after time, and now only the pulpit stairs remained unoccupied. These, one after the other, were filled, until, as a last resource, and to make room for just one more, my father took refuge in the pulpit, little thinking of the penalty to be paid soon for such an exaltation. Mr. Mackenzie got well into his subject, and made his sermon glow with life and interest as he described poor sick ones coming to an earthly physician, surrounded with bottles of medicine and ointments for all kinds of maladies. He had all these various bottles in full array on the pulpit around him. Suddenly he swept them away with both hands right and left as he introduced the Heavenly Healer, saying, 'Away with your quack nostrums! Away with them!' My father at his elbow was forgotten, and he, poor dear man, was in the third heaven of delight as he drank in the blessed gospel of Jesus Christ, when all at once the preacher's powerful hand in its backward swing swept like a sledge-hammer into his face, utterly blinding him for the moment, and making the sparks fly from his eyes like fireworks, and leaving him with a never-to-be-forgotten remembrance of that immortal sermon. Mr. Mackenzie, with his usual native tenderness, turned quickly round, exclaiming sorrowfully, 'O my dear brother, I hope I have not hurt you! I am so sorry!' It was certainly most instructive to see my father's attitude of distance and caution towards the preacher for the rest of the evening.

"This is but a peep at the popularity and work of Mr. Mackenzie in this out-of-the-way circuit; where trains and circuit horses were entirely out of the question; where distances were appalling; where roads, for the greater part, were very trying; and where the minister had of necessity to leave home for days together, and work his way back gradually from place to place. But none of these things moved our friend. Toiling and labouring on, he was faithful in little and in much; and with great reward he was then and is now crowned. It will be admitted that it is no easy thing to fill the Monmouth chapel, to command full and enthusiastic congregations. This honour was granted to Mr. Mackenzie. And how the country people all round the circuit delighted to hear him; and to-day, his name is with them as 'ointment poured forth.'

"My brother, who at that time was in his apprenticeship at Coleford, often accompanied him from Coleford to Monmouth and back for a week-evening service. Those otherwise dark and tedious journeys were illuminated and made special treats by rehearsals, orations, recitations of poetry and other good things from the lips and soul of him who did not hesitate thus to unfold to the eyes and ears of an apprentice lad what was to make him, as the future lecturer and preacher, the delight of people everywhere. Who can tell how many dear souls out in those country places were cheered and toned-up by the visits of this man of God, with his simple, cheery manner and his soul of music and praise. Many of them have gone on before, and to others of us heaven is all the sweeter for his presence there."

CHAPTER XV

The Wiltshire Mission — Rev. A. Barber's Testimony — Two
Sermons at one Sitting—Acting the Highwayman—Letters
to Mr. Thomas Elliott—"A Hard Cavil"—First Lecture:
The Bible—Admitted into full Connexion—Examination
Incidents—Visit to the Land's End—Good Times at Bowden
Hill.

AFTER labouring faithfully and with great acceptance for two years at Monmouth, Mackenzie,
at the Conference of 1862, was transferred to the
Melksham circuit, in Wiltshire. This circuit, like that
of the Forest of Dean, has undergone considerable
changes, and is now worked in three sections under
the general designation of the Wiltshire Mission.
This mission employs, at the present moment, seven
ministers and one lay evangelist. It directs and
sustains the work of Wesleyan Methodism, in other
words, Christianity in earnest, in forty-six towns and
villages of Wiltshire, including Melksham, Chippenham, Calne, Devizes, Warminster, Westbury, Malmes-
bury and Tetbury. In all these places there are
chapels or mission-halls, forming accommodation for
a total of about seven thousand people. The area of
the mission is wider than that of the original Melk-

sham circuit, though that was fairly extensive, including no less than nineteen places. The conditions of labour were here, as at Monmouth, hard and discouraging; long distances, small places, with a need of constant effort to sustain the life of the struggling churches.

The Rev. Alfred Barber says :—

" In the year 1862, the President of the Conference, the Rev. Charles Prest, directed me to leave the Higham Ferrers circuit, to assist my father in the Melksham circuit, who had broken down in his work. This brought me again into contact with Mr. Mackenzie, who resided as second minister at Chippenham. For months I was his colleague, and was a witness of his diligence and devotion. My father said it was impossible to stir his bile. Though very much tried, he never spoke an angry word. He was much from home; but in taking his country appointments he was most diligent and conscientious. His custom was to visit every house he could, and to pray with every family."

Of this conscientiousness in attending to the country places a somewhat amusing instance is related of him while in the Melksham circuit. One of the places at which in turn he had to minister was Tinhead, a romantic Wiltshire hamlet, not far removed, if tradition is to be credited, from the spot where good King Alfred burned the cakes; and where the Methodist chapel abuts on the far-famed Salisbury Plain, four or five feet of the chalk down having been cut away to make space for it. Owing to some other engagement, Mackenzie was, on one occasion, unable to take his appointment there. The matter was not forgotten, however, and, regarding himself as in their debt, at his next visit he had no sooner finished one service than he announced another to pay off the old score. And more marvellous still, and what probably could only occur in the experience of a preacher as racy as himself, it is stated that of those who had listened to the first sermon, only one failed to hear the second, and that because an engagement demanded her presence elsewhere.

An incident similar to this transpired, it seems, in the Gateshead circuit, during Mackenzie's period in it. Mr. John Burdess of Jarrow says: "I once remarked to a friend, in Mr. Mackenzie's presence, that the last ticket of membership I received in the Gateshead circuit was from the hand of Mr. Mackenzie himself, after he had preached us two sermons at one sitting. Mr. Mackenzie, in response to the remark, at once said, 'Ay, that was at Wreckenton.' He had come into the circuit in September, and previous to the visitation for the December tickets, he had failed twice to take his appointment at Wreckenton, on account of missionary meetings and other special engagements, and there were some complaints of neglect. So, on the occasion referred to, when he had finished his week-night sermon, he said, 'Now, friends, I have rather neglected you lately, so we will sing a hymn, and I will preach you another sermon.' He did so, and when it was finished, he remarked, 'Now, I have two classes to meet for tickets, and some of you may have to get up by the first caller, or I would have given you another.' He thus made himself straight with us at once, in accordance with his avowed principle of paying as he went on, and having no back-reckonings."

A correspondent, Jesse Warfield of Chippenham, says that Mackenzie's first service there was on a Wednesday evening, when he missed his way to the chapel, and arrived late. The first words in his opening prayer so impressed one man who was present that since then he has lived a Christian life, and become a useful local preacher. This correspondent adds that Mr. Mackenzie was always very kind to the local preachers and to the poor ; and that the Chippenham friends made him a present of a Bible when he left.

Devotion in Mackenzie always lived next door to humour, and as neighbours the two were on such intimate terms that they continuously exchanged greetings. One night, in this circuit, he had to join his colleagues on their way to a missionary meeting. Instead of waiting for them exactly at the appointed spot, he waylaid the phaeton, and, stopping the horse, called out in stentorian tones, " Your money or your life ! " This demand brought the full force of whip and umbrella down upon his shoulders from those who sat in front ; but the mistake was speedily discovered, and the would - be highwayman welcomed into the conveyance, and borne forward to expend the exuberance of his spirits in graphic and racy descriptions of missionary toil.

The following letters show the spirit in which Mackenzie, at this time, entered into the toils of his somewhat unpromising field of labour.

TO MR. THOMAS ELLIOTT.

CHIPPENHAM, WILTS, *March* 21, 1862.

MY VERY DEAR BROTHER,—Many thanks for your kind letter. I should be glad if the Lord would be pleased to appoint me

near you by and by. I shall not move this next year, as the good
work is going on. Another year will, with the blessing of God,
put the circuit into working order; and I do think that it will
be better to stay. They only give £100, and I keep a pony and
trap out of that. I don't get anything for the children, and *still
I have Plenty.* My dear brother, it is worth a great deal to me
that I had a few years in the pit ; that I know how to stick to a
"hard cavil," how to drive through nipped coal. She has been
cracking here for some time, and you may send the Barrowman
in when I get more in my head and also in my heart.

A "cavil," as has been already explained, is the
location appointed by lot to each miner at the
beginning of the quarter. "Nipped coal" is coal
which has been compressed between the floor of the
seam and the roof, and which, through the constraint
thus put upon it, has gained a tough, wooden consist-
ence, hard to deal with. At times the pressure is
so great as to crush the coal and make it break off
from the face in lumps or slices, with loud cracking
reports. This makes the work of the hewer much
easier, and this is what Mackenzie refers to above,
when he says, "She has been cracking here for some
time." "Barrowman" was another term for "putter";
and to ask to have the barrowman sent in was an
intimation that there was a good supply of loose coals
ready to be filled into the tubs.

TO MR. THOMAS ELLIOTT.

CHIPPENHAM, WILTS, *June* 25, 1863.

MY VERY DEAR BROTHER IN JESUS,—Many thanks for your
kind letter, it did me good to hear from you. Thanks be to
God that we are still found with our faces Zionward. Hallelujah
to God and the Lamb ! It gets better and better, and still we
look for good things to come. What a glorious hope is ours
while here on earth we stay.

The Lord *has*, *is*, and *shall* bless us in this circuit.   More than a hundred and fifty have joined with us, and they are doing very well.   May the Lord bless them for His name's sake !   If I am received into full connexion I shall stay here another year, God willing.   Could you come up and see us for a week if spared, some time this back-end, before the cold weather comes ?   Try, you will enjoy it, and also get a few souls brought to the Saviour.

It would appear from Mackenzie's Text - Book, already so often quoted from, that it was at Chippenham, on May 23, 1864, that his first lecture was delivered, the subject being the Bible.   This inference is confirmed by Mr. Barber, who says : " It was in this circuit that he first commenced to lecture.   His lecture on the Bible, given at Chippenham, was considered a great success, and attracted immense notice.   The place resounded with his praises.   No doubt he was assured he had a talent in that direction, and the necessity for aiding financially many a struggling cause, induced him to put his energies into that sort of work."

Mr. Barber also records the conviction, derived from frequent encounters with Mackenzie in later years, that amid the abundant labours which lecturing entailed upon him, there was no diminution of his piety.

The termination of the first twelve months of labour in the Melksham circuit brought to an end Mackenzie's four years of ministerial probation, and at the Conference of 1863, held at Sheffield, under the presidency of the Rev. George Osborn, D.D., he was received into full connexion.   At the Bath District Synod, in the preceding May, he was examined by the chairman, the Rev. Francis A. West.

Among the subjects of examination were Pearson on the Creed and St. Paul's Epistle to the Romans, and the questions were very searching. Mr. West spoke very strongly to Mackenzie on the necessity for reading and study, saying, among other things, "Tap an empty barrel, and what have you?" Mackenzie, who, with all his zeal, never lacked application, was not likely to come under this designation, and perhaps hardly relished the remark, observing privately of Mr. West, to another of the candidates, "He is a rasper!"

"The brethren," observed the venerable divine, "think you will be more useful if you control yourself, and take time to clothe your ideas." "Yes, Mr. Chairman," answered Mackenzie, "but there are so many of them, and they come so fast, that I haven't even time to get their shirts on." In an instant the fathers and brethren were convulsed. Mackenzie solemnly retired, while the chairman looked slightly disconcerted.

The Rev. Edward Dodds writes :—

"In 1865 Mr. Mackenzie paid what was, I believe, his first visit to Cornwall, and on Thursday, June 1, came to St. Just, where I was then stationed. He preached in the large chapel that night to a good congregation, from Luke xxiii. 39–43, and announced that he would preach the next morning at half-past five o'clock, before the miners went to their 'core.' At the appointed hour he was in the pulpit, and had a capital audience. He preached an excellent sermon from Matt. xi. 28, etc.

"In the forenoon of that day I had the pleasure of driving him to the Land's End, the coast scenery of which, and the sea breezes from the Atlantic, he greatly enjoyed. There chanced to be a professional guide on the spot at the time, who was one of our worshippers in the adjoining village of Sennen, and who freely discoursed on the stories associated with the locality. He told us of the folly of a gentleman who once laid a wager that he would ride his horse to the farthest point of that narrow promontory. The animal, becoming more nervous than its foolish rider, began to plunge. and go backward towards the southern end of the cliff; whereupon, perceiving the danger, the man slipped off the saddle, and the horse —the victim of the wild adventure—fell over and perished. Peter denounced the madness of the man who could attempt such a feat.

"But the next recital touched him deeply. The guide pointed to a flat piece of rock in the turf, and said that was called ' Wesley's Stone,' because thereon Charles Wesley had conceived the hymn numbered 59 in our hymn-book, the second verse of which begins—

> Lo ! on a narrow neck of land
> 'Twixt two unbounded seas I stand,
> Secure, insensible.

" Brother Mackenzie listened to the end of the story, then, planting his feet upon the stone, and with the Bristol Channel on our right, the English Channel on our left, and before us the great watery highway to America, he solemnly repeated a portion of the hymn, and then, taking off his hat, said, ' Let us pray.'

"He knelt on the stone and we on the grass, and immediately commenced to praise God for raising up the Wesleys, for the work they accomplished throughout the country, and especially in Cornwall, for the souls saved and the Societies formed, and for the continuance of the work by their successors. He earnestly implored a blessing upon Cornwall, upon the ministers and Societies in the circuit, upon myself and our companion. Prayer to him was seldom out of place, and he could engage in it readily and appropriately. That short open-air service was refreshing to us all. He lectured in the evening at St. Just, to a crowded congregation, on the Bible, and so finished services which were full of power and blessing."

The entry made by Mackenzie at the close of the record of the services held at Bowden Hill, in the Melksham circuit, is as follows: " Blessed be God for all the good times I have had here. The Lord has built us a chapel, and it is paid for, and His name shall be glorified. They made me a present of three pounds when I left."

From information supplied by Charles Maggs, Esq., J.P., of Melksham, it seems that the chapel here referred to was built between Bowden Hill and Lacock, that it might serve both places. It is now known as Lacock, and is comprised in the Melksham section of the Wiltshire Mission. This place, and the record left concerning it, are illustrations of how easy it was for Mackenzie's happy, grateful spirit to educe matter for congratulation out of what to many would have afforded only ground for discouragement. He blesses God for all the good times he has had at a place, not where there were crowds and cheers, but of which it is stated that a very meagre society and congregation have belonged to it through all its history. Perhaps it was their genial quality, rather than their numbers, that led their minister to write of them in the same gratulatory spirit that Paul manifests towards the Philippians. Mr. Maggs says he knew Mackenzie well, and though only a boy himself at the time, he remembers the crowds who flocked to hear him, and the hot haste to which he urged his pony, with a crack of the whip and a shout of " Hallelujah ! "

CHAPTER XVI

BACK TO THE NORTH—GATESHEAD—1865–1868

The Gateshead Circuit—Missionary Meeting Episodes—Fighting
a Bear—Lighting up the World—"Three Happy Years"—
New Chapels—Story of Whickham—"'Twas Peter"—Home
Life—Testimony of Rev. W. Calvert—A Lively Pony—A
Dashing Driver.

I HAVE a distinct recollection of the mingling of
trepidation and wholesome pride with which I
received the visit of the late Mr. Silas Kent of
Gateshead, who, on Friday, January 5, 1866, came
to invite me to take the place of third minister in the
Gateshead circuit, where Mackenzie was then labouring as second. I had been sent as supply to the
Bishop Auckland circuit at the previous Conference,
was but an inexperienced youth, and could not but
feel honoured at being asked to become co-worker
with one so widely popular as Peter Mackenzie.
Many happy colleagueships have smiled on me since
then; but for oneness of aim, thoroughness of brotherly
intercourse, constant co-operation on the part of the
people, and remarkable success, those Gateshead years
still wear for me by far the most shining garments.

Our superintendent was the Rev. Robert Haworth,
a man beloved wherever he laboured for his sincerity

and devotion, his large-heartedness, and his overflowing geniality.   In the sunniness of his nature he was hardly second to Peter himself.   What a treat it was to accompany those two men to a missionary meeting ! The circuit was large, so large that it included sixteen of those annual gatherings, and never, before or since, have I known anything to equal them for attendance, for enthusiasm, and general success.   The superintendent would open with a few cheery, heart-stirring words, such as were likely to put the meeting into thoroughly good humour, and then, when the " young man " had spoken, Mackenzie would finish up with an outpouring of humour, description, pathos, and exhortation such as only he was capable of producing.

A favourite story with him during those missionary campaigns was that of the man who, out in the Far West, when his wooden shanty was invaded by a prowling bear, escaped into the loft, drawing the ladder up after him, and leaving his wife below to battle with the dangerous intruder.   From the man above she received showers of encouragement as she contended with the bear.   As Mackenzie put it, " he fairly sweated with sympathy," and when the brute was slain, he hurried down and stood proudly over the carcase, exclaiming, " Isn't he a big one ?   Haven't we done well ? "   To see this incident dramatised in every detail by the inimitable powers of the speaker, with a running fire of withering comment on those who have nothing for a good cause but sentimental sympathy, was to gain possession of a picture such as the memory could never forego.

About two miles from Gateshead, the main road rises considerably as it passes through the small village of Sheriff Hill. From this point, on dark nights in winter, the lamps in the streets of Gateshead and across the Tyne in Newcastle formed a striking spectacle; and among the most effective passages in Mackenzie's missionary speeches was one in which he described, with gesture graphic as his phrase, the flashing of those lights into existence one by one, and then, spreading before us the map of a darkened earth, showed us the missionary lighting up one land after another, until the whole world was gladdened with a divine illumination.

Strikingly successful as were those missionary gatherings, the ordinary services were in interest and power but little behind them. The Sunday evening congregation in High West Street Chapel was so large, even as a regular thing, that forms had to be placed in the aisles, and hardly ever did one of those services pass without visible results in the form of conversions to God.

How successful those years were, and how refreshing to Mackenzie's own spirit, is evidenced by the record he has left concerning them : "Three happy years. In September 1865, 839 members, and in September 1868, 1500, with more than 200 on trial. And during the three years £4600 raised for chapels and chapel debts. To God be all the glory !"

New chapels were commenced, if not completed, during this period, at Usworth Colliery, Winlaton, Whickham, and Bill Quay, besides sundry alterations and enlargements. The erection of the chapel at Whickham was a case of more than ordinary interest. The services were held in what at other times was used as a butcher's shop, and for forty years the

Methodist cause had been exceedingly feeble. When the effort to obtain a new chapel was begun, there were only eight members in church fellowship, three of whom were over sixty and three over seventy years of age ; and owing to the predominating and unfriendly influence of the Established Church in the village, it had been impracticable for years to obtain a building site. All these difficulties were surmounted, however, and when, in a moment of youthful enthusiasm, the junior minister expressed a determination to raise by his own endeavours the sum of at least one hundred pounds, considerable sympathy was evoked, and generous help forthcoming.

The story of this effort would not be related here so fully were it not for the light it throws on Mackenzie's character, and on the high estimation in which he was held by the people generally. The photographs of the ministers were taken in a group as well as singly, and from the sale of these alone a profit of twenty-six pounds was added to the building fund. Then my generous colleague, one day on returning from a lecturing tour, handed me his gold watch-chain, which I exchanged at a jeweller's for three guineas. A sum of ten pounds was also realised on the sale of certain verses which, half in fun and half in earnest, I had scribbled concerning Mackenzie. The verses are given here, not because of any intrinsic merit they possess, their poetic quality being of the slightest, but because of the interest which the circumstances lend to them, and because the writer, having failed to suppress them entirely, and having met with several garbled versions at different times, concludes it is better on the whole, at whatever crucifixion of his taste, to let them appear as they were originally printed. When Mackenzie left the circuit, farewell tea-meetings were arranged at many of the places, and it was at such a gathering, held at Blaydon, that these rhymes were first recited, my magnanimous colleague receiving them with as much enjoyment as any in the audience.

'TWAS PETER.

LINES WRITTEN ON THE REV. PETER MACKENZIE LEAVING THE GATESHEAD CIRCUIT.

My numbers are feeble and small,
    And yet they may serve to portray
The likeness of one whom we all
    Shall love and remember for aye.

His figure was portly and good,
    His manner quite cheery and bland,
From your fingers he banished the blood
    When he gave you a shake of the hand.

His face was as happy and fair
    As the sun on a fine summer day;
His voice cut the throat of all care,
    And frightened ill-temper away.

His mind was a curious thing:
    The classic, the comic, the sage,
With a rush or a roll or a spring,
    Came out of this wonderful cage.

His heart was a nugget of love
    Dug out of the mine of God's grace,
To old friends it stuck like a glove,
    And for new ones could still find a place.

But, now, lest my verse should grow tame,
    I'll venture to alter the metre,
In order to tell you his name,
    Which was what? Was it Simon? No, Peter.

Who was it came to Gateshead town
When the Methodists were looking down,
Yes, came without his bands and gown?
        'Twas Peter.

Who filled the chapels very soon,
Both in the country and the "toon,"
And put the people into tune?
        'Twas Peter.

Who was it won the love of all,
The young, the old, the great, the small,
By ways that did their hearts enthrall?
        'Twas Peter.

Who gave you lectures on the Tongue,
The Sabbath, if I am not wrong,
God's Providence and Samson strong?
        'Twas Peter.

Who oft upon the Mission theme
Threw many a bright and witty gleam,
As from his lips the words did stream?
        'Twas Peter.

Who came to public meetings oft,
And made you laugh until you coughed,
With speeches neither small nor soft?
        'Twas Peter.

Who dashed along the road like lightning,
In Charlie's rapid speed delighting,
And many a timid spirit frightening?
        'Twas Peter.

Who christened babies by the score,
And gave them kisses one or more,
As loud as breakers on the shore?
        'Twas Peter.

Who is it now about to leave,
A thing we scarcely can believe,
Makes many a saddened spirit grieve?
        'Tis Peter.

> Who is it that when far away
> We'll think about for many a day,
> And for his weal and welfare pray?
>   'Tis Peter.
>
> Who is it that beyond the skies
> We hope to see with gladdened eyes
> Amid the light that never dies?
>   'Tis Peter.

Concerning Whickham, it only remains to be added that with the aid of photographs, watch-chain, rhymes, lectures, and subscriptions, the promised hundred pounds grew into about one hundred and twenty, and other friends helping freely, a pretty little chapel was reared on a suitable site, which has since proved the home of a successful Methodist Church.

An interesting peep into Mackenzie's home-life at this period, which may be taken as a type of what it was at all times, is furnished by the Rev. W. Calvert.

"In January 1866, I was sent to supply a vacancy that had occurred in the Gateshead circuit, where I had the great pleasure and privilege of living in Mr. Mackenzie's house until the following Conference. During those months he was to me more a father than a colleague. I think I had not been in his house two minutes before we were kneeling together in his study, and in his own impressive and original way he was praying that we might be happy and useful together. The next thing was heartily to assure me that I was welcome to the free use of any book in his library. It was generally at breakfast that he inquired about my studies, and when he knew that I had fixed on a new subject, or text, he would look through his excellent library, and bring down into my room two, three, or half a dozen books bearing on the subject.

"The unity of Mr. Mackenzie's character was perfect. He was the same bright, cheery, happy, racy man in private life as in public. Indeed, to spend one evening in his company was to know as much about his spirit and disposition as you would learn from a longer and more intimate association. I never saw him vary. I have heard him call up his eldest daughter in the morning, after this manner. Standing on the landing of the stairs, he would call out in stentorian tones, and with his own peculiar accent, 'Janet! Janet! are—you—in a—horizontal or a perpendicular position?' Or, 'Janet! Janet! can —you—read—small print?' In the same bright and cheery spirit he treated everybody through the day—wife, children, myself, or callers. By the way, when callers showed a disposition to occupy more of his time than he could spare, after the business in hand was settled, he sometimes dismissed them with prayer. He said, when the benediction was pronounced, they seemed to understand that the service was closed.

"His prayers in the family, if I may refer to them, were powerful and pithy, exactly after the style of his public prayers. I have heard him at the family altar name separately almost every place on the circuit plan, offering two or three brief petitions suggested by the need and condition of each place.

"Always happy and cheerful himself, he spread sunshine throughout his home. Now that we shall see him no more in the flesh, I have been thinking the old times over, and I have no recollection of ever having heard him say an unkind or uncharitable word to or of anyone. He was a living embodiment of the Christian spirit.

"As a companion and colleague, he was both delightful and devout. At Gateshead he kept a pony and trap. 'Charlie' was well fed and in good condition for work, and his master was a very lively driver. We used to drive to our appointments at no sleepy pace. When Charlie was going ahead in fine style one summer night, Mr. Mackenzie exclaimed, 'If John Wesley's doctrine of the resurrection of animals be correct, if the laws of heaven permit, I will have a race with Michael the archangel on the plains of heaven.' Once when we started from the stable, Charlie, being in unusually high spirits, turned the wrong way up the street and reared and pranced about considerably before Mr. Mackenzie could get him turned about. Years after I heard him give the following version of this little episode: 'Charlie started for the moon, but his hind legs refused to support the resolution.'

"When driving together once, he said, 'Do you know any grammar, Mr. Calvert?' I answered modestly, 'Yes, a little, Mr. Mackenzie.' His very geniality provoked reprisals. I was in no dread of my colleague's displeasure, and saw no reason why I should not turn examiner, so I said 'Do you know any grammar, Mr. Mackenzie?' 'Not a yard,' was his cheery reply.

"But our conversation was not all of this nature. It seemed perfectly natural and easy to him to turn at once from what was so bright and gay to a talk on entire sanctification, or any other serious and spiritual subject pertaining to our life and work.

"Mr. Mackenzie was a man to be loved, and the more you knew him, the more you loved him. His public gifts and character are well known, but to me it will always be a happy recollection that I admired and loved him most because of my knowledge of his private life."

Mackenzie's pony was a great assistance to us in our circuit work, for we had his permission to use it freely when he was absent from home. As an illustration of the happy terms on which as colleagues we lived and worked together, I may relate here how one Saturday evening I went to lecture at a country place, and how the kindly superintendent took the chair, and Mackenzie, in spite of his multitudinous engagements, went also, and sat on the platform, to clerk encouraging responses. One point urged in the lecture was the importance of each man having and maintaining an individuality of his own, instead of becoming a second edition of someone else, and it was very amusing, as we drove home together afterwards, to hear Peter exclaim, as he touched the animal lightly with the whip, "Now then, sir, get along, realise your individuality!"

He was a sure but dashing driver, enjoying immensely a rapid spin when the course was clear, the road good, and Charlie in fine condition. To a local preacher who sat beside him in the trap one day, somewhat alarmed at the pace, he said, "Don't be afraid, brother, you are as safe as if you were sitting in Gabriel's arm-chair."

CHAPTER XVII

SUNDERLAND—SANS STREET—1868–1871

Division of Sunderland Circuit — Rev. Thomas Vasey — A
Promising Appointment—An Apparent Failure—Misstate-
ments and Exaggerated Expectations — Tides of Spiritual
Influence—Sans Street Chapel—Memorable Watch-nights—
Extracts from Mackenzie's Text-Book—Attempt to Garrote
Him—Apocryphal Stories.

AT the Conference of 1868 the Methodist churches
of Sunderland were divided into three circuits,
Sans Street, Fawcett Street, and Whitburn Street.
To the first-named of these Mackenzie was appointed
as second minister. In the following year a third
minister was employed, and in that capacity I had
the pleasure of being associated with him once more,
with the Rev. Thomas Vasey as superintendent.

Mr. Vasey was one of the most devoted and powerful preachers Methodism has ever known. His memoir,
written by his widow, furnishes ample evidence of his
ability, his self-sacrifice, and his success in winning
souls. His ministry in Newcastle during the three
years immediately preceding had been characterised
by remarkable manifestations of power, and when our
work in Sunderland began, all hearts were big with
anticipation. For reasons difficult to divine, this

expectation was not realised. The distance between
Newcastle and Gateshead and Sunderland is only
twelve miles; the people were of a similar type, and
were kind and helpful; the ministers who had worked
so prosperously in the former places were working
here in the same spirit, and yet there came not the
same success.

A writer in the *Durham Chronicle* for November
29, 1895, referring to this period, says :—

"Twenty-five years ago Mr. Mackenzie was one of
the Sans Street circuit ministers in Sunderland. His
colleague was the Rev. Joseph Dawson, and the
superintendent was the late Rev. Thomas Vasey.
Probably never in all his ministerial career did the
deceased meet with a heavier disappointment than he
did then, for during the three years the congregation dwindled to almost skeleton proportions. Mr.
Mackenzie could not have been to blame for this; Mr.
Vasey was a very prince of preachers, and was to
have been nominated President of the Conference the
year he died; while Mr. Dawson (who happily still
lives) was one of the younger ministers of the body,
and a man of high promise. With Sans Street pulpit
so splendidly manned, a rare success was looked for ;
but, instead, there was failure so manifest and so
unlooked-for, that it all but broke Mr. Vasey's heart.
In any current criticisms on Mr. Mackenzie's circuit-
work proper, let the above facts be borne in mind.
Congregations do not always prosper, even under the
most favourable conditions in the pulpit. 'The wind
bloweth where it listeth.'"

This account, while kindly in spirit, and animated
by a praiseworthy desire to shield the memory of

Mackenzie from misunderstanding, betrays an imperfect acquaintance with the facts. There was disappointment, but not to the extent to which the writer seems to imagine. The congregations, either at Sans Street or the other chapels in the circuit, certainly did not dwindle, nor was there serious decrease in the membership. When Mackenzie came on the ground in 1868, the total number of members for Sans Street, Fawcett Street, and Whitburn Street, which up to that time had been returned as two circuits, was 1666; in 1869 it was for Sans street 794, and for the three circuits combined 1847, being an increase on the year of 181. In 1870 it was for Sans Street 864, being an increase of 70, and in 1871 it stood at 843, a decrease of 21.

The disappointment at not seeing sinners converted in larger numbers in Sunderland was undoubtedly great to both Mackenzie and his colleagues, and probably exercised a depressing effect on the health of Mr. Vasey, but it was a disappointment exaggerated by over-sanguine and perhaps not altogether reasonable expectations. The great wave of spiritual influence which had passed over Newcastle and Gateshead during the preceding three years was now subsiding, and it was no longer possible to be borne on its crest to wonderful spiritual achievements. As the critic just quoted observes, " The wind bloweth where it listeth "; and without attempting to account for the fact, it is sufficient to note what must have impressed every observant man, that there are tides in religious history, exhilarating in their glorious flow, depressing in their mournful ebb, but almost as far beyond our control as those that break upon the ocean strand.

A great thinker, speaking of the Divine Being and of His action in the spiritual world, remarks very justly: " Whatever He may be in Himself, His *manifestations to us* do not lie still before us in the sleep of a frozen sea ; they break out of this motionless eternity ; they sweep in mighty tides of nature and of history, with flux and reflux ; they are alive with shifting streaks of light and gloom ; and have the changing voice of many waters. And the clearer and more spiritual they are, the more marked is this fluctuating character : and they affect us, not as the dead of noon or the dead of night, but as the quick-flushing morning, or the tender pulses of the northern lights."

Sans Street Chapel at this period was suffering, and continued to do even more severely afterwards, from the fate that has overtaken so many fine old Methodist sanctuaries, when, owing to changes in the local surroundings, to fill and support them becomes increasingly difficult. But in spite of the movement towards the suburbs, the congregation was certainly not thin, and on the week-evening was often remarkably good. A few earnest workers stood outside every Sunday evening to give a kindly word to passers-by, and as the result, at one service as many as two hundred strangers have been known to enter and join in the worship.

The watch-night service in that venerable sanctuary was a sight to be remembered. The place was crowded, and as the mystic hour of midnight approached, men slunk in from the neighbouring public-houses and stood in the porch and aisles, impelled by an irresistible desire to spend the few final moments of the old year in what they felt to be a more sacred atmosphere.

I remember pushing my way into the crowded aisle on one of those occasions, after conducting a similar service elsewhere. Near me stood an elderly man, whom drink had made loquacious, and as Mr. Vasey went on speaking, he said: "Too long! too long! There are two other fellows in this town, Dawson and Bishop, both shorter; they make the round, he makes the square."

What Mackenzie's own estimate was of his sojourn in this circuit may be gathered in slight measure from the records he has left concerning the various places.

Sans Street.—Grand old chapel, and has been nicely filled, and many good times, but in prayer the people are feeble, most feeble; and but few have been saved during my sojourn.

Herrington Street.—The place is progressing slowly but surely, and will do well.

This was a new chapel in a new neighbourhood, and its subsequent history has fairly justified Mackenzie's prognostication.

High Street, East.—They want shepherding, and encouragement, and help. A few brought in.

Whitburn Street.—Kind, quiet people, with very little religious life or fervour among them. About half of them stand with their mouths shut when God's praise is being sung.

Ryhope.—Our kind friends gave me the *Life and Times of John Wesley.* Many blessings on them!

Seaham Harbour.—Generally good feeling, but little fruit. Unity wanted.

Seaton Colliery.—A few striving for the good of the cause.

It was while resident in Sunderland that an attempt was made to garrote Mackenzie. A few of us had been invited to spend the evening at the

house of one of the friends. Mackenzie's own house
lay about three hundred yards away, down a dark,
narrow lane with high hedges on either side, a
locality that has since then been entirely built over.
He had gone home for a season between tea and
supper to attend to some correspondence, and it was
while returning along the rather uncanny road that
two fellows sprang out upon him, and did their best
to relieve him of his watch and money. The task
was harder than they had bargained for. Striking
out vigorously, he sent them sprawling, and doubtless
begat in them the resolve that on their next exploit
they would select a victim with less power of muscle
and with less knowledge of how to use it. Mackenzie
returned to the company somewhat flurried and
dishevelled, and minus his hat, but little the worse
for the fray. A search was instituted immediately,
but neither then nor afterwards could any trace of
the assailants be discovered.

Several apocryphal stories have grown out of this
incident, such as his having been assaulted by a man
to whom he tendered half a crown, and to whom on
its refusal he administered a good thrashing, and his
having been set upon by three sturdy colliers who
wished to rob him of a collection-box, and others of
a similar nature. It is not surprising that round a
personality so remarkable there should gather a thick
incrustation of legend; but it is somewhat astonish-
ing, to use no stronger word, that people who profess
to admire his character and to honour his memory
should aid in the circulation of incidents that are not
only devoid of foundation, but calculated to place
him in an unenviable light.

CHAPTER XVIII

Removal to Newcastle—The Preachers' Meeting—Testimony of
the Revs. John Fletcher and William Jessop—Tribute in
British Weekly—Numerous Engagements—Letter to Mr.
Thomas Elliott—"The Philistines and Blucher"—Letter to
Eli Atkin, Esq.—In a Railway Collision—"The Block
System"—The Question of Compensation —Sympathy of
Friends—"Text and Notes"—Characteristic Comments.

THERE is only the river Tyne between Newcastle
and Gateshead, so that in removing from
Sunderland to the first-named town, Mackenzie was
returning to scenes and people with whom his residence
in Gateshead had rendered him familiar. Indeed, he
was by this time well known throughout the North of
England, as well as farther afield, and eagerly sought
after both as a lecturer and preacher.

The Rev. John Fletcher, who was superintendent of
the circuit when Mackenzie entered it, says of him:
" He came to me in 1871 at Newcastle-on-Tyne. As
a colleague, he was everything I could desire, and my
children adored him. He had engaged to take the
work as planned, and he faithfully kept his engagement. One week in three was a clear week, so that
he could go off from Monday to Saturday.

"On the weeks he was at home, he was very regular at the preachers' meeting, and mounted to my room singing the first verse of Hymn 630, generally reaching the door with the concluding lines

> When brethren all in one agree,
> Who knows the joys of unity?

And we realised the joy. I have lost a dear friend, and the world seems the poorer for his departure. My last interview was at Queen's Road, Peckham, on the 9th of last April. He preached from Psalm cvii. 7, I think the best sermon I ever heard him preach. Some of his week-night sermons at Blenheim Street Chapel were very good. My daughter speaks highly of his Sunday morning sermons—those, of course, I never heard."

The reference here made by Mr. Fletcher to his daughter concerns an appreciative tribute written by her for the *British Weekly*, at the time of Mackenzie's death, in which she says: "A Sunday morning discourse, preached in his own circuit chapel, showed him at his best—a man of native genius, true and robust piety, and manly humour. He was not a ranter by any means. There was good material, carefully prepared, in his sermons, and he worked steadily at preparation."

The Rev. William Jessop, Mackenzie's superintendent afterwards in the Shipley circuit, makes a remark similar to that of Mr. Fletcher in regard to attendance at the preachers' meeting.

"Though, owing to his eccentric course, he was unable to attend to the details of circuit work, he was seldom absent from our missionary meetings and other similar public gatherings. Knowing that his course as a Methodist preacher was somewhat abnormal, I intimated to him that he would be expected to attend the weekly preachers' meeting, and requested him to fix the day and hour according to his own convenience. He fixed it at twelve on Saturday, and considering that on the morning of the day he was often scores of miles away, it was remarkable that he was seldom absent, often coming in direct from the station, and bringing a ray of sunshine with him. When his attendance was impracticable, his inbred politeness and courtesy induced him to send a telegram."

How hard it must have been for him to attend to circuit work, and under what tremendous pressure he lived always, may be gathered from the following letter :—

TO MR. THOMAS ELLIOTT.

NEWCASTLE, *September* 21, 1872.

HONOURED AND DEAR SIR,—I should like very much to come over and see you and your kind family and the Swalwell friends again, and will try to do so before I leave the North. But for the present, I am so hard pulled at, that it is quite an act of charity to leave me alone. Week after week, month after month, at it, at it. If a beast were kept at it as I am, the officers of the Humane Society would be down on the Methodist Connexion for cruelty to animals.

What would you think of three services in Newcastle, two in Yorkshire, two in Wiltshire, two in Dorsetshire, and one in Bristol, all in one week? Never mind, the Lord is with us, and He is worthy of the best we can do. I had seven fresh ones to one class on Sabbath last.—"The best of all is, God is with us."—In much love.

A few years later, when in Leeds, some friends sought to lighten the labour of his correspondence in respect to these multitudinous and ever-increasing engagements. Mr. W. A. Millward, then resident with Mr. Eli Atkin of Newton Heath, Manchester, undertook to provide him a lithographed form of reply to applications for his services. Both gentlemen have since passed to their reward, but through the kindness of Mr. Fred. T. T. Reynolds of Chapel-en-le-Frith, I have been furnished with a letter of Mackenzie's bearing on the promised circular. It will be observed that the innumerable applications he was ever receiving are spoken of as " the Philistines," and the expected form of reply as " Blucher."

TO ELI ATKIN, ESQ.

LEEDS, *September* 22, 1893.

HONOURED AND DEAR SIR,—When I got here yesterday morning, I found the Philistines in great force. I had only two hours, but I drew up my reserved list, and slaughtered one-third of the fresh army ; the others, occupying a strong position, I had to leave in possession of the field. I again returned to the charge this morning, but their numbers having increased during the night, I was compelled to employ an electric battery four hundred miles long, which blew, as you may suppose, a number into the waste-paper basket. Tell Mr. Millward that my only hope of clearing the field is in the upcoming of Blucher. I am holding the fort, but the name of my tormentors is legion, for they are many.—In much haste.

It was during Mackenzie's residence in Newcastle that he was laid aside for a season through the effects of a railway collision. He used to remark humorously that no harm would have come to him if the gentleman who occupied the opposite seat had kept his place. Instead of that, as soon as the accident occurred he was flung violently against Mackenzie, and came perilously near doing permanent damage to the latter's nose and face.

Two gentlemen, one of them a doctor, visited him on behalf of the Railway Company, to ascertain the extent of his injuries and to report as to compensation. He presented a somewhat pitiable aspect, though partially recovered, for in addition to loss of flesh and colour, the centre of his face was still occupied by a batch of complicated strips of plaster, forming a substantial casing for the damaged nose.

The doctor, drawing his chair in front of the invalid said, insinuatingly and graciously, "Now, Mr. Mackenzie, tell us how this affair happened."

"Well," replied Mackenzie, instinctively throwing himself into one of his grotesque attitudes, with accompanying gestures, "I was travelling by your train, and we had just left Thornhill Lees station. In the same compartment with me was one of your officials, and we began to talk of the absolute security of the block system. Suddenly a great shock came upon the train, and my companion's block was pitched into my block, and the hard leather peak of his cap cut into my face just between the eyes."

Mackenzie went on, "The doctors have done their best to put matters right, and I have tried to help them by pulling the nose into its proper place. I have tried to walk straight through life so far, and I hope still to be able to follow my nose."

The late Mr. Ritson of Hexham, among others, called to see him during the period of his disablement, and found him laid in bed, reading a newly-acquired volume of theology. "I am reading this dry fellow," he said, "and when I am not busy with him, I spend the time in pulling my nasal organ to get it straight, so that when I get out again, I may not be likely to turn the wrong corner in the street." When urged by Mr. Ritson to seek compensation, he only enlarged on the kindness and skill of the doctor the Company had provided for him, and on the wonderful manner in which they had carried him "from Dan to Beersheba" for many years without doing him harm. The spirit that urges some people to try to squeeze out of a public company what they would be ashamed to ask from an individual received from him no countenance, and his answer, when pressed to demand a compensation to which he did not feel himself fully entitled, was truly noble: "No; I am not greatly hurt, and if I got compensation, I might find the money heavy when I came to cross the river."

The Rev. John Reacher remarks that his first close acquaintance with Mr. Mackenzie began in that sick-room in Newcastle where he was laid for a while after the accident. Mr. Reacher accompanied the stewards of the Leeds St. Peter's circuit—to which Mackenzie was engaged—on a visit of sympathy, and describes the interview as a loving and memorable one. Like Richard Baxter, the sufferer would have said, " Pain is pain," but his heart was glad. The sympathetic letters which poured into his chamber from near and far afforded him cheer; but he was directly and very richly comforted of God Himself; and there is reason to believe that the lessons of that " little while " of retirement were blessed both to the profit of his own soul and that of his subsequent ministry.

The Rev. George Barnley, who also called during that period, says: " He dwelt upon the kindness of friends who had sent him poultry, fruit, and other delicacies. Then he referred to many letters of sympathy which were lying near him. Some of them contained, besides words of affection, certain slips of paper of monetary value. Pointing to these, he said, with roguish emphasis, 'The words of kindness are very welcome. I like the *text*, and have no objection to the *notes.*'"

The records left of his work in Newcastle from his own hand are brief but characteristic.

Blenheim Street.—[In reference to his last service there.] In all respects a high day. To God be all the glory! A great many people could not get in. The collection more than as much again as last year, namely £37 odd.

Park Road.—I have had many happy times and a few souls.

Bentinck.—Only feeble. May the good Master bless them much!

Newburn.—Much room for improvement. No response, no amen. Dead and alive! Lord, bless them! They need it.

Throckley.—They have been good and reasonable. An odd soul saved now and again.

Ponteland.—Many good times, but little visible fruit.

CHAPTER XIX

Altered condition of St. Peter's—Hearty Welcome—Popularity in Leeds—Letters to Messrs I. Gibson, J. Holdsworth, and W. H. Briant—Humours of a Cornish Missionary Deputation —Bribing a Speaker—An Unfinished Meeting—Nehemiah a Home Missionary—Lecture on Ruth—Rev. John Reacher's Reminiscences—Kindness to Headingley Students—Rev. S. T. House's Tribute—A Happy Reply.

AT the Conference of 1874, Mackenzie was appointed to St. Peter's circuit, Leeds. The compiler of *From Coal Pit to Pulpit*, describing this appointment, remarks very justly : " St. Peter's, with seating capacity for about two thousand hearers, had seen better days. Once the stronghold of Leeds Methodism, it had dwindled to an almost insignificant position. Causes over which the officials could have no control had brought about a great change in the prospects of the Society. The environment of the chapel had changed, we had almost said *deteriorated*, in an extraordinary manner. Through the enormous extension of the clothing industry of the city, a vast number of foreigners have been attracted to it, and on the west of St. Peter's there is now a colony of some twelve thousand Jews, and on the east is the

Irish quarter, mostly Romish. Hemmed in between these two anti-Christian and anti-Protestant classes, there is little scope for evangelistic labour, and it is therefore not surprising to find that the permanent results of Mr. Mackenzie's labours here are not equal to his record in other places."

To this very sensible estimate of the situation may be added the remark that Mackenzie's labours had now assumed so Connexional a character and extent, that he was hardly the most suitable agent to work up an enfeebled cause. Such work requires a continuity and concentration of effort, a daily and almost hourly care, which the demands made upon him from the outside rendered it impossible for him to give. In spite of all drawbacks, however, his term of three years at St. Peter's was one of great profit and blessing to the people, and one which he himself could describe at its termination as having been " very happy."

The Rev. John Reacher, who was his superintendent, says :—

"In 1874 Mr. Mackenzie came to St. Peter's, and the circuit was prepared to accord him a sincere and most hearty welcome. A reception meeting was held, at which the attendance was very large, and the new minister won the hearts of all. He spoke like himself—now moving the people to smiles and now to tears. It was a good beginning, and his hold on the circuit never weakened. He rendered it a kind of service that was greatly needed and highly valued. Nowhere were Mr. Mackenzie's lectures more appreciated than in his own circuit. Popular all over the country, he was surpassingly popular in Leeds. On one occasion the town was lost in fog, and our friend told us that he had not been able to find a cab, a cart, or even a wheelbarrow, in which to come to St. Peter's. In spite of the fog, however, the chapel was crowded with sympathetic hearers, and they had no common treat."

The following extracts from his correspondence help us to see the man's wonderful outgoings and incomings at this time :—

TO MR. AND MRS. GIBSON, PETERBOROUGH.

LEEDS, *September* 4, 1874.

MY DEAR MR. AND MRS. GIBSON,—We got here to tea last evening, and they gave us a very hearty welcome. By the Master's help I will try to be a blessing to them. The Newcastle friends were very kind, and we left them in a good way—forty-seven added last quarter, one hundred and twenty-six on trial, £110 in hand, and a nice new ten thousand pound chapel ready for the roof. . . .

TO THE SAME.

LEEDS, *September* 25, 1874.

MY VERY DEAR MR. AND MRS. GIBSON,—We got here, and have had a most hearty welcome, and plenty of hard work. The services have been successful—last Sabbath packed, and a few souls for Jesus. The sermons for the missions also good—£38 instead of £14 at St. Peter's, and £25 instead of £9 at Richmond Hill. May the Lord grant us a good year ! . . .

TO THE SAME.

LEEDS, *October* 21, 1874.

MY DEAR MR. AND MRS. GIBSON,—If you can do with me, I had better return, so as to sleep all night at home by getting in by the 11.20.

I have just come in from Crawshawbooth, Lancashire ; good

day, and over £30. Eston on Monday; grand time, and £70 for the new chapel—it is a beauty. Last Sabbath places crammed and the Lord present and the collections doubled. I am off into the country to help one of our places with a lecture.—In much love. . . .

The following shows how he not unnaturally fretted sometimes under the routine which a circuit entails.

TO I. GIBSON, ESQ.

LEEDS, *May* 1, 1875.

HONOURED AND DEAR SIR,—I did hope to be able to come to you in the first week in June, but am hard fast. I don't know what to do. Our new five thousand pound chapel is opened, and we have to work it as best we can. The Super has brought me 400 tickets to renew. . . . I have collected for the cause this week by eleven services over £180. It is rather too bad to shut me up for the most of six weeks. I will see what can be done for you as soon as I can.—In much love. . . .

The next letter is evidently in reply to one who, having preferred a request, felt sure it would be granted.

TO MR. JOHN HOLDSWORTH.

LEEDS, *August* 7, 1875.

HONOURED AND DEAR SIR,—O man, great is thy faith! be it unto thee even as thou wilt.   P. MACKENZIE.

TO W. H. BRIANT, ESQ., WALSALL.

LEEDS, *November* 25, 1875.

HONOURED AND DEAR SIR,—I have not been able to find a day for Darleston. Our work here has been so irregular that we hardly know when a day is at liberty—Special Services and Missionary Meetings, etc. I have only one day out for a fortnight, and that is on a Friday.

TO THE SAME.

LEEDS, March 31, 1876.

HONOURED AND DEAR SIR,—I have ordered the C. D. V., and am waiting. We had a grand Quarter Day on Monday last—155 up, 90 on trial, stipends raised, money in hand. Hallelujah ! —In much love.

TO THE SAME.

LEEDS, April 5, 1876.

HONOURED AND DEAR SIR,—I have got a few C. D. V. for your bazaar. I will bring them on to Bradley on Monday. If it is not convenient for any of your folk to be over, I will send them by post. I have had a grand week so far, thank God. At Otley, last Saturday, we got about £40, which was good for a country town on such a day. In the country (this circuit) on Sabbath. Monday, opened, or rather preached on the third day of the opening at a little place in the Selby circuit, South Milford. They got £20 the first day, £14, 14s. 9d. the second day, and your old friend [himself] got them £47, that included the tea. I was in Cheshire yesterday. Beautiful day, and blessed time at a little place called Goosetree, in the Northwich circuit. I am in the town to-night, and to-morrow night here. The Lord be with you and your kindred !—In much love. . . .

TO THE SAME.

LEEDS, April 8, 1876.

HONOURED AND DEAR SIR,—Thanks for your kind communication. I have not forgotten our Hill Top friends, and have written to Mr. F——. I will do my best, but am hard up for spare days. This deputation work has thrown me back. Leave here on Monday, and not get back again until the 28th. —In much love. . . .

Through the kindness of the Rev. Joseph Nettleton, who has furnished ample notes, I am enabled to give a fairly full and interesting account of the " deputation work " referred to in the foregoing letter.

Mackenzie was appointed as Foreign Missionary Deputation to the Cornwall District that year, in conjunction with the Revs. Marmaduke C. Osborn and J. Nettleton. Peter was immensely popular in Cornwall, and introduced himself on the platform as the brown bread of the deputation, on which Mr. Nettleton would spread his Fijian butter, after which Mr. Osborn would cover it well with marmalade. He had prepared three speeches, and expected to work the round of the whole deputation with them. To his surprise, the people flocked in hundreds from place to place, so that there was a constant demand made upon him for new material. At Penzance he delivered the whole of his three capital speeches— one on the Sunday afternoon, one at the meeting on the Monday evening, and one at the breakfast meeting on the Tuesday morning. At St. Just he extemporised a short speech. The next day, at St. Ives, he requested Mr. Osborn to speak longer, and excuse him. He had plenty of material in his bag, but he had no time to look up his notes. Mr. Osborn declined the request, saying—

"I have arranged all my speeches over the District, so as not to repeat myself, and Mr. Nettleton has done the same. If I gave two speeches for one to-night, I should soon be in your difficulty."

Peter replied, "It is my first experience on a Cornish deputation, sir, and you must have bowels of compassion."

Mr. Osborn would not yield. Then Mackenzie appealed to Mr. Nettleton to change places in the programme, and allow him to speak last.

"Give them a swing of the clock with your many

Fijian facts," he said, "and I will give you a new hat. By the time you finish, I shall have a short speech ready."

Places were changed accordingly, and all went smoothly till just as Mr. Nettleton was finishing, when Peter sprang to the front of the platform and shouted, "No! you have five minutes more, or you do not get your hat." The people did not understand the meaning of the interruption, but, scenting some humour in the proceeding, they cheered long and loud. Mr. Nettleton filled up the five minutes with a Fijian boat-song, and then Mackenzie rose in fine form.

"You owe the most of that speech to me," he said. "Some of you listened to it with your mouths open as well as your ears. He has given you a round of the clock for the best new hat in Cornwall."

The incident was regarded as a mere bit of pleasantry; but when Mr. Nettleton was leaving Helston two days afterwards, his host placed a new hat by the side of his portmanteau, saying, "Mr. Mackenzie came this morning before you were down, and took your hat to Mr. Mitchell's shop to get the size for this."

The new hat was put on, and the old one left behind. Mackenzie had gone on before to preach at Hayle, and when he saw the new hat shining in the sun as the trap drew up at the door of Mr. Hoskings, he cried—

"Hallelujah! Here comes Thakombau with the swing of the clock on his head."

The missionary meeting at Helston that year had to be left unfinished. The chapel was packed, and many were unable to get in. Mr. Nettleton spoke first, on the material advantages conferred by Christianity on savage races, and the new markets opened up by missions for British manufacturers.   Mr. Mackenzie began :—

"Mr. Chairman, when savages get converted, they want Manchester calico, for they are no longer satisfied to be dressed in sunshine.   But we do not seek to convert them by this Society in order to sell calico.   Our object is not to make new markets for our manufacturers, but to bless the people and save their souls.   We must not have mercenary motives. Selfishness will spoil our work, and selfishness often spoils our prayers.   In a Yorkshire village a farmer and his son were converted, and, like good Methodists, they attended the prayer - meetings, and exercised their gifts.   After some months had passed, the farmer was taken ill.   The son went to the prayer-meeting, and pleaded for his sick father at home in bed.   His prayer was in good Yorkshire dialect, but it was mercenary—

> 'Heavenly Father, glorious King,
> Look upon my faather Jim,
> Tak' him to Thy Heavenly Throne,
> Then farm and stock 'll be my own.'"

The people went off into hysteria, or what they call in Cornwall "laughing happy."   It was impossible to quiet them.   Peter said, "Sing a verse, Mr. Chairman!" They sang several, but the hilarity had spread, and grew worse rather than better.

"Mr. Chairman," cried Mackenzie, "if anything will sober a Cornishman, it is a collection.   Make the collection!"

The experiment was tried, but the excited crowd

made it difficult, and as a last resource the meeting had to be closed with Mackenzie's speech unfinished and Mr. Osborn's not begun.

He soon got over his difficulty about speeches by converting his lectures into missionary addresses. He first gave Nehemiah.   Nehemiah was a home missionary.   He left the royal chaplaincy at the court of Shushan, where he had a big stipend, when he heard that Jerusalem had no circuit stewards to invite ministers, and the church property was in ruins.   He gave up the best appointment to help a poor struggling home mission station.   Here turning to his colleague on the deputation, Mackenzie said, " Mr. Osborn, a few years ago, when you were stationed at City Road, there was an appeal made for a minister for the Shetland Isles.   The people were poor and the chapels were dilapidated, and in their distress they appealed for a minister.   But, sir, I never heard that you offered to leave the Number One Circuit to help the poor Shetland Methodists.   Nehemiah would shame many of us in these modern days who choose the best circuits, and give the poor ones that need us most a wide berth, or visit them once a year at the anniversary."

The following has interest as showing that the lecture on Ruth was now in preparation :—

LEEDS, *May* 8, 1877.

MY DEAR MR. AND MRS. BRIANT,—I have put you down.   The Lord be pleased to grant us His blessing.   If the new lecture on Ruth be ready, you can have that.   If not, is there any other you would like ?   In much love. . . .

TO W. H. BRIANT, ESQ.

LEEDS, *July* 21, 1877.

HONOURED AND DEAR SIR,—I would gladly do as you wish, but as I am going into a new circuit, I do not think that I should leave on the Sabbath. I will do my best for sermon and lecture on a week-day.—In kind love. . . .

P.S.—Got £126 with Queen Esther the other week, on a Friday night, and £45 in Leeds, and £43 in Hull.

The Rev. John Reacher says :—

"During the Leeds period, Mr. Mackenzie's preaching varied considerably. When he was physically fresh, and when the subject suited him, he preached with great force, and the highest ends of preaching were secured. But there were times when he came to the pulpit weary and unready, and then the service dragged. In those years my valued colleague was at his best, probably, but he did too much. The super-intendent eased him all he possibly could at home, but his labours all over the land, added to his circuit work, caused him even then considerable strain. And he took no holidays, or rather, his holidays were spent in constant work. But he was grandly happy, and he made others happy. He beamed on all, for his spirit was full of joy. No tenderer, no truer man have I ever known. His pastoral visits to the sick were marked by rare insight and sympathy, and when the sick were also poor, he was a cheerful giver.

"When he got into a corner, as he often did, he had a wonderful way of securing help. One Sunday morning, at an early hour, he thundered at our door with his big knob-stick. His first words were: 'Now, my dear Super, if ever you helped a lame dog

over a stile, you must help me now.'   Then he went
on to describe how the bills were out as long as his
body announcing him to preach and lecture at various
places to-morrow and Tuesday and Wednesday, and
what was he to do, seeing that he was appointed at
the same times to Seacroft and Halton and Colton.
' Now, Mr. Super,' he said, ' if you will go for me, I
will give you a new hat.'   I undertook to supply the
Monday, but had not another free night.   ' Then,' he
cried, ' let us go to Mr. Brunyate.'   Mr. Brunyate,
who lived next door, was also plied with the offer of a
new hat, and, in short, between us we met the difficulty,
and sent our colleague away relieved.

"The wit and humour of Mr. Mackenzie were never
bitter.   At a meeting of ministers a brother entered
the room whom he did not know.   ' Who is that ? '
I told him.   ' Why,' said he, ' his beard looks like a
superannuated   scrubbing - brush.'   One day in my
hearing, a minister's wife laughingly asked him
how it was that he was so much more popular
than her husband.   ' Oh,' he replied, ' your husband
is a much better preacher than I am, but then
there is no accounting for tastes ; some people,
you know, like black pudding better than roast
beef.'

" His visits to Kingston-on-Thames, since my retirement, have been pleasant—very ; but when he was
with us in the autumn of 1894, it was evident that
his labours were costing him a lot of life.   His respira-
tion was more difficult.   But he was still the happy
man, the godly minister, the warm-hearted friend ;
and his lecture was as racy, as pithy, as biblical as
any we had heard."

It was while stationed in St. Peter's, Leeds, that Mackenzie allowed his naturally generous nature to flow out in a very kindly action towards the Headingley students, to show his affection and his appreciation of the service rendered by them to himself and his circuit. The Rev. J. A. Aldington, then at Headingley, says that Peter had made up his mind to invite the students to a supper in Leeds, but found on inquiry that the college authorities could not give their approval. "Then," said Mackenzie, "I'll not be beaten. If this cannot be, I will do something else for them." So, when the new edition of the Wesleyan hymn-book was issued in 1876, he presented each student with a nicely bound copy.

His chronicled notes on leaving St. Peter's are not voluminous.

St. Peter's.—Three happy years.
Richmond Hill.—Good times and loving people.
Garforth.—Good, kind-hearted people. I have had some good times, and a few souls.
Halton.—Good people. They like to help themselves.

LETTER TO MR. AND MRS. GIBSON.

LEEDS, *July* 14, 1877.

MY DEAR MR. AND MRS. GIBSON,—I should be very glad to visit you again, but, as I am removing, I have my fears. Here are 367 tickets to give before leaving this circuit, and the Wesley preachers told me not to promise out for September, as I would be preaching and giving tickets there the most of that month. We have done well here during the three years, and I have had some good times lately. Got about £100 at Haslingden last Sunday and Monday, and £126, 13s. 2d. with Queen Esther the other Friday night. I have been very hard worked, but am all the while in good order.—In much love.

TO THE SAME.

LEEDS, *July* 20, 1877.

MY DEAR MR. AND MRS. GIBSON,—I have just got in from
Hull. We had a Peterboro' time there. They began to prepare
me for a small do in the afternoon, as the friends were away.
But when the Kingston Chapel got such a number, they looked
amazed. They talked about downstairs and the low pulpit, like
a break-the-Sabbath shopkeeper with one shutter down, but the
number of people made them open out up and down. We had
a powerful time. The circus was full at night, all but behind,
where they could not see or hear. They took about £43 at night,
which was good for dull times. . . .

The Rev. Samuel T. House, one of his colleagues at
this time, bears hearty testimony to his character and
services. He says:—

"Speaking generally, Mr. Mackenzie did splendid
service in the St. Peter's circuit. When he entered
it, the people were dispirited, the circuit in debt.
Peter filled the chapels, lifted the circuit out of debt,
and gave the people new heart and hope, and new
confidence in themselves; and this not merely by the
large congregations he drew and the money he raised,
but largely by his habit of speaking encouraging
helpful words on all occasions. I can testify that he
was greatly beloved, and though much away from the
circuit, the people did not complain of his absence.
They said, 'We were glad to have visits from Mr.
Mackenzie before he came to the circuit, and we shall
want to have him after he has left it, and we must be
willing to let him visit other places.' I commend this
good sense to other circuits. Mr. Mackenzie did not
neglect his circuit work. Arrangements were made
by which he was nearly always present at the anni-

versary, missionary, and other public meetings in the circuit, which comprised nine chapels, and his colleagues had the pleasure of speaking to the large audiences that came to hear Peter. We had very little outside help during Peter's term."

This generous tribute of Mr. House to his former colleague may be fitly followed by an amusing tribute to Mr. House himself, which, unknown to him, Mackenzie bore. Mr. Henry Giles of Sowerby Bridge says that he and Mr. House were boys together. Meeting Mr. Mackenzie at Bristol, he said to him, "How is Mr. House?" "He is one of the best furnished houses in Leeds," was the quick and pleasant reply.

CHAPTER XX

LEEDS—WESLEY CIRCUIT—1877–1880

Removal to Hunslet—Not Standing in Anybody's Way—Letters to
Messrs. Briant, Gibson, Elliott, Higgins, and Jones—Lecture
in Dundee—Rev. S. R. Williams' Testimony—Brotherliness—Naturalness—Fidelity—Interview with Marwood—
Further Letters to Mr. Gibson.

THE appointment of 1877 did not entail a long
removal. Mackenzie remained in the same
town, simply exchanging circuits, leaving St. Peter's
for Wesley. In the fag and inconvenience of these
triennial removals, Mackenzie was too busily engaged
outside to take much part. Neither the holiday nor
the bustle common to such seasons was allowed to
break the continuity of his engagements. I remember
meeting him casually at a railway station at Conference time. To my inquiry as to the well-being of
his wife and family, he answered, " They are all well,
thank you. I left them busy packing. You see," he
added, with a mischievous twinkle, " I never like to
stand in anybody's way."

How difficult it was, even at the very beginning, to
make his circuit work square with outside engagements, and especially to preserve his Sundays for the
use of his own people, is evident from the following,

written from Hunslet, before he has yet opened his commission in his new sphere.

TO W. H. BRIANT, ESQ.

LEEDS, *August* 28, 1877.

HONOURED AND DEAR MR. BRIANT,—I am so sorry to find that it is out of my power to give the Sabbath. The minister is here, and advises me strongly not to leave on the Sabbath, or it will get me into hot water. You shall have sermon and lecture on the week-day.—In much love. . . .

The next give us hurried glimpses of how the work is progressing in his new circuit.

TO W. H. BRIANT, ESQ.

LEEDS, *October* 29, 1877.

HONOURED AND DEAR SIR,—I thank you very much. Will leave Ramsbottom a little before eight, and get into Manchester at 8.50. We had a glorious time here last night, many seeking Jesus.

TO MR. AND MRS. GIBSON.

LEEDS, *December* 3, 1877.

MY DEAR MR. AND MRS. GIBSON,—I am so sorry to have put you off from time to time, but so many things turn up in a new circuit that it cannot be helped.

We had a glorious time at Beeston last night. Some seeking the Lord, and in such earnest. The lecture last Monday was a great success. They got over £25, and that on a week-night; it would take them three Sabbaths to get it generally.

We have many classes to meet, seventy-five per quarter. I have met one this afternoon, and other three to meet this evening. I will not be able to give you a day before spring. All our missionary meetings are to be held yet. Much love to all. What month would you like best?

TO ISAAC GIBSON, ESQ.

LEEDS, *February* 11, 1878.

HONOURED AND DEAR MR. GIBSON,—I am so sorry that I cannot give you the 3rd of April, as it is fixed for Derby. But this I will do with pleasure if you think good. I have promised Limehouse (London) the 30th of April, Tuesday. You can have that, and I will let them have March 27. Glad to hear that you are looking up hopefully. We had a blessed time here on Sabbath—two fine cases, and others feeling. I gave them "Samson" on Tuesday last. They got £30, for which they were much pleased.

P.S.—I am giving "Ruth and her Relations" this evening in the circuit. "Queen Esther" has done well—collected £2830 in eleven months.

Here, again, we have a sight of hard work, good cheer, and glorious success.

TO MR. THOMAS ELLIOTT.

LEEDS, *February* 5, 1878.

MY DEAR MR. ELLIOTT,—I am sorry that I cannot answer your question about the Rev. ——, only having met him once. The Lord be pleased to send you the right man !

We are doing very well here. When I came in September, they only had eleven on trial—now fifty-seven. They were £82, 11s. in debt at the Quarter Board. Now all gone without effort, like snow in May.

I was in my old circuit last Sabbath, Burnley then—Padiham now (divided). The place was packed, though Dr. Punshon was at Burnley. One of the largest and the best love-feasts that I ever held. The Holy Ghost came down, and the gift of tongues was surely granted. O the power—*melting, moving, saving,* and *sanctifying* ! It was not the large chapel in Padiham, but the school chapel. The working folk would not let me leave them. They got £75, 1s. 1d., and about 35 souls at night. I wish you had been with me. One lady, when she got mercy, stood up, and such a shout—"I'll praise my Maker while I have breath!" Had you seen the hands held up to Heaven, the beaming face, the tears that tell the sins forgiven! But I have the lecture for our people here this evening, and am published far and wide, and the deputations trouble me, and here are 170 letters and two telegrams.—Much love. . . .

P.S.—I am afraid that the people will kill me before three years.

TO W. H. BRIANT, ESQ.

LEEDS, *February* 13, 1878.

HONOURED AND DEAR MR. BRIANT,—I never was harder put to it in my life. Two hundred letters to look after last week, and they are coming in a handful this morning. I am very full up to midsummer. Please drop me a line by and by. You will not expect me till after Conference. We had a grand time with "Ruth" in our third place—got about £20; and Tuesday week, gave "Samson" here; they got £30. Good for bad times! The "great gun" from London only got £18, so little folk should be thankful. We had two souls last Sabbath, and thirty-five the Sabbath before, in my old circuit, Padiham. They got £75, 1s. 1d. collections—school, chapel, and working men.—Much love and best wishes and prayers.

TO MR. THOMAS ELLIOTT.

LEEDS, *May* 17, 1878.

MY VERY DEAR SIR,—I should so much like to spend a day with you and your dear family, but am hard fast. They keep me at it night and day. This is the District Meeting week, you would think a poor old fellow would get a little quiet. Here is the week's work—Beeston, Sabbath morning; Hunslet for Stourton, afternoon; Stourton, night. Monday, class at three; Wesley, preaching at seven; Stourton, speech at 8.30. Tuesday, District Meeting at Wakefield; Wednesday, wedding at Wesley, Leeds, Hunslet; District Meeting at Wakefield, lecture at night at Stanley. Yesterday, attended the District Meeting, and preached and lectured at Wakefield. To-day, twice in the Birstall circuit, and to-morrow Band Meeting at Wesley. This is *a rest week.*

Please give my love to your dear family. You might drop me a line when I have had a *little* more *time* to *look* and *look* and *look* at it. Remember me to the friends. I hope the holy fire is *guarded* and FANNED and FLAMING.

TO W. H. BRIANT, ESQ.

LEEDS, *February* 8, 1879.

HONOURED AND DEAR SIR,—I am so sorry that our people will not let me out on the Sabbath. But you shall have sermon and lecture. We got over £50 at Keighley yesterday, and £45 last week with " The Patriarch of Uz," at Boston, on a wet night. Let us make the best of it, and please not to be offended.—Much love.

TO MR. SAMUEL HIGGINS.

LEEDS, *August* 16, 1879.

HONOURED AND DEAR MR. HIGGINS,—I will be at Wesley on Monday night.   Could we meet there, or would it be convenient for the doctor to have the baby baptized after at the house ?   Tuesday I am ticket-giving from 6.30 to 8.30, Wednesday the same. Thursday on for South Wales, etc. etc. Been to Beeston Hill and Shiney Row, and Newcastle and Stan-hope-in-Weardale this week. Thanking you and your dear family for all your kindness and honour you have put on me. I shall never forget it. I send you a Newcastle paper. We had a grand do. . . .

Much love to all your dear family, and not forgetting your own dear self.

The Rev. E. Ashton Jones says :—

" Mackenzie came to Dundee for the Young Men's Christian Association in 1879, to lecture on ' Esther ' in the Kinnaird Hall. I took the chair for him. His lecture was very graphic, and when he turned and exclaimed, " Who comes there ?' all the audience turned round, and a man who stood peeping in at the door withdrew his head as if he had been shot. On our way to the station he pointed out to me the street where he used to live, and where his parents kept a coal yard and dairy. He also told me that when a youth he was taken before the magistrates for ' riding some horses.' "

TO THE REV. E. A. JONES.

LEEDS, *October* 18, 1879.

REV. AND DEAR SIR,—I am filled up for this visit to Dundee, but shall be delighted to see you and my good country folk at the Hall on the 11th of November. I have a lot of love for you. Please get me a good turn-out, and I will remember you next time. I had 3000 at Oxford Place, Leeds, and 2500 at St. Peter's last Sabbath for the Missions. Good times !—Much love.

In November 1879, the Rev. Robert Haworth, who had been so happily associated with Mackenzie and myself in the Gateshead circuit, passed away. I was labouring with him in the Accrington circuit at the time, and wrote to apprise our former colleague of the loss. The following is his reply, in which the sister referred to is of course the widow.

TO THE REV. JOSEPH DAWSON.

LEEDS, *November* 29, 1879.

REV. AND DEAR SIR,—I have sent our dear sister a few lines to cheer her in her sadness. God be very gracious to her and the circuit and your dear self ! May the death of the good man be made a great blessing to many, as his life and ministry has been a joy and solace to multitudes of souls ! Yours in love.

The Rev. Samuel R. Williams says :—

" I had the privilege and joy to be associated with Mr. Mackenzie in Leeds in the years 1879 and 1880. The memory of that association cannot pass away, though there are few definite incidents I can recall of a kind that would interest the public mind. I can only give you general impressions then made, and still fresh and green. Let me note—

" 1. *His true brotherliness.*—There was not a trace of assumption or ' stand-offishness ' about him. In every relation of our common ministry he was frank, trustful, communicative ; always inclined to push another to the front, rather than take his own position there. In days of bitter sorrow and bereavement I found him a true yoke-fellow, full of generous and practical sympathy. Our preachers' meetings were generally held in his study, as being more convenient to him, and were ' seasons of grace and sweet delight.' The saintly wisdom of George Edward Young, and Peter's full - orbed *bonhomie* (both mirthful and shrewd) formed a blend of rare flavour and invigoration. On other occasions, when he and I were alone, he would start a consultation on some text he had in his mind, or some (perhaps historic) question connected with a lecture he was preparing. I cannot say that I ever helped him, for he could mostly give a great deal more than he got, but he always took the position of a learner rather than that of a teacher. How he gained all he possessed was often a puzzle to me, but he never talked of that of which he knew nothing. These private conversations and my measure of acquaintance with his public work have left the conviction that he never put all his goods in the window, but kept a well - stocked warehouse behind. He was a true, generous, disinterested colleague.

" 2. *Fidelity.*—He was not a semi-detached minister on his circuit. Necessarily he was often away, but never was a service left unprovided for: he took the utmost pains that nothing should suffer by reason of his absence, and if now and then a colleague had an extra class or two to meet, it was an event much more infrequent than might easily be supposed. Nor was his pastoral work made light of. On returning from a tour, he would bring a neighbouring cabman (nothing loth) into requisition for hours at a stretch, and thus cover much ground in limited time. A few minutes' cheery, helpful talk, with, invariably, the bit of simple, fervent prayer, left rays of sunshine behind in many a struggling home.

" 3. *Naturalness.*—He was not an imitator or an actor. Peculiarities of expression or gesture which he exhibited occasionally were not forced, but were part of himself. By the fireside, in his own study, he was just the same as people saw him in the pulpit or on the platform. Indeed, he had too solemn an estimate of his work to deliberately make a parody of it. One of his distinct characteristics was his genuineness. But he had no sympathy with the notion of religion making a man long-visaged or gloomy. He *enjoyed* religion himself, and lived a bright, happy type of it at home and outside."

The interest Mackenzie felt in all classes of men, and in all the sorts of experience that were likely in the remotest degree to augment his knowledge of human nature, and make him more capable of dealing with it as a moral teacher, is somewhat weirdly illustrated by an incident which Mr. Williams recounts. He says:—

" I called to see Mr. Mackenzie shortly after a noted malefactor had been executed at Armley gaol.

He said, 'Who do you think I've had here?'   'Nay,' I replied, 'how can I tell?'   'Marwood,' he whispered. 'I met him some time ago when I was out lecturing, and he promised to call and see me if he came into these parts.   Yes, and he brought his bag with him, and the *rope* was in it.   I got him to show it me, and I put my neck through the noose, but'—and he shook himself as he spoke—'it felt horribly cold and slippery, and I soon had it off again.'"

TO ISAAC GIBSON, ESQ.

LEEDS, April 25, 1880.

MY DEAR MR. GIBSON,—We have had a grand do at the Deputation, York District, this last fortnight. Up at *every place*, some of them as far as £20. The folk did flock out. As I will have to leave at 5.55 on Thursday morning for Winsford, near Crewe, please not to trouble Mrs. Gibson with folk to supper. I do think it will be better to get soon to bed, having to get up at such an untimely hour.

TO THE SAME.

LEEDS, May 1, 1880.

MY DEAR MR. GIBSON,—I found it all right. Changed at Bleswaith, and went right through to Winsford. They had a great day for them. I understood them to say £55, including about £27 which they got on Sabbath. That was good, and your people did well. It is nine years since I have been at Winsford (they say), and they have kept at me all the time. Here are about fifty letters left to be looked after. Three hundred and eighty-eight tickets to *give myself* the last time, and the District Meeting coming on. So you see they keep me from getting stiff. But I feel it a great honour that God has given me favour with the people. May I do all to His glory and with all my might!—Much love to your dear family.

CHAPTER XXI

BRADFORD—SHIPLEY CIRCUIT—1880–1883

Letters to Messrs. Higgins, Johnson, Gibson, Holden, Elliott—
Recollections of the Rev. Fred. A. Bell—Lively Preachers'
Meetings—"Face to the Wall"—Humours of His Corre-
spondence—Grim Humour—"Fetch Me at Eight"—An
Ambiguous Compliment—A Slow Love-feast—Comments
on the Places.

IN 1880 Mackenzie removed to the Shipley circuit,
his residence as second minister being at Saltaire.

TO MR. SAMUEL HIGGINS.

SHIPLEY, *September* 10, 1880.

HONOURED AND DEAR SIR,—Been to Bradford Preachers'
Monthly Meeting—good time I had to lead them in the
opening prayer, and my superintendent closed, so Shipley was
honoured. I did not tell you that Mr. Titus Salt called on the
chairman the day after the lecture, and left £50 to be put to it,
and said his brother would help. The chapel-keeper's daughter
told me he had chimed in with other £50. That is good and
kind and liberal. To God be all the glory !

TO MR. JOHNSON, HEADINGLEY.

SHIPLEY, *September* 16, 1880.

HONOURED AND DEAR SIR,—The present plan will be worked
out after the 17th of October. I will keep Mr. Camburn's letter,

and try to find a day.   But they have found me plenty of work here during the few days that I have been with them.   They are, however, so kind and courteous that they make us feel very comfortable.   Been to Charlestown this evening.   Mr. Edward Holden went with me to visit the people, and a grand time we had.   He knows them, and is much respected.   He can say Amen, and give the needy temporal support.   I could hear the silver sounding.   Such visiting is good for soul and body.   We have a good chapel at Saltaire and a strong Society.   They have got us a good house, Number 5 Victoria Park, and I hope to be happy and useful.

P.S.—This is 111 letters come in the fortnight.

TO THE SAME.

SHIPLEY, *November* 8, 1880.

. . . .   We like this circuit very, very much. The friends are *so kind*, and the congregations large.   A few dropping in, seats letting well, and the collections *up, up*. Thank God !   Three good times yesterday.   Missionary meeting to-night at Tong Park, this circuit, and at 2 A.M. Dundee. Tuesday, Dundee ; Dundee Wednesday (two nights) ; Aberdeen, Thursday ; here on Friday ; Clithero, Lancashire, Saturday. Not so bad for an old man, and not so many that could stand it, and keep up their strength, body and mind.   Many thanks to the Great Master.—Much love.

The following shows that the lecture on " Solomon " was being brought into shape and use.

TO THE SAME.

SHIPLEY, *December* 4, 1880.

HONOURED AND DEAR MR. JOHNSON,—I had not time to thank you and your dear good wife for the grand treat you gave us.   I did enjoy meeting your family and the friends invited. I think " Solomon " will go by and by.   I liked the spirit of the meeting, and felt well for a new subject.   I do hope that Mrs. Johnson will not have taken cold.—Much love.

TO ISAAC GIBSON, ESQ.

SHIPLEY, *December* 24, 1880.

HONOURED AND DEAR SIR,—All the compliments of the season to you and your dear ones. . . .

P.S.—We like this circuit very much. They got £27, 6s. 1d. with the new lecture on "Solomon," Tuesday last, at Shipley.

TO THE SAME.

SHIPLEY, *February* 2, 1881.

HONOURED AND DEAR SIR,—My good superintendent, Mr. Jessop, has been laid aside with a broken arm for six weeks. Last week I went at the letters might and main, but on Saturday night found 40 that I do not know what to do with for this year I see no prospect, no hope of my being able to give you a day. —Much love.

TO THE SAME.

SHIPLEY, *March* 24, 1881.

HONOURED AND DEAR MR. GIBSON,—How would Wednesday, 26th May, or Thursday do—Ascension Day? It is a very hard thing to find a day. I would have to return from Filey, and back again for London for Sabbath. I am very wishful to give you a day, but might do it better in June or July.

We are having good times at Shipley.—Much love.

TO THE SAME.

SHIPLEY, *May* 23, 1881.

HONOURED AND DEAR SIR,—We had a grand time yesterday at Frizinghall. They got over £24 and the Lord's blessing. . . . We are going to meet the President, and inter the body of our dear friend Simpson. Lord help us! Dr Jobson, and S. Coley, and Dr. Punshon, and W. O. Simpson missing—no ordinary men. —Much love.

TO THE SAME.

SHIPLEY, *February* 4, 1882.

HONOURED AND DEAR SIR,— . . . I have about 600 miles this week, and 10 services, six in the circuit and four outside.

We have added a few in the circuit each quarter.   About 90 on trial, and £109 in the bank.   Not so bad. . . .

TO THE SAME.

SHIPLEY, April 6, 1882.

HONOURED AND DEAR SIR,—I am sorry to find myself fast until July.   The Plan came to-day.   The Super is out so much, being Chairman of the district.   I sent off 470 letters last quarter, and here is such a hill that I have not had time even to read them. . . .

TO THE SAME.

SALTAIRE, June 3, 1882.

DEAR MR. GIBSON,—I sent the card, but could not stay on Saturday.   Preachers' meeting on Saturday, and three times on the following Sunday.   I ought not to be out on any Friday. But keep on *foolishly*, on until I am afraid it is now too late. . . . I am keeping better, but rather weak.

The following letter, though written some years later, has in it a reference to this period.

TO EDWARD HOLDEN, ESQ.

DEWSBURY, November 25, 1884.

HONOURED AND DEAR SIR,—I have put it right with the Band of Hope friends by giving them Tuesday, March 3rd.

Someone brought me your kind love the other day.   It will keep warm all through the winter, and onward till winter and frosts are no more.   Please to remember me to Mrs. Holden and the young folks.   Tell Mrs. Holden I have never *needed* or *taken* anything since she brought me out three years come May. . . .

Mrs. Holden says : " The reference in the phrase, ' I have never needed or taken anything,' etc., is to a serious illness which Mr. Mackenzie had whilst in the

Shipley circuit, in which we then lived, when it was my joy and honour to send him little things suitable for his weakness. He always declared that I had 'made him a teetotaller' (though he was *most* abstemious at all times) 'through having sent him supplies of Zoedone.'"

Through a curious coincidence the lady who lived in the house next to Mackenzie's was ill at the same time, and her affliction terminated fatally. The blinds being drawn, passers-by mistook the house for Mackenzie's, and a rumour spread abroad that he was dead. The evening papers published the false news, and letters of condolence were received. Having happily recovered, he preached in the Saltaire Chapel on the following Sunday, and said, "They had it reported that I was dead; but I am not dead!" and then, with a stride and a stamp of his foot on the floor of the rostrum, he cried, "Hallelujah! there is life in the old dog yet!"

TO ISAAC GIBSON, ESQ.

SHIPLEY, *December* 27, 1882.

MY DEAR MR. GIBSON,—I was so sorry to hear of your loss and trouble. The Lord be gracious to you at this time, your time of need. Help needed, sympathy needed, resignation and submission needed. Faith and trust in God and Providence will be firm as a rock.

Ill that God blesses is our good,
  And unblest good is ill,
And all is right that seems most wrong
  If it be His dear will.

So may you find it, and the New Year be the best you have ever known!—In much love.

TO THE SAME.

SHIPLEY, *February* 28, 1883.

MY DEAR MR. GIBSON,—I regret very much my inability to give you a day this year. The work has got the better of me, and I am hard fast. Here are over 40 places down, besides my circuit work; and in my last year they won't give me up. I have come this morning all the way from Liverpool to preach here this evening, and must return to Widnes again to-morrow. I sent off 182 letters last month, and this month they have got the upper hand of me completely—hour after hour, letters, telegrams, and deputations. You know I would come to Peterboro' if I could, but I am fast for this year.—Kindest love.

TO THE SAME.

SHIPLEY, *March* 10, 1883.

HONOURED AND DEAR SIR,—Your kind favour is to hand. Thanks for your kind sympathy. I will not get in till 4 A.M., I think, by leaving at 11.10. It will be better to just drop into the hotel for a few hours rather than keep you up all night. I cannot get to Dunstable this year. Mr. Hart was missed last year, and keeps ding-donging at me, so that for life's sake I must be out of it. Then here are Oundle, Doncaster, and Marsh, and High Wycombe, and Approach Road, and Foster Crozier's circuit, after three years' pegging and promising. In fact, there are about 50 places that I cannot get out of, and being in my last year, they keep me to my appointments, or make it too hot for me. This week I have had two ministers to help, the one to meet a class, and the other got six times the usual week-night congregation. Still the good kind Super has just been at me for not taking my work. He would not say a word, but some are always ready to cry out.

TO THE SAME.

SHIPLEY, *April* 13, 1883.

MY DEAR MR. GIBSON,—I got to High Wycombe all right, and had a good day, and at Cleckheaton the *Tongue* seemed to take after the old fashion. Kendall yesterday was very enjoyable.

Wonderful for them, they got £27, 10s. 0d. They had a "great gun" last week from Liverpool, and they got £14 ; £10 of it was sent from one man. They have not much money, but they have built a beautiful house for God, and He will bless them. —Kindest love to all your dear family.

P.S.—I have been at the letters from one o'clock till ten minutes past nine, and here is such a host.   Dreadful !

TO MR. THOMAS ELLIOTT.

SHIPLEY, *May* 23, 1883.

MY DEAR MR. ELLIOTT,—I thank you very much for your great kindness.   Had I been at liberty, and the Lord were to send me North again, how pleased I should be !   I remember 18 years since, when I accepted your kind invitation.   How soon the time has passed !   The Master help us to number our days !

I am engaged to Dewsbury.   Mr. —— will do well for you. I am pressing him.   He is afraid of the cold on account of his wife.   I never felt it colder than Yorkshire.   I will press him more and more, but he wants to go South.   The Lord send you the right man, and His blessing with him.

TO ISAAC GIBSON, ESQ.

SHIPLEY, *May* 25, 1883.

HONOURED AND DEAR MR. GIBSON,—You are more to me than any or all the Peterborough folk, and if I could have come for you, I would have done so.   But I have been put to it beyond all reason.   This is the District Meeting week, and I have had four sermons, two nights meeting classes, and three lectures.   It is fearful !

The Rev. Fred R. Bell gives an interesting description of his association with Mackenzie in Shipley :—

" My intimacy and friendship with Peter Mackenzie began with our colleagueship in the Bradford (Shipley) circuit after the Conference of 1880.   Our superintendent was the venerable William Jessop, a man very greatly beloved, and who, although a striking contrast to Mr. Mackenzie, had a sincere admiration and love for him. Our preachers' meetings were always lively times. We held them on Saturday, at noon, at the Super's house, and generally by that time Mr. Mackenzie would manage to reach home from his distant engagements. His cab would appear at the gate, and then we would hear the cheery voice in the lobby, 'God bless this house!' or 'Peace be to this house!' or some other salutation. Perhaps the Super would give Peter a sly dig at being late, or for running away from the circuit, but he always managed to laugh it off. On one of these occasions, it being a warm day, the Super was wearing an alpaca coat, and our friend exclaimed, 'Why, you're a *shining* character, an *illustrious* individual.' Of course the Super could do nothing but laugh good-humouredly, then we sat down and reviewed our work. No. 1 and No. 3 recited the prosaic routine of preaching and ticket-giving, but our popular No 2 would commence: 'Well, my beloved Super, I will go back to ———. On Tuesday I went to Sheffield and had a crowded house at ———. We got a thumping big collection, two pounds more than last year, when they had Punshon. Think of that now! I licked Punshon! think of that! Hallelujah!' And we sat and enjoyed it. But with evident sympathy for Dr. Punshon, he added, 'They said it was a wet night last year. Then,' he would continue, 'I gave them a lift at Gloucester, and took the mail for Bristol after lecturing, and I landed with my face to the wall!'

"'Where, did you say?' asked the bewildered Super.

"'To the wall, sir;' and, poking me in the side, he

would say, ' You know.'   It was then explained that
Wall was in the Hayle circuit, where Mr. Mackenzie
was always a great favourite.   Then it might be
Penzance for the Sunday and Monday, and other
Cornish towns, till, towards the middle of the week,
he would turn up in Lancashire or Newcastle to
breakfast for the Friday, and so home by noon on
Saturday.   Many times he had a ten days' tour of
this kind, and the marvel was his exuberance of spirits
and energy after such exhausting journeys.

" After dinner on Saturday, I now and again made
my way to his house, to assist him with his correspondence.   It was his habit to throw his letters on the
floor in the study when completed, and then, at the
end of a long spell, he would say, ' Now count them
up.   How many do you make of it ? '   Then the bell
would ring for his daughter to get him five shillings
worth of stamps, and put them on with, ' Lick them
well, hinny, lick them well ! ' and after that it would
be, ' Now, just sit a bit, to show there is no animosity ; '
and he would light his pipe, and we would talk about
the work he loved so dearly.   After a pleasant chat,
he would knock the ashes out of his pipe, and say,
' Now, just a word before we go,' and on his knees
would implore a blessing on the work and on our
respective families.

" The letters he had were sometimes most pathetic,
and he always tried to help a needy cause.   One day
an application came from a village Mutual Improvement Society, asking him to lecture for them, as they
had a debt of fifteen shillings, and wanted to buy
some books for their library.   ' Poor fellows ! ' exclaimed Mr. Mackenzie, and, ringing the bell for his

daughter, he said, 'Go and get a postal order for fifteen shillings, and I'll send it them, bless them!' To another who reminded him of a promise to come and lecture some time, and asked piteously that the date might be fixed, he would say, 'Tell him that to patient faith the prize is sure.' Writing to a brother minister about his arrival the following day, he once said, 'Shall arrive in time for the service at three. Shall want no *dinner*, but plenty of *grace*. You can eat the dinner, and I'll take the grace!'"

It was the custom during Mackenzie's sojourn in the Shipley circuit to hold a sort of camp-meeting on the wide romantic upland known as Baildon Moor. He and Mr. Jessop and others were driving to this gathering on a Saturday afternoon in an open cab. The day was fine, and Mackenzie was bubbling over with merriment. As they went on, a funeral came in sight — a hearse followed by a procession of mourners. The humour and laughter subsided, of course, for a moment, but just as the hearse was passing the cab, he leaned across to the driver, and said, "Fetch *me* at eight o'clock." His companions were horror-stricken for the moment at what seemed so ghastly an order, but their uncanny sensations wore off when they learned that the driver of the hearse was the cabman to whom Peter generally gave his orders, and that what he desired was to be brought from the meeting at eight.

At the March Quarterly Meeting, when invited to stay for a third year, he said: "Bless you, I thought you would have pitched into me, and given me the sack, but it is all right now. People ask me what kind of a circuit Shipley is, and I tell them it is A1.

It is the best circuit in Methodism ; there are one hundred and eighty trains in the day, and I can get away at any time."

In the second year of his stay, there occurs the following curious record about a love-feast at Shipley:—

Love-feast.—Never want another here. If I can I will get out of it. Good time, good feeling, and asked for the friends to begin—leading friends. The devil made them *sit still*. I leave them to him. Lord have mercy on them !

In spite of this and perhaps a few other untoward and discouraging experiences, he writes at the end of his term :—

Shipley.—Many times of refreshing. God be gracious to them !

Saltaire.—Many happy seasons, and some visible fruit.

Baildon.—Many good times, and good done, but the people much put to it with poverty.

Baildon Green.—Few members, but looking up and living to God.

Esholt.—A loving little Society, full of goodness.

Tong Park.—A good kind people.

CHAPTER XXII

DEWSBURY CIRCUIT—1883–1886

His Last Circuit—Testimony of Mr. Lobley and Rev. E. A. Jones
—His Aim—His Pastoral Work—His Popularity—Letters
to Messrs. Gibson, Andrew, Holden, Higgins, Stevens—
Foreign Missionary Deputation— Large Collections—Piles of
Letters—Not Worn Out.

IN submission to the trienni.'. jerk, Mackenzie left
Shipley in 1883, to find his next and final
settlement at Dewsbury. Writing of this appointment, Mr. D. K. Lobley, between whom and
Mackenzie there grew up a very warm friendship,
and who, along with Mr. Snowball of Gateshead,
acts as his executor, remarks :—

"Mr. Mackenzie came to Dewsbury in 1883,
and was welcomed very heartily at a large Circuit
Meeting held at Batley Carr. He was essentially
the Batley Carr minister, but laboured throughout
the whole circuit with great acceptance during the
three years of his regular term. We were told
before he came that the circuit work would suffer,
but we did not find it so. He was occasionally
away from his week-night appointments, but always
supplied the pulpit with one of the other ministers
of the town, either Methodist or Congregational, and

the golden piece was always paid for the help which they were glad to give.

"He was rarely from his work on a Sunday, and his pastoral work was quite up to the average. The fact is, he had such a good constitution, and was so strong in physique, that when other ministers were obliged to rest, he could still work on; and after his absence of a few days, preaching and lecturing, he would return to his circuit work as fresh as ever, and do more perhaps than some (always on the ground) had done during the previous fortnight.

"His congregations both on Sunday and week-day were very large, while all the funds of Methodism benefited by the collections taken up during his services. His sermons to his own people were strong appeals, deep in thought, sound in theology, and though his humour kept running out of his finger-ends, the principal object he had in view was the conversion of sinners and the building up of the Church. In the prayer-meeting which followed the Sunday evening services he is still remembered with very great joy by many of the friends he came in contact with. It was in such meetings that he was seen to best advantage. He threw his whole large soul into them, and one felt like Peter, James, and John on the Mount, for he seemed to take one right within the gates of heaven.

"At the missionary and other circuit meetings his presence was always a guarantee of a good attendance, a good meeting, and a good collection. One of the most wonderful things about him was the ease with which he could adapt himself to any kind of meeting. He often asked me what sort of meeting it was to-night, and would immediately begin to rehearse a speech for the occasion."

The Rev. E. A. Jones says: "He was highly esteemed in Dewsbury and the neighbourhood, and no one could attract such congregations. Even on a Friday night, the worst night of the week, I have seen the chapels crowded. One Friday night he lectured at Batley Carr, and although it was during an election, and raining in torrents, the place was packed."

TO MR. AND MRS. HIGGINS.

DEWSBURY, *December* 1, 1883.

DEAR MR. AND MRS. HIGGINS,—Many thanks for your kind letter inviting us to tea. I am so sorry that I will not be able to get over until lecture time. The work, the deputations, and the letters do keep me at it. I have just got in from Haslingden, and have to start for Morley, and back after the lecture. Chapel sermons here; Earlsheaton to-morrow; twice in Greenwich on Monday; Bedford, ditto, Tuesday; King's Lynn, twice, Wednesday; preach at Thornhill, this circuit, and give tickets, Thursday; Friday, preachers' meeting here. . . . On Saturday I preach and lecture at Longwood, near Huddersfield. What do you think of that for an old man? I have sent off 505 letters and cards in the last three months, and did not count the telegrams.

> O that every word and work
> Might proclaim how good Thou art.

TO ISAAC GIBSON, ESQ.

DEWSBURY, *January* 28, 1884.

MY DEAR MR. GIBSON,—I have sent Mr. Jones word that he can have a day in May, and not having filled in that month, thought you should have your choice. He will be dropping me a line, and my Super is very kind, and will help me to keep the day that you and Mr. Jones want for Peterboro'.—Much love.

P.S.—This is a good circuit in every respect. Grand house, stipend £185, large chapels, and congregations filling them up.

TO MR. AND MRS. GIBSON.

DEWSBURY, *February* 9, 1884.

MY DEAR MR. AND MRS. GIBSON,—I have got Wednesday, May 14, put down for Peterboro'. May we have the Master's blessing! We have had such a good Band Meeting. Got a soul last Sabbath, and all over the circuit we have been quickened and comforted. How soon the years have passed! God be gracious to you and your *dear ones*, and may you live to see a Golden Wedding Day, and still be fresh and green and growing. —Much love.

TO MRS. ANDREW, NEATH.

PONTYPOOL, *August* 30, 1884.

DEAR MRS. ANDREW,—I will come on about 12 noon on Tuesday. We have had *such good times* in Cornwall. The people came from far; some of them in strange-looking conveyances. The Lord was amongst us, and we felt it good to be there. I am looking for a good time here, and also at Neath. We have gathered the harvest, and now the beautiful showers are watering the earth. Glory to the Giver of all Good!

TO MR. EDWARD HOLDEN.

DEWSBURY, *November* 25, 1884.

. . . Thank God we are having a few brought in through the circuit. For four Sundays we have two persons appointed with each preacher—Sunday night, in all the places. They go and sing and speak, then in the chapel a short sermon, then the two join in and pray, and seek up the wounded, etc.—Kindest love.

TO ISAAC GIBSON, ESQ.

DEWSBURY, *February* 21, 1885.

. . . We have had about twenty brought in these last few days at Batley Carr, and some more seeking.

I go to York to-morrow with the Sheriff. He gives a tea to
all the Society. On Thursday we have the new chapel opened.
The last new one, at Eastborough, in Dewsbury, is doing well.
I had six or seven the first Sunday night.—Much love.

The next gives us intimation that another lecture
has come into existence.

TO ISAAC GIBSON, ESQ.

DEWSBURY, *May* 15, 1885.

DEAR MR. GIBSON,—Can you make Monday, June 15, do?
Sermon and the new lecture on "The Gospel of Christ and its
Counterfeits."   I have had to refuse 257, many of them needy and
worthy.—Much love.

TO THE SAME.

DEWSBURY, *June* 13, 1885.

HONOURED AND DEAR MR. GIBSON,—I will be with you on
Monday at 12.30.   Please don't ask anyone to dinner, as I want
a little quiet.—Kindest love.

P.S.—Sunday School sermons on Sunday last in this circuit;
Monday, twice at Tunstall; Tuesday, preached at home;
Wednesday, Cross Hills, preached and lectured; Thursday,
lecture at home; Friday, Selby, preached and lectured—a very
good day. They got £33. Big chapel here to-morrow. Then
Peterboro', then Towcester, then here, then Newcastle, then
Keswick, then home.

TO MR. SAMUEL HIGGINS.

DEWSBURY, *September* 11, 1885.

HONOURED AND DEAR SIR,—Thanks for your kind letter. I
trust we shall have a season of grace and sweet delight. I will
find my way to Becket Street in good time for preaching in the
afternoon.   Then you may put me into some corner or den, like
Bunyan, that I may get the lecture in good order for my dear
old friends. This is nearly 70 letters in a few days, and 13
deputations. It worries me very much when they come and sit

over me, and won't be said, Nay.   I had to refuse some 400 last Methodistic year, letters and all.—Much love.

TO MRS. ANDREW.

DEWSBURY, January 30, 1886.

MY DEAR MRS. ANDREW,—Your kind favour is to hand.   I will do my best to come when our mutual friend [Mr. Ritson of Hexham] can be with us.   I am very full of work.   Been to Bradford and Hull and Hanley and Pocklington this week.   We have had such unfavourable weather.   Still they got £45 at Bradford, and about £50 in Hull, and did fairly at the other places.   I am appointed Deputation in the York District in the fore part of April.   But after that, by and by, you may look for us.   We keep getting a few here, and have money in hand.   We should be thankful, and I trust we are.—Kindest love.

TO ISAAC GIBSON, ESQ.

DEWSBURY, March 29, 1886.

MY DEAR MR. GIBSON,—Your kind favour is to hand.   I would do anything for you in my power, but am afraid that I cannot get to see you before Conference.

I go on Foreign Mission Deputation work next week in the York District.   This being my last year, the good folk are putting nearly all the Sunday School sermons on me, and they look for me on the week-days.   I have given thirty-five lectures in the circuit this last two years and a half.

<pre>
June   2, Savile Town S.S. sermons
June 20, Batley Carr   „   „
June 27, Dewsbury   „   „
July   4, Moorlands   „   „
July 11, Thornhill   „   „
July 18, Earlsheaton   „   „
</pre>

And the last in July I am expected in Darleston, Staffordshire, but for the life of me cannot see how.

When you get all your arrangements made, you might drop me a line, and I will see about a week-day if it be possible, but please not to be grieved if I am fast and cannot get to you.   The

Super and Mr. Sholl change circuits, and will be at Conference, so I must stay in.—Much love.

TO THE SAME.

MALTON, *April* 13, 1886.

MY DEAR MR. GIBSON,—Just a line in haste. We are getting on very well with the Deputation work, up all round, although the times are bad. Sunday and Monday, York—Great do. Collection last night £160. We had Mr. Hill in the chair. He would give (with his brother) more than half. Still it was noble. Here they are in high expectations. Lord help us! I have an old colleague, Mr. Haigh from London, with me.—Much love.

TO MRS. ANDREW.

NORTHALLERTON, *April* 15, 1886.

DEAR MRS. ANDREW,—I am out on Foreign Mission Deputation work since the 4th. 'Will get back' on Saturday. You will be pleased to hear that we have had *such good* times, and the Master's blessing, and the collections up all along. The night before last, at Malton, nine pounds up, and the farmers here are hard up, some badly off. York Centenary, they got £160—it was wonderful. We are up this afternoon. They say that they have not seen such a congregation in the afternoon for sixteen years. . . .

TO ISAAC GIBSON, ESQ.

DEWSBURY, *March* 15, 1886.

HONOURED AND DEAR MR. GIBSON,—I would have sent a line a little sooner, but we have been so throng with the District Meeting at Dewsbury. We have had good meetings, but it has been wet. You will be pleased to hear that the brethren have kindly consented to let me free from circuit work after Conference. But no one knows the number of applications. . . . We got £48 1s. last Saturday and Sunday.—Much love.

TO THE SAME.

May 20, 1886.

MY DEAR MR. GIBSON,—Will you have the lecture on *John Bunyan, the Hero of Elstow, and his Pilgrims*, or the one on

Jonathan the Son of Saul, a Type of True Friendship? Sermon as before. Both lectures new—one three months, the other six. . . .

TO MR. R. STEVENS.

DEWSBURY, *July* 9, 1886.

MY DEAR MR. STEVENS,—Your kind letter is before me. When the good folk got to know I was likely to be a little more at liberty, down they came upon me, and off they went with 1886 and thirteen Sundays into 1887. Dear old friends like yourself have written for me to go spend a week or two, and let them have a Sunday and Monday, but it is no use, all is gone— The Isle of Man, and Cornwall, Bristol, Birmingham, Leeds, London, Liverpool, Manchester, Nottingham, Leicester, Luton, Darlaston, Workington, Berwick, Newcastle, Sunderland, Norwich, Lowestoft, Yarmouth, Outwell, Ashby-de-la-Zouch, Winsford, Sandbach, Burton, Bridlington, Scarborough, Filey, Driffield, Beverley, Hull, Barton-on-Humber, Gainsborough, Lincoln, Market Rasen, Exeter.—Much love.

P.S.—We had a good Quarterly Meeting, a little over a hundred up on the three years, three new chapels, and money in hand at the Quarter Board. I preached the Sunday School sermons in the great chapel. They got £87, 4s. 1d., about £14 up without a stranger. I have given the circuit forty lectures, and they got £45 with the last one, so your old friend is not quite worn out yet.

CHAPTER XXIII

What Retirement Meant—The Strain of Circuit Routine—Gift of Drawing-room Furniture—Rev. John Nayler's Incident—Characteristics of his Correspondence—Letters, 1886–1895 —Reading "Tam o' Shanter"—Baptismal Incident—Mackenzie as Chairman—Address to a Chairman—His Prayer for the Children—The Top of the Milk—"I've got my Eye on You"—His Letters Home.

AT the end of Mackenzie's term in Dewsbury he was permitted by the Conference to become a supernumerary minister, though such a term can hardly be applied to a man like him without a sense of absurdity. What it really signifies is, that he was released from the routine of a circuit, and enabled to devote his whole time to the wider work to which Providence had given him so emphatic a call, and for which he was so eminently fitted. The Methodist term for such retirement is, " to sit down "—an expressive phrase, but in Mackenzie's case laughably inappropriate. Seldom if ever has the Methodist ministry had in its ranks a man of such herculean power and irrepressible energy. For him to settle down into quietude and inaction would have been as feasible as for Etna in the height of an eruption to cease flinging out ashes and lava.

Liberating him from circuit trammels was simply empowering him to go forth to the work he loved with redoubled energy and with less harassment. It meant for him no increase of rest, but greater freedom of movement, and he often laughingly observed that he had never been off his feet since he sat down.

It is impossible to read the letters already given without realising that circuit work was in his circumstances a wearing and almost intolerable strain, and the true feeling in regard to his retirement is not surprise that it should come when it did, but regret that it did not come earlier.

When it was known that he intended to retire, the Dewsbury friends were very anxious to mark their appreciation of his character and of the service he had rendered to the circuit during his three years' labours. A meeting was called, and it was decided to · furnish his drawing-room for him. Of course in retiring a Methodist minister relinquishes the house and furniture which has formed part of his allowance, and has to provide a residence for himself—compelled to do towards the end of life what most men do at the beginning. In view of this the decision of the friends was thoughtful and graceful. A few of Mackenzie's friends at Batley Carr, Dewsbury, Savile Town, Mirfield, and Earlsheaton took part, together with one each from Moorlands and Ravensthorpe. There was no canvassing, the subscriptions being given quite spontaneously, and the presentation was made to him at Batley Carr, on August 14, 1886, by the superintendent of the circuit, the Rev. Charles Burbridge. The cost of the furniture, which included carpet, hearthrug, tiled hearth, and other requisites, was seventy-five pounds.

A glimpse of the grateful pride with which this gift was regarded by Mackenzie, as well as of his own obliging disposition, is given us by the Rev. John Nayler. He says :—

"At Bacup, in 1891, as one of Mr. Mackenzie's visits drew near, we found to our dismay that an important local event would clash with it. To get a man of his close and constant engagements to change seemed impossible, and some men so much in demand might have resented the suggestion, but, encouraged by our faith in his goodness, I arranged for an interview with him at Dewsbury. His buoyant step and cheery greeting as he entered the room were those of a man just back from a holiday, rather than of one only home from a week's hard toil and trouble. 'Come into the back room,' he said, 'where there's a bit of a fire.' Seated there, he at once generously placed himself at our disposal, and, handing over his engagement-book to me, exclaimed, 'There it is! see where I am, and what change we can make!' What a revelation that book was of incessant toil and travel! After some difficulty we were able to negotiate a change, and then I rose to leave. As we passed along the passage, he invited me into the drawing-room—a room so tastefully and beautifully furnished that it was a surprise to the visitor. 'What do you think of this?' said he, looking round with evident delight. 'These good Dewsbury folk gave me all these things when I settled down here.'"

The following correspondence shows us clearly how the hurry and rush of Mackenzie's life increased with

MR. MACKENZIE'S DRAWING-ROOM.

15

his retirement from circuit work. The fetters that fell from him were succeeded instantly by others of almost heavier metal. The struggle to retain even the Friday, his one day of rest, comes out pathetically, and the longing for quiet makes itself felt again and again through the stir and restlessness. His letters betray a curious lack of allusion to the great life of the world around him. No man was more interested in it, but the hurry crowded out the possibility of reference to it in his writing. Nor was there space in his experience for that kind of correspondence in which as in a mirror we see reflected the inner life of the writer. He lived necessarily so much in the glare that the rare gleanings of the shade remained a secret between himself and God, or found expression only in the rich personal experience and life that he carried with him into his public ministrations. There is almost a childish delight in his letters over the bulkiness of the collections, but it is only just to remember that one chief element in this was joy that the places, especially the poorer causes he sought to help, were being so largely benefited.

TO ISAAC GIBSON, ESQ.

DEWSBURY, *October* 22, 1886.

HONOURED AND DEAR SIR,—I have just got in from Boston. We had a good day, but my throat has been so bad for a week. I travelled through the night last week, two nights after lecturing, and was very hot and wet. They put me on three times in Manchester last Sabbath, and the Monday was a large gathering. They got about £100—£57 on the Sunday and about £50 more on the Monday. Then I had Stapleford and Dalston and Boston. Boston got £36. They told me I was at the top, congregations and money. I was thankful to get through. I go to the Isle of Man to-morrow morning. Do you know, the brethren have cleared me out up to Conference, and I am so far behind with old friends, that I am hard fast. I have taken 84 public services since I was set at liberty, so I may say I have been on my legs ever since I sat down.—Much love to all your dear ones.

TO THE SAME.

DEWSBURY, *December* 23, 1886.

MY DEAR MR. GIBSON,—I have just got in from Torquay and Plymouth and Cornwall. Thanks for your kind letter. I am only sorry that the brethren have got all from me up to Conference, and the Sundays up to 1888. I would enjoy a week-end with you, but it cannot be next year.—Much love to all your dear ones, and wishing you a happy and prosperous new year.

TO THE SAME.

DEWSBURY, *September* 9, 1887.

HONOURED AND DEAR SIR,—*D.V.*, I will leave Newcastle-on-Tyne at 7.40 and arrive at Peterborough at 12.30 on Thursday, September 15. I am looking for a good day. I have much enjoyed this week. I was at Heaton Moor Sunday and Monday. They got £47 for a sort of helper-up collection, without effort or charge. They were much pleased with the financial results. I go to Liverpool Sunday and Monday, S. S. sermons, Cranmer; North Skelton Tuesday, and Blyth Wednesday. Then I am longing to see you all on Thursday.—Much love.

TO MR. AND MRS. GIBSON.

LIVERPOOL, *September* 12, 1887.

DEAR MR. AND MRS. GIBSON,—We had a grand time here yesterday. They had not seen such a congregation for some years, and we had good done. The collection, also, was more at night than they got all day last year. I am at Kirkdale to-night with our old friend "The Tongue," and "Solomon" to-morrow. —Much love.

TO MRS. ANDREW.

DEWSBURY, *November* 12, 1887.

DEAR MRS. ANDREW,—Thanks so much for the beautiful card, and the good kind wishes for another year. God indeed has been good to me. I have been able to take 630 services right on, with the Friday and Saturday sometimes at liberty.

> O to grace how great a debtor
> Daily I'm constrained to be !

Kindest regards and many thanks.

For the long period of twenty - five years, Mackenzie's home at Neath (he called it home) was at Southfield, the residence of Mrs. Andrew. Mr. John E. Richards describes how one evening, to a few choice friends, Mr. Mackenzie read aloud there Burns' famous "Tam o' Shanter" with a force and expressiveness that were at times almost startling.

Mr. Richards also tells how Mr. Mackenzie, in 1886, baptized his little son, who at the time was hovering between life and death. Looking at the child as he lay on a cushion almost bereft of vitality, Mr. Mackenzie said, "Poor little chap, he may come round. I am sorry I dropped a big drop of water into his eye, but he merely closed the lid, as much as to say, 'None of these things move me.'"

TO ISAAC GIBSON, ESQ.

BLACKBURN, *February* 6, 1888.

HONOURED AND DEAR MR. GIBSON,—It was so kind of you to think of me when visiting Horncastle. We had a good time, thank God. Have you thought of the best Sunday and Monday for 1889? You put March or April down. I will be looking soon. The new book for 1889 has come to hand.—Much love to all your dear ones.

TO THE REV. E. A. JONES.

TYNEMOUTH, *May* 14, 1888.

REV. AND DEAR SIR,—I am so sorry that I cannot get through to Dewsbury so as to have the pleasure of going with you to Wakefield. I will have to go *viâ* York and Normanton. I can leave here by the 10.30 P.M., York 1.20 A.M., and go to bed till six, and get to Wakefield a little after 8 A.M. I may say without egotism that I will be one of the First Men at the District Meeting.

It was bright and fine here yesterday. Thank God, it is a great comfort to old people that have got through the winter. Thirty years have wrought great changes in the place and the people. It was a good time—collection double, and to-night to follow in the large hall in North Shields.—Much love.

TO THE SAME.

DEWSBURY, *December* 29, 1888.

REV. AND DEAR SIR,—All the Compliments of the Season to you and the dear ones. I am sorry that I cannot find a day for Dewsbury before June. I am at it every day, and ten of the Fridays they have got from me up to the former part of April. And I should not like to take a *Friday about here.* . . . I will not take Friday, the poverty of the land is made apparent, most painfully so.—Much love.

TO ISAAC GIBSON, ESQ.

WIGAN, *April* 11, 1889.

HONOURED AND DEAR SIR,—I would have answered your kind letter sooner, but have been out and overdone with work—twelve services last week and fourteen this. It is too much. It does not leave me time to rest and attend to the letters, etc. I can only give you two services on the Sabbath, and two on the Monday, if it will help the tea-meeting. I generally take twice on the Sunday and the lecture on the Monday night, but now and again I take three on the Sunday and the Monday. But I cannot stand three times on the Sunday. Will you have the new lecture on "The Wisdom of Esop and Others?" It goes very well.—Much love.

TO MR. ROBERT STEVENS.

DEWSBURY, *September* 12, 1889.

DEAR MR. STEVENS,—Thanks for your kind letter. The good folk have got *all* from me into November 1891.—With best wishes.

TO ISAAC GIBSON, ESQ.

DEWSBURY, *June* 30, 1890.

MY DEAR MR. GIBSON,—The new lecture, they say, is the best —"The Proverbs of Solomon and Others." Will you have it?... I will have to leave by the early train, so please don't invite anyone to supper. I shall get knocked up with thirteen services if I don't get a little rest. We had a good time here, Batley Carr, yesterday. They got £57, that was £11 up on last year, and £20 on the year before. I gave them three times, but it is too much, and I must give it up.

TO THE SAME.

SEDBURG, *August* 27, 1890.

HONOURED AND DEAR SIR,—I have booked June 29, 1891, for you. The Lord be with us! Good time at Cleethorpes Sunday and Monday. They got about £58, and at Lancaster last night we had His blessing.—Much love.

TO MR. ROBERT STEVENS.

ROCHDALE, *September* 17, 1890.

MY NEVER-TO-BE-FORGOTTEN,—Your old friend is so fearfully put to it, you will take the will for the deed.

TO CAPTAIN PERFECT.

DEWSBURY, *May* 29, 1891.

DEAR CAPTAIN,—We fully expect the pleasure of your company on Friday next, and have invited the ministers to meet you to tea. May we have a good time! If you get here between four and five, you can rest and be happy. . . .

On the occasion referred to in the above letter, Captain Perfect says that he went to Batley Carr to lecture on his seafaring life, at Mr. Mackenzie's special request, and with the understanding that he should take the chair. The ministers went to tea and also to the lecture, and there was a lively time. The captain learned afterwards that this was the only occasion on which Mr. Mackenzie had taken the chair at a lecture. The captain had years before taken the chair for Mackenzie, and before going to the lecture had been addressed as follows :—

"I hear you are chairman to-night. You are a sensible man, indeed *Perfect.* I cannot say that of all my chairmen. It has happened sometimes, just *sometimes,* that the dear man has read up on the subject, and of course had the first start, and when finished left me only bare bones. To-night it is Esther, lovely Esther, charming Esther. She has been a good woman to me. I have already got a fortune by her, and am expecting more. Don't you interfere with her. Never interfere with another man's wife. You are sure to get into trouble if you do."

That was Mackenzie's way of asking for a short speech from his chairman, and Captain Perfect remarks that of course when he reached the platform he was very brief indeed.

TO MR. J. SHIRLEY.

DEWSBURY, *December* 30, 1891.

DEAR MR. SHIRLEY,—I am so sorry that we did not book the day you named. I have again gone through the 1892 book, and you are not in it. The book is full to overflowing, and I cannot get them out.—Much love and the season's greetings.

MR. MACKENZIE'S STUDY.

Mr. Shirley says that on one occasion, when staying at his house, Mackenzie in his prayer asked the Lord that the children might be permitted to go to Llandudno that summer, a favourite place of theirs. Need it be added that ever afterwards he was remembered by them as the dear man who prayed that the little ones might go to the seaside.

TO ISAAC GIBSON, ESQ.

LEYBOURNE, *April* 29, 1892.

HONOURED AND DEAR SIR,—Your kind favour is to hand. I much regret that I cannot give the afternoon. I have thirteen services this week and thirteen next week, and the week before coming to you twelve. I am doing far too much. I have had to crawl about on two sticks. I don't like to give up, but I ought to keep the week to twice on the Sundays and four week-days. I have been as near done for as possible. I shall get home for two hours to-morrow before going to Padiham, Lancashire, to lecture, and will forward you the title of the lecture.—Much love and best wishes.

TO THE SAME.

HOLMFIRTH, *May* 3, 1892.

MY DEAR MR. GIBSON,—I will come on from Wisbech in time for a little quiet dinner and rest. It will make thirty-eight services without one day between. I hope it will not put your family about. Don't bring anyone till Monday.—Much love.

TO THE SAME.

KING'S LYNN, *May* 12, 1892.

DEAR MR. GIBSON,—I will leave Wisbech 10.34, arrive Peterboro' 11.26, on Saturday. Please not to trouble meeting me. I can take a cab. What a nice quiet day I shall have, *D. V.*!

TO MRS. ANDREW.

DEWSBURY, *May* 20, 1892.

DEAR MRS. ANDREW,—How are you? I hope quite well, and trust the spring and summer will be amongst the best that you have had. So may it be, please God! . . . I have been very well, only a little troubled with sciatica; but it has not stopped me. I had twelve services last week and fourteen the week before. That is not so bad for a supernumerary. . . .

TO MRS. ADCOCK.

DEWSBURY, *July* 29, 1892.

DEAR SISTER ADCOCK,—The grapes are here all safe and sound, and beauties they are. I think Father Adam could not have got better in the garden of Eden. I do feel grateful to you for all your great kindness. The Lord reward you with life and health and peace in this world, and glory in the world to come. April 11, 1893, is down all right, and may we have a good day! —With many thanks.

Mrs. Adcock relates that during his visit, on April 11th, he asked for a glass of milk. On the maid going to fetch it, he said, "The top will do as well as the bottom, my dear." When she came with it, he exclaimed mischievously, "Why, if you haven't brought me the *cream*!"

In 1894 Mrs. Adcock went to Castle Gresley to meet him, and to arrange for his next visit to Melbourne (Derbyshire). She was shown into the room where he was seated with a number of other visitors. When she had sat down, he turned to her and said, "I've got my eye on you." She replied, "Have you, sir?" In a few moments he remarked again, "I've got my eye on you." Somewhat bewildered, she inquired what was meant. Then he explained that he had been to a fresh place, and was put into a room, and left alone for quiet. He had not been there long, when a voice said, " I've got my eye on you." He looked around, but could see no one, and was just settling comfortably down again when the same voice exclaimed, " I've got my eye on you." He looked about him once more, and discovered a parrot in a cage, and knew at once where the sound had come from. And when the story was finished, Mrs. Adcock understood that what the strange remark meant was that he had not forgotten her application, but was looking out a day for his next visit.

TO MR. W. STARFORTH.

DEWSBURY, *March* 17, 1893.

HONOURED AND DEAR SIR,—Thanks for your kind and pressing letter. I only regret my inability to give you a day, owing to previous engagements. . . . I have 600 sermons and lectures booked. I would give you a day, if I had one, with great pleasure.—Kindest love and best wishes.

TO ISAAC GIBSON, ESQ.

FOREST GATE, E., *November* 15, 1893.

HONOURED AND DEAR MR. GIBSON,—I thank you very much for your kind wishes. I am thankful to say I keep very well. Twelve services this week ; six in London, four in Tunbridge, and two in Rochester. I have only had about eleven per week this last five weeks.—Much love and best wishes.

The following has reference to the death of Mr. William Ritson of Woodley Field, Hexham, an old friend of Mackenzie's, and a good friend to Methodism.

TO MRS. ANDREW.

YORK, *December* 1, 1893.

DEAR MRS. ANDREW,—You will be very sorry for the change that has taken place at Woodley Field, Hexham.   Hannah gone, and Mrs. Ritson gone, and now the dear, kind, *cheerful, liberal* old friend gone also.   I am so sorry. . . . He was anxious that I should give them a day.   I sent a few lines, and the next thing I heard was that he had gone home.   Well, through the mercy and merits of our Lord and Saviour, they have met to part no more, we trust. . . .

TO THE SAME.

LATCHFORD HOUSE, WARRINGTON, *January* 1, 1894.

DEAR MRS. ANDREW,—Just a line to wish you a very happy New Year in all respects.   We have very fine weather here, and great doings at the opening of the Manchester Ship Canal. Remember me to Mr. Richards and the rest.

TO ISAAC GIBSON, ESQ.

DEWSBURY, *April* 21, 1894.

DEAR MR. GIBSON,—The lecture on "The Nameless Prophet of Judah and his Wonderful History" is going well, so that is down for you on Monday, May 21. . . .

The next refers to Mackenzie's last visit to Peterborough.

TO MR. AND MRS. GIBSON.

CREWE, *May* 14, 1894.

DEAR MR. AND MRS. GIBSON,—I am here for to-day, and to-morrow, *D.V.*, London ; Wednesday, Folkestone ; Thursday, Ramsgate.   As it will be a long run from Ramsgate to Dewsbury, and back to Peterborough, I am thinking, if it be quite convenient to you, I will come on Friday evening and rest, and be ready for the Sunday.   If it is not convenient, just drop me a line to Ramsgate, and I will stay there and come on Saturday. —Yours with all good wishes.

The following are specimens of the brief but cheery missives with which, amid his many journeys and long absences, he brightened the hearts of the loved ones at home.

TO MRS. MACKENZIE.

RUNCORN, *April* 10, 1894.

DEAR MOTHER,—Safe here. They got £64 at Burslem. Was not that good, think you? Letters here. Thanks, and many of them. I go to Derby in the morning.—Much love.

TO THE SAME.

WALL, CORNWALL, *May* 21, 1895.

DEAR MOTHER,—Letters to hand. Grand time at St. Just's. They got £100. They thought if they got £15 or £20 it would be good, but they went far beyond. I have a long run up to Exeter to-morrow.—Much love.

CHAPTER XXIV

THE LAST DAYS

Failing Strength—Unreasonable Pressure—Apparent Forebodings—Letters to Mr. Shirley and Mrs. Adcock—"No Rest for Peter"—A Quiet Day—A Wave of Glory—A Severe Cold—Visit to Worcester—A Fatal Drive—Feebleness at Reading — Sunday and Monday at Darwen — Rev. E. Moulton's Account—Letter to Rev. Charles Mees.

TO the bulk of the Methodist people the news of Mackenzie's illness and death came with a shock of great surprise. He seemed so strong and lively, that sickness and death never entered even as a remote contingency into the popular conception of him. Such promise of continuance was present in all his speech and action, that circuits had not so much as dreamed of asking what they would do when he was gone. And yet to keen eyes the stalwart tree had begun to bend, its branches yielded with less elasticity to the wind, and its leaves, though still green, lacked somewhat of the old freshness. Of mental vigour there was not a trace of decay, but the outer walls of the tabernacle gave signs here and there of yielding to the strain. What a cruel strain it was! To what almost inhuman pressure were mind and body exposed! It cannot be defended.

Think of a man of nearly seventy years of age having thirty-eight services, and services such as his, without a break! There *must* and *ought* to have been some way of escape.

Forebodings of unfavourable possibilities seem to peer out in the following letters :—

TO MR. J. SHIRLEY.

BRISTOL, *May* 23, 1895.

DEAR MR. SHIRLEY,—Thursday, September 10, 1896, is down for you. *May we live and have a good time.*

TO MRS. ADCOCK.

MORECAMBE, *August* 26, 1895.

DEAR MRS. ADCOCK,—The grapes got to Dewsbury before I left on Saturday, and they were so sweet and good. Many thanks to you for all your kindness. We had a great day here on Sunday. Had to begin before the time, the place was so full. They got over £30, and the lecture to follow this evening. I wish you could get as much at Melbourne, on December 1 and 2. I am looking forward with pleasure to the visit. Please God to *keep me alive.*—With many thanks.

Mrs. Caleb Foster of Bowdon informs me that she saw Mr. Mackenzie at Redcar railway station on his way home from Skelton, and invited him to stay at her house for a few days for the sake of rest. He replied in his usual humorous way, "There will be no rest for Peter Mackenzie till he is dressed in a wooden suit and tucked in with a shovel."

To another friend who asked when he was going to give up work, the answer was, "When I drop."

How a day's rest was relished is shown in the following :—

TO MRS. ANDREW.

MARKET RASEN, *July* 15, 1895.

DEAR MRS. ANDREW,—We had a good time here yesterday, and I lecture and preach to-day. To-morrow, *D.V.*, I go on to Nottingham for Tuesday. Wednesday — Evesham. *That day,* however, is changed, as they have some great do in the town. So your old friend, if you please, will come quietly on for a cup of tea on Wednesday, arriving at 4.54. A day's rest is a godsend to me. I hope it will not put you about coming a day before you expect me. I will be on the ground for Thursday, and ought to give you a good sermon and lecture.—With all good wishes.

Of this quiet day Mr. John E. Richards of Neath says, that he read aloud to Mr. Mackenzie and Mrs. Andrew in the evening extracts from *Echoes from the Welsh Hills,* and that the time was one of great mental and spiritual refreshment.

Mr. F. Strickland of Scawby, Lincolnshire, sends an interesting account of Mackenzie's services at Scunthorpe in the August previous to his last illness. He was then apparently in good health and spirits. In the afternoon he preached on the Prodigal Son, and in the sermon, with his usual good nature, was ready to excuse, as far as possible, the action of the younger son in going off without, as he said, saying good-bye. " Poor lad ! " he said; " we must not be too hard upon him. He had on a new suit, and felt quite a dandy, and as rich as a millionaire." In the lecture at night, at which Mr. Strickland presided, Mackenzie was in good trim, and spoke with great vigour. When he had finished, and the collection

was made and the benediction pronounced, not one
person rose to go. "He said to me, 'Speak to them,'"
continues Mr. Strickland. "I answered, 'Who can
follow the King?' Turning to the choir, he said,
'Give us the last two verses over again, please.' The
choir had got up an anthem to the hymn, 'Talk with
us, Lord,' etc. When we came to the last verse—

> Let this my every hour employ,
>   Till I Thy glory see,

it seemed as if a wave of glory passed over the platform and filled the place. We all felt it, and the
lecturer said, 'Friends, I have come a long way, and
so have some of you, to be present, but it is worth it
all to hear that anthem.'

"If he had then any presentiment of his coming
end, he did not show it, save in the way in which
he seemed to feel the silent awe that for a few
moments rested on us all. This was one of his last
services."

It was while fulfilling an engagement at the village
of Sheepshed, on Tuesday, October 22, that Mackenzie
caught cold. Despite of this, he went to Bolton to
lecture on the Wednesday, and the Thursday found
him at Longton in Staffordshire. On returning home,
his family did their utmost to induce him to rest, but
he had many engagements. Besides, it had been a
lifelong habit for him to work off colds as the clouds
work off moisture by raining their treasures on others.
There comes a time, however, when the strongest
machinery yields to overstrain, and that hour had
arrived for Peter Mackenzie. He started for
Worcester on the 26th, where he had to preach on

the following Sunday and lecture on the Monday. Of this visit Mr. E. B. Storm furnishes an account.

"Arriving on Saturday evening at half-past six, he looked tired and feeble, and said he had not been well, and had eaten nothing for three days. He had a little tea upon his arrival, and rested until eight o'clock, when he retired to rest, saying he wanted to be equal to his work on the Sabbath.

"On Sunday he came down to breakfast refreshed, at nine o'clock, saying he had had a splendid night's rest, only waking at two o'clock, when he rose and spent a short time in prayer, sleeping again until half-past seven, when he got up.

"He conducted the service in the morning, and preached in his usual style and with much earnestness from Psalm cvii. 7. He rested during the afternoon, and in the evening again conducted the service, preaching an able and very instructive sermon on the Prodigal Son, from Luke xv. 12, 13, to an overflowing congregation, and at the close of the day he did not feel the fatigue or exhaustion that might have been anticipated. He, however, retired early to rest, and had a good night's sleep. He was more himself, in life and spirit, during the whole of Monday, and also took a fair amount of nourishment. He lectured in the evening on ' Absalom ' to a very large congregation in his usual style, and was never heard to greater advantage and profit.

"His visit here was greatly enjoyed, and was a great success, spiritually and financially. On Tuesday morning he left us at eleven o'clock for Winchcombe, looking much stronger, and quite free from pain, saying how thankful he was to feel equal to his work again."

It was on the way from Winchcombe to Cheltenham on the Wednesday that death discovered the vulnerable point in Mackenzie's armour, and drove his fatal shaft pitilessly home. Unfortunately for himself, and for the Church which could so ill dispense with him, he was driven in an open carriage, along an exposed road, through the piercing cold of a damp morning, and from the effects of that drive, despite the vigorous effort he made himself, seconded by the kindly attentions of many friends, he never recovered. From Cheltenham he travelled by rail to Reading, and Mr. H. Moon of that town reports that on arriving there it was evident that he was very ill, yet he would proceed with his lecture. The friends did all they could to dissuade him from going to Southampton the next day, and his hostess, Mrs. Edward F. Collins, spared nothing that could possibly benefit her guest. Mr. Moon feels assured that had he remained at Reading a few days under Mrs. Collins' kindly care. his life might have been prolonged; but he could not be persuaded, for, as · he put it, he would rather die than disappoint the friends. From Southampton, on Friday, November 1st, he journeyed to Banbury, Oxfordshire, and left there for Darwen in Lancashire on the Saturday. Of this visit to Darwen the Rev. E. Moulton writes :—

"Mr. Mackenzie reached Darwen from Banbury on the Saturday afternoon. I was not able to see him until after nine o'clock, and then for a few minutes only, as he was just retiring for the night. He looked worn and unwell. He said he had been on the point of writing me to say he could not keep his engagements. He complained of a long ride in an open conveyance over hills nine hundred feet high, and remarked, ' It has killed me.'   On the following day, Sunday, November 3rd, he preached morning and evening in Wesley Chapel, Darwen, and the friends spoke in the highest terms of the blessed season they had enjoyed.   During the Monday he remained indoors, writing letters, and reading and resting.   In the evening he lectured on ' Stirring Scenes in the Life of the Apostle Peter.'   It was an able deliverance.   During the lecture he leaned heavily on the book-rest of the pulpit, and at the close appeared exhausted and glad to sit down.   But he was cheery and responsive as usual.   I rode with him to his home, his host, Mr. W. Entwistle, J.P., of Rosehill, being confined to his bed with illness.   While in the carriage, he said he felt used up, and again referred to how he had been called upon to travel in an open conveyance the previous week.   He further said, ' You know I have been an abstainer thirteen or fifteen years, and I don't want to break my pledge, though urged to resort to stimulants.'   For several days he had hardly touched any solid food, and was then having only beef-tea and soda and milk.

" Still we had a quiet talk in his host's bedroom until about ten o'clock, when I said good-bye, no more to see my old friend in this world.   The next morning, about half-past seven, he left Darwen for Manchester. Mrs. Entwistle has since told me how very feeble he appeared on leaving, while he himself remarked that he hardly knew how to walk across the room. It was suggested that he should wait for a later train.

No, he would be all right when once in the train, and would go direct home, and not to Newcastle-on-Tyne, where he was expected that day.

"The decease of this brother beloved has been especially admonitory to myself. We stood shoulder to shoulder in the gallery of Talbot Lane Chapel, Rotherham, at the Public Examination of Candidates for Ordination, during the Sheffield Conference of 1863. On the following Thursday, August 5th, we stood in the same relation in Brunswick Chapel, Sheffield, and knelt side by side to be solemnly ordained to the Christian ministry. Since those days our paths have been much apart, but in most of my circuits it has been my joy to welcome Mr. Mackenzie. I mourn for him as a true friend and brother beloved."

Among the few letters written by the poor weary preacher from Darwen on the Monday, was the following :—

TO THE REV. CHARLES MEES.

DARWEN, LANCASHIRE, *November* 4, 1895.

MY DEAR MR. MEES,—Just a line to say I got to Banbury all right, and had on the whole a good time. Here yesterday, a grand gathering and a good time. I am a little better, but not *right*, unless it be old age coming upon me. To that we must bow.—Yours affectionately, P. MACKENZIE.

CHAPTER XXV

REST AT LAST

Overcome at Length—A Waiting Congregation—Doctors Sum·
moned—"In the Dry Dock"—Going in Haste—What Might
Have Been—A Brave Fight—Longing to Preach—Two
New Sermons—The Benediction—Sweet Sleep at Last—
A Large Funeral—Touching Tributes—Rev. J. S. Banks'
Address—Reflections of a Working Man.

THOUGH he had for days fought so bravely with
disease, Mackenzie realised, on leaving Darwen,
that it would be impossible longer to sustain the
struggle. The strong tide of his strength was
ebbing, never to flow again. A large congregation
had assembled to hear him in Clarence Street
Chapel, Newcastle-on-Tyne, but a telegram was read,
announcing that he was too ill to come. Among
the congregation, waiting to see the much-loved face
of her father, was his eldest daughter, Mrs. Snowball
of Gateshead, and wild were the steps and painful
the anticipations with which she rushed from the
building and hurried home when the sad announcement was made.

Meanwhile the poor tired traveller, who had been
joined by his second daughter in Leeds, had made
his way home to Dewsbury, where everything that

loving hearts could devise and loving hands could accomplish was done for his welfare. Dr. Cameron of Dewsbury was summoned, and for consultation, when the case grew more serious, Dr. Barr of Leeds.

On the day of his arrival home, he penned the following epistle, which proved to be his last :—

TO MR. E. B. STORM.

DEWSBURY, *November* 5.

HONOURED AND DEAR SIR,—I am in the dry dock. You sent me off bright and happy Tuesday week, but that drive was too much for me on the morning of Wednesday. It cut me up *fearfully*. I got to Reading and Southampton and Banbury, and Darwen on Sunday and Monday last, but it returned upon me on my way to Newcastle, and I had to return here.

I have to give up Newcastle and Leeds and Huddersfield. I am *breathing* better, and hope to have a *good night.*—Much love. From yours affectionately, P. MACKENZIE.

It was discovered that not only were his lungs affected, but also his heart, and the end came with a rapidity that was startling. And yet there was mercy even in the swiftness of its approach. No one could desire that a life of such fiery energy should burn itself out in a long-drawn flicker of weakness and suffering. Better, if he was to go, that he should go in haste. The "dry dock," as he quaintly phrases it in his last letter, was not the place for a barque with such energy in its timbers to linger in, and we may be glad through our sorrow that it went forth into seas of light without undue detention there.

One cannot but feel that had he rested earlier, he might have lived longer. Would that he had never taken that fatal drive! Would that he had been more prudent, and battled with the enemy at an earlier stage! Would that he had taken a refreshing holiday every year, and so hoarded a larger store of recuperative energy with which to ward off disease! But our lamentations are vain. He was so constituted that to work incessantly, and to push on as long as his vitality would hold out, was natural and almost inevitable. We regret the unwisdom; but we cannot help admiring the bravery of the fight, the pluck with which he resisted the final onslaught, confident almost that he could spike the guns of death. And when the strong form bent and bowed at last, and the quenchless spirit had to furl its wings, how patiently, and with what godly cheer he went through the few final days of weakness and pain!

On the Thursday week preceding his decease, he bade his family farewell, exhorting them to meet him on the other side. Twice he sat up in bed and prayed in a loud voice for them, for the church, and for his brethren in the ministry. To his eldest daughter, sitting by his bed and stroking his hand, he said, with a flash of the old humour, " Cheer up, Janet! I am better than two dead ones yet."

On Sunday, November 10th, he said, " I have had a happy life, bless the Lord, and I have enjoyed it. I do wish I could preach again. Oh, won't it be grand when I can stand in the pulpit and preach again. I shall enjoy it. I have made one new sermon and nearly another on my sick-bed." He also said, " I am firm on the Rock."

All through his illness the old spirit was strong

within him, and he was constantly either praying or preaching. It was pitiful to hear him ask the doctor when he would be able to preach again. Reminded that one of his grandsons in Gateshead was now on the plan as a local preacher, he exclaimed, " Tell him to press on. It is a noble work." He had begun a new sermon on the text, " Thine eyes shall see the king in his beauty; they shall behold the land that is very far off." And all through the night before he died, and during the ensuing day, it was the subject of his thought and talk. Just a few hours before he passed away, he clasped his hands and pronounced the benediction: " The grace of the Lord Jesus Christ, and the love of God, and the communion of the Holy Ghost be with you all."

Then quiet slumber came upon him, and thus, with the fragrance of the apostolic blessing on his lips, and with the benediction of his own good life behind him, having served his generation by the will of God, having blessed uncounted lives and won uncounted hearts, he fell on sleep. He died on Thursday the 21st of November 1895, having just crossed the threshold of his seventy-second year.

On Monday afternoon, November 25th, amid a vast crowd of mourners, and a sorrow that pervaded the whole town, he was interred in the Dewsbury cemetery. Among the many wreaths that made his grave a heap of flowers, was one that bore this significant inscription: " A mournful tribute to the memory of our highly - esteemed friend, from the Dewsbury cabmen."

A tribute of a similarly touching nature was paid

by a poor man whom Mackenzie's eldest daughter, on peering through the window in the early dawn, the morning after the funeral, saw stop on his way to work and look up at the house, and then, without knowing that he was observed, brush away with his sleeve the tears he could not drive back.

At the funeral service, held in the Centenary Chapel, Dewsbury, the Rev. J. S. Banks, Chairman of the Leeds district, delivered an appropriate address.

The name of Peter Mackenzie, said Mr. Banks, had long been a familiar one with all branches of the Methodist Church. He was a man by himself. He belonged to no class, he followed no model, and he could have no successor. He belonged to the ranks of the exceptional men whom God raised up from time to time in the history of His church for special work. The church needed such men, just as it needed ordinary men, and the church that was without them was very poorly equipped for doing God's work. The church that had them and did not know how to use them was narrow and unwise. We were told that in the Apostolic church Christ gave apostles, prophets, evangelists, pastors, and teachers. Pastors and teachers were the more numerous, essential, and useful, and have formed the prominent order in the life of the church, but the exceptional forms of service were mentioned first. Methodists, in looking back on the history of their church, were thankful they had that feature in common with the New Testament churches, and while they had always possessed pastors and teachers, they had also had men with special gifts for special service. They had had their John Nelsons, their David Stoners, their John Rattenburys, their Punshons, and their Peter Mackenzies. They had also had their Adam Clarkes, Richard Watsons, Jabez Buntings, and Dr. Popes, and, at the head of all, John Wesley. To these the inspired description applied, " By the grace of God I am what I am." Mr. Mackenzie could have used those words; no one had a better right than he. On the lips of the apostle they meant that God chose him from the first for special work. All the circumstances of his life worked together to prepare him for it. But Paul was typical of those servants of Christ who, not in great numbers, were raised up to do special work. They thanked God for men like Mr. Mackenzie—for his popularity, which was genuine, whatever anyone might say to the contrary. It was won by honest means and used for the most unselfish and generous ends. The power to speak straight to the nation's heart was God's special gift to His chosen servants. It was not difficult to discover the sources of Mr. Mackenzie's great popularity. There was his humanness. He never merged the man in the minister. When speaking in God's name, he was the opposite of formal, official, and conventional. There was about him robust manliness, but combined with it the most womanly and delicate tenderness. They would never forget his racy mother-wit. He saw at a glance what some only found out by the slow process of analysis, and put it before people in phrases and sentences that would not be forgotten. He was a magnificent master of assemblies in all things allied to human needs, smiles and tears, joy and sorrow, and his power to touch the heart proved him to belong to the class of exceptional men. There was an indefinable attraction about his personality which could not be put into words, though everyone could feel it. Mr. Mackenzie had it. In the early years of his ministry he was a mighty evangelist, and, had he continued in that line, might have been another David Stoner or John Rattenbury, but in his later days his steps were directed into another form of service. He had specially ministered to the needs of weak and struggling churches through the length and breadth of the land. His labours were enormous. Only an iron constitution could have enabled him to do the work he did. No one knew the amount of unselfish service rendered in this way. The Providence of God had determined the time and manner of his end. It was more merciful to him than a lingering period of inactivity. His last words were the apostolic bene-diction. There could be no doubt it was his. His work was of an extraordinary character. But his sorrowing friends and the sorrowing church could say, "The Lord gave and the Lord taketh away, blessed be the name of the Lord."

It may not be out of place to publish here a few sentences from a rather remarkable letter of a work-ing man, Mr. Henry Giles of Sowerby Bridge. He indulges in some friendly strictures on that sentence in Mr. Banks' address in which it is said that the Providence of God had determined the time and manner of Mackenzie's end.

"So far as the providence and will of God are con-cerned," remarks Mr. Giles, "is it not our duty to live as long as we can, especially when the expectancy of multitudes has been raised by a list of engagements that have been made for two or three years to come?

. . . When physically unfit for long journeys in bad weather, with a huge mass of stentorian oratory at the end of each, take counsel of thy wife and family, and rest a while! . . . If, under the circumstances, the return from the Potteries had not been so abruptly followed by a dash into the city of porcelain, and the modern apostle had been content a little longer with good Yorkshire relish, and had pushed on that Worcester sauce in the direction of Christmas, I see no reason why, with a little slackening of speed to the tune of common sense, the twentieth century, instead of the nineteenth, might not have been invited to the funeral. . . . I express my regret that for want of caution and apprehension on the part of our late minister and friend, about half a dozen Societies were benefited at the expense of, it may be, as many hundreds, and until it can be proved to me that those half-dozen last towns were in such extreme need of Peter the Great as for it to be worth his while to run such a risk at such a time on their behalf, I shall try now and again to imagine him still in existence, and saying, ' I assayed to go by a zigzag route to Southampton and back, but the Spirit suffered me not.' "

CHAPTER XXVI

Always a Gentleman—The Graciousness of His Letters—A
Coveted Fly—An Ungracious Correspondent—Difficult to
Scold—Rev. H. Jackson's Incidents—Gallantry to Ladies—
Consideration to Servants—-"Short Measure, Short Meat"—
Picking up the Doctor—The Bible and Bradshaw—"Nowt
to Do"—His Use of a Carriage—Consideration for an
Invalid—-Telling a Late Man the Text—Lecture on
Ritualism—Lord Bacon on Courtesy.

IN a conversation on Mackenzie, a few days after
his decease, Sir Henry Mitchell remarked to me,
" I always liked Peter. With all his brusqueness, he
had the heart and instincts of a gentleman."

Such was the verdict of all who knew him well.
His politeness was unfailing. It bubbled up in speech
and act like a perennial spring. His memory might
not be charged with rules of good behaviour, though
seldom did anyone notice a trip even in the smaller
points of etiquette, but there dwelt within him by
nature a well of courtesy that overflowed in streams
of gracious speech and bearing. Did we believe in
reincarnations, we might imagine that in his person
the soul of some Highland chieftain had found a
channel of expression for its chivalry. The heart of
politeness is a delicate consideration for the thoughts

REV. PETER MACKENZIE.

and feelings of others, and in this Mackenzie never failed. It breathes through all his correspondence. How brief the hurry of his life constrained his letters to be, and yet how courteous is their utterance! His pen seems to glide unconsciously into the shaping of gracious, even courtly phrases, though without a trace of the obsequious in its movement. However the haste of the day may injure the behaviour of many, clipping their speech into curtness and clothing their manner with a telegraphic abruptness, it was never allowed so to influence the bearing of this man, and yet life drove him at a speed to which she subjects only few. So rapidly did he rush along, and so beset was he by clamorous crowds, that it would have been easy and most excusable to drop the courtesies by the way, and so he would have done had they been merely tied on to him by the strings of a formal politeness, but as they were parts of his real self, the haste and friction only rubbed them .into a kindlier brightness.

It was undoubtedly this innate desire to please that helped as much as anything to keep him inextricably involved throughout his public life in such a network of engagements. He was the coveted fly to whom a thousand spiders, with the best of motives, were ever saying, "Will you come into my parlour?" and his lips were too gentle to frame a refusal, so day by day he was despoiled, but not devoured, and day by day he went forth with a merry hum to gather new wealth for the ravagers. The public which thus ransacked his brain and heart was not always as gracious in its bearing towards him. Mr. George Parkinson of Sherburn furnishes us with a case in point. During one of his visits to Mr. Parkinson's house, Mackenzie received a letter from a gentleman by whom he was held in high esteem, and who had at various times showed him much kindness. It was a respectful request for his services at an early date. Another letter by the same post was not quite so agreeable. The writer reminded Mackenzie of the time when he was not the Reverend Peter, when he was only a poor man, and how he could then come to a small place, and went on ungraciously to insinuate that now he was too exalted to remember old acquaintances. To both these communications he wrote a kindly reply, and, showing Mr. Parkinson what he had written to the grumbler, he said, " Poor fellow, he must have had the tic or the toothache, or his liver must be out of order. Things are not comfortable with him, or he would never have written like that. No, I know him well ; he has a *better* side, and I have written to his good side, his better self, and he will be sorry when he reads it, and our friendship will not be broken. They shall have a turn at his place as soon as I can."

This unfailing courtesy and good - nature on Mackenzie's part made it exceedingly difficult to pronounce even the gentlest stricture on what at times did seem a too frequent absence from circuit work, as well as a too lavish expenditure of his own strength. I have an amusing remembrance of how the Rev. Robert Haworth, in Gateshead,—himself one of the kindliest of men,—would fortify his mind with a charge of serious words to be given forth at the preachers' meeting, and how invariably when Peter, with glowing face and brimming soul, came within

range, the battery either hung fire, or was changed
into a cannonade of laughter and congratulations. To
scold such a man was as difficult as to scowl at a
cherub.

The Rev. H. Jackson kindly furnishes some
incidents illustrative of the inherent graciousness of
Mackenzie's nature. In the year 1888, he preached
and lectured at Warrington, his home being with the
late William Barlow, Esq., at the District Bank.
When he left the room after tea to prepare for
the lecture in the evening, the conversation turned
upon his idiosyncrasies, and special emphasis was
given to the fact that beneath much which startled,
perhaps even shocked fastidious people, there were
the characteristics of the true gentleman. In illustration of this was noted an incident that Mackenzie
himself had just related at table. He told how,
during the severe drought of the summer, he had
travelled one day with a lady, a perfect stranger to
him, but whose conversation evidenced that she was a
person of superior education. In the course of their
talk, she made some allusion to the withered condition
of the crops. In accordance with his usual endeavour
to give the conversation a spiritual turn, he remarked
on how much more the crops must have suffered when
it did not rain for the space of three years and six
months. "Oh," said the lady, "when was that, and
where? I never heard of that." "Now," commented
Mackenzie, in relating the incident, "what could I say
to the dear lady? I felt I could not pursue the
matter further without exposing to those in the
compartment her complete ignorance of a matter
known to every working man's child in the land, as

well as her indifference to the best of books, so all I could do was to make an observation on something we were passing, and so shunt the conversation on to quite another line."

"His words and manner," remarks Mr. Jackson, "as he told the story, seemed to all of us the very expression of that delicacy of sentiment which ought always to characterise the Christian gentleman. Truly grace had but refined a mind and heart that must have been fine by nature. Such courtesy was inborn, as if in the sometime collier there had cropped up a strain of some chieftain ancestor."

Attention was called during the same conversation to another illustration of his politeness that had occurred that very afternoon. The superintendent of the circuit and another gentleman had met Mackenzie at the Central Railway Station. A cab was called, and drew up at the steps, where the sidewalk is very narrow. The two gentleman stood for a few moments with the cab door opened across the curbstone, giving directions to the driver. They quite blocked the path, but before either of them was aware of the obstruction they had caused, they saw Mackenzie, with all the grace of a courtier, bowing, hat in hand, almost to the ground, in a manner that evidently both astonished and pleased a lady whose way had been hindered, offering their united apologies, and beseeching her to forgive their unintentional rudeness. All who saw and heard it said that the whole thing was done in a princely fashion, his apology being profoundly deferential, yet without a trace of effusiveness.

Quite in keeping with this innate delicacy was that unvarying practice of his, never to sit down after acknowledging a vote of thanks at the close of a lecture without proposing a similar vote to someone else, and never to leave a house in which he had been a guest for ever so short a season without giving the servants some acknowledgment in kindly words as well as in more substantial form.

A somewhat amusing instance of this consideration for servants is given in a reminiscence furnished by the Rev. John Nayler. He describes how, during Mackenzie's residence in Leeds, the Headingley students invited him to tea at the college, with the understanding that he should give them an informal address afterwards. One of the points of this address was the importance of brevity in conducting family devotions. A tutor at that time, very popular and beloved, was apt, in the fulness of his expositions, to become oblivious on such occasions to the passage of time and the exigence of domestic duties. Perhaps some thought of this was in Mackenzie's mind when he urged the students " to read short and to pray short." Once only, he observed, with the twinkle of a humorous recollection, had he felt justified in reading a long chapter at morning prayer. On his first visit to a certain house, where the family and the servant took their meals in the same apartment, he was quick to observe that the maid began her breakfast at a side table as he began to read, and that as soon as reading and prayer were over, the mistress said, " Now, Mary, clear away ! " He saw at once that for the poor girl " short measure meant short meat."

On his next visit to the house, he resolved that the maid should have ample time for a good meal;

so when she began her breakfast, he set to work on the 119th Psalm, and read on and on until a pause at the side table told him that Mary had eaten as much as she required, and was quite ready to join in the giving of thanks.

Dr. Sharples of Farnley relates how, on one occasion, having injured his foot, he was walking with some difficulty to visit a patient. Mackenzie, passing in a cab, knocked at the window, and beckoned the doctor to him. Finding that he was on his way to Burmantofts, and what was the nature of his errand, he bade the cabman drive thither, offering a prayer for the patient meanwhile. On their arrival, he put down the doctor, with a blessing on him and his patient, stating that he was going to a meeting at New Wortley, and would only be ten minutes late.

The gratitude of the man for the humblest service rendered him was very marked. I used with great comfort for many years a handsome travelling rug he insisted on pressing on me when we were together in Sunderland, in return for having taken week-day appointments to enable him to render service elsewhere, and many others can bear similar testimony. The Rev. H. Lefroy Yorke, M.A., remembers how, when a student at Headingley, he once preached for Mackenzie. Half a year afterwards, Mackenzie met him, and, referring to the service he had rendered him, said, "Here is a sovereign for you. It will help you to get some new books, which are always useful to students."

Mr. John Pearson of Halifax also sends an incident illustrating the same characteristic. He heard Mackenzie lecture in St. Andrew's Hall, Norwich, but knew him only by sight, not having spoken with him. On entering a train at Ely, next day, he found Mackenzie in the compartment, puzzling over a Bradshaw, having to change at March Junction, and to make his way into Lincolnshire for a lecture that evening. Very soon after leaving the station, the traveller heaved a deep sigh, closed his railway guide energetically, and said, " Thank God, the Bible is not like Bradshaw! The one I can understand, but the other I cannot." Mr. Pearson immediately tendered his aid, and, knowing the locality, was soon able to give him the required information, when he said, " Surely the Lord directed you into this carriage, and if you will write down your address, I will send you my portrait on my return home." The address was written, and within five days the photograph arrived, and is still greatly appreciated, though the incident happened eighteen years ago.

"Only once," writes the Rev. J. V. B. Shrewsbury, " have I seen our lamented friend's wonderful good-nature ruffled. A somewhat exacting invalid, who was receiving abundant attention from many friends, sent an earnest request that he would visit her. A cab was not to be had, and he had to walk nearly three miles to the cottage and back to his home, a hard task for failing locomotion. As he sat at the bedside of the invalid, she exclaimed, ' Eh, I'm rare an' glad to have someone come to see me who has nowt to do.' When narrating the incident to me afterwards, he exclaimed, with comic perturbation, ' Nowt to do? She should have seen the pile of letters I left unanswered.' This reminds me that on another occasion, having to call upon him between the afternoon service and the evening lecture, I was shown into his bedroom, and found the floor strewn with the débris of unanswered letters.

" In some of my circuits, his visit was an annual institution, and was the event of the year. On newly arriving in one circuit, I was unfortunately unaware of his usual home. Thinking him worthy of the best home to be obtained, I secured his location in the midst of luxury, where a private carriage would be at his service. The first use he made of the carriage, in driving to his appointment, was to call at his old and lowlier home, and give such an explanation as shielded me from blame, with exquisite tact, and as convinced his former host that he should expect to return to him on future occasions."

One rainy night, Mackenzie and a colleague were driving home in an open conveyance. On arriving at the toll-bar, the gatekeeper said his wife was ill, and would be very pleased if Mr. Mackenzie would kindly go in and pray with her. Of course he complied instantly. A few cheery words were spoken, and then prayer was offered, in which, with his wonderful consideration for others, he did not forget to ask that the invalid might suffer no harm from the damp clothes of her visitors.

Few things try a preacher's good-nature more than to be disturbed in a service. I once heard a popular minister, with a great reputation for saintliness, say in the most snarling manner, when a child disturbed him, " I wish some of you mothers had to preach, and then you would know better than to bring children to chapel." How different the flavour of the following incident! Mr. R. Sherwood of Selby first heard Mackenzie about thirty-three years ago. It was on the occasion of the opening of the village chapel of Thorpe Willoughby. Mr. Sherwood had been summoned to the dying bed of a member of his class, and consequently was only able to squeeze his way into the crowded chapel as the preacher was beginning his sermon. As soon as he was seated, Mackenzie called out, "My brother, the text is, 'Enoch walked with God.' I'm glad to see you." Mr. Sherwood adds, that on leaving the chapel, some-one said to him, "So you and Peter are old friends?" "No," he replied; "I never saw him before." One is not surprised to learn that the memory of that service has always been precious to him, and that he never missed an opportunity afterwards of hearing the preacher who treated him with such consideration.

The same considerateness comes out in another form in the following. When at Wood Green, Mr. J. W. Tabraham said to him, "I heard your lecture on 'Ritualism,' Mr. Mackenzie." The lecturer not replying, Mr. Tabraham said, "You recollect it, at Spitalfields Old Chapel?" "Yes, I recollect," answered Mackenzie, "but I never repeated it. I was afraid it would hurt the feelings of some good people."

In view of all that this chapter has tried to set forth, we may well close it by applying to Mackenzie the words of Lord Bacon: "If a man be gracious and courteous to strangers, it shows he is a citizen of the world, and that his heart is no island cut off from other lands, but a continent that joins to them; if he be compassionate towards the affliction of others,

it shows that his heart is like the noble tree that is
wounded itself when it gives balm ; if he easily
pardons and remits offences, it shows that his mind
is planted above injuries, so that he cannot be shot ;
if he be thankful for small benefits, it shows that he
weighs men's minds, and not their trash ; but, above
all, if he have St. Paul's perfection, that he would
wish to be an anathema from Christ for the salvation
of his brethren, it shows much of a divine nature,
and a kind of conformity with Christ Himself."

CHAPTER XXVII

THE MAN—HIS JOYOUSNESS

A Book of Joy—A Radiant Personality—Love of Singing—
"Child of a King"—Watching the Baby—Compelling the
Local to Lead—Beating a Speech out of a Brother—Looking
up Rinderpest Cases—A Treat for the Cathedral—"Repair-
ing Peter"—"Something like Tea"—Reminiscence of Rev.
T. Vasey—A Drive across the Moors—A Serviceable Devil
—Lecture on Satan—"Cool as a Cucumber"—Spreading
not the Gospel.

THE life of Peter Mackenzie was a book of joy:
every page sparkled with gladness, every word
danced, not a moping sentence intruded from cover
to cover. What a happy eccentricity was his! How
entirely free from the angularities that fret while they
surprise! Genius has a reputation for making companionship uncomfortable. The angles and abutments
that break it up into picturesqueness spoil it for sweet
human uses, and hence it frequently alienates as much
as it impresses. What saved the nature of Peter
Mackenzie from any such ungracious development
was its superabundant geniality. More sunshine
beamed out of him than radiates from three ordinary
men. You felt it diffuse through the room when he
entered, like daybreak dispelling the shadows. His
was not simply a buoyant, it was a radiant personality;

a little unchastened in its emphasis, perhaps, but never with the loudness of self-assertion.

Music, especially in the form of singing, always had a great charm for him. He could strum a little on the piano, and I remember well how, when we went together to a missionary meeting, if the home was one where he felt free to do so, he would invariably seat himself for a few moments at the instrument and rattle out some lively melody, accompanying it with cheerful words.

The Rev. J. V. Shrewsbury says : " On one occasion, after the night's lecture, when he was drenched with perspiration, he went upstairs for a change of linen, singing, as he mounted, a ditty beginning—

I'm the child of a king."

This changing of linen was, as is well known, an invariable practice. An hour's talk such as his would leave him bathed in perspiration even to his outer garments, and when in such a condition, he would playfully remark, " You see, I am not a *dry* preacher."

He broke into snatches of song as naturally as a bird, and a glad shout or a burst of melody would herald his approach to breakfast in the morning, before his bright face and polite bow broke in upon the waiting family. This strain of mirthfulness and mischief was in him from earliest days, and happily the black hand of a false - notioned piety was not allowed to wipe it out. One of his earliest recollections was of watching the baby when a wee boy. On the wall, above the cradle, hung an old-fashioned knife and fork box. The young Peter was climbing up to this in some daring manner, when he dropped a spoon upon the baby's face, and he used to relate with great gusto how he ran, as if for life, with his father and a promised thrashing at his heels.

Mr. J. M. Pallister of Harrogate, who knew Mackenzie well as a fellow local preacher, communicates two instances of this innocent mirthfulness.

A love-feast was to be held one Sunday afternoon at Billy Row, in the Bishop Auckland circuit, of which Peter was to be the leader. As he did not arrive in time, and the chapel was crowded, the local preacher who had officiated in the morning was requested to open the service. When Peter came, he slipped quietly up into the pulpit and sat down behind his substitute. The lattter wished to give place, but Mackenzie insisted on his going on, and when he attempted to turn round, he found himself unable to move, and had to continue the service, for the strong man behind had effectually pinioned him by holding his hands on his knees and pressing his thumbs tightly against his legs. Probably Mackenzie had learned this trick of another, for it will be remembered how Mr. Thomas Elliott held him in similar fashion during one of his earlier preaching efforts at Haswell.

The other story related by Mr. Pallister tells how Peter stayed one night at the house of a brother local, and how they both had to occupy the same bed. Mackenzie retired first, and had been in possession some time, but was still awake, when the other, who had been filling a distant appointment, entered the bedroom. The conversation turned at once upon the meeting of next day, at which both were advertised to speak. Mackenzie wished to know if the speech was ready. His companion replied that he did not intend to speak, his name having been published without his consent. To this Mackenzie demurred, and said there should be no bed for him till he promised to make a speech. The good brother, heeding not, continued to undress, and when ready, was about to step into bed, but the one already there objected, and drove him away with the pillow. An attempt to force an entrance at the foot was baffled in similar fashion. Eventually a truce was established, the rebel submitted, and the outline of a speech was jotted down. As soon as this victory was achieved, Mackenzie leaped out of bed, and both knelt in earnest prayer for a blessing on the services of the coming day. The reluctant speaker was well received at the meeting; and Mackenzie, whose turn came next, told the audience that he had beaten the speech out of his good brother with a pillow the night before, and whenever they wanted one twice as long, he would use the bolster.

Mr. Robert Alcock of Mansfield says: " Mr. Mackenzie came to Mansfield for nearly thirty years, and on nearly every occasion I was privileged to have him as my guest. No visitor could be more welcome, none shed a more radiant spirit in the home than he. His influence there was of the very best, touching with its own freshness and fervour all around. In the quiet of the home he shone as brightly as in the pulpit or on the platform. Those who knew him best loved him most; his memory to them will be most precious."

Mr. William Thompson of Newcastle - on - Tyne recalls two bright little irruptions of Peter into his shop, when carrying on business as a butcher. It was during the time of the cattle disease, and, entering one day, with the Rev. John Fletcher, he called out, "How are all here? We are just looking up the rinderpest cases. You have no foot-and-mouth cases here, so we will get on and look up others. Praise the Lord! Good-bye!"

Calling again one Saturday, he brought his stick down on the floor with a thud and a shout of "Hallelujah! Peace be to this house and prosperity to this shop!" Then, looking towards the sitting-room behind, he asked, "Is there anyone in?" "No." "Then let us go in and have prayer together. You can keep one eye on the business." In about two minutes, after a most comprehensive prayer, he went on his way, leaving his blessing behind him.

Once, when at Ely, Mackenzie was guided to the chapel by Mr. E. T. Atherton of Chatteris. On the way they had to pass the cathedral, and as they arrived at the front door, Peter called out, "Halt! stand at ease!" Then, turning to his companion, he said, "Atherton, I wish the bishop would allow me to preach and lecture in that splendid edifice. We would give the old place a treat; we would fill it to the brim."

Arriving in Aberystwyth one evening very tired and weary, and not in the best of health, he wished to be allowed—after having a glass of milk and biscuits—to go straight to bed, so that he might be ready to preach in the morning. He evidently found the rest and repose he sought, for on opening his bedroom door next morning, he began to shout "Hallelujah!" with much warmth and vigour. On being asked by his hostess if he felt refreshed after his slumbers, he said, "So much so, ma'am, that you must send in your claim to the Wesleyan Conference for repairing Peter."

"Ah," remarked Mackenzie, one day to his hostess at the tea-table, " this is something like tea.   I get tea sometimes so weak it can scarcely waddle out of the pot."

The constant joyousness of his nature made him always ready to enter into the gladness of things around, whether animate or inanimate.   He could not only weep with those that weep, but, what is often harder, rejoice with those that do rejoice.   Of the Rev. Thomas Vasey, I wrote, twenty years ago : "His gaiety was often like that of a happy child.   I remember accompanying him one day to a country village, where he had to preach, and as we walked through the fields, he took off his hat and startled with it some horses that were idly grazing close at hand, and then ran scampering after them, like a schoolboy out for a holiday."   That, in fuller measure, was the spirit of Peter Mackenzie.   He was brimming over with life and gladness, and I can hear yet the echoes of the hallelujahs that leaped like pistol-shots from his lips as, behind a spirited horse, he dashed along the road, a wonder to passers-by, who stood to watch as long as he was in sight.

Mr. John S. Stephenson of Hexham describes the vivid impression left upon his mind of the vivacity and joyousness of the man as he drove him across the moors from Blanchland in the Shotley Bridge circuit to Stanhope in Weardale, nearly thirty years ago. The air was bracing, the sky cloudless, and the combined influence of ozone and sunshine seemed to completely intoxicate him. He shouted and sang or broke forth into prayer in the exuberance of his joy. The moorland sheep, the grouse seated stealthily among the heather or rising on the wing, and darkening against the distant hills, awoke in him by turns the fervour of the poet and the enthusiasm of the sportsman. The mare they were driving, Fanny by name, was good in many respects, but required a considerable amount of whip. Towards the end of the journey, as they descended a steep hill into Stanhope, Mackenzie addressed the animal by name, expatiating on her many excellent qualities—her colour, her symmetry, her strength, her temper. " But," said he, with comic seriousness, " Fanny has a *saving* knowledge."

Mr. B. Halliday of Leeds once took Mackenzie over a cloth mill. Every department proved interesting to him, but what impressed him most was the machine in which old material was torn into shreds preparatory to being mixed with new wool, and then wrought up again into cloth. " That we call the devil," he was told. " The devil ? " he replied. " Thank the Lord, there's one devil who does a bit of good in the world."

His lecture on " Satan " was not infrequently connected with some accident. Sometimes, when this was to be his subject, his travelling-bag went astray, or his comb snapped in twain, or his bottle of scent was broken, or some other calamity befell him. He said to his colleague one day, " I thought His Majesty did not care to be shown up so plainly, and therefore had a spite against me, so I gave up taking him out."

Mr. John Foster of Selby, who had made Mackenzie a present of a light alpaca coat, met him afterwards at a railway station. The grateful preacher danced round him enthusiastically, and said, " Oh, you're the kind friend that gave me this nice coat. I have just come away from Conference, and whilst all the preachers were sweltering · away like tallow candles lighted at both ends, I was as cool as a cucumber all the time. Thank you ! thank you ! "

Mr. Wesley Bamford relates that on April 4, 1888, Mr. Mackenzie preached and lectured at Wardle, near Rochdale. On the following morning he was being driven to Rochdale by his host, Mr. James Stott, in a high two-wheeled trap. The horse was a very swift and spirited animal, and on this morning its pace was even more rapid than usual. Mackenzie, putting his hand quietly on Mr. Stott's arm, said, " A little slower, if you please, Mr. Stott. We don't want the gospel *spreading* this morning."

Once when travelling North, he was accosted at the railway station by a porter to whom he was well known.

" I am surprised to see you travelling North again so soon, Mr. Mackenzie."

" Ah yes, important business must be attended to. I am going to throw water on a snowball."

This to the porter seemed absurd, for it was now the month of June.

" I am going," said Peter, " to baptize a grandchild of mine whose name is Snowball." At which the train started, and Mackenzie sped on to Gateshead, where his daughter, Mrs. Snowball, resides.

CHAPTER XXVIII

THE MAN—HIS GENEROSITY

Lives that Enrich—Stintless Liberality—Rev. John E. Winter's
Incident—Peter and the Signalman—Kindness to a Porter's
Widow—Providing Tickets for his Lecture—Generosity to
old Mates—Returning his Fees—Giving away the Pie—
Peter meeting Paul—Helping a Mutual Improvement
Society — The Tramp and the Umbrella — " Be good,
Hinny "—Improving the World.

INTO the great ocean of human sorrow and need
there are lives that pour a ceaseless flood of
comfort and reinvigoration, giving a sweetness and
sparkle to waters that would otherwise be intolerably
heavy and bitter. Often without consciousness of
their high ministry they bear a wealth of gladness
down from the everlasting hills, which not only
enriches the sea, but bids the lowlands sing as it
travels thitherward. To this class belongs the life of
Peter Mackenzie. One of the deepest indentations
made on the memory of those who knew and loved
the man is the impress of his generosity. He gave
with a spontaneity and profuseness as natural as that
with which the tide flings the blurt of its spray over
the rocks on which it breaks. Providence favoured
him for many years with a well-filled pocket, but

forgot apparently to bestow with it an equally common quality—the power to button it tightly up. If any fault is to be found with him on this score, it must be attributed to the excess rather than the scantiness of his liberality. He gave to all men liberally and upbraided not, and pages might be filled with the generous outgoings of his heart and mind.

The Rev. John E. Winter says :—

"On July 2nd, 1893, I was driving to my appointment at Green How Hill, in the Pateley Bridge circuit. Overtaking a brother who was on foot, and who had every appearance of being one of the noble lay fraternity on his way to preach, I invited him to ride with me. He proved to be a Primitive Methodist local preacher, employed as a signalman on the railway. Our conversation turned on various Methodist notabilities.

"'So you know Peter Mackenzie, do you?' I said, in response to some remark.

"'Yes,' he answered; 'he is a very dear friend of mine. He has spent many hours with me in the signal-box.'

"'That is very strange. Where were you then?'

"'In Leeds. Mr. Mackenzie's house was not far from the box, and every now and again, when he had a half-hour to spare, he would come and have a chat.'

"'You would find him something more than a sociable man. I understand he was very generous, especially to you railway men.'

"'Yes, and he was exceedingly kind to me. My wife was delicate at the time, and Mr. Mackenzie, whenever he came back from his lecturing tours, would bring her a bottle of wine, or a fowl, or some other delicacy. The last time he called at our house, which was just before he left Leeds, he said, 'I quite forgot to get a duck for Missus this time, but here is something yellow instead.' So he put a half-sovereign into my hand. In addition to this, he used to give me many of his old 'togs' when he had done with them, and I have some of his old coats at home now.'"

Mr. David Proudlove, foreman porter at Holbeck railway station, says :—

"I am writing you to show the generosity of that noble-hearted, dearly beloved, sainted railway man's friend, the Rev. Peter Mackenzie. Arriving here by the ten o'clock train one night, he inquired very kindly about the widow and children of the foreman porter who was killed on duty here about three years before, and, pulling out half a sovereign, he said, 'Please give her this, but do not tell her where it came from. Say—The Lord sent it.'"

An incident impregnated with the same spirit, though manifested in another form, is communicated by the Rev. W. W. Walton :—

"I was stationed in the Fawcett Street circuit, Sunderland, from 1883 to 1886, and Mr. Mackenzie came to preach and lecture in Fawcett Street Chapel, I think in 1885. At that time we were suffering very severely from depression in the shipping trade. Many vessels were laid up, and thousands of men were out of employment. There was a charge of sixpence for admission to the lecture. After preaching in the afternoon, Mr. Mackenzie announced the evening lecture. Several working men were in the body of the chapel, and, looking at them from the platform, he said, ' I see there is to be a small charge for admission to the lecture. I am afraid many of my old friends will not be able to come, as times have been so dull; but I will leave forty tickets with the chapel-keeper, and forty of you can apply for them. I would like to see you at the lecture.' I thought this very considerate and generous, and evidence of his deep sympathy with his suffering fellow-men. I have often thought of it, and if you think it worth recording, you may depend on its truthfulness, as I was at the service and heard it myself. His lecture in the evening was on ' Elijah,' and was the grandest I ever heard him give."

Mr. George Parkinson of Sherburn says :—

" In visiting this locality, Mr. Mackenzie often met with old mates and acquaintances of his earlier years. With his kindly greeting he would join an inquiry into their circumstances, and often follow it by a generous outgoing from his pocket, managed so delicately as not to hurt their feelings nor to afford them opportunity to express their thanks. To some poor old woman, unable to get to the service, he would send half a pound of tea, and sometimes half a pound of tobacco to the poor old fellow who, he remembered, was fond of a smoke.

"Once, Mr. Alderman Stephenson of Newcastle had to preside at a lecture which Mackenzie delivered at Morpeth. The circuit had only one minister, and his visits to the villages outside were so infrequent that he could not afford to miss an appointment even for Peter's coming. When Mr. Mackenzie entered the vestry after the lecture, the steward put an envelope into his hand, saying, ' I was requested to give you that, sir.' On opening it, he found a five-pound note. Knowing how poor the circuit was, and how small the stipend of the minister, he turned to the steward and said, ' It's a very nice note. Kindly give it, with my best regards, to your good, hard-working superintendent.' "

The Rev. John H. Norton relates a similar instance. Mackenzie had been lecturing in a circuit in Norfolk. Before leaving, they said to him, " How much are we in your debt, Mr. Mackenzie ? " He answered, " You must give me three guineas." They did so, and, putting his hand into his pocket, he took out two more, and, handing the five to the minister, said, " Here, brother, you need this more than I do."

Mr. Norton adds : " On several occasions, when I have put into Mr. Mackenzie's hand a sum of money such as I thought his valuable services fairly entitled him to, he has returned a portion, and no persuasion would induce him to receive it back."

The Rev. George Alley of Belfast, after describing a visit of Mackenzie to that city to preach and lecture, says :—

" We had, of course, dealt generously with him for his valued services, and when parting with him at the railway station, he wanted to force a couple of the sovereigns we had given him back into my hand for the poor, and I had much difficulty in getting him to keep what he had got—not an extraordinary amount by any means."

Mackenzie never quarrelled with stingy people, but he never visited them twice. On one occasion, after a lecture, the trustees of the chapel paid him a miserably inadequate fee, and then followed him to the railway station, rejoicing in the success of their effort for the funds.

"Of course, you will promise to come again, Mr. Mackenzie. Do let us fix a date now, if you please."

Peter tried to evade the point, but as they still persisted, he said, from the carriage window—

"Well, now, Judgment Day is coming, but I reckon we shall all be very busy just then. Suppose we fix *the day after.* Good-bye."

The story is well known, and quite true, of how, when a poor starving woman came to the door, when he happened to be in the house alone, he took the pie that was cooking for the dinner of himself and family out of the oven, and gave it to the needy one.

He was coming down the street in Batley Carr one morning, and saw a little fellow who was poorly clad, and who looked hungry. "Hallo, my little man," he cried, "what do they call you ?" The boy, quite staggered, looked up at the gentleman, and replied, "Paul, sir." Mackenzie laughed, and then rejoined, "Take this sixpence, for Peter and Paul have met this morning."

When in the Leeds Wesley circuit, he was called upon to preside at the committee meeting of the Mutual Improvement Society.

"What is the business ?" asked Mackenzie.

"We are in trouble, sir," replied the secretary. "We cannot pay our way."

"What do your debts amount to ?" asked the chairman.

" Quite a sovereign," said the down-hearted young man.

" Well, cheer up, I'll give a *pound towards that*," said Peter, and the cloud vanished.

One day he was being driven from Leeds to Ilkley by Mr. W. Johnson of Headingley, in an open carriage. On the way he dropped his umbrella, and the carriage had proceeded some little distance before the loss was discovered. The horses' heads were turned, and on driving back, a tramp was overtaken, who was hurrying off with the missing umbrella.

" Can you lend me half a sovereign ? " asked Mackenzie of his friend.

" What for ? "

" Oh, just to give the poor fellow."

" A shilling is quite enough," remonstrated Mr. Johnson. " He seems to have been in no hurry to find the owner."

Mackenzie took the proffered shilling, added to it all the silver he had in his pocket, which happened to be half a crown, bestowed it on the tramp with a kindly word, and resumed his drive—as much satisfaction on his face as there was surprise on that of the recipient of his bounty.

The feeling that lay at the back of such apparently wasted kindness was a strong faith in the redeeming power of human pity, and is beautifully exemplified in another incident. On one of his many visits to Hexham, where he was usually the guest of the late Mr. William Ritson of Woodley Field, as he and his host were driving through the entrance gate, they were accosted by a poor woman, who solicited charity. Mackenzie anticipated the invariable generosity of his host by quickly handing the suppliant half a crown, and on observing the look of surprise and incredulous gratitude in her face at the sight of the coin, he said, " It's all right, hinny, *be good* ! "

Be good ! Yes, perhaps Mackenzie was right after all, and

> Men might be better if we better deemed
> Of them. The worst way to improve the world
> Is to condemn it.

CHAPTER XXIX

THE MAN—DIVERS TRAITS AND INCIDENTS

Geniality in Social Life—Testimony of his Hosts—Remarkable Memory — "Good Night, Washington" — Grapes for the President—Quickness of Repartee—"A little Grouse" and "Consumed on the Premises" — "That Clock Goes-tick"— Compliment to a Chairman—"You do look bonnie"—Peter reading Prayers.

IN the endeavour to picture Mackenzie as he was, we have set forth in clear light his courtesy, his joyousness, his generosity, and doubtless other features of his character have disclosed themselves more or less distinctly as our narrative has proceeded. To make the portrayal complete, however, it seems desirable to gather up into a final sheaf of general characterisation certain traits of mind and disposition that range themselves under no definite head, but which must be included in our estimate of the man.

In the social circle he was the embodiment of geniality; never obtrusive in conversation, but always ready to crown the remarks of others with some sparkling addition or comment. One of his hosts remarks :—

"We always found him a cheerful guest, and in his conversation he never reflected on the character and doings of other ministers or officials. Anything like tittle - tattle or scandal he had an abhorrence of. Coming home from an exhausting service, he would change and have a rub down, and then come out of his room to join us, as fresh and chatty as though he had done nothing at all."

Another says :—

" He was simple in his habits, not caring for luxuries, but enjoying homely fare, bread and milk being often all he would take for supper. Towards other guests who might be in the house at the time he was always very cordial ; and what struck me as remarkable in connection with these, was his extra-ordinary memory for faces and for incidents connected with previous visits. One guest, that he had met seven years before, he recognised at once, and put him thoroughly at his ease by mentioning a drive they had taken together, and some other matters associated with their former acquaintance."

Illustrative of this surprising power of memory, the Rev. John E. Winter relates the following :—

" Some time during 1892 or the following year, Mr. Mackenzie preached and lectured in the Town Hall, Pateley Bridge, in aid of the Mechanics' Institute. At the close of the afternoon service, I was standing in the vestibule, in company with Mr. Foster, a gentleman of Middlesmoor, and one of the leading Methodists there. We were watching Mr. Mackenzie as he came down the hall, shaking hands with dozens of people who crowded round him, and every now and then recognising a friend. Mr. Foster said to one or two of us, ' I wonder if Peter will know me. About nineteen or twenty years ago, he came to lecture for us, and I met him at the station and drove him to Middlesmoor, and I don't think he has seen me since. I'll try him.'

"On came Peter, still shaking hands. At last he caught sight of our friend. After a good look, he said—

"'I ought to know you.' Then, lifting his hand, 'Now, don't tell me. Wait a minute. You live up the dale?'

"'Yes.'

"'Do they call it Middlesmoor?'

"'Yes.'

"'You came to meet me when I was going there to preach?'

"'Yes.'

"'You drove an old white mare?'

"'Yes.'

"'You live on the top of the hill?'

"'Yes.'

"'Let me see—your name is Foster?'

"'Yes.'

"'How long is that ago?'

"'About twenty years.'

"'And I have not met you since?'

"'No.'

"Considering the numbers of people Mr. Mackenzie had seen," continues Mr. Winter, "and the many journeys he had taken in all kinds of conveyances, I thought this recognition of a gentleman after so long a period, especially as so many details were remembered, to be marvellous."

A well-known Methodist at Washington, in the Gateshead circuit, when Mackenzie travelled there, was a Mr. Dobson. He went many years afterwards to hear his former minister in Sunderland. From the platform Mackenzie raised his hand to salute him, but Mr. Dobson felt uncertain whether he was really recognised. He stood with the crowd outside, however, and Mackenzie, as he passed him, raised his hat, and called out, "Good - night, Washington." The name of the man had escaped him for a moment, but the name of the place remained and was made to stand as substitute.

Mr. Samuel Harse of Newport, Monmouth, describes how, on one of Mackenzie's visits to that town, he gave him a fine bunch of grapes. He left Newport for Conference, arriving in time for the opening. The President that year was the Rev. Charles Garrett, and at the first convenient opportunity after he had taken the chair, Mackenzie made his way to the platform, and presented him with the grapes which, in the kindness of his heart, he had carried all the way from Newport to Leeds for that purpose.

One night he had arranged to start for Aberdeen from Shipley by the late mail. It was the missionary meeting night, and after the meeting he went out to supper. Asked at table what he would take, he answered, "Just a little of the grouse, if you please, to take back again to bonnie Scotland."

A similar instance of quickness of repartee occurred when he was in the Gateshead circuit. Out one evening for a social hour, it happened that the host in a merry mood kissed his wife, the hostess, before the company. Turning to Mr. Mackenzie, he said, "Do you do anything in that line?" "They are all consumed on the premises, sir," was his ready reply.

The Rev. Fred Bell tells how, at a country missionary meeting, in the Shipley circuit, the clock stopped, and as a consequence Mackenzie's time was considerably entrenched upon by the previous speaker. The Shipley meeting was held the next night, and the Rev. J. C. W. Gostick was the invited stranger. The same minister who had been misled by the clock the night before was speaking, and, suddenly pulling himself up, he said, " I must hasten on, for last night the clock stopped, but that clock goes on."

Mr. Mackenzie called out at once—

" That clock *Goes-tick—Gos-tick.*"

The congregation caught the joke, and roars of laughter and cheers greeted the sally. Needless to say, the hint was taken, and the clock that called for Gos-tick, did not call in vain.

Mr. Bell also tells of a visit Mackenzie paid to Newtown, Montgomery. He says :—

" We had invited a county magnate to preside, a gentleman well known and highly respected, and who is at present a member of Parliament. He arrived at the house of Mr. Mackenzie's host after tea, while Peter was preparing for the lecture in his own room. Presently the happy voice was heard humming a tune, and, all radiant, he entered the room where the chairman was partaking of a cup of tea. Of course he had to be introduced, and the host performed his part with all graciousness. The chairman, who was in evening dress, rose and bowed with a pleasant smile, while Mr. Mackenzie, looking at him from head to foot, exclaimed, ' Praise the Lord ! You *do* look bonnie ! We shall have a good time.' Consternation at first took possession of us all, for we hardly knew how the stranger would take the remark; but he understood the position, and heartily enjoyed the pleasant reference to his appearance, and before the evening was over, he and Mr. Mackenzie were fast friends."

Mackenzie's readiness to adapt himself to circumstances is well illustrated by the following from Mr. Samson Turner of Whitstable:—

"I was a resident in the Hoxton circuit from 1861 to 1887. During that period it was our joy as a family to entertain Mr. Mackenzie on several occasions. They were seasons never to be forgotten. Our children would clap their hands in a frenzy of delight when they heard that 'dear Peter' was coming. He had a very happy way of winning the love and enthusiasm of the young people. They were instinctively drawn to him by the charm of his individuality and the generosity of his nature.

"He was with us on the Saturday evening after the death of the Princess Alice, and had to preach the following day, morning and evening. One of the chapel stewards informed him that the liturgy was used, and asked if he would like someone to read the prayers for him. I shall never forget the knowing look and the wonderful spread of the hands with which he answered, 'Thank you, good brother. I may be able to get through them, by God's help.' And so he did. It was a marvellous service. The power and pathos breathed into the old prayers will never be forgotten by those who heard them from the lips of Mr. Mackenzie that Sunday morning. When he came to the prayers for the Queen and the Royal Family, he broke out into extemporaneous supplication for Her Gracious Majesty, full of tenderness and sympathy, that her heart might be comforted under her great breavement. The congregation was melted to tears, and, I venture to believe, has never forgotten the morning when Mr. Mackenzie read the prayers at Hackney Road Chapel."

CHAPTER XXX

Methodism Rich in Preachers—Their Great Variety—Peter of no Class—Evangelical Character of His Preaching—The Mellowing of Time—God's Love the Groundwork—Not a Logician—Poetic and Practical—Choice of Subjects—Three Sermons : The Hebrew Children, Penitent Thief, Canaanitish Woman—Great Spiritual Power : Rev. Foster Crozier's Recollections—Diminishing Power of Emotion.

SINCE the days when Wesley and Whitefield attracted immense crowds by the charm of their fresh, energetic utterances, the Methodist Church has never lacked a succession of powerful preachers. Other churches may have surpassed her in the elaborateness of their ritual and the accuracy and profundity of their scholarship; but she has yielded to none in the production of men able to impress the popular ·mind and to win the popular heart. Such men have not been all of one type. Indeed, if there is one thing more than another in which the preachers of Methodism may claim to be differentiated from those of other churches, it is in their abounding variety. Whether it arises from the room afforded for the manifestation of individuality before entering on the ministerial life, or from the brevity of the preliminary training, or from the itinerating nature of the work, or from all combined, with the addition of causes difficult to enumerate, it is certain that there is about the Methodist ministry less trace of ecclesiastical set or class than is to be found elsewhere. Even within the compass of a moderately sized circuit there are generally to be found the most diversified specimens of character and method. But even had these classes existed, Peter Mackenzie could not have been made to fit into any one of them. He belonged to all, and yet to none.

His preaching, in its general trend, was of the evangelical order. It presented in popular form, and with fiery earnestness, the cardinal doctrines of sin, atonement, reconciliation, with all their collateral issues and practical applications to everyday life. This was its character most intensely at the beginning, nor did it ever greatly deviate from it. There was doubtless a toning down of phraseology in regard to what are called the last things—final judgment and future retribution. It is not meant that his views on these momentous subjects changed at their root, but that, as with most men, his expression of them gathered reserve and inwardness, evincing more of the spirit and less of the letter. It lay not in the tendency of his mind to philosophise on such matters, but the gracious invasion of humanism which has more or less affected all life and thought in recent days, could not but influence him, making it inevitable that the crude, the lurid, the physically terrible of his earlier efforts should be mellowed into quieter colour and less glaring outline.

From the first he had a profound conviction and

experience of the Divine Love as manifested in Jesus Christ the Son of God, and this may be said to have formed the groundwork of all his teaching. Whatever shifting lights and shadows may have played upon the landscape of his preaching, this bed-rock of faith in the largeness of the divine heart and the world-wide efficacy of the divine grace remained unchanged.

His mind was not of the logical order. It was not his to climb with eager foot the ascending slopes of an argument, tracking and smiting fallacies by the way, heeding no siren call of sophistry, and resting not until he waved his flag from the summit of a triumphant demonstration. Reason he did, but his attack was the light musketry fire of the line, aided by the squibs and rockets of a humorous sarcasm, rather than the ponderous broadside of heavily massed artillery. He was not analytical. To hound a truth into a corner and dissect it piecemeal, had he been capable of the task, would have yielded him small delight; and yet he would often pierce to the centre of a subject quicker than those who cut their way thither with the aid of microscope and scalpel. His mind was of the poetic order, with a copious dash of the practical. He loved the concrete—the form, the colour, the voice of things; and possessed, in large measure, that intuitive insight which, when it takes a practical shape, is known as shrewdness. He was sometimes conceived of as simple, innocent, easily to be imposed upon; yet there were few better judges of character. If at times he helped the unworthy, it was not because he was blind to their faults, but because his boundless charity constrained him to hope for better things.

This knowledge of and sympathy with human nature doubtless influenced his choice of subjects as a preacher. It gave him a leaning towards the delineation of biblical characters. His first sermon was on blind Bartimæus, and some of his happiest efforts were in depicting scenes and incidents in the lives of patriarch, or prophet, or apostle. Who that heard it could ever forget the thrilling power of his sermon on the three Hebrew children, where, speaking of Nebuchadnezzar's command to them to come forth from the fiery furnace, he asked, with dry humour, " What would he have looked like if they had said with Paul, ' Come and fetch us ! ' " or that on the penitent thief, or that on the Canaanitish woman, in which, among a multitude of other good things, he said, " She begged for a crumb, and Christ handed her the whole loaf and bade her cut for herself."

Of the spiritual and emotional power manifested in his earlier ministry, the Rev. F. Crozier furnishes a striking account :—

" During my first year at college, Peter came to see me at Didsbury, and at night he preached at Great Ancoats, Manchester, and of course I accompanied him. That service was one of the greatest triumphs I ever witnessed in my life, from any man, or ever expect to witness. I had previously heard the late lamented Dr. Punshon lecture on Wilberforce in the Free Trade Hall, when it was packed, and the vast audience, thrilled with his unsurpassed eloquence, rose *en masse*, and gave him round after round of deafening cheers ; but Peter (of course the two men are not to be compared) surpassed him in producing an overwhelming effect upon a great company of people. His text was—'It became Him, for whom are all things, and by whom are all things, in bringing many sons unto glory,' etc. The chapel, you are aware, has a double gallery, and was crowded. When the word 'glory' was reached, the preacher dwelt upon it in his own characteristic style, with question and answer. He instanced a penitent seeking the Lord and finding Him.

"'Have you found Him, brother?' he queried.

"'Glory!' was the reply.

"'Is he precious?'

"'Glory!'

"In the meantime there were low suppressed murmurs of 'Glory!' throughout the chapel, but Peter went on interrogating, and answering 'Glory!' the feeling all the while rising, and when at length he reached his climax, there was a burst of 'Glory!' with Peter's voice uppermost, which sounded as if it would rend the building.

"The prayer-meeting then commenced, and, as was his wont, Peter occupied the lower pulpit, held in an agony of prayer, his face quivering with agitation, without a dry thread upon him. The chapel, still packed with people, was veritably a Bochim: groans, tears, sighs, and loud cryings upon God were seen and heard on every side. Troops made their way to the Communion, which, though large, was again and again crowded, so that more than one hundred persons that night penitently sought the Lord. It was a never-to-be-forgotten display of spiritual power, and one feels glad to have lived and witnessed it. I can recall similar scenes in the villages of Durham, but none on such a grand scale as that at Great Ancoats, Manchester."

Regret is sometimes expressed that such scenes did not continue to mark Mackenzie's ministry to the end; but this betrays an incomplete consideration of the elements in the case. Two inevitable changes are lost sight of—the change in the preacher, and the change in the congregation. Speaking generally, every man, with the advance of years, grows less emotional in himself and less capable of producing emotion in others. Then there cannot be the least doubt that the dissemination of intellectual culture diminishes the potency of emotionalism in religion as in other things. The more men are dominated by reason, the less liable are they to sudden and sweeping irruptions of feeling. It is also probable that the multiplication of channels through which emotion can express itself—in literature, in art, in politics, in recreation, and in the wider swing of all social movement— has had something to do with lessening its outflow in more spiritual forms. Religion was the one main avenue in the past for the outgoing of feelings which to-day have no difficulty in finding a thousand outlets. When these and other things are borne in mind, it will be seen that to expect Mackenzie's preaching to produce the same results in 1896 as it did in 1852 is to expect what is unreasonable, if not impossible.

CHAPTER XXXI

Felicity of Illustration—Sources : Scripture and Life—"It's only a Tunnel "—The Old Goes, the Better Comes—"The Pope's Bulls "—Rev. James Todd's Recollections—Passing Through the Waters—" A Plant of Renown "—The Five Fingers Illustration—Perpetuity of the Lord's Prayer—The Planet a Hearse—Illustrations from Nature—Sunset and Night—The Serviceableness of Humour—From Smiles to Tears—His Sermons well Structured—Affluence of Words—Defects of Diction—General Excellence.

FELICITY of illustration was undoubtedly one of the most attractive features in Peter Mackenzie's ministry. It lighted up his preaching, filled it with windows, through which illumination stole into the densest minds, and lent to it a picturesque quality that made it easy to remember. The two main sources of his illustration were Scripture and everyday life. The glamorous region of classical mythology or the provinces of science and literature and art he less frequently intruded upon. In these he was less sure of his tread ; but across the picturesque landscapes of Bible story he could wander like one who knew his way, and along the high-road, and even into the bypaths of Christian experience, he could not only venture with confidence himself, but lead the blind by ways they had not known. The daily life of his hearers was an immense wallet into which he dipped a hand at every service, drawing forth treasures which all could recognise, for all had seen them before, though without discerning their spiritual significance. Especially was he at home in illustrating the bright and consoling aspects of divine truth. In depicting these, the intense sympathy and kindliness of his nature gave him vantage, and he was notably happy in showing the goodly provision that religion makes of cheer in the present and felicity in the future.

In the September preceding his death, he preached at Whitby from "And he led them out by the right way, that he might bring them into a city of habitation," and a lady who was present says :—

"One sentence in that sermon I will remember as long as I live, and glad I am that the last words I remember from Peter on earth were of such precious import. He was speaking tenderly and rapidly of those who thought the 'way' dark, rough, thorny; dark with sickness, trouble, bereavement, and loss. 'Chee—ee—ee—r up!' shouted Peter. 'It's only a tunnel ye're in! There's a hole out at the other end!'

"Often have these words returned with comfort and hope to my heart; and even now, when the darkening shadows close in, I seem to hear Peter's voice ringing from across the Jordan—'Cheer up! It's only a tunnel ye're in! There's a hole out at the other end!'"

To illustrate how in the mysterious working of Divine Providence the sudden removal of the old often introduces the new and the better into our lives, he told once, how, on visiting an old friend, a corn miller, he was amazed to find that the old mill had been destroyed by fire, and a handsome building had risen phœnix-like out of its ashes. On expressing sympathy with him in his misfortune, the miller answered, "There is no need for regret. The new mill has brought new machinery, and we are prospering better than ever." "Yes," cried Peter, in relating the story; "he could well afford to part with the old cranky, miserable machinery; he wanted to hear no more of its wretched noise, with its rang—shang—rang—shang—rang."

Preaching during the time of the cattle plague, when the Pope had just issued a message on the subject, his text being "The word is nigh thee," etc., he said, "Eat the word and digest it, and you will be fat and live when all the Pope's bulls have died of the rinderpest."

The following interesting account of Mackenzie's preaching, which furnishes further evidence of its illustrative quality, has been kindly supplied by the Rev. James Todd:—

"Mr. Mackenzie's death brings vividly before me the first and last times I heard him preach. A space of nearly twenty years separates the two. The first occasion was an anniversary service in a charming little town in Leicestershire. The chapel was full of country people, who evidently were at home with the preacher. But I was a stranger fresh from the serious, still atmosphere of Scottish churches, and so the tittering of the audience during Mr. Mackenzie's first prayer greatly shocked me. I could not endure it, and came out of the chapel at once. A gentleman followed me to inquire if I was ill.

" ' Yes,' I replied, ' very, to see such conduct in a place of worship.'

" ' Oh,' he said, ' it is not so bad as all that. Mr. Mackenzie is a good man. You will soon understand him. Come back with me now.'

" I took his advice, and have felt indebted to him ever since. The preacher gave one illustration of the Father's care that remains with me to this day. At that time there had taken place a swimming fête on the Thames. The daughter of some professor of swimming had given an exhibition of the art. So Mr. Mackenzie, who had seen it, treated us to a vivid description of the river banks black with onlookers, the young lady cleaving her way through the water hand over hand, the little boat following her, oared gently by her brother, and her father standing at the prow, anxiously watching lest any small craft thronging the river or any chance oar or paddle-box should strike his daughter. The instant any mishap occurred, or any weariness betrayed itself in his child, over he would leap to her assistance. ' Oh, the comfort,' cried the preacher, ' which the believer may have ! For hark to what his heavenly Father says—" When thou passest through the waters, I will be with *thee* ; and through the rivers, they shall not overflow *thee*." '

" On the last occasion, Mr. Mackenzie took for his text—' A plant of renown,' and he applied it at once to Jesus. He said :—

" ' We value a plant for its rarity. But none so rare as Jesus. The world has many poets, many preachers, but only one Jesus. Again we value a plant for its beauty. But none so fair as Jesus. He is the Lily of the Valley, the Rose of Sharon, the fairest among ten thousand and the altogether lovely. We value a plant also for its perfume. God has scattered sweet scents all over the earth. The smell of a beanfield in flower is better than all your lavender or Eau de Cologne. But what delights are comparable to the joys of His presence ? The joys that are at His right hand are pleasures for evermore. Still further, we value a plant for its healing properties. But can any heal as Jesus can ? There are rubs and bruises and wounds and rents and knocks and troubles in this world, but Jesus is a balm for every pain. He makes the wounded spirit whole. We also value a plant for its shade and shelter. What poor shelter the world gives ! A horse cowering beside a bare pole in an open field on a cold wintry day is a true picture of it. But the shelter of Jesus is manifold and sufficient— succour in temptation, sympathy in trial, and abundant consolation in sorrow. Lastly, we value a plant for its fruit. How many fruits has Jesus to give— pardon and peace and joy and love and power and purity ! O taste and see that the Lord is good.'

"Such are a few notes of a sermon enjoyed by a large congregation, on a week-day afternoon, in October 1895. I have not found it difficult to forget the grotesque descriptions and extremely funny stories with which Mr. Mackenzie so plentifully sprinkled his sermons; and I have ever found ample material wherewith to nourish faith and hope and love in human hearts. Many times, in visiting the sick or infirm after one of his services, I have seen faces brighten and care flee away at the recital of the good things in his discourse. On one occasion a kitchen full of working folk sat delightedly to listen to a rehearsal of his sayings. I am sure that many pilgrims through life will say of him, ' Mr. Mackenzie was eminent among the men who have been a comfort to me.' "

The Rev. W. Kendrew says :—

" I remember once hearing Mr. Mackenzie preach from Acts iv. 13. In the introduction he moved his audience, which was a large one, and composed of all classes of people, as I have seldom seen one moved. To illustrate the context, he held out his hand with the fingers spread abroad. ' There are five of them,' said he, ' priests, Sadducees, scribes, rulers, and elders. A committee—thumb, chairman of committee. They all point in different directions, but when they mean mischief they come together to put down the new religion.' And the way in which his strong fingers closed in, and the fist fell on the book, was so graphic, that it can never be forgotten."

He once remarked that the Lord's Prayer was not like a Bradshaw's Guide, done in a month, or a lucifer match which loses its head in the striking and becomes useless. It would serve through all time, the future as well as the past.

What an almost lurid grandeur there is in that sentence of his, when, in speaking of the death of our Lord, with its accompanying darkness and earthquake, he said, " And when He died, the planet dragged on its heavy course like a great hearse carrying a dead God."

While the world of everyday life was most familiar to him the world of nature was not by any means an unknown territory. " His glowing and vivid description of the sea and its ever-changing moods," remarks one, " will not be easily forgotten by many besides the writer."

Once, when describing with lofty eloquence a sunset, he wound up with—" It was just as if old Sol had forgotten to shut the door after him, and a flood of glory burst in."

This again shows his sympathy with nature :—

" When we have had a very hot day, the grass is almost withered, the flowers droop, and everything seems to get scorched up.　But the sun goes down, and the stars come out; the moon drives in the heavens, and it is very still and very calm.　What a transformation during the night!　When I went out one morning after a very hot day, my friend, Mr. Lees, near Birmingham, called me, saying, ' Come here, Mr. Mackenzie, and see what it is like.'　Instead of everything being dried up, there was the cabbage with the leaves covered with moisture ; the water filled my hand, and the leaves fairly crackled again. And so were the flowers, pretty and beautiful, covered with dew.　When the darkness is cast around you, you see the stars.　When the sun goes down, you learn lessons quite clearly that you can never learn in the days of prosperity."

Few men probably have used so freely as Mackenzie did the gift of humour in the pulpit.　His sermons sparkled with witticisms as the heavens do with stars. Humour was to him as the letting out of water— quick to flow, hard to restrain ; not that he was anxious to evoke merriment, but that the ludicrous side of things caught him so vividly that he must give it expression. To some natures any evidence of humour in the pulpit is objectionable. Such a view is contracted. Humour is as true and serviceable a human quality as pathos; and to evoke a smile, either in church or elsewhere, is quite as virtuous as to educe a tear. Perhaps the burden of this unintelligible world would grow more comprehensible if we made allowance for such a quality in the Divine Being. Our persistently serious view of the operations of Providence has not unlikely darkened out for us certain lines that would impart relief and meaning to the picture.

It is hardly to be denied that at times Mackenzie's humour was somewhat extravagant, and its points not always happily placed. Occasionally the laughter was a little coarse, and the fun bordered on the grotesque. One could not but be sorry, sometimes, to see the flimsy skirts of a jest flapping incontinently against the kingly form of a more than usually royal passage. All must have marvelled, however, at the swiftness with which smiles were melted into tears. His sermons resembled greatly one of those days in April when the sky is alive with sportive clouds, and the shadows seem to rejoice in chasing the shine across the grass.

These sermons were not the chance creations of the moment. They cost him days and weeks of thought on the rail and in the study, and were enriched with the gleanings of wide reading and constant observation. Nor were they flimsy and disjointed in construction. He was possessed of a methodical mind, and however much his humour and fancy might seem at times to bear him abroad, the careful listener would discern that he never failed to return to his main theme.

His spirituality, his sympathy, his pathos, his humour, his simplicity, his aptitude of illustration, and whatever other quality characterised his preaching, were all augmented and emphasised by his delivery. Great qualities are sometimes doomed to silence, or achieve only a maimed expression. Mackenzie suffered not in this respect. Voice, gesture, facial movement, all lent themselves powerfully to the forthputting of what was within. His fund of words being as ample as his supply of ideas, he was never threatened with bankruptcy in speech. On the contrary, his thoughts rushed forth with the vehemence of a mountain torrent; so rapidly, indeed, that the panting mind had to take refuge in a gasp of " Hallelujah ! " or " Glory ! " to gain breath for another effort. From an artistic standpoint this rapidity occasionally marred the perfection of the diction. The speed at which his speech travelled was too great to be sustained, and thus passages of eloquence which would have been overpowering if carried forward to a gradually accelerated climax, were often robbed of their potency by dropping into commonplace, or dribbling into a tag of undignified rhyme.

But he had neither studied for himself nor been trained by others in the art of oratory. What he said was natural, straight out of the heart, and the wonder is, not that he should miss some of the graces and effects of style, but that he should have attained to such a high degree of excellency and power.

CHAPTER XXXII

THE PREACHER—HIS PRAYERS

Unique in Prayer—His Devotion Natural—Variety and Comprehensiveness—Even the Humour not Discordant—Prayer at the Seaside — A Unique Thanksgiving — "Make them Eloquent" — A Cheap Smash — Prayer in a Strike—Pity for the Poor—"He means my Grandmother"—Prayer for the Prince of Wales—The Cow turned Minister — Pathetic Prayer at Conference Time.

NO characterisation of Mackenzie as a preacher would be complete that did not include a reference to his altogether uncommon gift of prayer. He prayed as the bee hums, as the light shines, as the stream flows, naturally and without effort. Devotion was to him what its feathers are to the bird—worn always, carried everywhere. Probably his prayers were frequent because they were so natural, and natural because they were so frequent: use became second nature, and nature fostered use.

I remember being greatly impressed with this when I first became his colleague in the Gateshead circuit, and when he took me round and introduced me to the friends. Hardly had we entered a house and exchanged a few words of friendly greeting before we found ourselves on our knees, and in a few moments ready to depart.   And yet it was not a scamper that fretted one with its hurry.   One felt it to be in order; for what in another would have seemed abrupt, was in him what the mind appeared to expect.   He was instant in prayer, and in everything gave thanks.   Prayer was a sort of divine perfume which sprinkled with its fragrance all that made up the days of his life.

What wonderful freshness and variety and comprehensiveness marked his petitions in the pulpit!   How he crowded them with life and common things!   Nothing was too insignificant to be included, and what in a less transparent and simple nature would have jarred upon us as irreverence, in him seemed but the familiar speech of a child with a trusted father.   Even the humour that would not allow itself to be shut out of his supplications struck not so discordant a note in those who knew the devoutness of his spirit.   Laughing words fell from him with a more hallowed accent than solemn utterances from less sincere lips.

One who heard him while on a brief visit to a seaside watering-place thus speaks of it: " As Peter prayed, instantly we and our needs were gathered up and presented to the Almighty Father: 'Lord, bless the dear people who have come for the rest and the sea breezes.   Refresh them, give them a good time, and when they go home to-morrow, let them find all just as nice and straight as if they had been there themselves.   Lord bless them!'   Not a soul in the building, besides the multitudes out of it, whose needs were not gathered up and expressed in like fashion."

At a harvest thanksgiving he poured out the fulness of his gratitude in this fashion: " The hills are tipped with purple, and the valleys are smiling with the golden corn nodding to the breeze, and the boughs are gracefully swinging, freighted with the precious fruits of the earth. Yes, Lord, the time was when the farmer's lad would ask for bread, and a thin miserable shive would be offered him, but, praised be Thy name, it is not so now, for when little Jonathan asks for bread, his father slashes off a big shive, and says, 'Here, Jonathan, there's more for the asking for.'"

At Dunstable he was once entertained by a gentleman in whose establishment there were several assistants, and amongst them two or three just beginning to preach. At family devotions these young men were supplicated for as follows: "Lord, make them eloquent! Give them an eloquence that shall flow smoothly as a river of oil, and be terrible as Niagara, an eloquence that shall blister the consciences of men and drive them to the atonement for healing!"

Preaching in a Yorkshire town on a dark, miserable winter afternoon, he cried out in his closing prayer: "O God, take care of the poor old men and women who have come to hear Thy word proclaimed on such a day as this. Take care of them as they go home this nasty, dark, murky afternoon. Preserve them from falling and breaking their legs in the slush and snow; though if they should happen to break their legs, and this causes them to give their hearts to Thee, it will be the cheapest smash they ever had in all their lives."

Once, when a strike was in progress, he prayed that it might be brought to an end, observing that when the little mouse in the pantry turned away from the meal-bag with a tear in its eye, it was time to settle the strike.

In the same spirit of pity for the poor which pervaded all his supplications, he once prayed for those "with little in them, and little on them." On another occasion he asked for a blessing on those who had to brew the same tea three times over.

Mr. Samuel Hartley of Halifax relates an incident which shows how the characteristic manner in which Mackenzie was wont to express himself in prayer arrested the attention and impressed the minds of little children as well as of older people. He was preaching in the old South Parade Chapel, in connection with the opening of a new chapel in the circuit, and in the opening prayer he prayed for the new place and the friends connected with it, that they. might have much spiritual success, and much of the presence and blessing of God in all their work and worship. Then he prayed for the givers, and especially for those who had been making sacrifices and foregoing little luxuries in order that they might have something to give towards paying for the new chapel. "Bless the old women and widows," he said, "who have been going without sugar in their tea, so that they might be able to have a brick or a stone in the building." Mr. Hartley's little boy, now a missionary in Ceylon, then about four and a half years old, who was with his mother in the pew, looked up into her face while the prayer was going on, and said to her, "Mother, he means my grandmother." It so happened that his grandmother had gone without sugar in her tea, and he knew it, although he did not know for what reason, and so, childlike, he came to the conclusion that it must be her for whom the prayer was being offered to God.

Mackenzie preached in Wesley Chapel, Lincoln, during the serious illness of His Royal Highness the Prince of Wales. In the morning service he prayed for the Prince, and among other petitions, asked that the Lord would convert his soul, " as it would do him more good than bagging a thousand grouse."

Mr. R. N. Dickens, who communicates the foregoing, says that in the evening Mackenzie related the following anecdote :—A man was feeding a cow when the cow rubbed its head against him, as if to thank him for his kindness. The thought occurred to the man— This cow thanks me for feeding her. God has fed me all my life, and I have never thanked Him for it. The thought led to the man's conversion, and, remarked Mr. Mackenzie, " The cow had that soul for her hire, and that seal to her ministry."

The Rev. R. H. Mole relates how he heard Mackenzie, two years ago, at Colwyn Bay. It was Conference time, and in his prayer the preacher referred, with great tenderness and pathos, to the sorrows of those who were leaving old friends, and entering on new scenes and labours. He spoke of the silent ones in the graveyard, left behind by the dear widows, who had gone with them through many changing scenes, and now the last change had come, and there would be the packing without the help of those who had been ready to tighten the cord and nail the boxes. " Bless the dear sisters, widowed and wearied. Let them have mercy by the way, let not one box be lost. The Lord be with them ! "

CHAPTER XXXIII

THE LECTURER—TOIL AND TRAVEL

The Platform to Mackenzie—List of Lectures—Money Raised
and Miles Travelled—Wear and Tear—In His Stocking
Feet—Letter to Mr. S. Wright—Visit to Farndale—Helper
of Small Places.

TO Peter Mackenzie the platform was simply a
wider pulpit, the lecture an amplified sermon,
so that much of what has been said concerning him
as a preacher in previous chapters will apply with
equal force to his qualities and work as a lecturer.
The subjects of his lectures were nearly all biblical.
as will be seen from the following list, which is not
chronologically arranged, nor are the full titles in all
cases given :—

  1. The Bible.
  2. Providence.
  3. The Tongue, Its Use and Abuse.
  4. John Bunyan, the Hero of Elstow.
  5. Elijah the Tishbite.
  6. The Proverbs of Solomon and Others.
  7. The Sabbath.
  8. Samuel.
  9. Jonah, the Runaway Prophet.
 10. Gideon, the Mighty Man of Valour.
 11. The Good Samaritan.

12. Joshua.
13. Satan.
14. Ritualism.
15. Nehemiah, the Cupbearer.
16. Samson, and his Feats among the Philistines.
17. Elisha.
18. Solomon.
19. David, the Sweet Singer of Israel.
20. Job.
21. Ruth and Naomi.
22. Jonathan, a Type of True Friendship.
23. Simon, the Galilean Fisherman.
24. Joseph and his Brethren.
25. Saul, the Man who Missed his Mark.
26. Abraham.
27. Jacob and Esau.
28. Balaam.
29. Moses, the Lawgiver.
30. John Nelson.
31. Noah.
32. Daniel.
33. Queen Esther.
34. John the Baptist.
35. Æsop's Fables.
36. Absalom.
37. The Gospel and its Rivals.
38. The Nameless Prophet of Judah.
39. Naaman : Or the Advantages of Disadvantage.

This is certainly an ample repertory, yet he could hardly have managed with less; for his popularity was such that his services were in demand at the same place year after year, and thus fresh subjects were constantly required.

What amount of money was raised for religious purposes through the labours of the lecturer it is difficult to estimate; for though he kept a journal of his engagements, the entries it contains are not sufficiently regular and full to enable the calculation to be made with accuracy and completeness.

It is interesting to find, however, that a calculation made in his own handwriting of the amount raised and the miles travelled between June 5th and November 4th, 1882, a period of five months, yields the following result:—£2367; miles, 7360. This gives us an average of £473 a month, or £5676 a year.

Even if we take an average of only £4000 a year, which would not be too high a figure, we reach the magnificent total of £120,000 raised by this one man's efforts during a period of thirty years. If, in like manner, we reduce the mileage from 1472 to 1000 miles a month, it gives us 12,000 a year, or in thirty years the enormous distance of 360,000 miles, —that is, nearly fifteen times round the world. Had this wandering prophet travelled in a straight line, he might have paid his respects to the Man in the Moon, and then, turning round, covered half the distance back again.

What a tremendous amount of physical wear and tear is represented herein! The long hours in railway trains, the waiting at draughty stations, the drives in open conveyances across wild country, on rough roads, the early mornings, the late nights, the constant change of food and beds, the nervous strain of standing every day before immense crowds and living in a whirl of excitement; all this, and much else, only a man of iron constitution could have endured for so long a period.

With what pluck and pertinacity he went about his work is well illustrated by an incident of which the Rev. J. Tessyman furnishes the particulars.

"The February of 1886 was very stormy. Mr. Mackenzie came on the 10th of that month to fulfil an engagement at Dunstable. I will venture to say he never more nearly escaped having to break an engagement. In order to reach us in time for dinner, he had to leave Dewsbury by an early train. It was dark, the frost very keen, and the streets so sheeted with ice that it was almost impossible to walk. However, Peter Mackenzie was not the man to be daunted even by formidable difficulties. He pushed on with vigour, as he always did, but only to find that it was a case of ' the more haste the less speed.' He stumbled, and slipped, and slipped again, and it was only with the greatest difficulty he could keep his feet at all. At the close of the lecture that night, he gave an account of the journey, and as nearly as I can remember his words, said : ' I stumbled on as best I could, sometimes holding on to a wall, and sometimes grasping a lamp-post to steady myself. I found, however, I was making little progress, and I was afraid of losing my train, so I took off my shoes and walked in my stocking feet. But this, instead of helping, hindered me, and I was worse off than ever, and already I thought I heard the whistle of the engine. But I was determined to get to Dunstable, so I pushed on with speed; but oh, would you believe it ? I came to a full stop ! I lost my feet, and down I went, right in the middle of the road ! My boots flew to one side of the street and my bag to the other, and my umbrella went right on towards the railway station, and there was I—the Methodist preacher— laid flat on my back, looking up at the stars.'

"Mr. Mackenzie made considerable capital out of

this eventful journey, and often related it at the close of his lectures. He got to Dunstable, of course, and had a good time."

Similarly hard experiences through the course of nearly forty winters must have been fairly frequent, though not always of a nature to lend themselves to so graphic a description.

Samuel Wright, Esq., of York, supplies an account of a journey with Mackenzie which is doubtless typical of hundreds more. Mr. Wright was chairman for him for many years, and the friendly relation between them may be gathered from the following letter :—

DEWSBURY, *April* 21, 1894.

HONOURED AND DEAR SIR,—I am so sorry that I cannot go to Bedale on May 17, as we had arranged. The District Meeting coming a week sooner has upset me. If you could kindly arrange, I have offered them Friday, June 15, 1894 ; but cannot go without your own dear self. I would be like a rod without a line, like a fisherman without his net, like a reaper without his sickle, like a writer without his pen. I will do my best for them for your sake. Much love and all good wishes from,— Yours affectionately,　　　　　　　　P. MACKENZIE.

Mackenzie as lecturer, and Mr. Wright as chairman, had been a standing arrangement at Helmsley for many years. On one of these occasions a deputation from the Kirby Moorside circuit came, beseeching Peter to visit a remote chapel situated in the romantic district of High Farndale, twelve miles from the circuit town. He agreed to go if his chairman would accompany him, and in due course the time for the promised visit arrived. Travelling from Helmsley, where he had lectured on the previous evening, to

Kirby Moorside, they were received by the station-master, a good Methodist, who quietly informed them that on so windy a day, and with such a drive as lay before them, they would never be able to keep their "top-hats" in contact with their heads. In reply to the statement that they possessed no other, he offered to lend them soft caps, which were gladly accepted. A man with a waggonette and a pair of horses waited to drive them to their destination, the road to which lay principally up the Farndale valley and across the moor, and glad they were that Providence had placed a man at the station capable of giving such good advice, when, as they drove across the open moorland, they saw the hat of a young farmer on horseback blown off, and carried far into the valley below. After a jolting drive of two hours in a wind which would hardly allow them to keep their seats, they arrived safely at the house of Mr. Frank, a well-to-do farmer, where they were hospitably entertained in thorough Farndale fashion. Mackenzie preached in the afternoon, and lectured in the evening, the people trooping in from far to listen to one of whom they had heard much, but whom in that outlying district they were not often privileged to see.

It was to such places, where his services were generally a financial windfall, as well as a spiritual inspiration, that he delighted to go, putting heart and hope into many a drooping cause. "It was his invariable custom," says an old colleague, "to give a small and weak place the benefit when a strong and feeble cause were in competition for his help. If Sheffield and Manchester were pitted against Kirby

Moorside and Stow-on-the-Wold, it was the smaller places that won the day. 'Give them the day, bless them—the other folk can afford to wait,' and so the larger centre was 'put off' a while, reminded that 'to patient faith the prize is sure.'"

CHAPTER XXXIV

THE LECTURER—DRAMATIC REALISATION

Two Methods of Delineation—How Mackenzie did with his
Characters—Not Two Selves—Swinging the Fiddle—How
the Lion Roared—Some Extravagances of Manner—Dramatic
Incidents—The Two Buckets—Shooting the Sun—Simplicity
and Humility.

WHAT were the qualities that lent to Mackenzie
such a charm as a lecturer? Foremost among
them, undoubtedly, stood his remarkable power of
dramatic realisation. He saw what he had to say,
and never failed to make others see it. He lived
with the characters he described, made a home for
them in his heart, knew them so thoroughly that he
could paint minutely every garment they wore, every
word they uttered, every feeling they indulged.
Some speakers stand outside their subject. They
analyse it, take it to pieces, show their hearers every
particle of its structure, every line in its conformation,
so that when the delineation is ended, not the thinnest
film of mystery remains. That is one method, and
for certain types of mind and certain aims of exposition it has great advantages. Exhaustive analysis is
to the man of science invaluable. But for the delineation of character, especially character pertaining

to a far-off age and country, another method is preferable, and this Mackenzie adopted. He did with his characters what the prophet did with the widow's child; stretched himself upon them, breathed into them the quickening of his own vitality, and thus was enabled to delight his audiences, not with wooden figures, but with living men and women, aglow with all the passion and feeling that make human nature of every sort and at all times an enthralling study.

This surrender of himself to his subject characterised his delivery down to the smallest detail of word and action. There were not two selves on the platform: one creative, personating Job or Moses or David; the other critical, watching to see that the personation was well done. On the contrary, the two were blended into one, and that one infused itself into every movement and gesture and utterance. The personality of the man, ocean-like in its breadth and vigour, flooded with a great tide of vitality all he said and did.

How he did thus yield body and soul to his subject is strikingly exemplified in an occurrence communicated by Mr. W. Parker of Felling, in the Gateshead circuit, at which place Mackenzie delivered his lecture on "Samson." Around him on the platform sat the singers with their instruments, and when he came to describe the havoc made among the Philistines by the Hebrew Hercules, he seized by the neck a large "bass-fiddle," and swung it round his head, as if it had been no heavier than a walking-stick, crying, "He slew them hip and thigh with the jawbone of an ass."

The Rev. John E. Winter tells of another lively experience during the delivery of the same lecture on a different occasion. It was at Spitalfields, London, in the year 1868. The chapel was crowded, and many gentlemen sat on the platform. Speaking of Samson's introduction to the lion in the vineyard of Timnath, he said, " Did you ever hear a lion roar, my friends ? " Then he began with a low growl, rolled his eyes and tossed his head, his hair being worn a little longer than in recent years. Growing more excited, he swung his arms, and by some means drew one arm out of his coat sleeve. Then he pushed aside the table, and began prancing round in a circle on the platform. Speedily his hands came perilously near the faces of the gentlemen who sat around, and who wisely gave him a wider berth. On he went, treading on the chairman's toes, tapping slightly on the ear of another, and stepping on the feet of a third. Every moment the circle grew wider, chairs and their occupants became all alive, and the audience, entering into the humour of it, cheered vociferously. At length one brother climbed over the rail on to the floor, and another one down by the steps. This created roars of laughter, and Peter, taking in the situation, enlarged his revolutions until, amid the enthusiasm of the audience, the platform was cleared, and the roaring lion left, like Selkirk on his island, monarch of all he surveyed.

This *abandon*, the losing of himself in his subject, was not only the secret of much of his power, but serves also to explain those vergings on the indecorous, almost the vulgar, to which at times he was perilously liable. Intoxicated with the enthusiasm of his impersonation, he occasionally allowed himself to be carried into an extravagance of utterance and gesture,

that detracted from the grace and dignity of his per-
formances.   Such lapses were regrettable; but where
in art or nature do we find the perfect, and what a
limitation of vision is ours when we see only the
fungi on the bark, and lose sight of the spreading
boughs and noble leafage that make the glory of the
tree.   There were people who went to hear him once,
and because of these minor delinquencies would never
listen to him again.   They were prejudiced henceforth; but to those who knew the true worth and
power of the man, these shortcomings were insignificant, no more than to the lover of the ocean is the
floating weed hardly visible in the magic movement
of the mighty waters.

There are many stories in circulation illustrative
of the dramatic nature of his delivery, and doubtless
the incidents on which they are based have occurred
on several occasions, and at many different places.
Lecturing at Reeth, for instance, on "Queen Esther,"
and speaking of someone wishing to see the king, he
exclaimed suddenly, "Just see who that is at the
door!" and two of the officials, one in each aisle, rose
and went to see who was waiting in the lobby.

In his lecture on "Simon Peter," he stopped abruptly,
and said, "Kindly excuse me, Mr. Chairman, for five
minutes.   I want to go down the street to see a poor
woman who is sick of a fever."   Then he moved
towards the exit from the platform, and the chairman
took up a hymn-book to announce a verse to be sung
in the meanwhile, and hardly felt complimented when
the lecturer turned round, and woke a thunder of
laughter and applause by remarking quietly, "It is
only Peter's wife's mother."

The Rev. John Nayler recalls hearing him on the platform of Oxford Place Chapel, on the occasion of the Wednesday morning meeting of the Leeds Missionary anniversary in 1875.

" What the point to be illustrated was, I do not now recall. Possibly it may have been the desirability of carrying on both home and foreign missionary operations, but what Peter did was to show how much better a man can carry two buckets of water than one. In the attempt to carry one the speaker staggered and wobbled about, and almost went over altogether. But when he got the two buckets, one on each side, to make his balance true, he tripped briskly and gracefully across the platform, the cheers of the audience attesting that the speaker's point was proved to a demonstration."

In describing a lecture which he heard afterwards at Bacup, Mr. Nayler says :—

" In the evening the Co-operative Hall was crowded by an audience representing the various churches of the town, and the proceedings were enthusiastic throughout. The Rev. Mr. Elsom, United Methodist Free Church minister, prayed at the opening, and Peter, as his custom was, responded audibly. When Mr. Elsom referred to the lecturer, and gave thanks for his rare gifts and devoted labours, and prayed that God would continue to bless him, the humble subject of these petitions was heard responding in pathetic tones, ' Ay! poor thing! Bless him! Amen! Do, Lord! Bless him! Poor thing! poor thing!'

" The lecture was ' The Gospel and its Rivals,' and in dealing with Agnostics and Positivists Peter's keen eye and ready wit went straight to the weak places

in these anti-christian systems, and the lecture was a
fine vindication of the 'glorious gospel,' and of the
lecturer's own glowing faith in its ultimate success
and victory.   Perhaps the most effective and dramatic
passage was that in which the brief triumphing of
the enemies of Christianity was compared to the glee
of a half-witted Scotchman, who, having conceived a
dislike to the sun, shot at it with an old blunderbuss,
and having raised a great smoke, rejoiced that he had
got rid of his enemy.   Peter's unrivalled powers of
mimicry appeared at their best in this scene.   Poor
' daft Jamie's ' glee over his weapon, his chuckle as he
heavily charged it, the flash and roar of the discharge,
and the clouds of smoke, amid which Jamie danced
and shouted, ' I've done for him !   He's gone !   He's
gone !' were as real as if we saw and heard them.
And when the noise and smoke had subsided, and the
sun was seen shining in undimmed brightness, no word
was needed to enforce the lesson.   The way in which
Mr. Mackenzie threw himself into that scene, and
leaped and capered and shouted, would have taxed
the powers of a young athlete, and was simply
marvellous in a heavy man, sixty-seven years of age,
whose limbs, when not spurred by his indomitable spirit,
already showed painful signs of stiffness and overwork.
The price the lecturer himself had to pay for these
great efforts was known to few, if any, although his
hosts, who saw how exhausted and bathed in perspiration he was afterwards, had some inkling of the truth.
The closing scene in the hall that night, as Mr. Edward
Hoyle, J.P., his host and chairman, tendered the
enthusiastic thanks of the meeting, with his own
warm eulogy of his friend, and the good man himself,

whom all were cheering, sat there with beautiful humility, and yet simple, childlike pleasure, murmuring, 'Thank you, Mr. Hoyle, thank you! It is very kind of you!' was characteristic of the man and his whole career. He lived his life and did his work amid an atmosphere of admiration and applause. Night by night crowded audiences delighted to do him honour. And yet he remained unspoiled by popularity and uncorrupted by opportunities of personal enrichment, and to the last he received a kindness with as much gratitude, and a vote of thanks with as much pleasure, as if such favours were quite fresh to him, and altogether beyond his deserts."

CHAPTER XXXV

Definition of the Humorous—Out of Time and Place—Mackenzie and Bible Characters—Gideon's Beginning—" Aaron off the Plan "—Noah's Gimlets—Boaz, Goliath, Gideon—Terseness —Dean Hole's Story—Terse, Witty Sayings—Mackenzie a Collector—Smart Hens—His Humour Consecrated—Emerson on the Orator—How much he is Missed.

PETER MACKENZIE was certainly not a classical scholar, and yet much of the humour that made his lectures so entertaining was in harmony with the classical conception of what constitutes the comic. Not that he had studied and mastered any canons on the subject, and sought to conform his speech and action thereto. It might have been an advantage to him if he had. To have known philosophically wherein the essence of the comic lies, what are its capabilities and what its limitations, might have saved him occasionally, as it would save others, from trying to coax a bright spark out of a dull ember, or from imagining that the blunt prod of buffoonery is as penetrating as the stiletto-thrust of wit. It is not meant by this for a moment that Mackenzie was simply a religious mountebank. He was sometimes so described, but only by men who had caught no more than the superficialities of his nature or the oddities of his manner, and who lacked either the patience or the capability to weigh the whole man.

What is it that begets in us the sense of the ridiculous, that loosens within us the springs of laughter ? Aristotle defines it as that which is out of time and out of place, without having in it the element of danger. When danger or pain intrudes, the comic darkens at once into the tragic. When words or acts occur in a way that we should never anticipate, as when a man holds up his walking-stick to keep off the rain, or puts his watch into the pan and looks at the egg to see how long it shall boil, the sense of the ludicrous begins to tickle us. We are conscious that such occurrences are out of harmony with the usual order of things, but they are out of harmony in a pleasant sort of way, and so we smile or laugh.

Much of Mackenzie's humour came within this definition. It excited our risibility by putting things out of their normal relations to each other and to the world around them. This was especially marked in his treatment of Bible characters. How continually and with what comic effect does he put them out of time and place in his lectures ! Probably they were never so dislocated either before or since. He flings them at one throw from Palestine to England, from the centuries before Christ to the days that are passing now. Confine them to their own age and their own clime, and they are grave and reverend personages, but clothe them in nineteenth century garb and gift them with nineteenth century speech and ideas, and they at once assume a different aspect ; their stately gravity disappears, and we discern in their faces unexpected gleams of merriment and good-nature. Who can restrain a smile when he is told that Gideon began his work by sharpening his hatchet and then holding a band-meeting with ten fine young fellows who had never kissed the calf or offered sacrifice to Baal; or that on a dusty morning Gideon's fleece was so wet that a whole bowlful of water was wrung out of it, and that any farmer in Lincolnshire would be glad to lift one so heavy?　One may be sober by nature, but it is difficult to sustain a reputation for gravity when informed that Aaron was knocked off the plan for a quarter for conspiring against Moses; or when assured that it was a good thing that Jacob was not in charge of a refreshment-room, as he charged so much for his porridge; or that a penny a week and a shilling a quarter would hardly have bought grease for Noah's gimlets.

In such examples we have men and things put out of their proper order in time and place; but without the introduction of danger to themselves or others, and so we are amused.　It is quite refreshing to walk with Mackenzie into an Old Testament harvest-field, and to be told that good old Boaz, when he went amongst the reapers, said, "The Lord be with you!" and they straightened their backs, and looked into his honest face, and answered, "The Lord bless thee!" and to be reminded that if we had a little more of that at the present time, we should have a better understanding between masters and men, and fewer strikes.　Who can help laughing when told that Goliath mistook David at first, and thought he was a little boy gathering mushrooms — or that

Gideon in his unbelief prayed, " O Lord, wool is a tremendous thing for attracting wet, but if Thou wilt make everything else damp, and keep the fleece dry, that will be a real miracle, and we will not ask any more ! " and that when they came to look next morning, they were wet up to their knees, and there was no brilliance of dewdrops on the fleece, and when Gideon squeezed it, poor man, it was as dry as the driest sermon that was ever heard.

One essential requisite in all humour is that it shall be terse. When the fun is long-drawn out, its fragrance evaporates before our nostrils have inhaled it. A story told by Dean Hole, and quoted in the number of the *Spectator* current as I write, will serve to illustrate this. It concerns an epitaph upon a tomb in Virginia. " A famous author residing in that State was bereaved of his wife, and inscribed upon her gravestone, ' The light is gone from my life.' Time not only modified his distress, but kindly and wisely suggested a renewal of conjugal bliss. An acrimonious neighbour had the bad taste to banter him on his engagement, and to express a surprise that he had so soon forgotten his words of lamentation. ' So far from forgetting them,' he replied, ' I remember and repeat them now, as originating and confirming the intention that you are pleased to criticise. I declared that *the light was gone from my life*, and it is for this reason that I propose to *strike another match.*' " This is offered by the Dean as an example of brilliant repartee, but it is hard to read it without feeling that the cumbrous preamble of the bereaved husband blunts somewhat the point of his reply. He is too slow in getting his match out of the box, and when struck, it does not make a very brilliant flash.

Many of Mackenzie's best things owed their sparkle to their brevity, as when the whale is made to say to the prophet, " Come in, Jonah, out of the wet ! " or when a lecture on " The Tongue " is begun by drily observing that " the subject is in everybody's mouth, more's the pity if it isn't "; or when of the pebble that slew Goliath it is said that " such a thing never entered his head before." Brevity and unexpectedness combine in such sayings, as also in that remark concerning Jonah, that, when swallowed by the whale, he was in the body in more senses than one. That, too, was a smart rejoinder, when, in reply to someone who was describing a person with a very big mouth, he said, " I should think such a man could sing a duet all by himself."

All the wit that sparkled in Mackenzie's lectures was not brewed on the premises. He was a collector as well as an originator. He had an eye for the comic in newspapers and periodicals, and his retentive memory enabled him to retain and adapt whatever in this way came under his observation and was likely to be serviceable. Perhaps there is a trace of such adaptation, a reminiscence of some Yankee yarn, in the following. Speaking of a Methodist preacher who changed his circuit every year, he said the whole establishment of the man had grown so accustomed to these annual pilgrimages, that, as soon as ever the Stationing Committee assembled, the hens came into the kitchen and laid themselves on their backs ready to have their feet tied for the removal.

The bitter and the cynical never entered into

Mackenzie's humour. It wore a broad, kindly smile, and the laughter it evoked never inflicted pain. Often indeed, his mirth had a semi-devout flavour, as when in one lecture he said: "I had some new potatoes for my dinner to-day for the first time this season, and how nice they tasted! Thank God that all the potatoes were not made in the days of Adam! If they had, we should have been eating old potatoes all our lives—did you ever think of that before?"

Whatever the form it assumed, and the elements of which it was composed, the humour of Mackenzie had upon it the touch of a higher consecration. It was the servant of God as well as the entertainer of men. Whether he made men laugh or weep, he did it in loyalty to a Master to whom he had dedicated all his powers, and in whose employ he delighted to expend whatever would gladden and elevate the souls of those around.

.   .   .   .   .

As we survey the man, setting in array before us his varied gifts and the force with which he exercised them, we cannot but feel that Emerson might have had such an one in his mind when, describing the orator, he says: "Or you may find him in some lowly Bethel, by the seaside, where a hard-featured, scarred, and wrinkled Methodist becomes the poet of the sailor and the fisherman, whilst he pours out the abundant streams of his thought through a language all glittering and fiery with imagination,—a man who never knew the looking-glass or the critic,—a man whom college-drill or patronage never made, and whom praise cannot spoil,—a man who conquers his audience by infusing his soul into them, and speaks by the right of being the person in the assembly who has the most to say, and so makes all other speakers appear little and cowardly before him. For the time, his exceeding life throws all other gifts into the shade,—philosophy speculating on its own breath, taste, learning, and all,—and yet how every listener gladly consents to be nothing in his presence, and to share this surprising emanation, and be steeped and ennobled in the new wine of his eloquence."

All this was Peter Mackenzie to the thousands who came from near and far to hang upon his lips, and of himself can never be written what he said in one of his latest utterances: "Do you want to know how much you will be missed after you depart this life? Fill a bucket with water, then put your hand in it, and push your arm right down until it is buried to the elbow, then draw it out and see what a big hole there will be left in the water."

As we gaze across the broad lake of life, now that this man has been taken, no staring gulf is seen in the midst, yet creatures of the brink must stoop lower for a draught, and many a laden boat labours more painfully to land because of the shrunken tide beneath its keel.

APPENDIX

THE MAN AND HIS WORK

The Memorial Sermon preached in the Wesleyan Chapel, Batley Carr, Dewsbury, by the Rev. Joseph Dawson, on Sunday evening, December 15, 1895.

"The cedars in the garden of God could not hide him : the fir trees were not like his boughs, and the chestnut trees were not like his branches ; nor any tree in the garden of God was like unto him in his beauty."—EZEK. xxxi. 8.

[Part of this sermon has been incorporated in Chapter xxv.]

THESE words are part of a poetical description of the king of Assyria in his pride and glory; but we are guilty of no violent perversion of their meaning when we apply them to him whose name and work we are met this evening to commemorate. He was indeed a cedar whose stature his fellow cedars could not hide, to whose boughs and branches were given a character that marked them off from all the other trees in the garden of God. He came to us, lived among us, and went from us as none had done before. *Uncommonness*, that is the note that strikes all that write or speak about him. He was the peak among the mountain-tops that had a shape and aspect entirely different from the heights around; the forest tree whose trunk and foliage found no fellow in all the woods. This all men could see, even if their glance rested on him but for a moment.

Methodism has never fallen behind other churches

in the manufacture of originals. Its annals are rendered picturesque by the advent and passage of many eccentric characters. In that respect this man is no wholly novel product, and yet he is singular, nay, more than singular — solitary. Others crowd him around, but his stature does not dwindle in the press; he towers higher and bulks larger than the rest. This arises from the fact that he was so full - statured a personality, and that the unique obtained in him so all-round a development. Not in solitary details or at scattered points, but up and down the column from pedestal to capital, there was the utterance of the unusual, the striking.

In churches generally, especially under the clasp of present-day organisation, there is a strong tendency to uniformity, to the production of men and women moulded according to one set pattern. We are more prolific of types than of individuals, and it is much easier to be one of a class than one who stands alone. What we have to thank God for in the case of Peter Mackenzie is a rich and powerful nature persisting, in spite of all the pressure of the external, in its own shape and swing. It is from this standpoint I am anxious to view him this evening. I would set him before you as one of the most unfettered and varied developments of Christian character and activity that this generation has been permitted to witness; as one who, while yielding gracious homage to the laws around, was yet a law unto himself; whose life, without any conceited affectation of singularity in its tone, produced a melody altogether distinct and unconformable. This will be the underlying tone colouring all I shall have to put before you of the man and of his work.

THE MAN.

Think of the broad, strong lines of his physical structure. What a powerful physique! What amplitude of chest and shoulder, what a keen eye, what strength and suppleness of limb! Vigorous from birth, even the hard labour of the mine served only to augment his strength. So powerful was he in bone and muscle, that I have known him split the panel of a door with a blow of his fist, and one hardly envies the would-be garrotters who one night assailed him in a lonely lane. Almost unbroken health was his portion, and muscular Christianity had never occasion to be ashamed of him. It was no doubt owing largely to the endurance and flexibility of his steel-like constitution that he was enabled for so many years to cut his way through such a forest of engagements.

Physical vigour is not everything in a preacher. It may be linked with mental feebleness or spiritual inefficiency; the epistle may be buried in the bulkiness of the envelope. Where it is not so, where physical power carries with it, as it did in this case, strength of mind and fervency of spirit, it becomes a most effective endowment.

This robustness and energy of physical nature was one of the main secrets of Mr. Mackenzie's overflowing cheerfulness and vivacity. It gave elasticity to his being, so that in all his contact with men and things there was a sort of joyous rebound. Many people are simply receptive to their surroundings; chilled or warmed by the things they touch. This man not only received, but gave. His touch was that of sunlight, sending a quiver of brightness and heat through all on which it fell. His life, after entering the ministry, was practically divided into three sections—that spent in the sanctuary, that spent in the home, and that spent on road or rail; and wherever you encountered him, whether his face beamed upon you from the pulpit, or whether you shared with him the pleasures of social fellowship, or whether he startled you with a happy greeting from the window of a railway carriage, there was always the same radiant personality, as if he had gathered up into himself all the summer and song of existence, and left the chill and the croak to less fortunate individuals. I remember well how his vitality and cheer, the spring and shine of his bearing in the Gateshead circuit, as we went in and out together for two years, conveyed to me the sense of a perpetual holiday. No need of the mountains or the sea; he was as the breath of both in himself. Low spirits and discontent, to weep here, or grumble there, or whine yonder never entered into the programme of his life. Sunniness and buoyancy were his perpetual attributes, the habitation and pose of his spirit.

And yet this cheerfulness was far from being the mere surface glamour of a superficial nature. He was not radiant because he was shallow, like a brook that glints perpetually because it is not deep enough to gloom. There were deeps in him where cloud-filled hollows or caverns of shadow could, if need arose, have claimed a space. But his natural bias, like that of the plant world, was towards the light. Instinctively as the trees, his soul turned sunward. He never saw the dark in men and things, or if he did, he never gave it accentuation. His glance might touch, but never stayed upon the gloom. Hopefulness and charity were as wells within him. Travelling so widely as he did, few men had such ample facilities for discovering and discussing the foibles of others; but it was never his to wound a reputation by a secret stab, or a sly innuendo, or a compliment that concealed a blow.

What a testimony to the inherent kindliness of his nature is that which his eldest daughter gives, when, in a letter to me the other day, she writes: "What I shall do without him I do not know, for he was always so kind. I never remember him saying an unkind word." That sounds a very simple statement, but what a meaning it encloses. We all know how kind and sympathetic Peter Mackenzie was in his public life; how his generosity flowed like a river, in channels

where that of others never made a track. We know
how he literally rained kind words and sunny looks
and generous gifts around him wherever he went in
his public ministrations ; but the simple words I have
quoted show us that this radiancy and warmth were
not laid aside, as they often are, on crossing the
threshold of his own house, that in the home he was as
bright and kind as out of doors. To have words of oil
and looks of sunshine for use abroad, and vinegar and
thunderclouds for consumption at home, is not an
unknown combination ; hence it gladdens us to be
assured, though few would have thought it otherwise,
that in the case of our friend, the sunlight of the hidden
corners was bright and genial as that of the open fields.
" He was so patient," continues his daughter, speaking
of his last illness. " If it was only a drink of water, he
would say, ' Thank you, darling ! What a comfort you
are ! ' "

And with this never-failing geniality, what a true
humility was blended. The pronoun " I " would never
have earned a livelihood if its employment had depended on the use he made of it. How seldom it
invaded his speech, and never with that blatant
assertiveness that so often characterises the man who
stands, or thinks he stands, above his fellows. What
impressed all who knew him, and none more than those
who knew him best, was an entire absence of self-
assertion. Indeed, his fault, if it was a fault, lay at
the other extreme—an undue self-depreciation. What
particularly and frequently impressed me was his un-
affected spirit of inquiry. He was always athirst for
information, and of the youngest would ask questions
with an almost childlike reverence. Of any ignorance
that life had not offered him opportunity to vanquish
he was never ashamed, and was always eager to replace
the ignorance with knowledge, even if it meant learning
from men and women greatly his inferiors in other
respects. This, my friends, was the man whose loss we

bemoan—strong, sunny, gentle, sympathetic, generous, brave, true, humble. A man whose manner a few criticised, but whose character all admired. A man whose presence was a benediction, and whom not to have known was to have missed one of the gladnesses of life.

What I have endeavoured to set before you so far were his natural qualities, the simple make-up of his nature as a human being; and now the question arises how far these natural qualities were influenced and modified by religion.

That Peter Mackenzie was an earnest Christian goes without saying, and that his Christianity permeated his whole nature, all he was and all he did, as thoroughly as moisture permeates a cloud, was patent to all who knew him. His conversion, when a miner at Haswell Colliery in the county of Durham, was a very decided one. It changed the whole current of his being and doing, and the fire kindled in him then only burned with purer, stronger flame as life went on.

But his religion, deep and pervasive as it was throughout, was yet of no conventional type. It had an accent and bearing of its own. No one ever dreamed of questioning his piety. It breathed from him at all points and at all times, imparting a sacredness even to the play of his humour, and a sort of holy grace to all the angles of his singularity. It was common for a congregation to smile as he entered the pulpit, but it was common also for them to feel a thrill of unaccustomed devotion as the fervency of his spirit laid rousing touch upon their souls. The impression made upon them was that there stood before them a man who, however unusual his manner and strange his speech, had touched the Divine, and himself grown holy through the contact.

Here was a saintliness not to be denied, and yet a saintliness of an altogether uncommon order. Not a trace of the ascetic, or the monastic, or the sanctimonious, or the fanatical, or the "unco guid" about it. All as natural and as real as the laugh of a child, or the song of a lark, or the dance of the daffodils. The natural parts with its grace when it takes upon it the manner of the artificial, and so does holiness when, striving to grow divine, it ceases to be human. The charm of this man's piety was its whole-hearted humanness, the warm, friendly embrace, wholly devoid of Pharisaical stiffness, with which it enfolded one. There was nothing of cloud, or class, or cloister, or drawing-room, or holiness as a special cult about it. It was an everyday, fireside, mother-tongue sort of sanctity, the religion that a little child would fall in love with, and that a bad man would envy and long to possess. The spiritual in our dear friend never extinguished nor even stunted the natural. All that was characteristic and wholesome in him before his conversion—the mirth, the wit, the humour, the heartiness, the generosity, the energy—remained, clad only with a richer grace and devoted to a higher end.

So common is it for what is called holiness to separate men from their fellows in thought and sympathy, and sometimes even in speech and attire; so common is it for it to drive them into narrow, exclusive paths in which they walk with unattractive bearing; so common is it for it to ban and quench a large share of the joys and graces and humanities of existence; so common is it for it to regard the world as the devil's hunting-ground rather than as one of the many mansions of the Father's house: so common is it for it to come as John the Baptist, clad in camel's hair, girdled with leather, and feeding on locusts and wild honey, rather than as Jesus Christ, eating and drinking, and mingling with publicans and sinners,—that it may be regarded as one of the distinct achievements of Peter Mackenzie's life to have set before us a type of saintliness high enough to evoke the reverence, and yet human enough to win the affection, of all on whom its influence fell. In this regard we may truly say that "the fir trees were not like his boughs, and the chestnut trees were not like his branches, nor any tree in the garden of God was like unto him in his beauty."

> He stood for us as none has stood before:
>   Unique in spirit and in outward bearing,
>   The best of other spirits amply sharing,
> Yet hewn distinct as cliff on ocean shore.
> As cliff? nay, goodly land, where evermore
>   The winds blew fresh, the clouds with happy daring
>   Wove hues and fantasies beyond comparing,
> And earth and wave a matchless glamour wore.
> The land is with us still, but dulled and faded,
>   We see it through the mist of memory now,
> Its glow is gone, its sun by gloom enshaded.
>   O stalwart friend of God and man! know'st thou
> That griefs uncounted have our hearts invaded?
>   The birds sing not; for night is on thy brow.

HIS WORK.

So much for the man, let me now speak to you of his work. That work divides itself naturally into two parts: the specially evangelistic effort with which it began, and the more general service into which in a few years it enlarged. It was not long after his conversion that Mr. Mackenzie began work as a local preacher, and a demand for his services soon set in, for which the supply was all too limited. In the villages, throughout an ever-widening area, he was eagerly sought after to conduct special services, and was sometimes absent from home for six weeks at a stretch. I remember well the first time I heard him in my own native village in that same Durham circuit. I sat as a youth of about sixteen in the chapel, and have never forgotten how the flash of his piercing eye impressed me as he discoursed in a powerfully dramatic manner on, "Lo, He cometh with clouds, and every eye shall see Him, and they also which pierced Him, and all kindreds of the earth shall mourn because of Him."

During the first few years of his ministerial life, his work was mainly of this evangelistic character, and was very successful. Those who began the Christian life as the result of his earnest and graphic appeals were many, and are to be found still in large numbers scattered throughout the land.

Then, as his popularity extended, and the demand for his services increased, as his own powers developed and his view of the situation enlarged, his work assumed a wider and more varied character, and the practice of preaching on week-day afternoons and lecturing in the evening was begun—a form of labour in which he has toiled with greater assiduity and success than any other public speaker for over thirty years.

This departure of Mr. Mackenzie from the specially evangelistic work with which his preaching life began, is often spoken of with regret, and apologies of various sorts are made for it by his friends. I think, if you will give it fair and ample consideration, you will find it to have been an entirely natural development.

Mr. Mackenzie was a circuit minister when the practice was begun. Now, a circuit minister, however so disposed, cannot devote the whole of his time and energy to the holding of what are called special services. Such services would cease to be special if he did so, and whatever gain might accrue from their irregular character would terminate. It is true that Mr. Mackenzie might have been employed in this manner beyond the boundaries of his own circuit, as certain special men are employed to-day; but that arrangement does not seem to have been suggested, for the time of District and Connexional evangelists was not yet. In a circuit, moreover, there is always need of money for the prosecution of various kinds of Christian work, and the man whom Providence has gifted with the talent for raising it cannot be allowed to remain unexploited. People would as soon dream of leaving a diamond field or a gold mine unworked as of leaving such a man unused. How natural, then, in view of all these considerations, for our friend's talents as a lecturer to be discovered and cultivated, and for the demand for his services to go on increasing until he came to be one of the most eagerly sought and widely known platform orators of the day.

I fail to see why any regret should be felt or apology needed for this development. Peter Mackenzie was so many-sided, large-natured, liberally-gifted a man, that it required both platform and pulpit to afford him full expression. Evangelistic preaching at its best offers a somewhat restricted field for the exercise of intellectual and other gifts. It necessarily means ringing the changes on a certain number of truths, or on certain limited aspects of the truth. In such work Peter Mackenzie was, and would doubtless have continued to be, for many years eminently successful, but that alone would never have moulded him into the man whose loss we bemoan to-day. Our friend was not simply gifted with special talent, he was a genius, with all the fulness of endowment enfolded in that much-debated word; and the hall-mark of genius is the power and inspiration it possesses to cut its own way through the world, unhampered by usage and opinion. It has always been the custom for staid, slow-going onlookers to criticise the track in which genius treads; but it has also been the custom for these same onlookers to walk in the said path themselves, or to sing praises to it a generation later.

Be it also borne in mind, in considering this matter, that Peter Mackenzie never gave up preaching the gospel. He did that almost every day of his life, and with unabated earnestness. There would doubtless come changes in his mode of presenting the truth, as there come to all men as their minds grow and their outlook widens. Even those who deplore a change in our friend have probably, in proportion to their size, changed quite as much as he did. I have no doubt that, like most of us, he grew less crude and contracted and dogmatic as the years went on ; but having heard him before he entered the ministry, and many times since, to within a year or two of his death, I am free to testify that there was the same fervour, the same simple-heartedness, the same desire to bring spiritual blessing to his hearers as marked his earlier days.

Then think further of the benefit this larger work of his brought to the Methodist Connexion, and through the Connexion to the community at large. What struggling churches it succoured and strengthened, delivering them from financial pressure, and so freeing their energies for spiritual service. Add to that the cheer, the stimulus, the influx of hope and courage which every visit of his brought with it, and you will be slow to believe that, in pursuing the course he did, he was not divinely guided.

The intellectual qualities that Mr. Mackenzie brought to the accomplishment of this work were of a very exceptional and diversified kind, and of much higher quality than is commonly supposed.

In the forefront is to be placed the wonderful magnetism, the electric quality of his nature, that lent a thrill to every movement of his body, and a distinction to the simplest utterance of his lips. His burly form was charged with soul down to the finger-tips. Word and gesture flashed with it as a diamond scintillates with light. The vitality and regnancy of spirit that grasps men, that bears them down like a wave, was his in no small degree. You could not be in his presence for five minutes, could not see him move or hear him speak without being arrested,—surprised, or startled, or attracted,—or in some way compelled to yield attention. In the pulpit and on the platform this magnetic force had free play, and, combined with a fulness of sympathy and power of dramatic rendering, imparted a vividness and reality to the portrayal of character and incident that was ofttimes very amazing.

And what shall be said of the humour and pathos
that in his sermons and lectures were so marvellously
interblended? How wonderful the rapid alternation
of sunlight and shadow in his speech! Few men have
lived nearer the fountain of laughter and tears. The
quaintness of his prayers would often wake a smile, to
be followed instantly by a tug at the heart and a gulp
in the throat. Nor, to those who knew and understood
the man, was there any suspicion of irreverence; for
the rush of earnest feeling made it evident that here
was one who, though he might speak in strange phrase,
spoke straight from the heart. Prayer is one of the
outgoings of our religious life that is in constant
danger of crystallising into set forms, and Mr. Mackenzie
did well in showing, though unconscious that he was
giving the lesson, how possible it is to approach our
Father in heaven in a perfectly natural manner, and
with perennial freshness of utterance and almost
extreme comprehensiveness of detail, and yet with
absolute reverence of spirit.

The frequency, too, of this man's prayers, the almost
torrent-like irruption with which they broke into his
life, deserve a passing note, though time will not allow
of enlargement. The annals of Methodism may be
able to furnish us with illustrations of men who have
spent longer periods at once upon their knees; but not
with one who surpassed this man in the frequency and
fervour of his supplications. Prayer was indeed his
vital breath, and it is no enlargement of the fact to
say that he mingled devotion with all the activities of
his life as naturally and thoroughly as in a landscape
the shine is blended with the shade.

His magnetic charm and humour and pathos have
already been adverted to, but these were not by any
means the sum of Mr. Mackenzie's endowments.
There was, in addition, liveliness of imagination, shrewdness and sanity of judgment, considerable insight into
character, and a happy knack of delineating it in

forcible phrase. The realistic manner in which he was able to clothe the East in the garments of the West, and to make the men and women of olden time live and talk like the men and women of modern days, was something never to be forgotten by those who saw and heard it.

To claim for him academic culture, or theological precision, or philosophical breadth, or perfection of style, or the finer arts of oratory, would be unwise. It would be vain to expect such things of a man who came straight from the mine into the ministry, and that not until after he was thirty years of age, and married. It would be a great mistake, however, to imagine, as many seem disposed to do, that he was entirely unlettered, and depended for his effects on little else than oddity and humour. He was from the beginning to the close of his ministry an earnest student, and probably read twice or three times the number of books on any given subject, as many of those who credited him with a comprehensive ignorance. I remember distinctly procuring for him, at his request, when we were together in the Sunderland, Sans Street, circuit, the best and latest works on Old Testament history and character, to aid him in the preparation of his lectures, and that was a practice he kept up to the end. His own thought was continually enriched with the best in the thought of others, though no commodity imported from abroad was allowed to pass forth again until it had received the imprint of his genius.

And now, without dwelling further on our friend's qualifications, I want you to note how in work, even as in character, he stands apart, with a niche and a chiselling altogether his own. The charm of his speech, and the hold it took upon the masses, did not consist in its stately or florid rhetoric, nor in its ordered and argumentative arrangement. As a speaker he cannot be classed with any other either general or Methodist orator. Something he had in common with them all, and yet something that differentiated him from them all. What probably marked him off, and made him unique as a public speaker, was his wealth of humour, his energy of utterance, his oddity of gesture, and, above all, the width and intensity of his sympathy. As the true artist in fiction communes with the creations of his fancy until they become to him living beings, so did he with the men and women whom he set himself to understand and portray.

But the great distinction of his work, as of his nature, was the deep and broad humanity that pervaded it. In his treatment of biblical characters in sermons and lectures, there was a reversal of the ordinary method. The usual mode is to study these men and women through a veil of Oriental associations. Mr. Mackenzie tore away this veil, and set them before his audience in British, nineteenth-century, and often in Methodist habiliments. Samuel, Saul, Jonah were made to figure as itinerant preachers, Esther as a modern housewife, and Paul perhaps as President of the Conference. Historical consistency was violated, archæological accuracy defied, theological prepossessions and traditions disregarded. Why? Not because the lecturer was an iconoclast, delighting to shatter the images of the past, and to demolish the carven niches in which a reverent regard had placed them. Not at all. Our friend was no wanton image-breaker. He brought the dim, dusky East into the hard, bare light of the West, not to strip away its charm and glory, but to make it brim and throb with the life of the present. Some of the mystic glamour might depart in the process, but that did not enter into the intention of the speaker. When he made those old-time heroes sit with us at the same table, share with us the same toil, talk with us in the same speech, it was not to rob them in any degree of their rightful dignity, but to make us realise more intensely that we are of one common kith and kin. When the Apostle James adduces Elijah as an illustration of prevalence in prayer, he reminds his readers that the prophet was a man of like passions with themselves; and to bring home to his hearers the community of soul between themselves and those who lived in the far past, was one of Mr. Mackenzie's main objects, and one in which he strikingly succeeded.

That he should violate certain canons of exposition in achieving success is a comparatively small matter, if he succeeded in driving home the main truth. There are quite enough teachers who go to the opposite extreme, who speak of Abraham, Isaac, and Jacob, as if they were men of an entirely different mould, and dwelt in an entirely different world. In the vividness of his portraiture, in the clearness and enthusiasm with which he painted their life down to the minutest detail, and found parallels for all they thought and did in what we are thinking and doing now, our friend did sometimes skirt the bounds of probability, and perhaps occasionally exceed the limits of propriety; but when all that is admitted, it still remains that we owe him a generous tribute of thanks and appreciation for the manner in which he made the common mind apprehend the fact, that the men of the past were made of the same stuff as the men of the present, that they trudged along the same great road of life, and had hearts filled with the same hopes and fears as ourselves. In short, he made us realise the strength and wholeness of their humanity; and the ocean of human feeling that flooded every creek and cranny of his own nature, gave the task in his hands an ease and a success to which it seldom attains in that of others.

Such was the man, and such his work.

> God made him as the ample mountains make
>   The torrent strong enough to dig its own
>   Brave way o'er shelving rocks, thro' gullies lone,
> Till hushed to slumber in some lowland lake :

What force 'twill win, what tuneful echoes wake,
　　What impress give to bordering soil and stone,
　　To heart of prophecy is all unknown ;
Unled it shall its way through boulders break.
　　So, fresh and full, he came from God's own hand,
And down life's mountain carved his proper track,
　　Sped glad and tireless through the waiting land,
To carry fulness where they suffered lack.
　　Nor have we one in his blank space to stand,
And call as he our elder Kinsmen back.

The lessons of this man's life are many, but at this moment, we sum them up in one. Let each of us be as true to Jesus Christ, and as true to his own self, as Peter Mackenzie was to himself and his God, and the world will be cleaner and stronger for our presence. We want no one to imitate the manner of the valued worker whom we mourn, but we want all to catch his brave, unselfish spirit. Who will be baptized for the dead ? Who will take up the banner that has fallen from his grasp, and wield the sword with which he fought so valiantly for the King? Who among you young men will do as he did—give yourselves first to the Lord Jesus Christ, and then to the service of humanity, living your own life, cultivating your own bit of ground for God and man, creating for yourselves every day a larger soul, a wider circle of influence, an ampler sphere of labour, until it comes to be said of you at the last, as we now say of him—" The cedars in the garden of God could not hide him : the fir trees were not like his boughs, and the chestnut trees were not like his branches ; nor any tree in the garden of God was like unto him in his beauty."

PRINTED BY MORRISON AND GIBB LIMITED, EDINBURGH

NEW AND RECENT BOOKS.

PETER MACKENZIE: His Life and Labours. By Rev. JOSEPH DAWSON. Crown 8vo. With three Portraits and eighteen other Illustrations. 3s. 6d. *Fifteenth Thousand.*

"A straightforward, honest piece of work, fairly picturing every phase of the preacher's work, and expressing a ready sympathy with his remarkable character. . . . Mr. Dawson's book is a worthy monument of an individuality as noble as it was eccentric."—*Sheffield and Rotherham Independent.*

A STRING OF CHINESE PEACH STONES: Being a Collection of the Tales and Folk-lore of the Hankow District, which eventually becomes a story of the Taiping Rebellion in Central China. By REV. W. ARTHUR CORNABY. More than one hundred Original Illustrations. Demy 8vo, 496 pp., cloth extra, gilt top. 10s. 6d.

"This book is the revelation of a new world of thought and feeling, of literature, romance, and history. . . . The book is an education in the art as well as in the life and ideas of the Chinese."—*The Scotsman.*

OXFORD HIGH ANGLICANISM AND ITS CHIEF LEADERS. By JAMES H. RIGG, D.D. Demy 8vo. 7s. 6d.

"No one who desires to understand some of the more important chapters in the religious life of the England of this century can afford to pass this volume by."—*The Critical Review.*

THINKING ABOUT IT: Thoughts on Religion for Young Men and Women. By ALBERT H. WALKER, B.A. Printed on antique paper, in crown 12mo. Bound in art linen, gilt top, 2s. 6d.

"This charming volume. . . . The tone is pure and high, the teaching devout and practical, and the language plain and scholarly. No fitter book could be found to meet the case of thoughtful, but undecided, young men and women."—*Hastings Observer.*

NEW VOLUMES OF "BOOKS FOR BIBLE STUDENTS."

SCRIPTURE AND ITS WITNESSES. By Professor J. S. BANKS. Author of "A Manual of Christian Doctrine." [*In the Press.*

THE BOOKS OF THE PROPHETS IN THEIR HIS- TORICAL SUCCESSION. Vol. I. "To the Fall of Samaria." By Professor GEORGE G. FINDLAY, B.A. Small Crown 8vo. 2s. 6d.

"If the others are as good as this Professor Findlay will have given us a notable contribution to this momentous question. We shall await the other volumes with some impatience, and we thank him for this instalment of an important work."—*Aberdeen Free Press.*

THE MINISTRY OF THE LORD JESUS. By Rev. T. G. SELBY. Author of "The Imperfect Angel." Small Crown 8vo. Second Thousand. 2s. 6d.

"Mr. Selby has written a book that is worth reading and re-reading. It is full of true and pregnant and deep things, and towers grandly above much that seeks to pass as a reflection of the teaching of Jesus."—*British Weekly.*

IN THE BANQUETING HOUSE. A Series of Meditations on the Lord's Supper. By MARK GUY PEARSE. Large Crown 8vo. Printed in Two Colours. 3s. 6d.

PARENTS AND TEACHERS SHOULD READ

SCRIPTURE TRUTHS MADE SIMPLE. By Rev. J. ROBINSON GREGORY. Forty-Six Illustrations. Small crown 8vo. 2s. 6d.; gilt edges, 3s.

"An admirable little book of sermonettes for children. What is chiefly remarkable about them is their variety and aptness of illustration. The language, too, is excellently suited to a childish audience, clear, nervous, and simple. Teachers of junior classes in Sunday Schools would do well to note it."—*The New Age.*

GATES OF IMAGERY: Illustrations of Scripture Truth. By Rev. J. MARRAT. Post 8vo. 2s. 6d.

"All who are called upon to address the public will acknowledge this to be a treasury, and the general reader will find in it endless entertainment. It is the best book of its class that we know."—*Wesleyan Methodist Magazine.*

THE LIFE OF THOMAS COLLINS. By Rev. S. COLEY. Abridged by REV. SIMPSON JOHNSON. Crown 8vo. 1s. 6d. *The full edition is still on sale. Crown 8vo, 3s. 6d.*

THE HERO OF RUFFORD. A True Tale. By REV. JAMES A. MACDONALD. Crown 8vo Ten full-page Illustrations. 2s. 6d.

"It will do anyone good to read this book. Its literary merit is exceptionally high."—*The Christian Million.*

HER WELCOME HOME. By SARSON C. J. INGHAM. Author of "The White Cross and Dove Pearls," etc., etc. Illustrated. Crown 8vo. 2s. 6d.

"A fine story, true to life, and charmingly interesting from start to finish."—*Lincolnshire Free Press.*

AT AUNT VERBENA'S. By MARGARET HAYCRAFT. Crown 8vo. Illustrated. 1s. 6d.

JOHN ROWAN'S TRUST. By EDITH M. EDWARDS. Crown 8vo. Twenty-eight Illustrations. 1s. 6d.

LION, THE MASTIFF: The Story of his Life as told by himself. By A. G. SAVIGNY. Illustrated. Crown 8vo. 1s. 6d.

"A charming story of dog life. Few will get to the end of the book with perfectly dry eyes, and all will be sorry that it is so short."—*Sword and Trowel.*

ETCHINGS FROM A PARSONAGE VERANDAH. By Mrs. JEFFERS GRAHAM. Twenty-three Illustrations. Crown 8vo. 1s. 6d.

THE CIRCUIT RIDER. A Story of the Heroic Age of American Methodism. By Rev. J. EGGLESTON. Crown 8vo. Illustrated. 1s. 6d.

FROM COBBLER'S BENCH TO PRESIDENT'S CHAIR. The Story of Samuel Bradburn. By Rev. BENJAMIN GREGORY, D.D. Crown 8vo. Portrait and six whole-page Illustrations. 1s.

THE POACHER TURNED PREACHER. The Story of John Preston of Yeadon, a Famous Yorkshire Local Preacher. By Rev. BENJAMIN GREGORY, D.D. Crown 8vo. Seven Illustrations. 1s.

ROBERT FORWARD; or, A Life's Regret. Describing the Evils of Juvenile Gambling. By HARRY LINDSAY. Author of "Rhoda Roberts," "Tested by Fire," etc. Crown 8vo. Twelve Illustrations. 1s.

CHARLES H. KELLY, 2, CASTLE STREET, CITY ROAD, E.C.;

AND 66, PATERNOSTER ROW, E.C.

LIBRARY BOOKS.

One Shilling Each.

Uncle Frank's Library.

ILLUSTRATED.   SMALL CROWN 8vo.

MISS GRAHAME'S MEMORIAL, AND OTHER STORIES.

NELL, THE CLOWN'S WIFE. By GRADIDGE.

SINCLAIR'S MUSEUM, AND OTHER STORIES. By W. J. FORSTER.

SKIPPER GEORGE NETMAN. A Story of Outport Methodism in Newfoundland. By REV. GEO. J. BOND.

PICTURES AND STORIES ABOUT THE EARLY CHRISTIANS. By ANNIE F. PERRAM.

SKETCHES OF EARLY METHODISM IN THE BLACK COUNTRY.

THE POOR BOY OF THE CLASS. By HELEN BRISTON.

THE NARROW ESCAPE, AND OTHER STORIES FOR THE YOUNG. By W. J. FORSTER.

WITH STEADY AIM; or, Herbert Ford's Life Work. By W. J. FORSTER.

ONE TOO MANY. By E. M. EDWARDS. Frontispiece.

MATTHEW WINDROD; or, The Methodists of Casterwell.

MY BROTHER JACK. By EMILIE SEARCHFIELD.

ROOKSNEST ABBEY, AND OTHER TALES. By JENNIE CHAPPELL.

UNDER THE JUNIPER TREE. A Story for Boys. By W. J. FORSTER.

TELL ME A STORY: YES, I WILL. By HELEN BRISTON.

HEARTSEASE AND MORNING GLORIES. By JENNIE CHAPPELL.

KING ALFRED'S LAST CHRISTMAS, AND OTHER STORIES. By FANNY SOPHIA HOLLINGS.

ELIZABETH GAUNT. A Tale of Monmouth's Rebellion. By FANNY SOPHIA HOLLINGS.

THE KNIGHT'S MOVE, AND OTHER STORIES. By W. J. FORSTER.

SARA'S CHOICE; or, No Vain Sacrifice. By ANNIE F. PERRAM.

WHEN HIS YEARS WERE FEW. By EDITH CORNFORTH.

THE HIGH RIDGE FARM. By SARA MOORLAND.

BROOKSIDE SCHOOL, AND OTHER STORIES. By MARGARET S. HAYCRAFT.

THE FOUNDATION SCHOLAR, AND OTHER STORIES. By JENNIE PERRETT.

MICHAEL THE TAILOR. By REV. M. GALLIENNE. Translated from the French by REV. C. de P. GLIDDON.

CHARLES H. KELLY, 2, CASTLE STREET, CITY ROAD, E.C.;

AND 66, PATERNOSTER ROW, E.C.

LIBRARY BOOKS.

One Shilling and Sixpence Each.   Crown 8vo Series.

MR. SAM AND HIS TALKATIVE CLOCK. By Rev. W. WIGLEY HAUGHTON, Author of "Parson Hardwork's Nut, and How He Cracked It." Illustrated.

CECIL WILFORD: A Soldier's Son. By Edith M. EDWARDS. Illustrated.

ELBERT'S RETURN. A Story in which the Hardships, Trials and Sorrows which befell an Idle Boy who was foolish enough to run away from a Good Home are faithfully set forth. By Rev. DANIEL WISE, D.D. Crown 8vo. Numerous Illustrations.

MAGGIE FAIRBURN. By Rev. J. FEATHER. Illustrated.

THE HAND ON THE HELM. A Story of Irish Life. By Rev. F. A. TROTTER. Illustrated.

THE STAR IN THE EAST. A Story. By R. ROWE, Author of "Diary of an Early Methodist." Illustrated.

WAYSIDE WISDOM; or, Old Solomon's Ideas of Things. By Rev. JOHN COLWELL. Numerous Illustrations.

THE TWO HARVESTS. By ANNIE RYLANDS. Frontispiece.

THE LITTLE WORLD OF SCHOOL. By ANNIE RYLANDS. Illustrated.

JENNIE AND HER CHARGES. By ANNIE RYLANDS. Frontispiece.

MILLIE'S DISAPPEARANCE AND WHAT CAME OF IT. By M. E. SHEPHERD. Frontispiece.

COURTENAY HARRISON'S EARLY STRUGGLES. By M. E. CROWTHER. Frontispiece.

GO WORK. A Book for Girls. By ANNIE FRANCIS PERRAM. Illustrated.

THOSE WATCHFUL EYES; or, Jemmy and His Friends. By EMILIE SEARCHFIELD. Frontispiece.

AURIEL, AND OTHER STORIES. By RUTH ELLIOTT. Frontispiece.

'TWIXT PROMISE AND VOW, AND OTHER STORIES. By RUTH ELLIOTT. Illustrated.

A VOICE FROM THE SEA; or, The Wreck of the "Eglantine." By RUTH ELLIOTT.

FOOTSTEPS IN THE SNOW. By ANNIE E. COURTENAY. Illustrated.

THE DAIRYMAN'S DAUGHTER. By Rev. LEGH RICHMOND, M.A. A New Edition, with Additions, giving an Authentic Account of her Conversion, and of her Connection with the Wesleyan Methodist. Illustrated. Gilt edges.

THE PILGRIM'S PROGRESS. By JOHN BUNYAN. Illustrated. Gilt edges.

PICTURE TRUTHS. Practical Lessons on the Formation of Character, from Bible Emblems. By JOHN TAYLOR. Thirty Illustrations.

LIBRARY BOOKS.

One Shilling and Sixpence Each.   Crown 8vo Series.

THE SOLDIERS OF LIBERTY. A Story of the Siege of Leyden. By E. P. WEAVER. Illustrated.

CHILDREN OF THE COURT AND TWO LITTLE WAIFS. By F. M. HOLMES. Numerous Illustrations.

JACOB WINTERTON'S INHERITANCE. By EMILIE SEARCHFIELD. Illustrated.

SYBIL'S REPENTANCE. By Mrs. M. S. HAYCRAFT. Illustrated.

LENA AND I. By JENNIE CHAPPELL. Frontispiece.

THE FOUR FRIENDS. By FRIBA. Author of "Miss Kennedy and Her Brother." Illustrated.

NINA'S BURNISHED GOLD. By EMILIE SEARCHFIELD. Frontispiece.

WINDMILL HOUSE. By EDITH CORNFORTH. Frontispiece.

JOHN MARRIOT'S IDOL; or, The Scarlet Geranium. Frontispiece.

LIFE IN A PARSONAGE; or, Lights and Shadows of the Itinerancy. By W. H. WITHROW, D.D. Frontispiece.

MAY'S CAPTAIN. By HELEN BRISTON. Three Illustrations.

PATTY THORNE'S ADVENTURES. By Mrs. H. B. PAULL. Illustrated.

THE NEW HEAD MASTER; or, Little Speedwell's Victory. By MARGARET HAYCRAFT. Frontispiece.

THE BASKET OF FLOWERS. Illustrated. Gilt Edges.

DRIERSTOCK. A Tale of Mission Work on the American Frontier. Illustrated.

MY MISSION GARDEN. By Rev. S. LANGDON. Twenty-Six Illustrations.

PUNCHI NONA. A Story of Female Education and Village Life in Ceylon. By Rev. SAMUEL LANGDON. Numerous Illustrations.

SIAM AND THE SIAMESE. Described by American Missionaries. Illustrations and Map.

IN THE TROPICS; or, Scenes and Incidents of West Indian Life. By Rev. J. MARRAT. Illustrations and Map.

THE BELOVED PRINCE. A Memoir of His Royal Highness the Prince Consort. By WILLIAM NICHOLS. Nineteen Illustrations.

THE SCOTTISH COVENANTERS AND THEIR SUFFERINGS FOR RELIGIOUS LIBERTY. By Rev. T. J. MACARTNEY. Illustrated.

CHARLES H. KELLY, 2, CASTLE STREET, CITY ROAD, E.C.;

AND 66, PATERNOSTER ROW, E.C.

LIBRARY BOOKS.

Two Shillings Each. Crown 8vo Series.

DEAN-HURST. By Sarah Selina Hamer, Author of "A Chronicle of Old Leighton," "Barbara Leybourne," etc. Crown 8vo. Eleven Illustrations.

DR. BRENT'S NEIGHBOURS. A Tale of Two Homes during the Great War. By Dora M. Jones. Crown 8vo. Numerous Illustrations.

PINK ROSES, AND OTHER STORIES FOR LEISURE HOURS. By Margaret S. Haycraft, Author of "The New Head Master," "Springtide Reciter," etc., etc. Crown 8vo. Twelve Illustrations.

"WITH A GLADSOME MIND," AND OTHER STORIES FOR LEISURE HOURS. By Margaret S. Haycraft, Author of "Pink Roses," etc., etc. Crown 8vo. Twelve Illustrations.

HAWTHORNVALE. By Rev. J. Cuthbertson. Crown 8vo. Illustrated.

SPRATTIE AND THE DWARF; or, The Shining Stairway. A Story of East London. By Nellie Cornwall. Crown 8vo. Illustrated.

GRANNIE TRESAWNA'S STORY. By Nellie Cornwall. Crown 8vo. Frontispiece.

DICKON O'GREENWOOD; or, How the Light came to Lady Clare. A Village Picture in Martyr Days. By Kate T. Sizer. Crown 8vo. Illustrated.

AVICE TENNANT'S PILGRIMAGE. A Story of Bunyan's Days. By Kate T. Sizer. Crown 8vo. Six full-page Illustrations.

THE PRIDE OF THE FAMILY. By Anne E. Keeling. Crown 8vo. Five Illustrations.

CASTLE MAILING. A Yorkshire Story. By Anne E. Keeling. Crown 8vo. Five full-page Illustrations.

ANDREW GOLDING. A Story of the Great Plague. By Anne E. Keeling. Crown 8vo. Three whole-page Illustrations.

THE OAKHURST CHRONICLES. A Tale of the Times of Wesley. By Anne E. Keeling. Crown 8vo. Illustrated.

THE "GOOD LUCK" OF THE MAITLANDS. A Family Chronicle. By Mrs. Robert A. Watson. Crown 8vo. Five Illustrations.

TINA AND BETH; or, The Night Pilgrims. By Annie E. Courtenay. Fifth Thousand. Crown 8vo. Illustrated.

MISS MEYRICK'S NIECE. By Evelyn Everett Green. Crown 8vo. Illustrated.

MY BLACK SHEEP. By Evelyn Everett Green. Crown 8vo. Three full-page Illustrations.

RAYMOND THEED. A Story of Five Years. By Elsie Kendall. Crown 8vo. Frontispiece.

FRIENDS AND NEIGHBOURS. A Story for Young Children. By Elsie Kendall. Crown 8vo. Illustrated.

VALERIA, THE MARTYR OF THE CATACOMBS. A Tale of Early Christian Life in Rome. By Rev. W. H. Withrow, D.D. Crown 8vo. Illustrated.

THOSE BOYS. By Faye Huntington. Crown 8vo. Illustrated.

JAMES DARYLL; or, From "Honest Doubt" to Christian Faith. By Ruth Elliott. Ninth Thousand. Crown 8vo.

CHARLES H. KELLY, 2, Castle Street, City Road, E.C.;
AND 66, Paternoster Row, E.C.